A Lady Awakened

A Lady
Awakened

CECILIA GRANT

BANTAM BOOKS
NEW YORK

A Lady Awakened is a work of fiction. Names, characters, places, and incidents are the products of the author's imagination or are used fictitiously. Any resemblance to actual events, locales, or persons, living or dead, is entirely coincidental.

A Bantam Books Mass Market Original

Copyright © 2012 by Cecilia Grant
Excerpt from *A Gentleman Undone* by Cecilia Grant © 2012 by Cecilia Grant

Published in the United States by Bantam Books, an imprint of The Random House Publishing Group, a division of Random House, Inc., New York.

BANTAM BOOKS and the rooster colophon are registered trademarks of Random House, Inc.

This book contains an excerpt of the forthcoming book *A Gentleman Undone* by Cecilia Grant. This excerpt has been set for this edition only and may not reflect the final content of the forthcoming edition.

ISBN 978-0-553-59383-9
eBook ISBN 978-0-345-53252-7

Cover design: Lynn Andreozzi
Cover photograph: Marie Killen

Printed in the United States of America

www.bantamdell.com

9 8 7 6 5 4 3 2 1

Bantam Books mass market edition: March 2012

For Shirley
the alpha and omega of beta readers

Chapter One

 $\mathcal{N}$OT ONCE in ten months of marriage had she wished for her husband's demise. Nor would she be glad of the occurrence even for a moment. Even for this moment. To do so would ill become her.

Martha sat straighter in her chair, smoothing her black skirts. One's conduct might owe more to principle than to sentiment at times, admittedly. But principle could be relied upon. Principle steadied a person; braced her up through those same occasions, in fact, where sentiment made only a sluggish kind of mire to sink into.

She finished with her skirts and folded her hands on the tabletop. "Well," she said into the silence of her sunlit parlor. "This is all legally sound, I don't doubt."

Mr. Keene gave a little bow from his place at the table's foot, affording her a glimpse of the bald spot atop his head. He did not meet her eyes and had not done so since beginning to read. A faint sifting sound came from the papers before him, as his hands lined up the corners and made other adjustments of no particular purpose. Really, he ought to stop that.

Across the table her brother sat tight-lipped, his jaw working as if to swallow something of fearsome dimension. His temper, that would be. To his credit, he always did try.

"Speak, Andrew." She knew well enough what he would have to say. "You're liable to do yourself some injury otherwise."

"I'd have done injury to Russell if I'd known what he was about. A thousand pounds!" He spat out the sum like a mouthful of spoiled porridge. "One thousand, from what began as ten! What kind of man would speculate with his wife's settlement?"

A man half lost in drink apparently would. To take just one example. She drew a fortifying breath. "It's not as though I'll be penniless. I'll have my dower."

"No dower house, though, and but a tenth of what you brought into the marriage. I'm sure I'd like to know his reasoning." This, rather pointedly, to Mr. Keene.

"I wouldn't have encouraged the investment myself," came the solicitor's reedy voice as he went on shuffling papers. "But Mr. Russell had a taste for those things. His will with the first Mrs. Russell was similar: her portion invested in private securities, and all the rest arranged in hopes of an heir." An heir, of course. If there was any man on earth more eager to get an heir than her husband had been, she should like to see him.

Well, no. In fact she wouldn't care to see that man at all. She unlaced her hands and touched her fingertips to the tablecloth. Very pretty, this cloth. Linen, from Belgium, and no longer hers.

"I wish I'd had my own solicitors see to your marriage agreement. I would have had nothing to do with this *trust*." More bad porridge. "Father's people were worse than useless. I ought to have done it myself."

"How could you have managed?" One had neither time nor patience for this sort of nonsense. I wish I'd done this; I would have done that; I ought to have done some other thing. Blind alleys, those were, leading straight to the swamp of sentiment and nowhere else. "You had your hands full settling Father's estate. Those were difficult days for us all. What's done is done. We needn't say any more about it."

Andrew held his tongue, then, but his eyes—large, liquid, dark as day-old coffee—glowed with strong opinions. She angled her head politely away. So indecorous, to let the mood of any moment run rampant across one's face. So undisciplined. For all that she had those same eyes, she'd long since schooled them into sphinxlike calm. It really wasn't hard.

"So when is she to be turned out of her home?" he said upon reaching the limits of forbearance. "How soon will this other Mr. Russell expect to take possession? Of course you will come to stay with me and Lucy," he added to her without waiting for the solicitor's reply. "When we go to the country you may even have your old room."

And live as a dependent child again, for all that she was one and twenty. A burden to him and his wife. Something stirred in the pit of her stomach: tiny fragments of mutiny, chasing about as pointlessly as rubbish in a windstorm.

Mr. Keene inclined his head so as to show her the bald spot again. "In these cases, we generally don't proceed until the widow assures us there is no possibility of a son."

Well, there wasn't. Her body had resolved that some three days since, and brought her the news in its usual fashion. For all of Mr. Russell's most vigorous efforts, on her and presumably on his first wife, no child had ever resulted. Now no child ever would.

Was she expected to say so on the spot? Mutiny stilled her tongue. If she left the matter in some doubt, she could get a few more weeks here. Maybe as much as a month.

Of course if she were truly mutinous . . . well, one heard tales of what desperate childless widows occasionally did. Lurid tales, difficult to credit. What woman could ever be so desperate? Probably it was all some myth got up and passed about by wishful men.

She lifted her chin. "I will send you word when I know that question to be resolved." She could see to the servants, at least. Mr. and Mrs. James Russell would bring servants of their own, making some of the Seton Park staff redundant. She would take what time she needed to get them placed out.

Andrew fidgeted silently for the several minutes Mr. Keene took to gather up his papers and make polite remarks, and when the solicitor was finally shown out, her brother quitted his chair with vehemence. "For the love of God, sister, will you never speak up for yourself?" He strode away to the table's other end. "It's not right, how you've been served in all this. Why must I be the only one with the fortitude to say so?"

A familiar coolness blossomed in the middle of her chest and seeped outward. "I see no question of *fortitude*." She measured out her syllables, and folded her hands atop the table again. "I could speak of injustice, I suppose, and indulge myself with some show of outrage, but none of that would change the facts of my current situation, would it?" Her voice grew flatter and flatter, like pastry dough under a most adamant rolling pin.

"Not now, it wouldn't." He flung out his hand in an impatient gesture. "But this whole thing might have been averted. For the life of me I'll never understand why you married the man. Why any young girl would marry a widower twice her age when she—"

"He was nine and thirty. Hardly in his dotage. And no, you're not likely ever to understand." What eldest son could? He would never be faced with the prospect of a parasitic existence. He would never come to make those reckonings in which girlish fancy had no place. He would only pity her, provokingly, and wonder at her wrongheaded choice.

As though a love match were the only viable kind of marriage! As though humanity had not prospered for countless generations through unions of other kinds; through respectable alliances between people who happened to prize other things above unbridled feeling!

Her hands had come unfolded and two fingers were tracing over and over a bit of openwork in the tablecloth. She stilled them. Laced the fingers firmly again. Sat silent.

Abruptly her brother heaved a sigh. "I'm sorry, Martha." She could hear the change in his voice, though she kept her eyes on the tablecloth.

He came round to stand behind her chair. One hand settled on her shoulder. She lifted her chin and looked hard at the wall, where peonies marched in a cheerful red-and-white pattern.

"I'm sorry if I offend you." He was all uncertainty now, casting about for the right way to comfort so perverse a little sister. "Sorry you've had this misfortune, and sorry I wasn't more help to you. But I'll help you now, if you'll let me. You'll have a good home with me and Lucy."

The wallpaper's peonies shimmered for a moment, and threatened to swim. She might have been seven again, and he eighteen, that same hand on her shoulder as awkward as a turkey on a pigeon-perch. They'd done this before, though that day they'd sat side by side on the stone wall where he'd finally found her, and the halting words of consolation had all to do with Heaven, and their mother's soul.

I'm sorry, too. I wish I could want what you offer. I don't know why I can't. She swallowed, and kept the words down. "You were so kind to come," she said.

"You've been a great help indeed. These past few days should have been much more difficult had you not been here. I'll write to you when I . . . I'll write to you." That was her one toe dipped in the wallows of sentiment, and quickly drawn out again.

He left for London. When she'd waved at his carriage all the way to where it turned from the drive onto the road, she dropped her hand and began to walk. Away from the house she went, south toward the swelling hills. The August sun showed no mercy to a woman in full mourning, particularly one who covered ground at her pace. So be it. She walked faster.

Soon she was ascending, feeling her stride shorten as she started up the face of the highest hill. Somewhere nearby she could hear the discourse of sheep, plaintive and petulant by turns. A dog barking as well, and a man's voice giving terse commands. Round a fold in the hill she came upon them: one of her tenants training a new dog by guiding it round and round a clutch of three disgruntled sheep. Mr. Farris caught sight of her and removed his hat, and then she must stop to make conversation.

One could say only so many things in praise of a sheepdog. She said them all, while the tenant turned his hat round between thick fingers, nodding with a sage expression. "My Jane set me to ask, if I should see you," he said once these pleasantries were concluded, "whether we may expect you to stay on here."

"I'm afraid it's unlikely." More than unlikely. But her answer to the tenants must coincide with the answer she'd given Mr. Keene.

"There's many will be sorry to hear." He whistled, and the dog reversed direction, circling in its half-crouched stance. "Jane says it's to you we owe the new roof."

"Well, chiefly to Mr. Russell's generosity." She bent

her head and brushed a speck of something off her sleeve.

"The first Mrs. Russell never did take any interest in improvements. Nor did he, before you come along. So says Jane. She gives you the credit."

"Her good opinion honors me." She brushed another speck before raising her head. "She's well, I hope? And the children?"

"Aye, everyone's well." He made a signal with his hand and the dog changed direction again. "Ben and Adam look forward to the school opening."

"The school?" Delight surged up from her toes, flushing out the morning's disappointment and boosting her voice into some very strange octave. "They weren't on Mr. Atkins's list, the last time I spoke to him. Will they be attending after all?"

"Just three days out of the five, to start. My youngest girl as well. Everett's boys will help me out some, and my boys help him, and we'll scrape by with the rest of it."

"Do you mean the Everett children will go to school, too?" She wrestled her voice back down to a range that wouldn't frighten the sheep.

"Three days out of five, aye. Maybe more in the winter."

"I'm so glad to hear it. You do your children a great service by schooling them."

"Well, they've got some cleverness." He shrugged and turned his hat over again. "Pair that with education and a boy might choose his own course."

She recognized one of the many lines of persuasion Mr. Atkins had rehearsed with her, and couldn't suppress a smile. She'd done some good at Seton Park, even in her short stay. She'd been useful. When discontent threatened to overtake her, she would remember the new cottage roofs, and her part in realizing the curate's long-cherished scheme for a tenant school.

She'd like to remember her improvements to his scheme, as well. "What of your Laura, and Adelaide? They'll be attending the class on Sundays, I hope?"

"I cannot say they will." He set his head on an angle and rubbed the heel of his hand along his jaw. "We'll need them at home all the more with their brothers going to school."

"Of course." She'd heard this same discouraging response more than once. "Still, it's only an hour of instruction, once a week. Perhaps in time you'll find you can spare them after all."

"Perhaps. Just now I've got Laura learning more of this work." Mr. Farris nodded toward the dog. "She takes to it, you know. Ordering creatures about."

"Well, a gift for command is certainly to be admired." Cultivated, as well. A girl of such talent deserved education, more education than the reading and ciphering with which feminine schooling began and ended. She would speak to Mr. Atkins tomorrow. A stronger case must be made to these parents, and with her time here cut short, he must be the one to make it.

$\mathcal{T}$wo weeks ago, and for every Sunday of her married life, she'd sat beside Mr. Russell in the first pew on the right-hand side of St. Stephen's church. This morning she sat three back on the left of the aisle, a gesture intelligible only to herself. That front pew was for the proprietors of Seton Park. She would sit there no more.

One saw things differently from the third row. One could see the spot where sunlight through the east wall's lancet window struck the tile floor, for example. One could make a study of the backs of people's heads. She shouldn't have known, in the first row, which of her neighbors washed behind their ears and which did not. From the first row, too, she should likely never have seen the stranger. She might have heard him, hastening up the aisle to an empty spot even as the rest of the church fell silent at the entrance of the curate through the vestry door. But she should certainly never have turned to glimpse the tall, finely clothed figure that slipped into the pew across from hers.

Neither did she turn now. People who came late to church deserved no notice, which fact one might wish could be impressed on those neighbors who were throwing furtive glances his way. Her peripheral view of him, as he seized a prayer book and thumbed vigorously through its pages, was more than sufficient, and she dismissed him altogether when the service began.

Mr. Atkins preached earnest, unaffected sermons, perhaps a bit longer than one might privately prefer, but usually with a worthy point to make at the end. He'd chosen for his text today the story of Mary and Martha, those sisters who differed on the proper way of receiving the Savior's visit to their home—rather a confounding verse, endorsing, as it seemed to, the dereliction of duty. But she could bow her head and await the worthy point, and the end.

A child's muffled giggle imposed itself on her attention some few minutes in. The little boy in the pew ahead of hers was craning to look at something over his shoulder. She followed his gaze and met with the figure of the stranger, sound asleep and listing a few degrees to the left.

Had he no notion of setting an example? She sent a quick look of reprimand to the little boy, who turned hastily forward, and then she marshaled her disapproval on the slumbering form across the aisle.

He dozed on untroubled, his head lolling at such an angle as to present her with a view of his hair, which grew in waves and had the pale raw hue of fresh-split boxwood. What features went with it, she could not tell.

The turn of his neck left them to her imagination, not that she had any intention of imagining.

His posture spoke all over of indolence. Long legs he had, bent grasshopper-like to cram between his own pew and the one in front. His hands sat slack on the hymnal in his lap, still open to whatever place he'd been at when last he was awake. Doubtless he was one of those men who came to church primarily for the chance to subject everyone to his singing voice.

He subjected her now to something else: a snore, low and subtle like the buzzing of some wayward insect, but still, unmistakably, a snore. Then another, just in the pattern of the first.

Well, really. Why even bother coming to church? She faced front again. Mr. and Mrs. James Russell could have the pleasure of dealing with him. Worthier things must claim her own attention. The sermon, for example. Or the state of her prayer book, which smelled of dank winter even on a summer day. All the prayer books in St. Stephen's had that smell, and this one, as she paged through it, revealed the additional offenses of dark spotting and pages warped by too much damp. A pity she'd never got round to having Mr. Russell replace—

Her skin prickled all over. Someone was watching her. Someone to her right. In one quick move she brought her chin up and around and looked into dark blue eyes; eyes the color of some faraway ocean. The stranger, just woken, his head nearly righted and his countenance revealed.

Sleep disheveled his features still. His cheek had a crease where it had lain on his shoulder. A curling lock of hair fell slantwise on his forehead. Beneath the disarray were aristocratic bones, a reddish full mouth, and lashes she could have seen from six pews away.

He blinked, and blinked again. Then his whole lower face melted into a smile, for all the world as though he'd glimpsed her across a ballroom and was hopeful of an introduction.

No. Worse than that. She turned quickly away, the blood already coming up in her cheeks. Women who woke in his bed saw that smile. Sleep-liquored. A bit surprised to see her. Ready to see more, just as soon as she'd oblige.

She put down the prayer book and folded her arms, hiding as much as she could from his view. The air on her bare neck felt suddenly like an uninvited caress. August or not, she wished she'd worn a shawl.

Once or twice more her skin prickled, but she kept her eyes fixedly forward, even when the service ended and the pews emptied about her. She was the last to pass through the doors onto the threshold, and last to shake the curate's hand, and thank him for his edifying sermon.

At close range, perhaps even more so than when he was in the pulpit, Mr. Atkins looked precisely the way a churchman ought. His austere build lent an extra measure of dignity to his plain dark vestment, and his coloring was such that one might make a true likeness of him with only white paper and a bit of charcoal: charcoal eyes, charcoal hair, and thick black brows whose natural slant gave a melancholy cast to his pale, angular features.

"I think it a fine text," he said in reply to her compliment, gentle mischief just evident in his smile, "though perhaps I shall have to choose livelier passages in future, for Mr. Mirkwood's benefit. If he sleeps through my sermon on David and Goliath, I suppose I shall have none but myself to blame."

"Is he a neighbor?" Over Mr. Atkins's shoulder she could see the stranger, a good quarter-mile already down the path that would lead to the road. "I don't know him by sight or by name." He moved with a springy ease, hands thrust in his coat pockets.

"They own the property east of Seton Park, though we've rarely seen them there. Not at all, I believe, in your time, and even now it's only Mr. Mirkwood the younger come down. But I've spoken too long without asking how you do." The curate's voice changed. "I did not expect you to be about so soon."

His eyes would be keen, if she should look up into them. They would invite confidences, entirely respectable confidences such as were common between parishioner and pastor. "I do well enough." She shaded her face with one hand as she followed the receding form of Mr. Mirkwood. "Thank you for asking. May I help you put things away?"

"Certainly you may." Here, too, he was keen. He understood reticence and met it with a graceful respect.

Back inside the church Mr. Atkins busied himself with papers at his lectern while she collected books from the pews. Mr. Russell had not thought it suitable for the mistress of Seton Park to perform such tasks. But now she had only her own wishes to consult.

She picked up the hymnal Mr. Mirkwood had used, and locked her arms round all those she'd gathered. "I must confess an ulterior motive." Feet set, she faced the pulpit. "I hoped to discuss the school."

His hands went still for a second or two. "Ah, yes. I did expect this." He set aside his papers and lifted his chin. "Come take a seat." With one hand he gestured her to the first pew as he came down from the pulpit. Then he leaned against the pew opposite, folding his arms. "I understand Mr. Keene was at the house yesterday."

"He was." She set the stack of hymnals in her lap. "I find the estate is very likely to pass to Mr. Russell's brother James. I shall probably be here but a few weeks more."

"There's some chance it may pass to you, though?" His upper body inclined slightly toward her.

"Some very little chance." This was getting complicated. Lies so often did. "The question should be resolved within the month."

"Ah." Understanding colored his face and he took a sudden interest in the floor.

"At all events we face the prospect of my departure." Onward. No time to indulge in embarrassment. "And in view of that, I should like to recommend certain actions in regard to the school."

"Yes, of course." He nodded, gaze still lowered, as though he were expecting her to say something grave indeed.

"Enrollment in the class for young ladies is not what we had hoped. But I've had an idea." She had, surprisingly enough. "If you were to point to those places where one may find Scriptural support for women's learning, these families must listen, I should think, and see the notion's merit in a way they otherwise might not." His eyes had slowly risen to hers, and the slant of his brows gradually steepened, putting urgency into her words as she went on. "Consider your text of today. Christ bid those sisters leave off their womanly pursuits, didn't he, and learn from him the same as any disciple. If on your next visit to the Farris cottage, or the Cheathams, you could remind them of—"

"Forgive me, Mrs. Russell." He held up one hand, and his face was all resignation and regret. "But surely you see the school cannot go forward, given what you've told me."

"Not go forward!" Her heart lurched halfway up her throat. "But why?"

"Whether or not to have a school will be Mr. James Russell's decision if you do leave us, and he might not consider it a worthwhile use of his funds."

How could he so quickly give up what he'd so long worked for? "But if you began the school—I imagine he shouldn't actually be in residence here for several months yet—he might accept it as something already in place."

"And he might not." His voice, like his gaze, was soft, sympathetic, and utterly unyielding. "Think of the disappointment if I were to get the school going only to have to shut it down several months later. I can't do that to the tenants."

He made a good point. But something like mutiny stirred up in her again. She'd pared away bits of her soul for his school. One did not do such a thing in vain. "What if . . ." She searched the floor for inspiration. "What if I were to write to Mr. James Russell, and tell him all about the school, and perhaps secure his support in advance?"

A glance at him caught the change in his face: he was guarded, indeed, but she could see how ready he was to grasp at any bit of hope. "Do you know very much of him?" Caution kept his speech short. "Do you think it likely he would approve?"

"Mr. Russell spoke of him sometimes, enough for me to gather he's an amiable man, at least." It might be true, that last bit. Why should he not be amiable?

"If you would undertake to write . . . If your own interest so compelled you . . ." The weight of his hope forced her attention down to the hymnals in her lap. The stack needed straightening. "I have the greatest respect for your powers of persuasion. You know I spent months working to convince Mr. Russell of the merits of educating his tenants, but I do not believe he would have agreed to it in the end without your intercession."

Two books slipped from her lap and went skittering into the aisle. She bent to reach for them and nearly collided with Mr. Atkins, suddenly kneeling there before her. "I'm sorry," she said, rather stupidly, as there had in fact been no collision.

He looked up. A faint whiff of almond came to her: he must use soap of that scent. A smile—modest, decent, kindly—played round the edges of his mouth. "The apology ought to be mine." He lifted the books. "You've labored to no purpose—I haven't actually been in the habit of putting these away."

She took the hymnals and sat up straight. "You ought to." Her finger traced along one's failing spine. "Especially in the winter. The damp is bad for paper."

"Indeed I ought." He got to his feet, brushing absently at his cassock.

"These need to be replaced, at all events. Perhaps I will ask Mr. James Russell to approve it." She forced a smile and he smiled back, his eyes lit with a trustful gratitude of which she had long since ceased to be worthy.

$\mathcal{T}$HERE WAS a new man in church today," said her maid that evening while taking down her hair. "Across the aisle from you—did you see him?"

"Mr. Mirkwood, you mean. His family owns Pencarragh, just to the east." She tipped her head forward as the hairpins were drawn out. Perhaps Sheridan could draw out her stupidity with them. What had she been thinking, to propose a letter to Mr. James Russell?

"Mirkwood, aye." In her dressing-table mirror the maid's blond head bobbed once. "Sir Theophilus, as will be, once he's finished driving his father to an early grave."

"I see you know more than I. Is this the fruit of below-stairs gossip?" She couldn't work up any stronger admonition, with her mind so urgently occupied.

There had to be some way to secure the school's future; some sounder scheme than a mere written plea. Mr. Atkins's flattering faith to the contrary, she was no persuader. His thanks ought to go to the bottle, for Mr.

Russell's imperfect recall of what he had and had not authorized. She should have accomplished nothing without that.

"You know Sarah, who makes the sauces?" Sheridan's voice looped and fluttered among her thoughts like a cheerful unreproached bird. "Her sister works in the house there, and she said Mr. Mirkwood had come to stay not by his own choice but by his father's."

"As a kind of banishment?" This finally drew her full attention. What sapskulled father, and what sapskulled son, could view the Sussex countryside as a penance?

"Banished, to be sure." A handful of hairpins dropped musically onto the silver tray at her right. "Put away from the temptations of London, in a place where there's little chance for deviltry. Cut off from his allowance too, I've heard, so no running down to Brighton for the amusements."

Deviltry. Amusements. This much, she could have guessed. "I am sorry to hear it." She found her maid's eyes in the mirror. "However we need not sustain the life of a man's misdeeds with discussion, or with any notice at all. We will merely hope he may profit by his stay in Sussex." Not very likely, though, if he continued to sleep through church.

Sheridan picked up a comb and eased it into Martha's hair, ducking her head in a chastened way, but her smile suggested she was indulging, still, in agreeable thoughts of Mr. Mirkwood and his transgressions.

Undoubtedly one might have done more, in ten months, to curb the maid's affinity for gossip and plant some foundations of decorum. But to regret that now would be no good use of her time. Indeed, she might perhaps employ the trait to some advantage.

"Do you know anything of Mr. Russell's brother James?" she said. "Do the older servants ever speak of him?"

"Mr. James Russell." A muscle twitched in the girl's cheek; her features otherwise went neutral. "Why do you ask?"

"He stands to inherit Seton Park, and I have certain matters to discuss with him in advance of that." This time she felt a tiny catch in the comb's movement, though Sheridan's face betrayed nothing. "He didn't come to the wedding or to Mr. Russell's funeral, so I must rely on others' impressions." Three, then four, then five seconds went by in silence. "You've heard some reports of him, I think?"

"Sometimes the older servants have said things." The maid's eyes flicked up to hers in the mirror, and down again.

"And what have they said? I beg you will be frank with me." A chill was creeping up her backbone. What could instill this sudden reserve in the same girl who'd chattered so readily of Mr. Mirkwood's disgrace?

Sheridan's mouth pursed. She set her head on an angle and watched her hands combing. Finally, she spoke. "They say he ruined two housemaids here when he was a young man."

"What?" The chill flooded every part of her now. "Who says so?"

"Mrs. Kearney. She was second housemaid then. She says it was only her pockmarked face kept her safe." Her lips went tight together; her hands divided out a lock of hair.

"Safe from . . . being lured into a degraded connection, do you mean?" Or safe from something worse?

"Wasn't much luring in it." Like huge malign hailstones the words fell, a few at a time, while Sheridan worked the comb through. "He went into their rooms at night and told them they'd be dismissed if they said anything about it. And then the two were dismissed all the same, because of what condition they found themselves in."

"Was he never brought to justice?" The threadbare whisper exactly suited that woman she saw in the mirror, pale as the white lawn chemise she wore. And the question was a foolish one. Nobody held such men to account. Women could only pray for mercy, and bear what came.

The maid shook her head, not bothering to reply in words. "Not that he'll ever lay eyes on me," she said after a moment. "There'll be no place for me here if you don't stay." She set the comb aside and busied herself in plaiting the combed-out hair. "Only I was hoping you would. All the servants were. I suppose things would have come out different if you'd been blessed with a son."

"Different indeed." Martha lowered her eyes from her blushing mirror image. "But as we've known these few days, all chance of that is . . ." She stopped. Here came the mutiny again, boiling up from somewhere deep in her belly and confounding all her words.

She raised her chin and met with her reflection as her breaths went quick and shallow. Sheridan's reflection, too, the sweet springtime face paired with eyes that already knew too much of the world.

Women could only pray for mercy . . . That wasn't true. Women could do more. A desperate woman could do more.

Women could only bear what came. But a chance had come. A chance had come and looked her in the eye that very morning.

In the mirror her blush was receding, her features settling into the lines of calm resolve. This could end in a dozen different kinds of disaster. There'd be no guarantee of success. And how to get through it without losing all claim to principle, she couldn't begin to imagine.

So be it. She could wait for Providence to come to these women's aid, or she could make use of what Providence had already put in her path. "Sheridan." She twisted to face her maid squarely. "Tell me again about Mr. Mirkwood. Tell me everything you know."

Chapter Two

Who is Mrs. Richard Russell, and what business can she have with me?" Theo Mirkwood held the card—the first to appear on his tray, since coming to the country—between two long fingers and turned it critically this way and that. Black lettering engraved on white. No border, no artful script, no little curlicues or flowers; nothing, in short, to betray any hint of its owner beyond her name. Or more precisely, her husband's name.

"She is your next neighbor," said Mr. Granville, "the mistress of Seton Park."

Theo sat back in his chair and bit into a piece of buttered toast, the card still balanced between his first and second fingers. Across the table his land agent—no, his father's land agent—sorted diligently through the many tedious-looking documents he'd brought along. "She must have left it at some ungodly hour this morning," he said, flicking at one corner of the card with his thumbnail. Decent paper. Crisp. "Do you know her?"

"A little." The man barely looked up from his work. "She's been among us less than a year, and was unhappily widowed a week and some since."

He stopped chewing. Perhaps it was some other

widow? But no, Seton Park, now he recalled, was the name of that property just to the west, where the field-stone church stood. "A week, you say." He swallowed. "Why the devil is she calling on anyone, let alone an unmarried gentleman?"

"Mrs. Russell is the properest of women. I'm sure it must be some matter of business, as you said. And I should think a new neighbor would feel flattered by her notice, and overlook any lapse in her adherence to the strictures of mourning."

"Flattered. So I am." What else could he say? The length of his term here depended on the reports this man would make to his father. He read the card again. "What happened to Mr. Richard Russell?"

"Thrown from a horse and broke his neck. Most unfortunate. Are you nearly ready to begin?"

"Yes, why not?" He sighed and set the card by his plate. "Instruct away." *Drag me down with your details into the next circle of this forced rustication,* he might have stylishly added, could he be more flippant and less mindful of making a good impression.

But in a short time he had ceased to attend the agent's droning. Sunlight filled the breakfast parlor, bringing with it a most agreeable drowsy warmth, and his tea was warm, and the buttered toast was warm and furthermore could be spread with three different kinds of jam. He had only to nod and occasionally raise his eyebrows in an approximation of attention, between bites of toast, while his own thoughts drifted back to yesterday morning in church.

What an odd business that had been; the widow and all of it. Arriving late as he had. Falling asleep. Forgetting himself for the space of a smile.

Like so many things that appeared at first blush to be his fault, these ones were not, really. New habits took time. Sunday services were so infernally early. He'd expected more singing, and a shorter sermon.

" . . . and here you see what economies we've achieved by blocking up the unneeded windows and reducing our tax." Granville was foisting some document on him.

"Most impressive." He glanced at the paper and plucked another piece of toast from the rack. Who ever heard of an unneeded window? In his London lodgings he always kept the curtains wide. The light was particularly fine at this time of year, mellowing in preparation for the change to autumn. Some afternoons it lured him back into bed, sweetly as a woman might.

He ought not to have smiled at that widow. Speaking of women and their lures. What man could blame him, though? Such a delightful waking apparition she'd made, so grave and erect in her widow's weeds, but paging through her prayer book like a child looking for the pictures. Then when she'd swung about to face him, with the eyes of a startled deer, he'd liked her better still. He could imagine teasing her on the topic of her truant attention, and submitting while she scolded him for falling asleep. He could imagine a most enjoyable roundelay of teasing and submission, culminating in a most thoroughly . . .

Granville had gone silent. For how long? He scrabbled at the paper before him. "I beg your pardon," he said, "I was working my way through these window-tax calculations and I'm afraid I missed the last of what you said." He dug hard. "Something about fencing?" Why fencing, though? Surely there was no parlor within miles, and besides it wasn't quite fashionable. Boxing was a gentleman's exercise, these days.

"Several sections of fence are due for repair, yes. In addition to the two or possibly three cottages that will require new thatching before winter."

"New thatching, by all means." Christ. He couldn't

sound more witless if he tried. He'd never see London again at this rate.

He put the window paper down and his hand brushed the plain little cálling card. He picked it up. "Would it be proper for me to return this call, under the circumstances?" Oh, that was good. An appeal to the man's judgment coupled with concern for propriety.

"I should think it a civil thing to do. You might make time this afternoon."

"This afternoon. Quite. Are we nearly done with these papers?" He felt some renewal of cheer. A polite call was surely not beyond his abilities. He'd make a better impression on this widow than he'd done in church, and a good impression on Granville into the bargain. And the more good impressions he could make, the sooner he'd be out of this exile and back in London where he belonged.

$\mathcal{T}$HE WIDOW Russell apparently took her at-home retirement so far as to abstain from receiving guests in the formal parlors: Theo was shown to a pink-papered upstairs room where she sat in an armchair whose chintz upholstery featured roses twining daintily on a white ground. She was head-to-toe in black, of course, and for a moment he had the very odd impression of a spider lurking in a rose bouquet. But she could not be blamed for the black, one must recall. She would probably make a fine ornament to this room, in some other color, and at all events, to be decorative was surely no widow's first concern.

She rose from the chair to shake his hand. Her eyes skimmed across his before settling somewhere near the level of his collarbone, and when the greeting was done she turned away altogether, gesturing at a small rosewood table on which sat a pot of tea and a plate holding two kinds of cake. "I was having tea when you were announced," she said, sitting again and arranging her skirts. "May I offer you a cup?"

"That would be most pleasant, thank you." Rather forward of her, offering to share her refreshment. But maybe things were done that way in the country. And the cake looked very fine. He sat in a second chintz chair, at an angle to hers, and tugged off his gloves.

The footman brought another cup and plate and she picked up the pot to pour. Did he imagine, or was she avoiding his gaze?

He cleared his throat. "I'm told your loss was very recent." Maybe he ought to have said that sooner. "I'm sorry to hear of it."

"Recent indeed, and sudden as well." She poured, watching the level of tea in his cup. "Your condolences are kind. Do you take milk or sugar?"

"Neither, thank you." Well, this was interesting. Granville hadn't evinced much grief, either, in speaking of the affair. But people didn't always wear those things on their sleeves. If she felt grief's opposite, she wasn't showing that either.

"You've come from London, I hear." She looked up to hand him his tea, and finally fixed her eyes full upon him.

For the barest instant he felt confusion. It scrambled over his skin and all about his innards. Such eyes she had! Dark and wary as some woodland creature's; he remembered that from church. And she looked at him now as though . . . well, he really had no idea what.

"London, indeed." He took the cup with a bow. An interruption came—a maid appeared at the door with temporary need of the footman, and they both went away—and he swallowed some tea, using the moment to reclaim his self-possession. "Have you spent much time in the city yourself?" he said when the servants had gone.

"Only part of one Season, when I met my husband." Behind her composure was a concentrated attention, and beyond this . . . Secrets. Many, many secrets churned and simmered at the back of that bittersweet-chocolate stare. "I fear Sussex may seem rather dull in comparison to what you must be used to." Slowly she raised her teacup to her lips and drank, her eyes never leaving his.

Good Lord. Did she have any idea how that looked, to a man? Well, obviously she didn't. If she'd meant it that way there'd be invitation in her posture; sweet insinuation curling round the edges of her voice. And besides, she was respectable. And a widow. Whatever her secrets, they weren't for him.

"A bit more sedate than London, to be sure." He shifted in his chair, angling slightly away from her. "But I've occupations enough."

"You're studying some of the responsibilities of a baronet, you mean. So I've heard." Her hands, so starkly pale where they emerged from the black sleeves, set down her tea and arranged two cake slices on a plate. She had deft, delicate fingers. Slightly chilly, though— he'd noticed that, even through his glove, when she shook his hand. A man could warm those hands between his own and then—

And then nothing. He wouldn't let his mind roam there. He was better than that, surely. "Land management, yes, and things of that nature." He accepted the plate, and the silver fork she held out with it. "Keeping the fences in repair. Seeing to the windows. Window-tax. Assuring that things are optimal in that regard. In every regard." He crammed a bit of cake into his mouth, chiefly to stop himself talking before he could sound any more of a coxcomb.

She took a forkful of cake from her own plate and

chewed it, a grim sort of compression about her lips. That was a shame, because the fullness of her mouth disappeared when she tightened it that way, and also because even a person in fresh mourning ought to be able to give in to the enjoyment of a good piece of cake. "Do you like it?" she said, once swallowing.

"Oh, yes, it's superb cake; thank you." It was. Lemon cake, sweet and bracing both at once.

"No," she said, a slightly pained expression flitting across her face. "Your studies, I mean. Learning what will be your duties one day. Do you find that engaging?"

"Oh, quite. Without a doubt." She could repeat that to Granville the next time she saw him. "I find such studies suit me altogether."

She ate more cake, silently. Her glance switched back and forth between himself and her own plate, causing him to feel a bit like another menu item, and one of dubious provenance at that. "You're to be commended, I'm sure," she finally said, and allowed a hint of a smile. "If I were in your place I don't know but that I'd be scheming to get myself to Brighton."

"To Brighton?" This was . . . unexpected. And the curve at the corner of her mouth made him hungry to see her smile in earnest.

"To some more vibrant setting." She dissected the cake with her fork as she spoke, withholding her eyes from him again. "To some place where I might be in company with more . . . spirited people. With more varied pursuits. Being used to that sort of thing, I imagine that's what I'd prefer. If I were a young man." Poor innocent, imbuing a faddish bathing-place with all the cosmopolitan glamour her own life must lack.

"I'm sure Brighton must be thoroughly delightful." He set his cake down and drank more tea to mask what he knew was an indulgent smile. "To a young lady as well as a young man."

That wasn't the right answer. Her face told him so. But why should there even be a right answer in such a discussion? More things were going on here than he could fathom, quite.

"I'm told the shops are very fine in Brighton." Now she sounded as though she were willing him to levitate from his chair and deposit himself in that town this minute.

"I shouldn't doubt it." He put his cup soundlessly back in its saucer. What in blazes was she about? Was she hinting that he ought to remove himself from this neighborhood? But she'd just met him. Could a single smile in church engender such disfavor?

"Amusements, too." She took up the strainer and leaned over to pour him more tea. "One hears the amusements in Brighton are just those such as young men most enjoy."

He considered her words as she poured. Also, he considered the view down her bodice. Speak of the amusements young men most enjoyed. She wore no fichu or shawl, and he could see just enough to gauge how one breast would fit in his hand. Plenty of hand to spare. Her endowments were modest and his hands were large. Nothing wrong with that.

Not that it mattered, of course. "If I could be of service to you by sampling Brighton's amusements and confirming these reports, I would, gladly." Wonderful what a look down a lady's gown could do for his spirits. "However I'm not likely to get there on this stay."

"Because you lack funds, you mean, now you've no allowance." She said it softly, replacing the strainer on its little dish.

Ah. A gossip. Her early call at his house took on a new cast, unflattering to both of them. Eager to gawk at the London scapegrace, was she, and draw out some new stories to retell among her friends? Well, she must look elsewhere for her satisfaction. "I confess I cannot see how that could be any concern of yours." He made his voice cool as well-water, and took a forkful of the second kind of cake. Walnut, merely serviceable. It did not increase his charity.

"Pardon me." She sat very still, her hands in her lap. "I should never introduce the subject of money but that this time, it does happen to concern me."

What sort of nonsensical guessing-game was this? "I'm not a subtle man, Mrs. Russell. Whatever you've got to say to me, you'd do better to put it plainly." He abandoned the cake and took up his replenished tea.

"Plainly, then. Plainly." She took a deep, deliberate breath and leveled all her attention on him. "I can get you funds, Mr. Mirkwood, in exchange for something from you. I need to conceive a child."

Only by heroic will and quick use of his napkin did he prevent a mouthful of tea from spewing straight into his lap. He choked and sputtered, and groped for the fresh napkin she held out to him as his teacup met its saucer all clumsy and percussive.

"I'm prepared to pay five hundred pounds for your assistance regardless of the issue, and fifteen hundred more if it should result in the birth of a son."

"Stop. Stop." He mopped at his mouth. "Do I understand you aright?"

Her brows drew together. "I really have no way of knowing that. I hope so."

"I understand you to have just proposed to engage me as your whore." He gave one last cough. "Is that correct?"

Disapproval thinned her lips again. "The better analogy is to a stud animal. My concern is only with the issue. I have no expectation of pleasure."

"Fine distinction." He stared at her, hard. "You mean to pay me to bed you."

"Unless you know some other way of getting me with a child, yes, that will be necessary," she said, clearly displeased with his slow grasp of the situation.

Slowly or not, though, it was all coming clear. The private room. The vanished footman. Her keen attention. Probably even the fichu omitted, and that glimpse down her bodice. Good God. How had he not seen it?

He had to laugh, then. He brought the napkin to his eyes and shook his head, and finally abandoned his chair to go to the end of the room and back. "Forgive my loss of composure," he said. "It's not often one finds oneself a player in such a ripe sort of melodrama." He took up a place behind his armchair, leaning his elbows on its back. "Shouldn't you have seduced me first? Or drugged my tea, and let me wake up chained to a bed?"

She colored, and looked more disapproving yet. "This is a business arrangement. I should like to conduct it accordingly."

"Business arrangement. That's the name you give to circumventing your husband's last wishes with a fraudulent heir?" If she thought he wouldn't catch on to *that*, she could think again.

"Yes." She lifted her chin to look steadily up at him. "Much depends on my circumventing them."

The secrets danced in her gaze like motes in a shaft of sunlight. Oh, but she was pretty. And she intrigued him. And this was absolutely not how he was meant to be spending his time in Sussex. "Hell and damnation," he muttered, and turned his face away. One finger ran absently over the chair's chintz, tracing where a rose was embroidered in. "Why me? I suppose you've heard I'll rut with anything that moves." He shot her a look. Little call for delicacy now.

"To be quite frank, I have heard you spoken of as a sensualist." The word sounded wicked, delectably wicked, on her prim soft lips. "I presume you were accustomed to keeping a mistress in London. You must know they're thin on the ground here, and even if you could find one, how would you keep her without funds? I offer you the essential benefit of a mistress without the expense. In addition, of course, to the remuneration I mentioned." He could picture her practicing those words. She'd probably even written them out beforehand.

Obviously he ought not to do this. For what reasons, though? He pushed away from the chair and went to stand before a painting on the opposite wall, the better to banish distracting thoughts of her lips. This wasn't one of those rooms with grandiose portraits of dead ancestors cluttering every surface. In fact only the one painting hung here: a study of a sunlit meadow, rolling off toward the horizon. Competently executed, but who would ever look at that when the same thing might be seen out the window, alive with breezes and butterflies? "Your plan depends on a son, I presume." He kept his back to her. "What if I got you with a daughter?"

"You'd be five hundred pounds the wealthier."

"And you that much the poorer, with another mouth to feed." Yes, *there* were solid grounds for declining her offer. "I cannot like it." With a shake of his head he started back toward the chair. "I've taken care not to spawn any children thus far, that they might not be brought up in circumstances of privation. I surmise your husband's will must have left you in a disadvantageous situation indeed if you're willing to resort to such measures to thwart it."

"But there's no risk of privation." She'd been ready for that objection. "A daughter would be entitled to a portion, and we could live comfortably enough with a brother or sister. Indeed my brother has already offered me a home."

"Then why do this?" He sat down again and reached

for what was left of his tea. "Why not go to your brother
at once?"

Her hands folded one over the other in her lap and she
went perfectly still, all light shuttered behind her dark
eyes. "Because that is not what I choose to do." The
words had such clean edges, she might have sliced them
on a tiny guillotine. "I have reasons beyond personal
avarice. I will not speak of them to a stranger, but you
may believe I have them."

"Hmm. You'd have done better with me if you'd
claimed avarice. I like a woman who takes what she
wants." He said it looking into his teacup, though, and
his voice sounded unsteady to his own ears. Because
somewhere in her last utterance she'd grown rather
magnificent, all will and determination behind the tea-
table manners. Like some dire, forbidding fairy in a
story, letting slip her mild disguise at the crucial moment.

What if she was like that in bed? Stern and exacting,
but soft to the touch. Hell. That could be good. That
could be interesting, and very, very good.

He sat back in his chair, crossing one long leg over the
other, and put aside his tea. She remained motionless, as
though husbanding her energies to meet his next refusal.

Or his assent. No harm in imagining. He could free
that creamy skin from its dour wrappings, if he just said
the word. He could discover what those elegant hands
had it in them to do. He could get her on top of him—
she'd like to be on top, fierce fairy, murmuring her stern
commands—with her hair falling like a curtain against
his cheek, and . . . "What color is your hair?" he said, as
every last wisp of it had been banished beneath her cap.

Two faint creases came between her brows. "Will that
make a difference?"

"It might." Shameful. He ought not to toy with a lady
that way. Not when he knew a hundred better ways. He

shifted in his seat. What reasons remained to refuse her, exactly? Well, if Granville got wind of this—if his father got wind of it—he'd be bundled off somewhere even more remote, and probably for the remainder of his natural life. But besides that, what reasons?

She raised one hand to her cap-strings and hesitated. He could see her groping after strategy. He could nearly hear the clatter of her thoughts, like all the looms in a Lancashire mill. Her hand lowered again and her head tilted, giving her an air both coquettish and defiant. "You may learn the color of my hair easily enough," she said. "But not by asking."

"Ah. Now you begin to speak a language I understand." A smile rose from somewhere elemental in him, coloring the words. "How often would you expect my services? If I were to agree to this?" *If.* Because he might not. But Lord, she was lovely with her head so angled and her every resource bent on how to get him into bed.

"Once each day. We'll have nearly a full month." Her speech accelerated with ill-concealed eagerness. "And I had hoped we might begin today."

"As a conclusion to this call, I suppose." Why not? Hell, really, why not?

"If you can contrive it, yes."

He was contriving it even as she spoke, conveniently enough. He'd been contriving it on and off for the whole of the visit. "Well, Mrs. Russell." He uncrossed his legs. "You seem to have bought yourself a whore." Swiftly, before she could correct his terminology, he rose up and leaned over her, resting his hands on the arms of her chair. Her mouth was even prettier at this distance. Was there some way to make her say *sensualist* again?

"What are you doing?" She blinked up at him, eyes dark with disapprobation.

"I thought to begin by kissing you."

"That won't be necessary." Uncertainty suddenly shaded her face. "Unless you require it?"

"Not at all." He straightened. This was getting better and better. "Which way is your bed?"

"Through that door, and then the door after." She rose from the chair and edged past him, her hem whispering over the toes of his boots. "I'll go now. You may follow in twenty minutes. There's some claret on the sideboard there, if you think it would be helpful to you."

"Helpful?" What kind of milksop did she suppose herself to have hired? "Darling, the day I need claret to help me come up to scratch is the day you may begin digging my grave."

So smartly answered, she could make no reply. After a short, inscrutable hesitation, she passed through the door and closed it behind her. Twenty minutes later, he followed.

*S*HE MUST have rung for a maid in that time because he found her in the bed, presumably unclothed, clutching the sheet nearly up to her chin. At his entrance her glance fell on him briefly before sliding away to the wall behind him.

He moved closer. Her hair, freed from its cap and freshly unplaited, fanned out on the pillow in kinks and slight waves. Honey-colored hair, just on that border between blond and brunette. The kind of hair that went luminous under sunlight, but kept its secrets indoors.

All secrets, this woman. And some of them were for him after all. "Mrs. Russell," he said, and brought her eyes back to his face.

"Yes?" If she had a different voice for the bedroom, she wasn't using it. Yet.

"I suspect, from what I can see of you, that you're a beautiful woman."

"Yes. Very good. Thank you." Her cadence hitched and hurried as though she spoke a foreign tongue.

And likely it was foreign indeed to her, the language of seduction. Few husbands went to the trouble. He reached for the edge of the sheet. "Let me look at you."

Her fingers tightened their grip on her covering. Her wary eyes narrowed. "Is this . . . will it be . . . useful, in . . . preparing you?"

"Useful. Yes. Helpful too." He smiled, all knowing reassurance. "May I, please?"

She closed her eyes and loosened her grip, and allowed him to draw back the sheet.

Something went stuttering in his vitals as he laid her bare. For as many times as he'd done this—seen a new woman naked—one would think he'd learn to take it in stride. One would think the thrill might wane with repetition. But good Lord in Heaven, it knocked his breath out every time.

So many different ways women had of being beautiful. Mrs. Russell's beauty was of a kind that spoke in whispers, veiled her like mist. As though she had some hope of keeping it to herself, and granted her curves might escape a careless man's notice, so gradual were they. She wanted a discerning lover. One who saw all her sensual promise. One who knew how to tease out the voluptuousness from an understated form.

Well, she'd picked the right man. No expectation of pleasure, indeed. Here, here, and here, he could do things to delight her. Here, her slight, supple body would arch and twist.

His forefinger touched down on her breastbone and traced a leisurely path between the ribs, into the hollow of her navel, and on down, just to the patch of light-colored curls. "Turn over," he said, his voice already gone thick.

Her eyes flew open. "I did not authorize anything out of the ordinary," she said, the words shrill with alarm.

"I only want to look. I promise we'll fornicate face-to-face like Christians." He couldn't quite mask his laughter. "But let me finish looking."

She frowned at him but did turn over, and he took in the rear view of her: the surprising angularity of the shoulder blades, the long, graceful indentation of the spine, and the unfailing wonder of that last little inward arch at the lower back—the best place to touch, on a clothed woman—where her body seemed to gather itself before curving out again in its tasteful way.

"Will you be needing to do this every time?" The pillow partly muffled her voice.

"Impatient, are we?" He unknotted his cravat. No reason to make the lady wait.

"Impatient to get a child. Surely you must be prepared by now."

Prepared. Really. If she spared him more than half a glance, she'd know a thing or two about *prepared*. But perhaps her husband had always come to her in the dark, and made her shy of looking. Some marriage beds went that way, all furtive and grasping, the very satisfaction cloaked in shame.

She would learn better pleasures now. With an efficiency only to be gained through much practice, he shucked his clothes. "You may turn over again if you like."

She did, and looked at him, and looked away, just as she would if she'd been foolish enough to gaze straight at the sun, or at one of those gods a mortal could not bear to behold. Apollo, or someone. Mercury. Whichever was the broadest-shouldered, and most generously equipped.

He knelt on the bed, running his gaze up and down her as he would some sumptuous private repast. His first widow—Sussex had its surprises after all—and he her hired paramour. His hand twitched impatiently; he reached out and settled it on one exquisite breast.

The fit was exactly what he'd calculated, mounding into his palm and the first joint of each finger. Cool, smooth, and sure to be sweet, like some confection— twin confections—made up special for him. Made up and then offered, artfully, in that one tantalizing glimpse against a ground of black crepe. Clever little seductress. He'd never stood a chance.

"Business arrangement, you say." The words came without thought, the way they always did after a certain point, and his voice dipped down to its most intimate range. "But you meant me to see these, didn't you? You meant to tempt me with them." He lifted his palm away and traced, with two fingers, the graceful arc that made the underside of her breast.

Her lips pressed tight together. She stared up at the canopy, cheeks flushing. No, she'd not heard this kind of talk before.

"Well, it worked." Words, voice, and fingers all conspired to caress her. "I saw what I could and imagined the rest. Just as you intended I should." Her chest rose and fell in one quick breath under his touch. "I imagined the cool silk of your skin. I imagined the colors. Ivory and rose." One hand braced on the mattress to hold his weight as he leaned lower, closer. "I imagined your scent." He closed his eyes and inhaled, slow and luxuriant. "Like fresh flowers." Like lilac-fragranced powder, to be more exact. Had she dusted it on for this very moment?

Short, shallow respirations—he was near enough to hear them now—were her only response. She was anxious, and not ready. But they had all afternoon. And he had ways.

"We'll start slowly." He eased back and lowered himself to lie beside her, up on one elbow. "Will you tell me some things you like, or would you prefer I find them out by trial?"

A second or two went by with no sign she'd heard him. Then the two creases came again between her brows. Her eyes snapped from the canopy to his face. "What?" she said.

"As slowly as you wish. As many little attentions as you need." His voice sought out its most soothing, buttery pitch. "Where might you like me to begin? Your neck?" He brushed his fingers there. "Your ears? The soles of your feet?" Ladies liked that, to have their feet stroked.

Her eyes widened for a particle of a second, and then looked grave again. "I didn't hire you for pleasure. I'm not paying you to do those things."

"But I like doing those things." Poor woman was shockingly ignorant. "They're common between a man and his mistress. And they'll help to make you ready."

"I'm ready now. You may begin as soon as you will."

Muscles pulled crazily round his mouth as he fought to contain his merriment. "No, darling." He touched a fingertip to one unripe nipple. "I meant—"

"I'd be obliged if you could accomplish this without laughing at me." Her face darkened with all the sternness he'd imagined, but none of the hunger he'd supposed would go with it. "I know what you meant. But men can manage without that. You can manage. Can't you?"

Why in hell would you want me to? He bit that back. He'd offended her already with his laughter. "Was this your husband's way of proceeding?" He spoke casually, looking down as with one hand he tested the beginnings of his own wetness. Probably enough to make do.

The silence vibrated with her uncertainty. For three full seconds he believed she might really answer. "My

husband's way of proceeding need not concern you,"
she then said. *Yes,* in other words.

So. He'd have a great deal to teach her. But this moment, with his fingers working to stroke dampness up
and down his length, he found himself perfectly willing
to oblige her impatience. "As you wish," he said, and
rose up over her.

She moved her legs apart, closed her eyes, and went
limp beneath him even as she curled one hand into a fist
at her shoulder. Bracing herself, unmistakably.

"Don't be frightened." He eased his hips forward so
she could just get the feel of him. "I know it's rather
large, but I can assure you no lady has ever had the least
difficulty with—"

"I'm not frightened. For Heaven's sake." Her eyes
stayed shut and her cheeks turned a shade of red he
would not have thought possible. "Please do begin."

Well, then. He flexed and pushed, and met with muscles clenched hard against him. No pliancy. No easy entry. He'd have to use some force, unless . . . Drawing a
deep, ragged breath, he made one last try. "Won't you
let me do a few things to relax you, if only for the sake
of—"

"No. We've discussed this more than thoroughly. Can
you just get on with it, please?"

Her words hung in the air like a chill mist, and a sudden awful slackening came in the flow of blood to his
pertinent regions. Could he really put himself somewhere so inhospitable?

Oh, for God's sake. He was a disgrace to whoredom.
To stud-animaldom as well. What bull ever felt a moment of concern for whether the cow actually desired
him? Quickly he moved into position. Put a hand down
to brace himself. Filled his lungs again. And with one
mighty push, he was in. Mere mechanics would take

care of the rest. Enough times in and out would get him there. Her tight grip on him—had he ever been so exquisitely sheathed?—might get him there even sooner.

She ought to touch him, though. Her right arm lay slack on the mattress; her left bent to keep that fist at her shoulder. "Can you put your hands on me?" he said in a hoarse whisper. Hark at him, asking politely when the occasion called for command.

But she did what he asked. And then he wished she hadn't. Her hands fell at random places on his back and stayed there, passively riding his rhythm like a pair of dead fish tossed by the sea. Or rather, one dead fish. The other still curled tight, like a brittle seashell with its soft sensate creature shrunk all the way inside.

Didn't matter. Didn't matter. Pleasure was gathering force in him now and he need only keep up the motion; shut out the sight of her impassive, closed-eyed face; shut out the disagreeable novelty of finding himself undesired. He could look at her hair. Better yet, at her breasts, her pretty breasts, bouncing daintily on his every thrust. Good. Perfect. They answered to him now, those same parts she'd used to tempt him, and other parts must answer to him in time. Her whole body would dance to his tune; her face would contort, *yes*, in savage ecstasy. He could see it so clearly, he could nearly hear her wanton cries, and finally all thought fled and the sweet sharp oblivion came as he delivered up the first installment of her purchase.

God. His chest heaved. That had been some work, after all. He rolled off and sank down on the other side of the bed, bringing his breathing back to normal. A month of this. Devil take it. How did he get himself into these things?

"Was that . . . typical?" came a voice from beside him. "As to duration?"

"Typical?" He raised his head from the pillow to peer down at her.

"It was not, perhaps . . . briefer than usual?" Her forehead showed slight furrows. She studied the bed's draperies again.

"As I recall, you were eager to get the seed and be done with it." His head dropped back to the pillow. "If you want a marathon, ask for a marathon." Ha. Not likely, that.

"No, I have no complaints. In fact, I was pleasantly surprised."

Well, that makes one of us. He wouldn't say it out loud. He sat up and grasped for his pillow. "Here. You'll want to lie on this." Her face softened with uncertainty as he slipped his hand under the small of her back.

"Oh." She settled her hips on the pillow. "I see."

He leaned back on his elbows. How long was one obliged to linger, in this sort of arrangement? He didn't like to be rude. Perhaps he ought to have given this whole thing a bit more thought.

With nothing particular to say to the woman at his side, he looked about him. Pink paper in this room too. It was a smallish bright room, white draperies pulled back from the bay window and pale pink paper on every wall, with a pattern of darker pink flowers. Foxglove, they looked like. Poison. Digitalis. Odd thing to allow into one's bedroom.

"I was married ten months," the widow said, unbidden, "and I never conceived a child."

"None that was lost early, even?" He turned back to inspect her afresh.

She shook her head, lips pursed and eyes still on the draperies above.

This was not at all propitious. "Did you and your husband have regular relations?"

Her face snapped into the already-familiar lines of disapproval as she angled it toward him. "You cannot really be expecting me to speak of that."

"I assure you I've no interest in a narrative account. I'd only like to know I haven't been set on a fool's errand. I presume you must have some grounds to believe the problem lay with him and not with you."

"He had a wife before me, and she never gave him any children in ten years. I think the problem must have been his. Don't you think so?" Under her words, in the keenness of her gaze, he sensed the slightest shadow of urgency. She wanted reassurance, and she had no one from whom to get it but him.

"Yes." God, but a woman's need always made him go soft at the core. "I certainly should have drawn that same conclusion in your place." He sat up to reach for the sheet, rumpled down at the foot of the bed, and pulled it up to cover her.

"Do you know very much about it?" Her eyes left his face to watch him tucking the sheet the way she'd done, nearly to her chin. "About getting children?"

"Not especially. As I said, my efforts have always tended rather in the other direction."

"You knew about lying on a pillow, though. That's more than I knew." She shifted under her cover, settling herself more comfortably and looking skyward again.

"Well, one hears of things that may make a difference." Idly he smoothed the sheet over her body. "Time of day. Phase of the moon. Whether or not the woman attains release."

"That last is not true." She spoke straight ahead of her, as though to convince the canopy. "I really don't see how it could be true."

Already he knew better than to argue. "Things you eat and drink might make a difference," he said instead. "Parsley, nettles. Other things. You'd probably do better to ask a woman." He stroked away the sheet's last rumple, over her thigh, and sat up again. "But I shouldn't worry if I were you." His clothes lay in a haphazard pile on the carpet; he'd been in a hurry, he now recalled, to get into bed and begin. "You're young and apparently in sound health, and you have me for a partner. You'll breed without trouble." Those were the words she'd want to hear. "Now shall I call tomorrow at this same time?" He stood.

"If that is convenient for you." Her eyes traveled over his body and her forehead etched itself with two or three severe lines.

"What? Do you see something amiss?"

"No, I only . . ." She raised her eyes, sober and intent, to his face. "I may assume, may I not, that you would never have agreed to this if you harbored any sort of dissolute disease?"

Thus were his kindly impulses repaid. "I told you I've been careful." He bent to retrieve his shirt, and pulled it on over his head. "I've confined myself to reputable courtesans and decent adulterous wives." He picked up his pantaloons; they snapped angrily as he shook them out. "And for the love of reason, next time ask that question *before* you let a stranger debauch you."

"I wouldn't say you debauched me, exactly," was all she had to murmur in reply. Theo could not have argued if his life, her life, and every life in the British Empire depended on it.

Chapter Three

$\mathcal{D}$ID SETON Park really employ all these women? Some of them, Martha had no recollection of ever seeing in ten months. Yet here they were, seated in concentric ranks round the dining-room table, faces turned expectantly to her.

"Thank you all for coming." Her voice sounded high; insubstantial. One wished for an authoritative contralto of the sort Miss York had always deployed so effectively in the schoolroom. "I'm sure you will be wondering what changes await you in the wake of our recent sad loss." Several of the older women nodded. Several of the younger ones looked a bit stunned at being addressed by the lady of the house.

To call such a meeting was irregular, certainly. But *irregular* rang quaintly in the ear, she found, once one took the step of hiring a libidinous wastrel to perform in one's bed.

"You will have heard rumors, I don't doubt, and perhaps none of what I say this morning will come as news to you. I say it, though, to make clear where my allegiance lies. To have certain things open between us." She paused to take a sip of tea. Or not tea, exactly, but a concoction of nettles Sheridan had been so kind as to brew for her. The maid sat one row out from the table now, and gave a small encouraging smile as Martha's eyes landed on her.

Decidedly she needed all the encouragement she could get. "Here are the facts," she said, and, over the rabbit-like racing of her own heart, managed an account of the will and the hope for an heir—a legitimate heir, of course, as the unseemly truth was better kept secret—and the consequences if that hope failed. The bit about Mr. James Russell was news to no one. Mrs. Kearney, the housekeeper, had obviously made his infamy known.

"This was years ago, mind, and I have no evidence he continues so corrupt." Her pulse beat strongly still, but steadily. More like a running horse than a bolting rabbit. "If he has reformed, then perhaps I wrong him." She set down her tea and spread her fingers on the white damask tablecloth, leaning forward. "So be it. I will take that risk, before I will risk the safety of any of you by leaving you ignorant of the facts. So I tell you." She looked from face to face to face. "Because if I were one of you, I would want to be told."

What an odd sensation: like the little fountain of sparks that went up when a stick broke in the grate. Something—who could say what?—seemed to have broken in the middle of her, and those sparks went charging all through her blood, warming her limbs and bringing color to her face. "What to do hereafter is your choice." The words came now as though she'd waited all her life to say them. "If you wish to seek a new situation at once, I'll give you a character and whatever other help I can. If you'd rather wait until the question of an heir comes to some resolution, I'll inform you as soon as I know any more of that matter. You have my promise, in either case, that I'll do everything in my power to prevent your falling victim to such a man."

If only *everything in my power* could have taken some
grander shape! If she could face down Mr. James Russell
with a sword in her hand and an army at her back, for
instance. Or lead every last one of these women to safety
through smoke and flames. She ventured a smile round
their ranks—they were all watching her as though she
were some wild-eyed stranger come to impersonate
the mistress—and reached for her nettle brew again.

She would do what she must. Lie still and bear the
breaching of her body by a stranger, and then hope the
stranger's seed bore fruit. Sacrifice came in different
shapes, for a woman, and if it brought about the proper
result, that would have to be grandeur enough.

I'VE ARRANGED all the books that will be of most value
to you in this row." What a pathetic place the library
looked, with no family in residence to fill its shelves with
novels and leave periodicals lying about. Mr. Granville's
collection took up only two shelves and a half, and
doubtless each work was duller than the last.

"I like the ceiling." Theo threw his head back to study
it, hands in his pockets and feet planted apart. "Barrel-
vaulting. You don't see that often. Gives the place a sort
of Roman look, wouldn't you say?" The built-in book-
shelves all arched at the top, echoing the ceiling's curve,
and what furniture there was had clean, classical lines.
He could approve of this room, if it were given a little
life and perhaps a mosaic-patterned carpet.

"Roman, quite." Granville was brandishing something at him; he could see it from the corner of his eye.
"Here's a work I think will make a good general introduction, and from there you might progress to any of
these others."

He took the pamphlet and cast an eye on its cover.
The Utility of Agricultural Knowledge to the Sons of the

Landed Proprietors of England, and to Young Men in-
tended for Estate-Agents; illustrated by what has taken
place in Scotland. With an Account of an Institution
formed for Agricultural Pupils in Oxfordshire. By a
Scotch Farmer and Land-Agent, resident in that County.
God help him now.

"That's neatly tailored to the occasion, isn't it?" He
sank into the nearest armchair and flipped a few leaves.
Page of oppressive text succeeded page of oppressive
text.

"My thoughts exactly." The man beamed as though
he'd written the accursed thing himself. "Now, will I
disturb you if I stay here and do a bit of work?" He
gestured unintelligibly. "I'd like to finish this map of the
parcels available for enclosure, and I'm afraid the gate-
house hasn't any surface suitable for such drawing."

"By all means, stay and work." Parcels? What parcels? Had he dozed through some discussion of that?
And would Granville expect him to make a petition for
enclosure? Splendid. Another opportunity to display his
ignorance. He bent his head over the book and watched
sidelong as the agent settled himself before a slanted table on which lay a great sheet of paper all marked in
pencil. Drawing maps looked a good deal more interesting than the *Utility of Agricultural Knowledge.* But
then, what didn't?

"I called on the widow yesterday," he said after several pages turned.

"Mrs. Russell?" Granville glanced up. "And how is
she?—I haven't seen her since the unhappy event myself.
I expect her spirits must be low."

"I think so." He had yet to see her smile, now he
thought of it. He wouldn't count that sham quirk of the
lips by which she'd lured him into discussion of Brighton. "But I don't suppose I'm the best suited to judge,

just meeting her. She strikes me as being of a sober temperament altogether."

"To be sure." The other man held up several pens, examining their points in the light. "A good, serious-minded woman. Not so interested in the lighter things as some women are."

"I received that impression as well." He turned another page, its papery whisper a punctuation to his thoughts, though he'd read none of it.

"She had business to discuss, then?" The best pen selected, Granville set the others aside and uncapped a bottle of ink.

"Yes, she had a number of things to say." *Was that typical? As to duration?* "Concerning land, and land management, and so forth."

"Very good." He dipped his pen and set to inking over the pencil lines. "If I don't overstep my bounds in saying so, I believe this is exactly the sort of acquaintance Sir Frederick had in mind when he put you here in Sussex."

"Do you?" Theo bent his head a little lower over the *Utility*.

"If I don't overstep." The pen scratched faintly across the paper, a muted accompaniment to Mr. Granville's words. "He hoped for you to absorb the influence of respectable people, I know. None more respectable than Mrs. Russell. Did you happen to discuss cottage roofs?"

"No, I don't recall that being among the topics we canvassed." *May I assume you're not harboring any dissolute disease?*

"Pity. They replaced all the cottage roofs at Seton Park this summer. There might be some value to you in hearing her account of it."

"Ah. Well, next time, perhaps." Or perhaps when Hell froze over. A sad day it would be when he had nothing more compelling to discuss with a woman than the replacement of cottage roofs.

Today would go better with Mrs. Russell. It could scarcely go worse, of course. But the more he'd thought on the topic, the more clearly he'd seen that most, if not all, of yesterday's difficulties could be ascribed to her anxiety. She'd probably never lain with any man excepting her apparent lummox of a husband; certainly never with a stranger, and she would have been so wound up with hoping he'd agree to her bargain, how could she possibly relax? Today he would come to her as a known quantity, his cooperation secured. That would make all the difference.

"The call did her good as well, I don't doubt." Granville paused in his inking to consult a paper on which he appeared to have made some notes. "It's a sad thing, in my opinion, that widows should live so secluded just when society might be most welcome. Never venturing abroad; only waiting for what callers might come. And I don't believe she has a very broad acquaintance."

"Then I'll do my best to not neglect her. As propriety allows, of course." He rubbed a hand across his mouth to cover an imprudent smile. They were conspiring against him, the virtuous people of the world. Plainly they did not want him among their number. Well, who was he to battle on when such might was arrayed on the opposing side? Between respectable Mrs. Russell bribing him into her bed, and worthy Mr. Granville all but ordering him back there, what could he do but succumb?

*S*HE WATCHED him undress this time, from her place in the bed where she'd gone before him. His clothing looked expensive—probably one of those indulgences that so affronted his father—but it was at least tasteful. He removed an impeccably tailored coat of sage-tinted wool; then a waistcoat whose more vibrant green quite became, one must allow, his fair coloring and dark blue eyes. "Is that Irish linen?" she said of his shirt, just to be saying something, and "Yes, in fact, it is," he answered before lifting it, a bit slowly, over his head.

Clearly he was expecting to be admired. He would be used to it, well-proportioned man that he was. His musculature altogether outpaced what she had seen in Mr. Russell, though Mr. Russell had set no very difficult standard to surpass. That mattered to some women. Muscles and so forth. Those taut flat ones across his stomach, for instance. Or the ones that stood out on his arms. Women who didn't place the proper priority on a man's character had doubtless taught him to be vain of his physique, and even a woman of principle could enjoy, on some aesthetic level, the picture he made with his shirt removed.

Then he let his pantaloons fall, and that was the end of the enjoyment.

In its place welled up that same dismay she'd known on her first viewing, some ten months past, of a naked man. Whose idea of good design was this? Why those awkward angles, and what could be the necessity for all that hair? If one believed, as the Bible and the Greek myths had it, that man had been created first and woman after, then one must conclude there had been some dramatic improvement in the process following that amateurish first attempt.

Where she was molded, he was rough-hewn. Where her form curved with logic and precision, not to mention breeding parts tucked neatly away, he looked rangy, haphazard, his male parts an ill-placed afterthought. Like the last leftover bits of clay scraped together, rolled into primitive forms and stuck onto the middle of him, the stones in their rough red sack and that improbable appendage dangling to the fore.

Or not dangling, at the moment, but standing alertly

up, all expectation, all dumb demand. So had Mr. Russell's done, with tedious frequency. Her husband's appendage had stiffened and sought her out regardless what she felt or thought, and for this, finally, she could not respect it.

Nor could she now respect Mr. Mirkwood's exemplar, despite its apparently remarkable size, and the jaunty air suggesting confidence of its welcome anywhere. It bobbed once or twice when he straightened from stepping out of his clothes, then settled into stillness. She glanced up at him. He was watching her, hands on his hips, satisfied to be the object of a lady's scrutiny. "It's all yours, darling, bought and paid for," he said with what was probably a rakish smile.

What on earth did one say in reply to that? It wasn't even accurate—she hadn't paid him yet—but really, the less said on this subject, the better. Yesterday had been rather excruciating in that regard. *Your skin is like silk. You smell like flowers.* He must seduce chiefly on the strength of his good looks. He couldn't expect to overcome any lady with poetic invention.

Withdrawing her gaze, she moved over a little and held up the covers on one side. He slipped in beside her, appendage leading the way, as indeed it must lead him through much of his business in life. Instead of proceeding to the task, though, he propped his elbow on the pillow and his cheek on that hand, and angled his face to address her. "Where did you grow up?" he said.

Now what? "In the north part of Cambridgeshire."

"We're neighbors, then. My family estate is in Lincolnshire." He set his hand on her rib cage, fitting each finger into one of the spaces between. "I'm exiled to a mere minor holding here. How many brothers and sisters do you have?"

"Three brothers and a sister. Why do you ask?"

"I want this to be easier for you today." His voice was

light; conversational. His fingers flexed comfortably in the channels between her ribs. "I think if we can talk for a bit, and begin to grow acquainted, your body might not resist so hard as it did yesterday."

She could feel a scorching blush spread from her ears to her cheeks. "I think it would be better if you just went ahead. If we delay you might lose your readiness." Too, an increased acquaintance with him was not likely to help his cause. But she wouldn't say so.

"My readiness?" He grinned as though she'd made some joke especially for his benefit, and brought his mouth down by her ear. *"It's called an erection,"* he whispered, "and I assure you I'm in no danger of losing it."

Was she to congratulate him for the accomplishment? With some remark upon its immensity, no doubt? Men had the strangest notions. "I'd really prefer we begin now. We can converse afterward if you like." She put her knees apart and closed her eyes. Vague noises ensued: he must be readying his male parts, as he'd done yesterday. A moment later, it began.

Martha gave a small sigh, just to herself. This again. Presumably this was enjoyable with a man one desired. Absent desire, she was left only with the weight of another body on hers. Strange skin against her own, with hair in strange places. Hip-bones pressing into her, and everything pressing into her. Seeking entry; seeking and . . . gaining it, *there,* on one long slide.

He breached her with less trouble this time, her body apparently resigning itself to its fate. The rest was much like yesterday, and much as it had been with Mr. Russell. The same farcical action took him to his crisis: haunches heaving in a style reminiscent of some rutting dog, or ram, or any of those other creatures to which she had always supposed a man superior. He bent his head to the pillow, his breath warm and moist and labored against her ear. Close by her ear too were the sounds he made:

five grunts and four groans she counted today, spaced gradually closer together, and gradually more urgent in tone until on the last harsh animal utterance he gave up the seed, and it was done with for another day.

He helped her onto the pillow again, strong hand under the small of her back. That was kind of him. He'd been kind to show her this pillow business in the first place. She ought to be polite to him, at least. She took a breath. "On what subject would you like to converse?"

Sidelong she could see how his head turned to consider her, though she kept her own eyes to the canopy. "You're quite young, aren't you?" he said. "Not much past twenty, I should think."

Propriety, one must recall, had different boundaries in an association like this one. A man would expect such familiarity with the woman he bedded. "I'm one and twenty." She cleared her throat. "Though my sister is fond of saying I've never been young."

"Your husband must have been older by a good margin. He had a wife for ten years, you said." His curiosity was like an impertinent touch exploring the shape of her cheek, her neck, her shoulder. "How did he land you? Some claim on your father?"

She whipped round to face him. "Inconceivable as it may be to a man of your youth, some young ladies will choose an older man of their own free will. Some weigh factors other than mere sentimental indulgence in making that choice."

"I'm six and twenty. Not so very young." Either he'd missed the reprimand, or he'd had so many in his time that he could now absorb one and move on with barely a blink of his ocean-blue eyes. "What factors weighed with you, then? Please don't say security. Given the outcome, I'd have no choice but to pity you."

"Save your pity." She could hear the words emanating from some polar region, calm and cold and distant. "My father was dying. My mother had died long before. My immediate choice was to marry, or to live as my brother's dependent."

"I'm sorry." His eyes glittered at her. On closer observation one perceived bits of gold scattered throughout the blue.

"Thank you. But I was not so well acquainted with my parents as to be very deeply bereaved."

"Now I'm sorrier still." Like sunlight sparkling on ocean waves, the gold in his watchful gaze.

"You needn't be." She angled her face skyward again. "I had a thoroughly competent governess."

"Sorry you had to choose a husband under such circumstances, then. That must have been difficult." His manifest curiosity was patting at her again, like the hand of a blind man trying to work out just who she was.

"I should have had to marry sooner or later. And I'm not romantic. I'm sure one husband is very like another." She tugged at the sheet, to shield more of herself from his scrutiny, but it caught: he had a fold of the fabric pinned underneath him.

"I doubt that." His hair brushed against the pillow, a sibilant whisper, as he turned to gaze at the canopy with her. "Women are all so different. I expect husbands must be as well." His scent wafted to her with his movement. At the forefront was something not his own. Something piquant. Citrus. His shaving-soap, most likely. Behind that were other scents, murky and male. Her bed would smell of him when he had gone. So would she. "You don't miss him, then. Mr. Russell."

"I never said so." She tugged again at the sheet. "And I must say I don't approve of such forward conversation."

"Forward?" His impudent classical profile gave way to his impudent full-on stare. Even sidelong she could see the gold flecks in his eyes dancing with merriment.

"Which one of us is paying the other to be naked in her bed? I shouldn't speak of *forward* if I were you."

"Depend upon it, I am painfully aware of how I have lowered myself, and need no reminding. Notice, though, that I stop short of asking you exactly what prompted your banishment, or whether you miss your most recent mistress. I am not *forward* without good cause."

"My banishment isn't so interesting a tale as you suppose." Classical profile again, and this time he lifted a hand to inspect his neat fingernails as he spoke. "No cuckolded husband baying for my blood. No gambling away the heirloom silver. Only I'm an expensive son to keep, and therefore trying to my father's patience." He ran a thumb over the edge of one nail, back and forth, as though he'd found a ragged spot there. "The precipitating incident, if you would know, was my expenditure of two months' allowance to buy a single snuffbox. Sèvres." His glance cut over to her. Without quite realizing it she'd turned on her side to watch him speaking.

"That does seem extravagant." Wasteful, in fact, and foolish in the extreme.

"Particularly given that I don't use snuff." This bit he delivered to his hand, which was now touching thumb to fingertips, one by one. "My father shared your assessment, though in stronger terms. So here I am." He let the hand fall. "And no to the other."

"I beg your pardon? No to what?"

"My mistress. I don't miss her." He indulged in a tremendous catlike stretch of his limbs, shifting all the gravity in the bed and finally liberating the sheet. "I've never yet missed a lady from whom I parted. I have a habit of forgetting all women save the one who is directly before me."

"That is . . ." She rolled several over-strong words round in her mouth as she adjusted the sheet. "Unfortunate."

"That depends on which woman you are." He needn't sound so satisfied.

"I should think it unfortunate for any woman who relied on your constancy."

"Yes. I avoid that kind, as a rule." He sat up and swung his feet to the floor. "The same time tomorrow?" he said over his shoulder.

"The same time, but a different place." She'd nearly forgot to tell him. "We'll be meeting in another room henceforward, at the other end of the house. You can come in a side door and go up a servants' stairway where you won't be seen."

"Very good." He stood, catching up some clothing on the way. "I have abundant experience in that sort of thing."

One did not encourage such remarks with an answer. She lay on her pillow and watched, silently, as he stepped into drawers and pantaloons and pulled the shirt of Irish linen back over his head. Only when he sat to put on his boots did a topic present itself. "Do you own any top boots?" she said. "They're better suited to the country-side than your Hessians."

"More to your taste, are they?" He favored her with a sly half-smile. "I did happen to have a pair made, and I can certainly wear them next time if you desire to see me in them."

How much of this nonsense would she be obliged to endure? "I was speaking of practical matters, of walking through pastureland and such. I have no preference as to what you wear."

"Then obviously I haven't worn the right thing yet." He stretched his booted legs out before him as though for her viewing pleasure. "Now tell me how I'm to find this room where our trysts will go forward."

*　*　*

*Y*ou might give it out that you'd had a boy, and dress her in boys' clothes. I've heard of such cases." Thank goodness for an unshockable maid. Not once had Sheridan questioned the enterprise, or so much as raised an eyebrow. She'd been resourceful, too, in such matters as finding the way for Mr. Mirkwood to come and go unnoticed in future, to a bedroom in the house's closed-up east wing.

"But the truth must come out eventually, mustn't it?" Martha frowned at her reflection. With her caller gone on his sated way, she sat at her dressing table, waiting for her hair to be put back up. "A girl couldn't live her whole life under that pretense. Sooner or later the facts would reach Mr. James Russell, and I'd lose the estate and be in great trouble besides."

The maid pursed her lips and watched her own hands plaiting. "There's switching goes on as I've heard of."

"Switching?" Almost certainly she'd rather be kept in ignorance of this.

"Where an heir is badly wanted." Their eyes met in the mirror. "You find a boy baby of near the same age, and when yours is born, if it's a girl, you switch them."

"I couldn't change my child for another." Her hand went inadvertently to her heart. "I can't believe anyone would."

"People who want for money will do all manner of things." Sheridan pinned up the first plait. "Some, especially those with too many children, might be glad to give one to a fine home in exchange for some payment. If you had a girl, you could get a boy that way, and keep your own child too, and say you had twins. You might get a boy that way in any case." The maid spoke softly, eyes averted.

"If I don't conceive a child of my own, you mean." She would have thrown herself away for nothing then.

"I've heard of it. A lady puts on padding under her dress, to look as though she were increasing, and—"

"Yes, I see how it would be managed. I shall have to give that some thought." She picked up a hand-mirror from the tabletop and turned it over and over and over again. Please Providence it wouldn't come to that. Buying some desperate woman's baby. That might be more than she could do.

And yet it might, perhaps, have been the more prudent course. Women did die of this. One's own mother, to take the obvious example. Women of insufficient bodily fortitude lay down in childbed and never got up again.

Nothing whatsoever to be gained by dwelling on that. "Were you able to air out the rooms in the east wing?" she said, and spoke thereafter of mundane things.

WITH HER hair all arranged and her dress restored, she went for a walk. The late-afternoon sun shone steady and warm, and her wanderings took her, as they so often did, to the low, uninhabited cottage set aside for Mr. Atkins's school, where she found the door standing open and the curate himself within. He stood at one end of the building's single room, bent over a table where he was sawing a thin strip of wood.

From the corner of his eye he must have noticed her: he looked up, smiled, and waved her in, setting down his saw to reach for the coat hanging over the back of a nearby chair.

"Don't stop your work on my account." She hesitated at the threshold.

"Oh, there's no hurry to finish this." He shrugged into his coat. On the tabletop were stacked a dozen or so schoolroom slates.

"Will you use those in your school?" She scraped the

soles of her boots as well as she could on the grass, and came into the room. He'd spent a good hour on hands and knees, she knew, scrubbing the brick floor clean.

"Some school will. If not ours, I'll find another who can make use of them." Over his shoulder he said this, as he'd turned away to button his coat. The simple gesture of modesty sent an ache to the middle of her chest. She wore traces of citrus scent still.

"Well, as to that, I've posted the letter to Mr. James Russell, and I'm hopeful of a favorable reply." She said it quickly, before he could turn to face her, and when she reached the table she bent her head to examine a slate. Lying to the curate wasn't like lying to anyone else.

"Your kindness has long since surpassed my power to give thanks. But I do thank you." He'd finished with his coat and took a step back to the table.

"Are you putting frames on these?" Foolish question. Obviously he was.

"To make them uniform, yes." He picked up the new subject with a will. "I've acquired them from all over, and some don't have frames, as you see. Some have broken frames." He lifted one to show her. "I shouldn't want any pupil to have a poorer slate than any other. It may sound like a trifle, but the latest scholarship in the field tells us these things matter." His hands straightened a pile of short slats cut from his wood strip. He wanted to be working again, clearly.

"I can see the way it would matter." Martha stripped off her gloves. "Now how may I be of use?"

A smile came to his eyes first, and sifted down to his mouth. He looked up from the table. "Have you any practice with a penknife?"

"Very little. You'd better give me some inconsequential task."

"No task is inconsequential. You're speaking to a churchman, recall." He picked up a knife from among a little arrangement of tools. "My humble worn slates come with humble worn slate-pencils in need of better points. Would you be so good as to sharpen them?"

So she pulled up a chair and set to paring one stubby slate-pencil after another, while he measured and marked his wood strip against the slates, sawing off new pieces and arranging them in sets.

Could any other congress with a man be so agreeable as this? He had his work to do, and she had hers, and nothing stirred the air between them but the soft scrape of her knife, the intermittent rasping of his saw, and a noble shared purpose.

The curate's wife would be fortunate, as wives went. She would spend many such hours. And as to marital obligations, likely a churchman would exercise his rights with a becoming modesty. Without so much fuss and fanfare as other men found necessary. Afterward, he and his wife would lie side by side and talk. He might try out bits of the sermon he was making that week, and ask her opinion. She might tell him what she'd observed in visiting the cottagers that day. Together they would confer, and hatch plans for bettering the lives of everyone in the parish.

Citrus wafted to her nose, as though to remind her she had no right to think of a virtuous man. But citrus could take its counsel elsewhere. She could think, if she chose, of the objective advantages of marriage to a clergyman, particularly an upright and considerate one. One who might come to his wife's bed some nights with no other purpose than to talk. To know what were her ideas and judgments, and to share his own with her.

A wife could look forward to those visits. Then, perhaps, to the other visits. He might touch her in different places one night, and chance across the place that governed her satisfaction. Then he would wish to please her, and she might help him discover how.

Martha shifted in her chair and gave a tiny shake of her head. She, herself, would not do any of these things. She could see Mr. Atkins glance up at her movement, but when she neither spoke nor raised her eyes, he went back to his work. Better that way. This way. Better for a woman to see to her own satisfaction, as necessary, and to keep independent of men as far as she could.

She lifted her sharpened slate-pencil to blow stray shavings off its tip. "Did you say you'd read studies recommending the uniformity of schoolroom supplies? I'm sure I should like to hear all you can tell of your reading." Indeed, if her plan succeeded and she kept her position here, she could share ideas and opinions with him whenever she wished. She would have no cause at all to envy the curate's wife, or, for that matter, any man's wife.

Chapter Four

$\mathcal{P}$EOPLE LIVE there?" Theo stared openly at the first of the cottages. "I've seen better pigpens."

"I don't doubt it," Mr. Granville said. "And I have every confidence you'll take care not to repeat such a remark within earshot of those people who do, in fact, live here."

"Well, of course." The admonition stung, then irked him. He'd never had the least intention of insulting the cottagers' homes in their hearing.

But the house and its grounds were appalling. He'd formed no precise expectation, having spared a thought for these buildings only when Granville spoke of them, but he'd had a vague idea, he supposed, of something pastoral, something like those tenant farms on the Lincolnshire estate. Tidy little yards, with ripe fields beyond. Robust children running about in plain but clean clothing. A fresh scent of grass and meadow flowers, perhaps, or, alternately, a whiff of some savory stew being readied for the family dinner.

What he had not expected, first of all, were geese. Geese and their leavings. But the foul gray creatures ran rampant over what grass remained, and on passing through the gate, he was grateful for Mrs. Russell's advice to change his Hessians for top boots. To pick his way from gate to house, avoiding all the geese's evil handiwork, should have required a St. Vitus's dance of sorts, entirely unsuitable for the tenants' first glimpse of him. So he fixed his eyes straight ahead and stepped forward. One goose approached, stretched out its neck, and hissed at him, a distinctly triumphant look on its face.

"This is the Weaver family," said Mr. Granville.

"Weaver," he repeated, to show he was paying attention. "What sort of house is that? It looks as though it were made of mud." That was charitable. Its walls suggested the dredged-up contents of a cesspit.

"Nearly so, in part. The studs are wood, and between them is clay mixed with straw. Not as smart as stone or brick, perhaps, but durable enough. It's stood for a hundred years and more. I expect it had some sort of whitewash at one time."

They were close enough now that he could hear a crying baby—the sound made each hair on the back of his neck stand up—and, as though the picture of squalor had needed any embellishment, a sizable pig came lurching round the corner of the house and made for the front door, with every appearance of expecting to accompany them inside.

"Why do you suppose the pig is permitted in the yard?" he asked at a discreet volume, before Granville could knock on the door. "And the geese?"

"This is all the land they have." The man gave him a quizzical look. "These are hired laborers, mind, not tenant farmers such as you may have been accustomed to at Broughton Hall."

Ah. Laborers. Another fine point he'd missed. Still, one would think they could pen the geese.

Granville knocked. The pig edged closer. Closer, too,

came the sound of the crying baby as whoever was holding it approached the door. He took off his hat, and
Granville did the same.

"Mrs. Weaver, good day," said the agent, a bit loudly
to allow for the baby's increased volume as the door
opened. The pig heaved forward, but Theo blocked it
with one boot. "May I present Mr. Mirkwood, the proprietor's eldest son? I'm showing him round the estate
today." With surprising agility, the pig feinted left and
then surged right. He just managed to get his boot in
front of it again, prompting an indignant barrage of
squeals and grunts to round out the general cacophony.

"Come in, then," said Mrs. Weaver. "Pleased to meet
you, sir," she added, without any perceptible effort to
convince.

Well, he was not particularly pleased to meet her, either. Her or her squalling baby or, for that matter, any
one of the numerous children now to be perceived in the
cottage's dingy interior. They were probably worthy
enough folk, after their fashion, but what had he to say
to them? No more than he had to say to the pig, who
now voiced its grievances from the other side of the
closed door.

Mr. Granville and Mrs. Weaver spoke of the weather
and the recent harvest, leaving him to look about. It was
a cottage of only one story, a large room in front and
two doors on the back wall leading to whatever consti-
tuted the rest of the house. Sleeping-quarters, probably,
for those Weavers who merited better than a pallet on
the front-room floor, and then some sort of pantry or
larder. The place could use a good cleaning, beginning
with the kitchen table, on which sat the apparent remains of dinner along with a healthy visitation of house-
flies. One would think some of the numerous children
might trouble to clear the dishes.

The children appeared to number ten altogether. A

few girls, a few boys, and a few young ones of indeter-
minate gender in smocked dresses and unshorn curls,
they disposed themselves listlessly about the pallets and
other poor furnishings. One or two spared him a sullen
glance. Largely he was ignored.

Who could approve such children, with no visible capacity either for industry or for childish dissipation?
Granted they lacked many of the advantages he'd enjoyed as a child, but a tidy house could boost their spirits prodigiously, and *that,* at least, was in their power.
Someone ought to tell them so.

A small one roused itself to cough several times, and
sank back into lassitude on its pallet. Probably it was ill
with something pestilent. Probably this whole room was
rank with contagion. If he had been their parent, he
should have insisted they go outdoors and breathe better air.

Some movement in the corner caught his eye: one of
the children was not quite idle. A round-faced girl, fifteen or so, sat in a chair with her head bent, her attention all absorbed by something in her lap. Needlework,
perhaps? A diminutive pet? But no—she had a piece of
gold paper and was folding it with great care and concentration. A favorite pastime of young girls, if his own
sisters were anything to go by. So many hours they'd
spent in this occupation, turning out the most marvelous things: swans, castles, ingenious little men with
jointed limbs. They'd grown out of it, though, by the
time of reaching this girl's years.

As he watched, she folded the paper in half, lining up
the corners. Then in half again. Then two times more, to
make a small square with a thickness of sixteen sheets.
She looked at it, turned it over, and unfolded it: to
eighths, then quarters, then halves, then all the way out.
The creases, he could see, were nearly worn through.
She smoothed the paper in her lap and began to fold

again, in just the same pattern, with the same force of attention.

Some need of the baby's drawing Mrs. Weaver away, he leaned near to Granville and spoke in an undertone. "The eldest girl is simple?"

"Indeed," his agent answered with a curt nod, managing to suggest quite plainly that the question would better have waited until they were gone from the house.

So he said nothing more on the subject. The cottage looked different, though, now he knew it contained this sadness. By such an age his sisters had progressed to more intricate crafts—somewhere he had a box Mary had made for him, all pasted over with strips of paper rolled into pretty spirals—and progressed, too, to an interest in gowns, and the balls they should wear them to, and the eligible young men they should meet there. Of course no girl in this cottage was likely to attend balls, but the simpleminded daughter might have to remain here always, watching her younger sisters grow past her to contrive their own establishments.

Those sisters who survived to adulthood, that was. He was obliged to make that emendation as the small smocked one fell into another coughing fit. What an arrogant fool he'd been to judge them. Probably half these children would never see sixteen.

He'd worked himself into ridiculously low spirits by the time they left the house, and nearly tripped over the pig, who had taken care to put itself in his path. "What do we pay Mr. Weaver?" he asked as they passed out of the yard.

"Eight shillings a week, same as all the laborers." Granville had to close the gate twice before it latched.

Eight shillings sounded like a pitiful wage. One couldn't be sure, though, not knowing the price of a loaf of bread, or, for that matter, anything practical at all. "Is that all they have to live upon?"

"Mrs. Weaver and the older children work at the harvest, and earn some then. And the children might make a few pennies picking rocks for a neighbor, or keeping off the birds from a crop. Nothing much to speak of. They do receive some supplement out of the poor rates."

So it *was* a miserable wage. "Why do we not simply pay them more, and not depend upon the parish to keep them out of poverty?"

"It's a difficult thing." Granville looked older out of doors. He must be forty or so, but the sunlight gave him a worn appearance. Perhaps this topic did too. "Wheat is fetching only sixty-six shillings a quarter this year, sharply down from what it was a few years back. No telling where the price will go."

"Is this not a profitable piece of land?" The concept was an outright novelty. Why keep property that didn't bring in a good income?

"Barely, now. It's not large enough to ever be truly lucrative. Not on the scale of your Lincolnshire estate."

"I see." He fell into silence. *Not large enough to be lucrative.* Could enclosure of adjacent land cure that? He might raise the question, later, when he'd studied a bit on the subject and had a look at Granville's map. More hours in the library. Splendid. He should be a soft, bookish-looking fellow indeed by the time he was judged responsible enough to be admitted back to London.

He met other families: the Knights, the Tinkers, the Rowlandsons, and the Quigleys, all more modest in size than the Weaver clan, and with better-mannered pigs. The last cottage they passed over as it belonged to a bachelor, who was then out in the wheat field with the other men.

Could there be anything less fitted for engaging a man's interest than wheat and its cultivation? Perhaps he should have felt differently if he'd seen the field before harvest, rippling rows of gold in the middle of Sussex green, but today, as he and the agent approached it over a rise, he saw the wheat bound in shocks, waiting for whatever happened next to wheat, stark on the stubbled-over ground. So much of the stuff, and still not enough to make a good income.

Mr. Granville presented him to the men there, the husbands and nearly-grown sons of the families he'd visited. They were suitably sturdy, outdoor-looking specimens, most of them, save for one elderly, slow-moving man who proved to be the bachelor Mr. Barrow. Their hands, when he shook them, were coarse and callused, and Mr. Barrow's seemed furthermore a bit crabbed. Surely his working years could not be many more.

Several minutes of agricultural discussion transpired. Something about prospective tariffs, and how these could give an advantage in market to the domestic crop. More remarks upon the weather. Nothing of note. Theo stood with his hands behind his back and his head up, a bit removed from the conversation as was fitting for a landlord, until the time came for everyone to bow and restore his respective hat. "The smaller families with older sons are fortunate," he said as he and Granville moved along. "Two or more wages, and fewer people to divide them among."

"The shape of your family makes a great difference, doesn't it? I'm sorry the Weavers have no grown-up sons." They were walking a path that followed a rail fence now, and from time to time the man rapped at some part of it, presumably to test the soundness of its joints.

"Mr. Barrow has no family at all? Not even nieces or nephews, I mean?"

"No." This brought an extra gravity, he could see, to Granville's weathered features. "He had sisters, I know, but they married long ago and settled somewhere far north."

"No one to take an interest in caring for him, then."

"It's not as uncommon a case as one might like it to be. Reminds a man of the importance of marrying. Not a man of independent means, of course—you may look after yourself and then pay others to do so, if you choose."

This sounded a dismal prospect. He must remember to think seriously of marriage, in five or ten years, and in the meantime, to ingratiate himself with his sisters' children. "But Mr. Barrow," he said. "There will come a time—soon, perhaps—when he can no longer earn a wage."

"Aye, and after that, a time when he cannot keep house, and a time when he cannot care for himself." Granville stopped, having found a place in the fence that did not make the proper reply to his knock. He rapped at it again, and then took out a pencil and a folded bit of paper to make some note.

Theo waited. "What happens to such a man at that time?" he said when the agent had finished.

He shook his head without looking up. "If a man does live to that age, and has no connections, like as not he ends in the workhouse infirmary."

"Workhouse." The one word was all he could manage.

"There's one in Cuckfield, a bit to the north and west of here." A small silence followed, then Granville spoke again. "It's as difficult an end as you may imagine, for a man who's supported himself and stayed out of debt all his life." He put away his pencil and walked on.

What more could be said on the subject? Nothing at all. The sun shone hot already through the still summer air, and by the time they returned to the house he felt as though he had walked a dozen miles with something heavy—the Weaver pig, perhaps—strapped to his shoulders. Thank the fates he had his amusements in the widow's bed still before him today. A man with responsibilities needed some place to escape them.

*H*E ARRIVED promptly at half past the hour, letting himself in without a knock as though the place were his own. "You found the room," said Martha, watching him from her armchair.

"With a woman waiting for me there? Of course I found it." He pulled the door shut with a little smile in appreciation of his witticism. "It's convenient as can be. There's a woods straddling our properties with a path through it that lets me out just feet from your side door. Altogether discreet." While sharing this information he surveyed the room, blinking in its relative dim. Discretion had dictated just a sliver of space between the drapes.

Whether he would approve of the furnishings had not come into her mind when she'd chosen this set of rooms, but they did rather suit him, now one thought of it. The sitting room was larger than her own, with a grand marble fireplace and everything done up in blues and grays. Blue-and-gray carpet, blue-paneled walls, sapphire-and-silver striped damask on the massive chairs and sofa. In better light, his eyes would probably appear to advantage against these colors.

"This is decidedly more opulent than your rooms," he said, coming over to where she sat and dropping into the facing armchair. He looked proportionate there. Not overlarge and ill contained, as he'd done in her own spindly-legged furniture.

"My rooms suit me. And to many, many people, I'm sure they would represent opulence beyond imagining."

"Quite." He propped his elbows on the chair's arms, steepled his fingers, and studied them. If anything was in his mind, he made no move to share it.

She sat straighter. "I see you've changed to top boots today."

"To be sure. Trousers as well." Immediately he brightened at the new topic, and stuck out one leg before him, twisting the boot back and forth. "What they lack in elegance, they make up in a certain virility, wouldn't you say?"

"I really don't know. I hope you did not wear them for my benefit."

"No, dear." He swung his foot back down beside the other, and untwined his fingers to stretch out his arms. "I was busy about my land this morning, and wore them for that purpose."

Here was a promising change of subject. "Were you doing some work on the land, you mean?"

He shook his head. "Walking about with my agent, merely, and getting acquainted with things." His gaze went somewhere past her, perhaps to the stripe of light between the drapes. "We grow wheat, it would appear," he added after a moment. One hand moved restlessly on the arm of his chair.

"Some of my tenants do, too. And of course they raise sheep."

"You have tenants, then? Not hired laborers?" A thoughtful frown was working itself into his brow, which certainly gave his countenance a novel aspect. "I find only the latter on my land. Not the former. And none of them have sheep."

Was he expecting a reply? One couldn't quite be sure. "I don't suppose you've much room for farms, besides your own. Your property is of modest size, as I recall."

"At present, yes." The frown turned itself to her, as though he were considering her anew. "Would you happen to know very much about enclosure?"

"I'm afraid not." She leaned forward. "But I could

look through Mr. Russell's library. He may have had books on the subject, or even records of enclosure here."

"No, thank you. I have books of my own." His attention subsided from her, and settled on the arm of the chair where his fingers still worked, tracing the silver stripes between the blue. What was occupying him? She should have expected him to invoke the purpose of his visit by now. He'd certainly been eager enough the first two times.

Abruptly his hand dropped to spread over the chair's arm, his fingers no longer fidgeting. "I find some of my people are partly dependent on the parish relief," he said, and looked up, angling his head to face her indirectly. "Are any of yours?"

Was he . . . embarrassed? The thought woke a strange clumsy tenderness in her. Perhaps he was embarrassed, and troubled, by the conditions in which people lived on his land.

"I've never known any to be on relief." She took care to make the words gentle. "But other families in the parish are, I'm sure. If you like I could ask my curate—"

He held up a hand and shook his head, eyes turned once again to the chair's arm. "Never mind. Only I don't quite like it, you know. Asking every landholder in the parish to provide for these people who ought to be my own responsibility."

"Tenants, too." The words slipped out before she could calculate their effect. "The tenant farmers pay the poor rates too."

"Even better." He laughed, a sharp, humorless sound. "You see my ignorance. But at least I have some idea of what a gentleman ought and oughtn't to stand for, and it plain strikes me as a shabby way of doing things. Doesn't it strike you?" On these last words, he raised his head to face her again, eyes lit with earnest appeal.

He could not have said anything more right; anything

more exquisitely tailored to win her sympathy, her support, her better regard. The call for her opinion alone should have softened her, but the admirable sentiment demanded the warmest sort of reply.

"You refer to duty." She moved to the forward edge of the chair and clasped her hands before her. "And yes, beyond the duties we all owe to one another, I do believe a landowner has a special obligation to his tenants or laborers, to make their lives comfortable and worthwhile as far as it lies in his power to do so." Such a rush of satisfaction, to know she was saying the right thing in her turn. His eyes were steady on her and the worry was leaving his brow. "We have so many opportunities to do good for these people. You may think yourself ignorant now, but that's the beginning of wisdom, isn't it?"

"Is it?" He was almost smiling. "I'm sure I don't know."

"Of course it is. If you thought yourself already informed, you shouldn't be open to learning. And you *will* learn." He needed to hear this. He needed encouragement. "Ten to one you may distinguish yourself, once you've begun. Many young men have done so, I'm sure. Even young men of fashion. It's a fashionable pursuit these days, isn't it? The study of agriculture?"

"I should certainly hope so." Now he was smiling, unmistakably, his whole face newly awash with that light a woman's faith and fostering could kindle. "Go on."

"At all events a sense of duty is a commendable beginning. Even without you know how to improve the land, duty might lead you to make a difference in your laborers' lives just by calling on them, and knowing their names, and paying those other routine attentions that tell a person of humbler station how he . . ." Her speech broke off. As she spoke he had suddenly sunk out of his chair to kneel before her. Now he caught her clasped hands and gently prised them apart, turning the palms up and stroking his thumbs over the inner sides of her wrists.

Oh. Not a new light, after all. Just the usual one. Disappointment plummeted through her like a stone, with chagrin at her own foolishness chasing it all the way.

"Go on," he said, though from the vector of his attention anyone would think he was bidding her wrists to do something or other.

"I don't believe you're listening." Her voice dropped a good dozen degrees in warmth.

"Not to the words." He bent his head to brush his lips over the thin, blue-veined skin. "But you're rather lovely when you speak so. All ardent and crusading."

Could any woman on earth really welcome such a remark? Maybe a woman with susceptible wrists could. Probably he was used to women who gave themselves so thoroughly up to pleasure that they'd welcome any thoughtless thing he said.

She let her hands go heavy in his grip. It was easy. She felt heavy all over. "I've finished speaking," she said. "We may as well go to bed, if you're ready."

*H*E INSPECTED this room, too, as he removed his clothes. Taking in the blue brocaded drapes, the pattern of the wallpaper, the enormous bed, his reflection in the room's several mirrors. When he appeared to have catalogued it all, he came to bed.

He was quick. One must credit him with that. Comparatively tidy, too. He did not, at least, perspire heavily and shower her with his thrashing about, as had been Mr. Russell's unfortunate habit. He managed his business with purpose and dispatch, just as she'd like him to, and in future she must remember to be grateful for this, and not waste time wishing for him to be better.

*   *   *

ℬUT HE could be worse. On the fourth day he insisted she not ring for Sheridan, that he might undress her himself.

To protest that this was an unearned intimacy should have been absurd, everything considered. So she submitted, with the same silent stoicism that had borne her through Mr. Russell's occasional like whims.

He must have taken that for encouragement because the next day he wanted to undress her again. This time he worked with deliberate leisure, as though he believed himself to be whetting her anticipation. And he spoke, incessantly, while he worked. Once more her skin was said to resemble silk, and her limbs and other parts were praised for their shape and proportion. Then, as though she could not have come to the conclusion on her own, he held it necessary to inform her of the exact effects her bodily charms had upon him.

Thus did he like to unburden himself to her. When he might have confided cares and nascent ideas, and been rewarded with that warm, steadying support she would gladly give in return, he chose instead to say trite things such as any man could say, and take as his prize that congress in which only her body need be present. She could have been any other woman, lying beneath him with her legs apart, and his enjoyment should surely have been just the same.

Not that it mattered, she thought afterward, resting on the pillow. As long as he brought the seed, she could bear whatever he brought with it. Whatever further indignities he might feel moved to propose, she would endure with patience and resolve.

*   *   *

A MONTH. FIVE days down, some five and twenty to go, counting the present occasion.

Twenty-five days. How the devil was he going to get through them?

"Wrap your legs around me," Theo muttered, and her hands tightened briefly on his shoulders as she complied.

Her brow had creased when he'd lifted her, fully dressed, to a seat atop the conveniently sized chest of drawers, but she'd said no word of protest. Then she'd made a study of her hands while he stripped himself naked before her, and a study of the ceiling while he gathered her skirts up and found his way in. Lord only knew what she was studying now. The backs of her eyelids, like as not.

She took no pleasure in compliments. She didn't care to be disrobed. She didn't want him to touch her in any particular place. What was a man to do with such a woman?

He angled his head to avoid any glimpse of her placid, patient face, and caught their reflection in the room's largest mirror: pale urgency against somber black. Not so difficult, really, to imagine a different set of motives for the exotic tableau, at this distance. Not so difficult to see a shameless widow and the man she had to have at any price. Not at all difficult to picture the frantic lust mounting up in her as she watched him remove the last of his clothes, the hunger that drove her to forsake the bed and take him here, in full mourning, defiling her husband's memory and the sanctity of widowhood itself. That much did she desire him.

"How long am I to keep my legs like this?" As though she were posing for a bloody portrait and beginning to develop a cramp. Did she *want* to render him unable to perform?

"As long as it takes," he said through gritted teeth. But that was uncivil. "Stop if it hurts. If it's uncomfortable." He slowed his motion, that she might more easily unwind her legs if she so wanted.

"No, it isn't. I only wondered if you still required it." Curse her husband for allowing her to perpetrate this kind of talk in the bedroom. Next she'd be asking whether he expected to finish soon.

"I do require it." He breathed the words into her ear. "But harder. Wrap your legs around me harder."

Her legs tightened deliciously on him as she hooked her knees a little higher over his hips. In the mirror, he watched his fingers steal up to play on the length of thigh exposed between stocking-top and rucked-up skirts. "Do you have any idea how erotic this part of you looks?" He whispered against her cheek, nudging her to turn and see it for herself. "Silky white skin, bare amid all that black. Do you see?"

Silence. Apparently she thought he spoke for his own benefit. Why did he keep trying? Why should her enjoyment matter to him, when it plainly didn't matter to her?

And what if he were to creep his fingers up the inner side of her thigh, farther and farther until they found her sweetest bit of flesh? The woman in the mirror would like that. She'd sigh, and tilt her hips to ask for more. Hell, the woman in the mirror already had her legs locked round him, urging him to grind against her there.

That woman, he could tease. He took his hand from her leg and gripped the dresser's edge. Both hands held on there, bracketing her and steadying him as he slowed; drew almost all the way out, tipped his head back, and closed his eyes. Good. Let her wait and wonder.

"Is something the matter?" That *voice*. If he looked now he'd find her watching him with quizzical distaste. The sight could murder all his efforts.

"Nothing's the matter. Please don't talk." Oh, he'd regret that later. Never a safe thing to say to a woman. But he needed to keep that mirror-widow clear in his mind, to see her eyes widen as he went back in with excruciating slowness, deeper and deeper until his groin brushed against her where she liked it best. Then he took himself away again, to keep her hungry, and hell and damnation, it felt so good.

He drew a shuddering breath and let his head fall forward. When his eyes opened they met with her fichu, black and forbidding. Without a word he bent to catch it in his teeth—one could easily imagine a gasp of excitement in place of the continuing silence—and dragged it out from where it was tucked into her dress.

A sudden catch in the linen stopped him. She'd pinned it. *Pinned* it. By all that was holy, what kind of woman pinned in her fichu prior to an assignation? But never mind—he found and freed the pin, and pulled out the cloth and dropped it beside her. More bared flesh to enjoy in the mirror now, her bosom rising and falling with each delicate breath.

He turned from that vision and sank to meet the swell of her breast with his lips, trailing kisses over its buttersmooth surface. Just as she wanted him to. Just as she'd been dreaming he would from the moment she first spied him there in church and made up her mind to have him, in bed and everywhere else, to have him and have him and have him, propriety be damned.

In small pulses he started to move again, and meanwhile dipped his tongue down into her bodice to feather it across one nipple. She stiffened, in every place but the right one. Good God. Had he ever met with such a pair of recalcitrant nipples in all his life? Could they continue so utterly unmoved by anything he did? With a desperate groan he brought up one hand to tug down her neckline, and took the nipple entirely into his mouth.

A spasm of unmistakable revulsion shot through her. "Is that *necessary*?" she said, as a society matron might address a man who broke into drunken sea chanteys at her dinner table.

"No." He jerked his head away from the offended bosom. "And don't talk. I beg you." How had he come to be in this nightmare? Any ill-chosen word from her now might bring it all down in shambles; mortifying, unprecedented shambles. Even to look at her risked a stalling in his blood. So he closed his eyes and, God help him, he thought of other women.

Of Mrs. Cheever and the way she would cling to him, if she were here atop this dresser, because his ministrations robbed her of her very balance. Of Eliza, who would arch away in an agony of helpless delight. Of women, numberless women, who would rake his back with their nails, and women who would bite down on his bare shoulder.

She was paying for seed. He would give her seed, by whatever means he must contrive. Onward he drove his hips, a mere priapic machine now, thinking of women who would whisper filthy things in his ear. Delectable filthy things, all invitation and command.

Better. Much better. He dropped his head to her shoulder and thrust harder. If he'd kept his head up he might not have heard it, but, his ear being just on a level with her mouth, he could not miss the one faint sigh, a thorough and walloping expression of patience tried.

The sound pierced him, true as an arrow from the bow of . . . whatever was Cupid's opposite. And he stumbled like a wounded stag. He hauled in a breath. "Can you please . . . not . . ." How would he even finish the plea? *Can you please make some effort to hide your disgust? Can you not act so explicitly as though you're waiting for me to just be done?* He moved faster. If he could just finish while he still had—

"Not talk, do you mean? You said that already. And I wasn't." She had no idea.

"No, I didn't mean . . ." Little energy to spare for words. "I'm sorry; it's just . . ." Bloody hell, he really was going to lose it; he could feel it beginning to crumble like a derelict chimney. "You just make it . . ." *Impossible. A punishment. A back-breaking chore.* "So hard," he finally got out.

Like a plucked string she snapped away from him. "There is no need for moment-to-moment descriptions of your state," she said, her voice frigid with disapproval.

Mother of God. Could she really be so stupid? Couldn't she feel it herself? "No, I mean *difficult*. You are making it . . . difficult . . . to proceed." He couldn't look at her. To own the fact aloud was so, so much worse than he could have imagined.

Again he felt a snap in her; a violent start as she saw her mistake. For the span of a breath it seemed possible she might recognize her wrongs and do something, anything to help him recover and finish the job. Then she spoke. "I can't see that I'm to blame." Her voice rang cold and uninterested as ever. "It's not as though I do anything to prevent your sport."

That was the end. He slipped out of her, he knew that much; slipped right out as useless as a dead eel. The rest was something of a blur. His hands, pushing blindly at the legs still crossed behind him. He must have got free because he staggered, under all the weight of masculine disgrace, to the nearby wall. Her fatal last remark rang in his ears and *No*, he thought, *It's not as though you do anything at all! I may as well be swiving a propped-up corpse!*

Those were the words he thought. Or . . . maybe . . . the words he said.

He breathed hard, ragged, in the silence, and worked to bring the wallpaper's fleur-de-lis into focus. Christ. Shit. Had he said that out loud?

He ventured a look at her. Damnation. He'd said it out loud.

"Hell," he muttered, now leaning his forehead against the wall. "I'm sorry." He glanced back.

"No, it's . . ." She sat very still, drained of color, staring at the floor. "*I'm* sorry. I'll try harder."

"No!" He wheeled away from the wall. "For God's sake, can't you see? What pleasure do you suppose there could be for a man, in bedding a woman who has to *try hard* to bear it?"

No reply came. Of course none came. She withheld herself at every opportunity; why should she give it up now? Even to look at him appeared to be more than she would grant: she merely sat, watching the toes of her slippers, with all appearance of waiting for him to finish out his indulgence of temper and get back to work.

That was more than he could do. With a shake of his head, he leaned down and picked up his trousers where they lay on the floor.

She saw. "What are you—"

"It's gone." He cut off her panicky words with pleasure. Let her panic. Let her be the uncomfortable one in this bargain, just once.

"Is there no way you can—"

"No. No way. It's gone; it's done." He watched her sidelong as he stepped into his trousers; saw her thinking hard, quickly as she could.

"I believe there are some erotic novels in the library," she said at last, her gaze fast on her slippers. "Perhaps you could—"

"No. I could not." One hand held up his undone trousers; the other scrabbled for his shirt, waistcoat, and cravat. "If I can't stay hard with my cock in a woman, I surely can't expect to look to erotic novels for the remedy."

She flinched at the language. Good. With his clothes

gathered up he went away to the mirror. In the glass he could see her, as he pulled the shirt over his head and thrust his hands through the sleeves. A strange bawdy spectacle she made, skirts still bunched above her stockings, legs still splayed. If she had other ideas for how he might arouse himself again, she did not offer them. She only sat with her head bowed, and finally, slowly, drew her knees together and plucked at the skirt to cover herself.

She looked . . . so small, sitting there alone. He closed his eyes. *Do not pity her, you idiot. Do not.* But his temper had always been a quick one: by the time his waistcoat buttons were all done up, he felt sorry to have made her look like that.

Still she did not speak. He wound his cravat without the usual flourish. What must it have cost her to mention the erotic novels? How many were there? And how did she know? Had she come across them by accident one day? Or were they perhaps flaunted before her?

Damn his stupid sympathetic heart. What accommodations had she ever made for him? If he'd been her husband, he probably should have resorted to erotic novels too, sooner or later.

He wished he hadn't called her a corpse, though. That outburst had in no way alleviated his mortification, nor was it likely to inspire any feelings in her that could help him with what was proving to be a labor worthy of Hercules. And it ought to have been, he thought, now sitting in an armchair to pull on his boots. The first labor, to make all the later ones seem easy. Even the Hydra would be as child's play, against the memory of breeding Mrs. Russell.

His clothes were all on now, save for the hat. He sat for a moment longer. Perhaps he would think of something to say. Perhaps she would speak.

The silent seconds ticked by. Finally there was nothing

to do but stand and reach for his hat. He cleared his throat. "Shall I come again tomorrow?" The words sounded so loud in the room's leaden stillness.

"If you please," she said to her toes.

He left, then, and heavy thoughts of tomorrow went with him. Tomorrow and the tomorrows beyond, nearly a month of them to get through before his commission was complete.

Chapter Five

*S*URELY THIS congregation would run her out of church and chase her down the road with torches, if they knew what was the substance of her prayers. But she'd reckoned with that likelihood from the start.

Please forgive me as far as You are able. Martha opened her eyes to see the pale knuckles of her hard-clasped hands, and shut them again. *Please take into account that I am not, if one defines the word precisely, guilty of Lust. Please understand why I had to do this, and what was at stake. In addition, please compel Mr. Mirkwood to glance this way and notice that I am without my fichu.*

Not that she expected the sight to galvanize him with such desire as would sustain him into their appointment this afternoon. But he would see it, one hoped, as a signal of her willingness to . . . not *try*, because he didn't want her to *try* . . . but to step away from her fixed position and meet him somewhere along that distance separating her wants from his.

Was that the same as trying? Why must this business have so many arcane rules? Don't *try*. But don't do nothing; else you are no better than a *corpse*. Even in her own inward voice, the word slapped her. Not so painfully as yesterday, when it had come like a hard open hand to her face. Given time its power might fade further. One hoped.

She opened her eyes again, angling her bowed head to peer across the aisle. He wasn't looking at her. He sat straight and attentive today, his dress subdued, his countenance solemn, his prayer book opened to the right place. No one would ever guess he was a man who put women on top of odd furniture and expected them to enjoy it.

She couldn't enjoy it. Exotic acts with an unprincipled stranger. He oughtn't to expect that of her. But he did have a right to expect civility, and there, admittedly, she'd been remiss. She'd do better next time. If there was a next time. She'd be polite, and solicitous, stifling all uncharitable sentiment for the duration of his call.

If only he would look at her! She might even smile, quick and private, and he would know to expect a better welcome this afternoon than he'd had in the past.

But he didn't look. When the service ended he slid from his pew and made for the door without once turning his eyes her way.

Would he even come to call today? He must—he'd asked if he ought—and yet what if, upon reflection, he'd decided he just couldn't continue with her?

She sat still in her pew, last to leave the church again. Mr. Atkins might notice her missing fichu, and wonder at her. As well he ought. She was a crude, grasping woman, reduced to attending Sunday services uncovered in hopes of catching a man's eye. She'd disgraced herself, stooping to such a ploy, and gained nothing for her disgrace. Desperate as it was, it hadn't been enough.

THEO PLUCKED at the roadside hedge as he walked home from church, crushing its leaves and throwing them away. Someone would have a devil of a time cleaning his gloves. Perhaps he would ruin them altogether. The prospect left him strangely unmoved.

He sighed aloud and scattered a handful of broken leaves. She'd robbed him of the one thing he did well, the widow had. That was the worst of it. He could laugh off his own ineptitude in those pursuits for which he cared nothing, as long as he could count himself a virtuoso in more important matters. But how was he to think of himself, faced every day with the way she shrank from his practiced touch? If he wasn't a man who knew how to please women, then what was he at all?

The rumble of cart wheels came up behind him: he stepped closer to the hedge and lifted his hat as some farm family drove past, festive in their Sunday best and animated as though they were bound for a pleasure-party instead of just come from a sermon about a farmer struck dead while celebrating his bountiful harvest. The man and several of the boys raised their hats in return. One girl waved, and ducked her head shyly when he waved back.

Such charming looking people. Why couldn't their sort live on his land, instead of the sullen Weavers? But some of the laborer families had seemed congenial enough, and perhaps even the Weavers improved on acquaintance. He ought to give them that chance. He might expend a little energy on duty today, and see where it took him. If he met with more disaster in the afternoon's appointment with Mrs. Russell, he could at least have some sense of effectuality in other areas.

The plan coalesced as he finished his walk home. Call on the laborers and pay them attentions, the widow had said, and this much he could certainly manage with competence. He set the cook to wrapping up some parcels of beef and tea and even a few lumps of sugar while he went about the house gathering up other odds and ends. A sense of benevolent purpose swept through him, bringing his first real relief from that debacle of yesterday afternoon. He would win these people over with his gentlemanly condescension, and reports of it would surely reach Granville's ears and help his greater cause.

An hour later he climbed the rise to the Weaver cottage with a slowing step. The calls had not gone precisely as he'd envisioned. He'd made a beginning, to be sure. No one could doubt the pleasure and surprise with which each humble housewife had received his parceled gifts. But neither could anyone miss the lingering distrust that met his visit. The husbands were all away at work—he ought to have anticipated this, by the absence of these families from church—and the wives answered his polite remarks and queries with uneasy monosyllables, for the most part.

Well, one more stop would finish his tribute to duty, for better or worse. He pushed the gate open and went in.

Even from this distance the baby's cries were audible, making no great incentive to approach the house. The eldest daughter stood at one side of the yard, emptying a pail into the pig's trough. She glanced up as he latched the gate, and dropped her eyes again before he had time to tip his hat. Poor thing. She must have come to expect neither courtesy nor any notice at all from such callers as the family did have.

He crossed to that side of the yard and took off his hat. "Good day," he said.

The girl curtseyed silently, never raising her eyes from the pig, who applied itself to the trough with fierce purpose.

"How do you do?" He replaced his hat. Perhaps she was a mute?

"Well, thank you." She spoke without expression, as though it were a practiced response, and still her head was inclined swineward.

So he considered the animal too. "How is your pig?" he asked after a moment.

Here was a question for which the girl hadn't any rote answer. She pursed her mouth, concentrating. "She's wicked," came the eventual reply.

"Really?" She certainly smelled wicked. "What wicked things does she do?"

For a half-second her eyes rose to his. "She sits on her young sometimes."

"Well, that is wicked indeed." To say the least. "What can be done?"

"I hit her with a stick. Then she might get up."

"But she doesn't, always?"

She shook her head. Theo took a moment to imagine it: the sow's impassive bulk, the squeals of the desperate piglets, and this girl, powerless, despite her stick, against the brute whims of nature. Every day spent in the country made London look a little better, and no mistake.

"Well." Enough about the pig. "I've come to call on your family, and brought some things. And I brought something in particular for you."

She did not ask what it might be, or look anywhere but at the pig. Only her posture betrayed a heightened attention.

"I wasn't sure, you see," he said, rummaging through his bag, "whether it was the gold or the paper you liked, so I brought you some of each." He pulled out a length of gold ribbon. "I've no idea why this should have been in the house—some long-ago ladies must have left it there, I suppose—but I'll make no use of it, and neither will Mr. Granville." He put it in her hand.

She dragged it between two fingers, wordlessly, end to end. Then back the other way.

Now this was more the thing. Next time he'd direct all his efforts at charming the children, and like as not win their parents' approbation into the bargain. "You might use it to decorate your pig, if she ever mends her ways enough to deserve such a treat." He nudged the animal with his boot. "It would look rather handsome in a bow about her tail, wouldn't it?"

A dimple appeared in the girl's cheek, and she shook her head.

"I must defer to your judgment. But here is paper, too, as I mentioned." He drew out a little sheaf of it. "It's wallpaper, actually, so it's all patterned. Flowers, birds, leaves, whatnot." He riffled the papers to show her. "And they're heavy. They'll keep a crease well, if you wish to fold them. If you wish to make a fan, for example. Have you ever made a fan?"

She shook her head again, eyes fast on the paper.

"I'll show you. It's not at all difficult, else I'm sure I wouldn't know how." He took a sheet of paper and handed her the rest. "It's best to use a tabletop or some other flat place if you can," he said, setting down his bag and putting a foot up on the trough, "but one can make do." She watched as he started to fold the paper on the makeshift work-surface of his thigh. "Fold an inch or so from one end; now turn it over and fold back another inch. That makes a pleat, do you see? Just keep turning the paper over and folding back another inch until it's pleated all the way to the end." No telling whether she fully grasped this, but it had been the easiest thing he could think of to fold.

"Pinch it close at one end when you've finished, and open out the other, and you have a fan." He held it up and fanned himself, causing her to dimple again. "If you like, you can even punch a hole here, where it's pinched together, and tie it with a string. My sisters used to run ribbons through and wear them on their wrists." With this, undoubtedly, he had exhausted the subject, so he closed up the pleats and held it out to her.

She examined the pleats, then pinched one end and fanned herself experimentally.

"Just so, yes." Well, *that* had come off as it ought. Now to make the best of his meeting with the other Weavers—but before he could begin, the girl drew a second piece of paper from the sheaf and pushed it toward him. "Would you like me to make another?" he asked.

She nodded, and moved a step closer to watch.

He was two pleats into it when he heard the cottage door open and Mrs. Weaver cry, in a terrible voice, "Christine, come here now!"

The girl scrambled away and he understood, in an instant, what her mother had seen: his back turned to the cottage, her daughter too near him, and both their heads bowed to watch his hands doing something in the vicinity of his lap.

Good God. Could she really think—Good God. He held up the paper and groped for words that could explain—but the woman didn't even look at him now. She was talking rapidly to her daughter, who a minute later hurried back to him, or rather to just within arm's length, the ribbon and the rest of the paper in her outstretched hand, her face turned aside. He could only take it all from her and watch her run away again.

Sick, febrile heat roiled through him, flooding his face with guilty color. *Idiot. Idiot. Idiot.* Why had he not stopped to think of how this might look? And yet how should it have occurred to him? Never in his life had anyone thought him capable of such infamy.

The longer he stood red-faced and wordless, the more culpable he would appear. Also, the greater the chance he would cast up there before them. Mechanically, he took up his bag and forced himself across the yard to where Mrs. Weaver stood, her baby's rageful howls the only mitigation to a dense, choking silence.

"I'm sorry for any offense." His hat felt huge and ungainly as he took it off; his head felt horribly exposed. "I've been calling on the families today, and brought things such as I thought they might be able to use." Her gray eyes, now he was near enough to see them, betrayed no evidence of sympathy or any other human sentiment. "I noticed your daughter folding paper when I was here before, and I had some lying about at the house. I was showing her how to fold a fan." Even the truth sounded like some nefarious trick to lure a child. "May I give the paper to you instead? And you might give her a piece when you wish?"

"Christine, go into the house now," she said without turning, and the girl obeyed. "Mr. Mirkwood." Her tone was flat and forbidding; her stare would do a basilisk proud. "We've no need of your paper. Christine don't want gifts of any kind."

"As you think best, of course." He put it back in his bag and found the meat and tea. "I'll just give you these," he said, drawing them out, "same as I brought to the other families."

"No." She moved the baby from one shoulder to the other. "Thank you, no."

He ought to be angry. He had every right to be. He'd come here with honorable intentions, and indeed, he could feel the first sparks of anger struck within him— but they were promptly smothered by thick, poisonous shame. What man could stand under Mrs. Weaver's awful gaze and not suspect a monster lurked deep inside him after all? God in Heaven, never had any person looked at him so.

As briefly as possible he wished the woman good day and started back to the house, his stomach curdling every step of the way, his leftover presents shifting about in the bag that should have been empty by now.

So much for good intentions. The panic in her voice, when she'd flung open the door and called her daughter

away from him! *Don't think of it.* He stopped and
screwed his eyes shut, and his stomach pitched and
reeled like an unmanned vessel on a stormy sea. *Think
of something else.* He opened his eyes and walked on.
But no innocuous subject could hold his thoughts: back
they slipped again and again to the scene he would have
escaped, and finally he gave in and was ill, helplessly,
shamefully ill at the border of his own back garden.

MR. FARRIS said you weren't planning to enroll your
girls in our class for young ladies." Martha pinched a
weed from among a stand of parsley plants and stretched
out her arm to drop it in the pail.

Across the row of herbs, Jane Farris nodded once.
That the mistress insisted on helping with some chore
whenever she called was probably trying enough to a
tenant-wife. To introduce this conversation, in place of
their usual minimal pleasantries, must make a further
imposition on the woman.

So be it. Mr. Mirkwood was due to arrive in an hour,
and if she sat about waiting she would surely run mad.
"I was sorry to hear it. I confess I had your Laura and
Adelaide in mind, when I suggested to Mr. Atkins that
he make some provision for the older girls. They're both
so bright."

"They both read already, though. Lizzie will go to
school with her brothers. Do you see any yellow in the
parsley there?"

"No, it all looks quite fresh still." She tossed in another few weeds and moved on to the peppermint, where
she paused to lean in and breathe its crisp scent. "The
very purpose of the class, as I saw it, was to prevent a
girl's education from stopping with mere letters and
numbers." Another breath of peppermint. Wonderfully
clarifying to one's thoughts. "We live in a time of such

great change, don't we?" She picked up the one hand-spade and set to extracting a tenacious weed. "I'm sure Mr. Atkins isn't the only country curate who's taken note of the trends, and seen the use of more schooling for our boys. One can't help worrying, though, for girls who grow up with the expectation of marrying a farmer, only to find so many farm-boys gone into trades, and educated so far beyond them."

Aha. She'd scored a hit. The tilt of Mrs. Farris's bonnet hid whatever expression was in her eyes, but her mouth had drawn itself into a thinking frown.

Now to press the advantage. "It's not like a generation ago, when a husband and wife might both have had a few years in infant-school, and the rest of their education on the land. I expect a young tradesman might be inclined to look to some merchant's daughter, with a bit of schooling, when he goes to take a bride." Emphatically she threw her weed in the bucket and gave back the spade. "And if he does choose a barely literate farm-girl, he will be deliberately making an unequal marriage."

"No good ever comes of that." From side to side the woman's bonnet swayed.

"No, never." She dusted her hands and moved along to the fresh-laundry fragrance of lavender. "I shouldn't like to see it happen to any of our Seton Park girls." From under the funnel of her own bonnet, she stole a glance at Mrs. Farris. "It *is* only for an hour, the class. And only on Sundays, and I expect Mr. Atkins will build many of his lessons on spiritual topics. Geography of the Holy Land, and so forth." Now she was spinning thread out of air. She really had no idea what lessons Mr. Atkins would make. "At all events I hope you'll consider it."

"So I shall." Mrs. Farris picked up the pail and plunked it down farther along the row. "I don't want any man to think he's marrying beneath him, in taking one of my daughters. I'll think on all you've said."

Martha dug her fingers silently into the soil. Had she just managed some successful persuasion, after all? Indeed she seemed to have done. She might make this same case to more tenant wives, given time—if only she would have that time. If she had not already thrown away her chance.

She brushed at a dirty patch on her skirt. She'd best be gone soon, to allow time for changing into her second set of mourning before he came. Though perhaps he wouldn't notice. Perhaps he wouldn't come. She might change into her clean gown and sit on that chair all afternoon with no one to see it, with no company at all but the memory of her every mistake.

How did they do it, those men who did such things? Theo trudged up the wooded path that would take him to the side entrance of Mrs. Russell's house. Right and wrong aside, how could they even forge ahead where they were not wanted? The widow's indifference had been enough to kill his own appetite and render him wholly ineffectual. How on earth did a man scrounge up lust in the face of terror and perhaps even frantic resistance?

Scrounging up lust. He stopped to lean his weight on a pathside tree. Within minutes he was going to have to find a way to do just that. How, though? The memory of Mrs. Weaver's cold stare; the girl's guilty confusion as she gave back the presents, might pollute his every carnal impulse for the rest of his days. Certainly for as many days as he must contend with a lover—the very word mocked him—who offered none of that warm welcome that could make a man's appetites feel wholesome and right.

He pushed away from the tree and walked on. One dogged foot and then the other, through the copse, across the bit of lawn, and before he knew it he was opening the door to that sitting room, hat in one hand, heart unhopeful.

The climb upstairs hadn't been quite long enough to accustom him to the indoor dim, and he blinked stupidly for several seconds as he cast about the room in search of her. His gaze lit upon her at last, and he blinked more stupidly still.

Small wonder he'd missed her. He'd been looking for the usual black shape, in her usual striped chair. But today she sat on the sofa, facing him, and she wasn't wearing black. She wasn't wearing . . . very much of anything at all. No cap, to begin with: her hair fell loose about her shoulders, dark gold rippling against the pale pink of a dressing-gown that skimmed over her form, apparently with no other garment between.

Definitely with no garment between; that became clear as she rose from the sofa. The fabric shifted here, clung there. His hat slipped from his fingers and tumbled to the floor. The gown's sash, he saw, was not even fastened— only her clutched hands kept her covered—and he went very still and began silently to pray, the kind of prayers to land a man who-knew-where in the hereafter.

She took one step forward. She swallowed. For a small eternity she hovered where she was, on the verge of doing something, and he could only wait, and pray harder.

Slow as a spring thaw, slow as a tide, slow as clouds scudding across the calmest of skies, her hands glided up the gown's two edges and drew them back, over her shoulders, baring her to his sight. The garment caught for one scant second at her elbows, then it slipped all the way off and she left it behind, walking toward him.

Hell and all its devils. Everything else in the room just dissolved, until only the sight of her remained. He'd seen her naked before, of course, but . . . no, scratch that, he'd never seen her naked before. Not like this. Dimly he recognized that she was *trying*—that this was exactly what he'd told her he did not want—and he knew, as his mouth went dry and his short hairs stood on end, how utterly hollow his own words had been.

She moved deliberately, with an excruciating slowness that made the scene feel as if it were playing out underwater, or in a dream. Her shoulders sat square, her head upright. He raised his eyes to hers and saw a jittery, almost sickly expression. Like a French aristocrat doing her best to be brave on the way to the guillotine.

Stop. You don't have to do this. Somewhere on the way from his brain to his tongue the words expired. He could envision, with perfect clarity, crossing the room to catch up her discarded gown and draping it gently, reassuringly, over her shoulders, but envisioning was as far as he could go. Well enough. Kindly, caretaking impulses had got him precious little of late.

And fear or no fear, on she came, and he willed her, with everything he had, to keep coming. *You can do it, Mrs. Russell. Just four more paces now . . . and three . . .* He could help her, of course. He could take a step toward her, and reduce the distance she had to cover, but it seemed important she finish what she'd begun.

Now two paces . . . now one . . . His right hand rose of its own accord and fitted itself to her breast as she reached him. The nipple lay soft, as always, in the palm of his glove, but no matter. She'd planned this. She'd spent time thinking of what he would want. She'd probably chosen the dressing-gown she supposed he would like best, and she'd put it off immediately because she knew he would like that even better. She'd felt fear and gone ahead anyway, and this kind of effort, a man could live with. He could live with a great deal of it.

She had no idea what to do next—he could feel that—so he sent his other hand round to the small of her back, and gathered her in. Her body was relaxing in the shelter he made, letting go the tension that had so tightly strung her, and she felt . . . Oh, but she felt splendid against him, naked where he was clothed. Thighs against his trousers. Chest against his coat. Breast curved neatly in his palm. Neither of them had spoken since his entrance into the room, but he suddenly had something important to say.

"I'm not going to make it to the bed. Do you mind the floor very much?"

She shook her head and he bore them both down to the carpet, one hand already working his trouser-buttons free. For a moment she looked vulnerable as a butterfly, pinned to the floor underneath him, wide-eyed, uncertain, exposed. Her bare toes brushed against his boots and then he was in her, the freed buttons pressing marks into her flesh with each thrust. There would be marks on her back, too, rasped in by the rug—he ought to prevent those; ought to take some care; maybe cradle her up off the floor just enough to—but she slipped her hands under his coat, *trying* again, and then—oh, God— hitched up her legs and locked them round his hips.

And he was lost. He gripped her shoulders and ravished, hard and quick, half expecting her to cry out in protest, but she only seized his shirt in handfuls and wound her legs tighter.

Yes. Take it. Take it all. Don't refuse me. Take every last foul bit. He plunged, again and again, into a frenzy of lust and shame and blessed, blessed relief. She didn't refuse. She didn't recoil. She kept his shirt tight in her fists and stayed with him as he gave her everything, everything he had to give from every bright and dark place in his soul, until nothing remained to give but the seed, and he gave it, and sank down, and lay still.

* * *

WELL. SHE hadn't expected that. She hadn't really known what to expect, but . . . Well.

He appeared a bit stunned by it himself. He lay as though lifeless on top of her, his head sunk heavy past her shoulder. "Forgive me," he muttered stiffly after a minute or two.

"There's nothing to forgive." If he knew how she had feared this act wouldn't happen again, he would surely laugh.

"Yes, there is." He rolled off her, onto his side, and fumbled at his trousers, putting his parts away. "I'm sure I've left you raw in more places than one." His eyes sank from hers for a moment, to find the first few buttons, and when he looked up again he must have seen her confusion. "If your back doesn't sting already, it will soon."

Her back. That seemed unlikely. But who was she to question?—undoubtedly he was better versed in these things than she would ever be.

"I'm truly sorry." His voice softened and slowed. His eyes looked stricken. "I'm not like that, usually."

"I didn't mind it. It went quickly."

His head dropped back to the floor and he sighed. "No, I pride myself, usually, on leaving a lady with something more to delight in than the brevity of my attentions."

Delight was a strong word. But admittedly one might have use, in certain hours, for the memory of his quick, furious surrender. The desperate need with which he'd come to her, almost as though he were seeking some carnal salvation. One might fold these qualities in with one's collection of vague imagined scenes for reviewing in private, and one might find some pleasure there.

No need to say so to him. She bent her knees up to tilt her hips. "Can I trouble you to fetch a pillow before you go?"

"I've no intention of leaving you stunned and naked

on your sitting-room floor." The suggestion brought him out of his pensive manner: he hauled himself to his knees.

"I'm not stunned," she began, but before she could get further he was bent over her, and then one of his arms was cradling up her shoulders, and one hooking under her knees, and the carpet receded beneath her as he rose to his feet. Without comment, as though he frequently managed women this way, he carried her to the bed and used one knee to pull back the covers. Then he set her down, arranged the pillow, and drew the covers over her.

I didn't give you permission to do that, said some unruly part of her, but she shushed it. He looked odd, lingering at her bedside. Not so blithe as usual, not so sanguine. Probably still berating himself for using her so hard as he'd done.

She might grant him a kind of pardon. Why not? "Will you stay for a few minutes?" She moved over and touched her hand to the empty side of the bed. "You look as though you could use a rest. And I'd be glad of the company." Not entirely untrue.

It was the right thing to say. One could see a weight come off his shoulders and his troubled brow. He sat, wordlessly, on the edge of the bed and pulled off his boots. Then his coat. He let it fall on the floor and climbed under the covers, otherwise completely clothed.

What could have cut him up so? Really, the coupling had not been so bad. "You've had a trying day, I think." She studied his profile. Maybe he'd like to confide.

He laughed, a sharp exhalation with very little voice. "Darling, you can't imagine."

If you'd just tell me, I wouldn't have to. She let that rebellious thought float up and away. He wasn't her husband. He had no obligation to share anything with her. "I'm sorry for it," she said.

"Don't you be sorry, when you're the one with a back

rubbed raw on the carpet." The covers went slack as he twisted toward her. His eyes raked back and forth, working to read her face. He took a breath. "You were afraid of me, I think."

"Not at all. I never have been."

"What was it, then?" With a jerk of his chin, he indicated the other room. "You looked near to illness, approaching me. You've never looked like that before."

"Oh. Yes. Well." She swallowed, and felt the color rising in her cheeks all over again. "Of course I was afraid you would refuse me, and end our bargain."

But that wasn't the whole truth, and he knew it. He waited, his eyes steady on hers now. In the silence he touched two gloved knuckles to her arm and stroked just above the elbow. *Stop that.* No. She wouldn't wound him with any objection.

"Also, I suppose I was afraid of appearing ridiculous." A few at a time, she got the words out, her voice awkward even to her own ears. "I have not been in the habit of doing such things. I feared this would be obvious to you, and you would find me ridiculous as a result."

Already he was struggling to keep a smile in check. She pressed her own lips together, and trained her attention on the canopy, and submitted to the quiet caress of kid leather against her arm. "Ridiculous," he repeated. "Do you think you looked ridiculous?"

"Yes. I do think so." Like some clown's pantomime of a wanton, lurching clumsily through such foreign motions. Her cheeks might burst into flame at the memory.

"Was my response, in your recollection, the response of a man who found you ridiculous?" Still that smile laced itself through his every word, though he was clearly striving for gravity.

She allowed herself a glance at him. "I think I may have overestimated what would be your discrimination in this matter."

"Oh, very nice." The smile spread unconstrained to all quarters of his face. "And now you see me to be a mere gluttonous beast, do you? A pig who doesn't notice whether his trough be full of trifle and sweetmeats or spoilt curds and potato peels."

"I certainly shouldn't go that far. I don't think you're at all like a pig."

"Quite right." He stretched out on his back with a satisfied air. "More in common with a horse. Or so the ladies say."

That was in exceedingly poor taste. One oughtn't to find it amusing. But she understood his mood. Each of them had feared the bargain was irreparably damaged, and each was giddily relieved to have salvaged it. "I'm glad to see your spirits are restored." She brushed a hand over her mouth. Sympathy or no, her smile, if he glimpsed it, would only encourage him to a hundred more advertisements of his masculine largesse.

"For the moment, because I'm occupied with agreeable topics." Sideways he addressed her, his head pressed back into the pillow. "I expect my morale to sink again once I'm at home and back to the grind."

So that was the trouble. With new resolve she angled herself toward him. "Is it so dismal, studying the management of an estate? I recall you saying such study suited you."

"Yes, I hoped to create a good impression. I didn't realize yet how little you cared for my respectability." A smile flickered over his lips, but found no purchase. "The truth is I have neither interest in nor aptitude for this subject. Mr. Granville has both. Why should he be burdened with teaching me what I don't value, and why must I spend my hours in learning responsibilities I never intend to assume? Land agents exist so that gentlemen may be spared all this care and tedium, I'm sure."

How to word this constructively? She frowned at the

far wall. "I consider you rather fortunate to be under his tutelage." No reproach. Only suggestion. "Sometimes I think men don't properly appreciate their privileges. If I were lucky enough to have someone teach me about land, I'm sure I should do my best to learn."

He pivoted toward her again, and this time came up on one elbow. "Are you in earnest? You really find this business interesting?"

"Of course I do. It's the best work a person in your station, or mine, can have: to make the land fruitful, and benefit all the people who live upon it, and demonstrate that we were born for something better than leisure."

"What an odd little woman you are." He picked up a lock of her hair and rubbed it between kid-sheathed fingers, watching her gravely all the while. Hair against a glove made a soft squeaking sound. "I wish you wouldn't ever wear a cap," he said.

Always, he would turn a conversation to corporeal matters. The fact wasn't nearly so distressing now she knew to expect it. "I'm in mourning."

"Yes, I know." No glimmer of a smile; he looked as solemn as an archbishop. "But I wish you wouldn't wear it. I like the sight of your hair."

"Well . . . perhaps I could take it off before you come to call." A small concession. No great breach of propriety. "If you think to do so would be useful."

"I'd like that." His voice was low, nearly a whisper.

"Then I'll try to remember, in future." Her own voice went low too.

"Yes," he said, and brought the lock of hair to his lips. "Do that. Try."

$\mathcal{H}$AVE YOU had much conversation with Mr. Mirkwood?" Martha spread her fingers to hold the map firmly against the schoolroom wall.

"Almost none. You?" Mr. Atkins had tacks in his mouth; she probably oughtn't to ask him questions.

"A little. He called last week. We've spoken a bit." She steadied her stance on the chair. The more untruths one scattered, the harder it was to keep track of them. But then she'd come here with an untruth as her purpose; with the flatly false news of a letter from Mr. James Russell approving the school. And Mr. Atkins, of course, had believed her and commenced to celebrate by putting up things on the walls.

"And what impressions have you formed?" he said now in his tack-impeded way.

There was the question, certainly. She could have answered with ease a week ago. Now she hesitated. "I'm not sure I'm acquainted enough to judge. He seems a good-natured man, but one does hear certain reports of what were his habits and pastimes in London."

The tacks clicked out onto the curate's palm. "I try to put little stock in such gossip. People have a way of rising, or sinking, to meet one's expectations. And he is, I think, a very young man. Still forming himself." He set a tack and lifted the hammer in his other hand.

"A man may be young, and conduct himself in a seemly way." She spoke up over the pounding of his hammer. "*You* have not used youth as an excuse for careless living." And they must be nearly of an age, Mr. Mirkwood and Mr. Atkins.

"Well, the Church will make a man serious, even where other things have not already made him so." He stepped down from his chair and when he looked up at her his eyes were lit with something not serious at all. "As to Mr. Mirkwood, I'm inclined to give him the benefit of the doubt. Did you see he stayed awake for my entire sermon yesterday?"

"To sleep through it would have been shocking. We can all profit, I'm sure, by the lesson of that foolish man and his new barns."

"Next week I think I'll be addressing *Train up a child in the way wherein he should go*. I've been meditating on that verse, for obvious reasons, and reading over John Wesley's sermon on the same subject. I cannot agree with his conviction that a child naturally inclines toward wickedness. So I must compose my rebuttal." He set the tacks back in his mouth and picked up his chair, moving it from her left side to her right.

What a generous man he was, with charitable thoughts for everyone, and how sorry she would be to lose his good opinion if her duplicity was ever made known. She watched him step up, spit out the tacks, and hammer in another. He held his head back on an angle, looking down his long nose at the work of his hands, and she knew from months of watching him at various industries that this was to thwart a lock of hair that always wanted to fall into his eyes.

"There's that one done," he said with a last tap. "Does it look straight to you?"

"Surely you ought to have asked that before you pounded in the tacks!"

"Surely, yes." He stepped down, and so did she, and they both considered the map from several paces away.

Like the slates and pencils, it had come secondhand and a bit shabby. He'd pressed out the creases as well as he could, with a warm iron—that had been her idea—and inked over where the print had faded, but nothing could be done about the exuberant scrawl of some schoolboy's name, STEPEN, across the south Pacific. Probably it was meant to be Stephen. He ought to at least have learned to spell, before despoiling property in that way.

"My brother and I had a map like this when we were boys." He set his hands against his back, elbows bent behind him. "Nowhere near this size, but all the same countries and oceans, as you may imagine. We learned all the names."

"Including Stepen?"

"Stepen excepted. John Wesley would have strong words for that boy, I'm sure." He smiled absently, still gazing at the map and no doubt savoring memories of the first time he'd traced the long coast of Africa with a finger, or seen how Italy took the shape of a high-heeled boot. Now he would help other boys—and girls—to those same discoveries.

She lied, and that was wicked. She lay down with Mr. Mirkwood, and that was a terrible sin. She sought to cheat a man of his inheritance, and that was probably a jailable offense. But watching Mr. Atkins, his face alight with the pleasure of good work to be done, she could not feel sorry in the least.

*   *   *

*S*TAND AND deliver, Mrs. Russell. I've had the devil's own erection this past hour at least." Mr. Mirkwood shut the door behind him and used that same hand to toss his hat into a corner. His other arm was full of books.

"What have you got, there?" Most certainly she did not stand.

"Erection. I've just told you."

"Those books, I mean." Really. "That rolled-up document."

"Afterward." Four long strides brought him to the sofa, where he unceremoniously dumped his armload and began on his coat buttons. "Why are you still dressed? I was hoping that business of yesterday might become a regular arrangement."

And so it went. With quick sure hands he undressed them both, moving nearer the bed with each discarded garment until they were naked, and settled in the sheets.

He took his pleasure carefully today, as though to atone for yesterday's loss of self-command. His eyes stayed fixed to hers, watching, she felt sure, for any symptoms of discomfort. Even when she closed her eyes to escape his gaze, she could feel him watching. It felt . . . strange. Different. Mr. Russell had never taken such care. Not even the first time, which had been uncomfortable indeed, nor the second, when she'd still been feeling the effects of the first. *I'm sorry,* he'd said, but he'd exercised his right nevertheless. So husbands did.

"Go on," she said, eyes still shut. "Truly, it doesn't hurt." Doubtless there were better answers to make to a man's tender restraint. But she no more knew how to make them than she knew how to speak Portuguese, and besides they had no place in this bargain. She only set her hands at his shoulders, because he liked to be touched, and she heard in his breath the moment when he left her behind to go to his crisis, just as she wanted him to do.

Afterward, he explained the books. "They're all about aspects of agriculture. Crop rotation. Yields and prices. I'm meant to study them, but I find they can't command my interest. However I've had an idea." He was lying on his stomach; now he raised up onto his elbows. "You might read them, since you do like these matters, and then make reports to me. In particular if you find yourself having insights, write them down. Tell me how a serious person ought to respond to this material, that I may make that response for Mr. Granville."

One hardly knew whether to laugh, or to rap him across the knuckles. Neither, perhaps. People rise or sink to meet your expectations, Mr. Atkins had said. What if she expected better from him? "I would like to read those books. You're very good to remember my interest. But I think you'd do better to read with me than to rely on my reports. Perhaps we could spend an hour or so in study each afternoon, after we've conducted the other business."

$\mathcal{T}$HE OTHER *business*. Three days later, the words still lodged with him. She received him politely now, with none of that awful disapproving resistance, but plainly the arrangement was indeed mere business to her. If she had carnal appetites at all, they slumbered soundly.

He yawned and stretched his arms, and felt his shoulder blades indent the carpet. She'd unrolled his enclosure map on the sitting-room floor today, a vase, a saucer, and two books serving as paperweights, and to join her at that level had seemed the companionable thing to do. This study-hour routine had proven quite restful, actually, as most days he reclined on the sofa, half-dozing to the music of her crisp modulations as she read aloud.

She glanced up at his movement, and glanced down again. "One of these outlined patches appears to be between your land and mine, if I'm interpreting the drawing correctly. I'm not entirely sure where to imagine the boundaries of Seton Park. But if it's the place I'm picturing, I believe some of my tenants pasture their sheep there." She frowned thoughtfully, and didn't look to him for any reply.

Theo pushed a hand through his hair. The carpet was not nearly as conducive to rest as the sofa had been, though it did vary one's view of the room. Rather a fine bit of plasterwork about the ceiling's border. Italianate, if he didn't mistake. Scrolling and so forth. He yawned once more, fist at his mouth. "Do you know what we ought to do?"

"No." She spoke straight down into the map. "We did that already today. We're supposed to be studying now. Surely you can curb your appetites until tomorrow."

"What a wicked, wanton mind you have." He rolled onto his side and propped his head on his hand. Her stern schoolmistress manner provoked him in more agreeable ways, now he was used to it. "I didn't mean any such thing. But now you've put it in my head, haven't you?"

"Then you must put it out again. May I suggest a brisk walk." This, too, was delivered to the map, with unruffled authority. Almost certainly she was beginning to derive some little enjoyment from this routine, some satisfaction in strictly correcting his errant wanderings. More satisfaction might follow in time.

"You're in luck, then. A walk was precisely what I meant to suggest." Her chin came sharply up, but he wouldn't let her dissuade him. "We'll take the map, and see these parcels for ourselves." One after another, he shoved the paperweights aside. "I'll go round and call at your front door, and we'll undertake to find this bit of land that lies between your property and mine. What could be more respectable?"

She hesitated. The mantelpiece clock ticked, and the map creaked and whispered as he rolled it up. "You'll conduct yourself with absolute discretion if we encounter anyone?"

"Discretion such as you can scarcely imagine. I shouldn't be half so popular among the married ladies of London without I possessed that skill." He winked at the reprimand gathering in her countenance, and got to his feet. "The fresh air will do us good, I promise you. Do you know we've been acquainted eleven days, and only seen each other indoors? I'm sure that's not healthy, and besides I should like to see how you look under sunlight. Give me fifteen minutes to go round and come up your drive."

𝓕IFTEEN AND some minutes later they were outdoors, and—well, he still could not say how she looked in the sun. She wore a black bonnet that swallowed her features whole. He should have had to lean down to peer in and see her, first stopping her for the purpose as she was marching beside him, across her great lawn and toward some slopes to the east.

Their paces matched up surprisingly well, considering how ill-matched they were in every other respect. She walked with a determined, mile-eating step that kept her even with his longer, more leisurely stride. Together they might walk to the ends of the earth, though conversation would falter long before they got there.

"Do you look forward to being a baronet?" she said after several minutes of silence.

"Not in the least." He took the map from under his elbow and switched it to his other side.

"No?" The bonnet's funnel swiveled his way; he could see her chin and lower lip preparing to judge him.

"No, dear. I'll have more responsibility then, with no appreciable gain in privilege."

"Perhaps you'll find yourself equal to the responsibility, when it comes."

"A man may be equal to all manner of things, and prefer not to undertake them." Yes, there went the thin straight mouth of disapprobation. "But I spoke flippantly. Responsibility or no, the fact is I cannot contemplate with any eagerness the event that will make me a baronet, so I cannot look forward to my baronetcy." Suddenly she was no longer at his side, and he craned about to find her stock-still behind him, her chin lifted to finally show all her face. "Please tell me you're not astonished by that sentiment," he said.

Even in the shade of her bonnet he could see her cheeks coloring. "Not astonished. A bit surprised, perhaps. You mean to say you love your father."

"Not necessarily. There's a great stretch of ground between loving a man, and wishing for his demise." He walked on and heard her follow, a step or two behind as though she were wanting to study him, and fit this new bit of knowledge in with the picture she'd already made. "But I suppose I am rather fond of him." Now he'd confuse her further still. "I made up my mind to be so, and he hasn't succeeded in dissuading me yet."

"Not even by banishing you for something so small as a snuffbox?"

"It wasn't just the snuffbox, you know." He bent to pluck up a long blade of grass, and to avoid her eyes. Had he just heard her take his part against his father's? "I've been a bit of a wastrel all round. Not good for much." He'd always owned up to the fact readily. It was good for a laugh at White's. But for some reason it didn't sound nearly so amusing out here in the country. "I do intend to be better, eventually." He twirled the grass-blade between thumb and forefinger. "To be upstanding and respectable and so forth. Certainly by the time I'm a baronet."

"If you know you can be better, why not be better now?" Ah, here came the lecture. So much for taking his part.

"Think a minute, darling. What would it profit you if I were to reform now?" He bent his head to flash her a smile, and knew she took his meaning by the way her bonnet tipped down and her conversation ceased.

Well enough. He tossed away the grass-blade and they went on. With or without talk, it was a beautiful day to be walking with a woman. Some overnight rain had left a fresh scent in the air, and woke a few languid late-summer flowers that dotted the grass, white and yellow and purple punctuation on a great page of green. Birds swooped down and up again, calling to one another in a regional dialect unlike the birdcalls one heard in Lincolnshire. At the top of the nearest hill he could see how a breeze stirred the grass as though some large invisible hand were going through it with a comb.

"We want to go up and over that hill." She pointed, her black glove stark against the blue, blue sky. "The place I have in mind is just on the other side."

They climbed slowly—what perverse devil had decreed that widows must wear so much black, even in weather like this?—and reached the hilltop to look down on a minor kind of valley, green and studded everywhere with sheep. A dog barked at the sight of them and raced up the opposite hill to where a girl sat in the shade of some trees. "That's one of my tenants," Mrs. Russell said. "One of the Everett daughters, I think."

She put another step of distance between them. "And a little way beyond those trees is your hedge."

So this land could be his, perhaps, if he chose. Though it didn't look very promising for wheat or any other crop. And the girl would lose a grazing place with the advantage of a shady overlook. He put the map away under his arm. "Why do you suppose your husband didn't enclose this himself?"

"I'm afraid I haven't any idea. Mr. Russell didn't often speak about that sort of thing." She turned her head to face him, and looked for a moment as though she would say more. But after a short pause, she only proposed crossing the valley and greeting the shepherdess.

The girl had a book and a basket with her, in addition to the vigilant dog, and as they drew near she closed the book and shoved it half-hidden under the basket, which rendered the volume a good deal more interesting than it otherwise should have been.

Apparently Mrs. Russell thought so as well. Once the introductions were through—the girl proved, indeed, to be a Miss Everett, and honored to make his acquaintance—and they'd all taken seats in the shade, he could see the widow's attention straying again and again to that corner of the book peeping out from under the basket, even while she made all the necessary inquiries into the girl's health, and the health of assorted family members.

They formed a pretty picture, the young widow with her dark eyes and dark dress, and the younger shepherdess, blue-eyed, with reddish-blond hair and a sprinkling of freckles over the bridge of her nose. He'd sat a bit apart from them, to lean against the trunk of a tree. The dog, a shaggy brown-and-white herding sort, sank down beside him and rested its chin on his leg just as though it belonged to him, its ears perking this way and that as the ladies spoke.

They spoke without much ease. Miss Everett seemed a bit in awe of Mrs. Russell, who didn't help matters with the topics she chose. Sunday school was broached. Schooling of every sort came in for praise, and so did the general concepts of duty and application, and so did the parish curate, who was apparently plotting to inflict a school upon the children of his flock. The poor girl could only nod and murmur agreement, and twist her hands in her lap, bereft of her book, while the widow launched her next offensive in support of education.

Clearly she hoped to inspire her listener to some enthusiasm on the subject, but she went about it all wrong, bludgeoning the girl with *worthy* this and *diligence* that, and never giving the smallest sign that she cared to hear anyone's opinions but her own. Not so different, really, from the tone she took with him.

"Perhaps Miss Everett is rather an adherent of self-education," he put in at a moment when the widow had paused for breath. He smiled at the girl, encouragingly as he could. "You were reading something, I think, when we approached. I fear we keep you from it."

"Oh, no, I was only reading to pass the time." She blushed and looked more miserable yet. "Nothing in the way of education."

"A novel, I suppose?" Mrs. Russell quickly caught up this new thread, and when the girl nodded, she continued with fresh purpose. "Certainly there are more substantial things a young lady can read, but most novels do no real harm. One may begin with tales of romance and suspense, and proceed eventually to reading Shakespeare, or Homer, or some other thing to elevate the mind."

Good Lord, she was bad at this. Couldn't she see the girl growing smaller with mortification over her poor novel, and shrinking from the prospect of these elevated things the widow would foist on her? He leaned for-

ward, and worked his fingers into the ruff at the dog's
neck. "A novel, eh?" he said to Miss Everett at a conspiratorial volume. "Was it *The Monk*?"

Her face convulsed with nine parts alarm and—he'd
almost stake his soul on it—one part mirth; meanwhile
the widow whipped round to fix him with her sternest
stare.

"No?" he said. "Was it *The Italian*, perhaps?"

Four parts mirth to six parts alarm: he was making
progress. "It wasn't anything like that," the girl said, finally drawing her book out from its hiding place. "I'm
only reading *Belinda*."

"Ah, *Belinda*. Let me see." He took the volume and
flipped to its opening pages. "Oh, this won't do. You
want the original version. Lucy marries an African plan-
tation servant, and Belinda nearly marries that Creole
fellow, the West Indian. Very scandalous. The author's
father disapproved, and so she revised it." He returned
the book and sat back, scratching the dog along its jaw.

"How do you know any of this?" Mrs. Russell had
grown saucer-eyed listening to him. "How do you know
of *The Monk*?"

"Older sisters." He felt, and fought, a most unseason-
able impulse to wink at her. "When I was a boy, my
sister Sophia was caught with a copy and nearly dis-
owned. How could I not seek it out, after that?" And
how do *you* know of *The Monk*, he barely refrained
from adding.

"I'm convinced that's exactly opposite to the lesson
your parents intended." She would surely have drawn
herself up to a more terrible height, but that she was
already sitting, as was her habit, straight and strict as a
judge.

"Then they ought to have given me more interesting
things to read." He shrugged, and slouched a little far-

ther. "You ladies have the advantage of us entirely, with your novels."

These last words apparently reminding the widow of Miss Everett's presence, she turned to address the girl again. "Mrs. Edgeworth's books amuse and entertain, undoubtedly, and she is to be commended—as is any lady novelist—for finding a means of income and independence. But if you care to read a more ambitious sort of novel, you ought to try *Waverley*. It's just come out this summer and it's quite well regarded. The author has drawn what I believe is a very accurate picture of Scotland in the middle of the last century. You may borrow my copy."

"*Waverley,*" the girl repeated. Behind her attempt at a smile was all the enthusiasm of a housemaid getting set to scrub out the chamberpots. "What story does it tell?"

"It's true to history, an account of that period in which many of the Scots people hoped to enforce a Stuart claim to the throne. Perhaps you're not versed in that, not having had the advantage of schooling. But *Waverley* is such a novel as could address gaps in a person's knowledge of English history, while simultaneously imparting a lesson through its hero's progression from sentimental fervor to a more reasoned, practical view of the world."

God in Heaven, she made the thing sound like a sequel to *The Utility of Agricultural Knowledge*. "Has it got a love story?" He would prompt her in the right direction.

She paused, considering in her fastidious manner. "I suppose it does. Mr. Waverley comes to feel a regard for two different young women, each worthy in her way. The one, I think, is intended to embody a sort of Jacobite zeal while the other—"

"Has it got battles, or a quest? Does your Mr. Waverley risk his life for high ideals?"

"Well, there are battles, of course. One could hardly

set a story in the Jacobite rebellion without them, and as I've said, the author seems scrupulous in regard to the accuracy of the setting."

"Very good." He nodded at the shepherdess. "You look like a reader of sturdy constitution. You must read this novel and tell me whether there's a good story in between all the accurate and elevating parts. I'm afraid those virtues are a kind of poison to me, and I need some other reader to go before, like one of those fellows who tastes a king's suppers."

He did know how to get what he wanted from women. Most women. The girl flushed prettily under his attention, and agreed to precede him with *Waverley*. The widow, who had at first frowned as if ready to say something scolding, observed this outcome, and studied him with a thoughtful mien, and said nothing after all.

From there the conversation went more easily. Mrs. Russell spoke of his errand in visiting her, and unrolled the map to consult with Miss Everett on how the land before them corresponded with what was drawn, and on which families would be affected if this land should pass out of their use.

Theo sank against the tree until he was near to recumbence. The dog rolled over and eyed him expectantly; he scratched its belly with an absent hand.

He didn't want any families to be affected. He didn't want this bashful, novel-loving girl to be the worse off for his having come to the country. Would every parcel on the map be like this? Behind the neatly inked rendition, just an opportunity for him to dispossess people who'd done nothing to deserve it? And yet if the addition of land could increase Pencarragh's prosperity, and put an end to relying on the poor rates for his laborers' upkeep, then surely he must consider enclosing.

He frowned at the dog, who returned his look with drowsy unconcern. So many times he'd worn such a look himself, before he'd come to Sussex and learned the weight of cares.

*Y*OUR COTTAGERS must be very fond of you," Martha said when they'd taken their leave of Jenny Everett and marched north into open pasture.

Mr. Mirkwood laughed without much perceptible humor. "Must they? I wish someone would tell them so." He was more than usually handsome in the out-of-doors, moving with the vigor of an animal turned out from captivity. Jenny had looked quite smitten.

"I can't believe they're not fond of you. You were so good with Miss Everett just now. You knew all the right things to say."

"I guessed." He shrugged.

"To set her at ease the way you did is no commonplace skill. As I believe I demonstrated myself."

"You do come off a bit like a draconian governess." Over his shoulder he smiled at her, robbing the words of any sting.

"I suppose that's to be expected. I was raised chiefly by a governess, though I should never call Miss York *draconian*. Sensible, rather. Proper." Strict, of course, but within reason.

"Indeed." His step slowed so that they walked exactly abreast. "At what age did you lose your mother?"

"I was seven. But she was unwell for all those seven years. Preparing for the next confinement or recovering from the last." The words came out rather tentatively. One really need not provide this level of detail. "There ought to have been three more children after me. But none of them survived, and the last took her with him." Though truly, little had remained of her by the end. Five children living, five more deceased, and Mother further diminished with each birth and each loss.

"And your father never remarried?" Round the brim of her bonnet she saw his white gloved fingers hitching the rolled map higher under his arm.

"Oh, no. It's a bit of a wonder he ever married at all, he had such a retiring nature. Shut up in his study with his Bible and philosophy books most days."

"Who was there to love you, then?" Without any discernible hesitation he asked the question, and without any attempt to hide the swell of sympathy in his voice. Wasted sympathy, roused on behalf of a little girl she'd long since left behind.

She crossed her wrists behind her back and laced her fingers tight together. "I am in no doubt of having been loved by both my parents. My siblings care for me as well. And Miss York managed my upbringing quite capably. If I am draconian, or ungraceful, in such interactions as you witnessed today, the fault is entirely my own, I'm sure."

The conversation lapsed. She would not look at him, and risk meeting with more sympathy in his indiscreet eyes. She marched on, unlacing and relacing her fingers, until he spoke again.

"Don't suppose you've seen an accurate example of how I interact with my own laborers. Talking to someone else's cottagers is different, I don't doubt. Too, you were there. She shouldn't have been so much at ease if I'd come upon her alone."

"Of course. I hadn't thought of that." A single gentleman landowner had a whole different set of challenges, didn't he? Maybe she could be of use. "Perhaps one afternoon I could go with you to call on your own people."

"Perhaps." He wheeled out ahead of her, as though to slip from under the burden of solemnity, and walked backward, facing her, eyes lit with irreverence. "Will you badger the ladies with lists of recommended reading? Will you make a sermon on the virtues of education?"

"I might make such a sermon to you." Impudent man, he would deserve it. "Have you given any thought to educating your laborers' children?"

"No more sermons today." He caught the map in his hands and proceeded to twirling it round and round like a parading soldier's musket. "No more thought. Altogether I've had a pleasant afternoon, and I should like to finish it in just this style, walking about with you under the sun and the sky."

So she said no more. Hope burned strong and steady in her, though. No more sermons *today*, he'd said. That left tomorrow, and quite a few days besides. With persistence, and encouragement of his better qualities, what improvements might she not set in motion, on his land as well as her own, before the month was through?

*I*F HE were a cottager—which he must remember to be thankful more often that he was not—Theo would keep a house, he hoped, not unlike Mr. Barrow's. The very yard told of thrift and order, with the geese and pig confined in separate makeshift pens and a neat kitchen garden visible back of the house.

The door stood open to take advantage of the early evening breezes. One could afford that little luxury, of course, when one's pig was not at liberty to march into the house. He stopped on the threshold and knocked.

He'd come home restless from Seton Park, and gone from room to room looking for something to do. All that study and tramping about ought to have left him tired, but he found, instead, that he wanted to be busy. Industry probably became a habit, if one allowed it to.

"Come," a voice called, and he went in.

Sunlight slanted through clean windows to show the

spare, tidy kitchen he remembered from the one time he'd called there to find no one home. Mr. Barrow sat at the table, doing something with a needle and cloth. A plate of food sat near him.

Country hours. He ought to have learnt by now. "Forgive me." He stopped where he was and made an apologetic bow. "I didn't mean to interrupt your supper. I'll call another time." He hadn't any particular purpose in calling, anyway; just a vague notion of seeing whether he couldn't have as cordial a conversation with one of his own people as he'd done with Miss Everett.

"Supper?—not at all." The man pushed up from his place at the table, sweeping another place clean. "Only something to take the edge off. Will you sit? I'll fetch a plate for you." He bustled off with such speed as his age allowed, reaching down a tin plate from a shelf that ran across the kitchen's back wall, and some paper-wrapped foodstuffs from another shelf, this one hanging by chains in the room's center so as to foil even the most ambitious and sure-footed rats.

Yes, he must remember to be thankful he was not a cottager. Thankful for a life in which rats were dispensed with by somebody else, kept away from his meals by methods of which he could remain blissfully ignorant. Thankful for dinners eaten from patterned china on tables laid with linen, and thankful for numerous inventive courses rather than the heel of bread and unprepossessing hunk of cheese now set down before him.

He inclined his head again, and maintained the angle long enough that it might pass for a private observation of grace, in case that was the tradition in this house. When he looked up, Mr. Barrow's eyes were on him, icy blue, crevassed at the outer corners, and lit with the keen expectancy of a young boy waiting for a puppet-show to begin.

You knew all the right things to say, the widow had

said. Well, with a pretty young girl, yes. But how did one make conversation with a man of Mr. Barrow's age and station? He glanced about him for ideas. "What do you do there, with the needle and cloth?" He nodded toward the heap of abandoned work.

"Mending." The man reached for a bit of it and turned it over to show him. "Here's a shirt that's grown a hole in one sleeve. I'm putting a patch on."

"You do that yourself?" The moment it was said, he heard the stupidity of it. Of course the man did his own mending. With no wife and no servants, who else was to do it? "I mean, I'm sure I shouldn't know where to begin." He crumbled off one corner of the cheese and took a bite. It tasted faintly of chalk. No, not so faintly. He set the rest down, and tried his best to chew and swallow what was already in his mouth without tasting any more.

"You begin by threading the needle, and for me that's the difficult part. Eyes not so good as they once were. After that, it's just a matter of getting the patch to lie straight." Mr. Barrow's fingers, knobby about the knuckles and not inclined to lie straight themselves, pressed the patch smooth and he poked the needle up from inside the sleeve. He reached for his bread and bit off a piece. "Sorry the food isn't better," he said after swallowing.

"Oh, I'm not very hungry." He could feel shamed color rising in his face. Had he been that obvious, with the cheese? "I have supper yet to eat and I don't want to fill up."

"Not a practiced liar, are you?" Mr. Barrow was smiling, eyes on his needle. "You want to pick one excuse: you're not hungry, or you need to save your appetite. The two don't mix."

"I'm sorry." He groped for a neater balance of truth and tact. "I suppose cheese must be a matter of particular partiality. One grows up eating a certain kind, and no other region's can taste quite right after that."

"Now, that's a bit better." The man's smile creased deeper into his cheeks. "But you'd best marry a girl you won't ever need to lie to." He jabbed at the cheese on his own plate. "This is vile stuff. I know. I grew up on a dairy farm."

"Did you? Was that here in Sussex?" He leaned forward and planted his elbows on the table. Here, maybe, was the way to make conversation with a person of advanced years: not by thinking of any right things to say, but by drawing out the person's life story and accumulated wisdom; by asking the questions one might have asked one's own grandparents, had they been hale enough to survive to such an age.

Mr. Barrow made the task easy. With glowing animation he recounted tales of life in Sussex, a half-century ago, and threw in his decided opinions on the modern manufacture of cheese and butter, and, for that matter, bread and tea, with all the rubbish nowadays added to stretch product and profit.

Theo listened. He'd expected the life-story bits to be compelling, of course, but even the business about cheese was interesting, more interesting than it had any right to be, and what was more, it sounded like just the sort of thing that would interest Mrs. Russell.

He might carelessly drop such pearls of learning in their next sitting-room conversation, and see if her face would light with studious bliss. Or whisper them to her in bed, in hopes she'd look at him as a woman looked at a man who knew all the best ways to surprise her.

Or he might simply bring her here to call, and sit back while she and the old man spoke of such matters as she seemed to enjoy. She would make thoughtful, measured replies, and Mr. Barrow would perhaps be impressed by this example of modern womanhood, with her serious bearing and her devotion to bettering her estate.

A prideful wave of pleasure flushed through him at the thought. Fool. What had he to be proud of? What had he to do in the scene but sit back in a corner, idle as always, and watch two worthy people come to esteem one another? And still, pleasure warmed him as the time limit for a polite call came and went, pleasure simmered in him as shadows crept across the kitchen floor, and prideful pleasure chased along as he finally legged it back to the house, so late he had no time to even dress for supper.

Chapter Seven

M̶R. KEENE shifted in his chair. He folded and unfolded his hands on the tabletop, making her wish she could give him some papers to straighten. "I'm sorry, I tell you frankly, to come on this errand," he said, and Martha knew what subject he would have to introduce.

"You mustn't apologize for doing what duty demands. I expect Mr. James Russell wishes to know whether the prospect of a direct heir has yet been ruled out?"

So miserable he looked, bowing, a shaft of afternoon sunlight glancing off the bald part of his head. Shame on Mr. James Russell for tasking him with this mortifying inquiry. Shame on her as well, of course, for cooking up the circumstance into which he must inquire.

Three weeks and two days now since Mr. Russell's passing. She lowered her eyes and brought her voice down too. "I cannot say beyond a doubt, and of course things are tenuous in the early weeks. But I should have expected to know by now if there were *no* such prospect."

"I see." She stole a look at him. He straightened, as though grasping for fortitude. "Then I must proceed to the next part of my commission, and prepare you for the likelihood of a visit by Mr. James Russell himself."

A tiny cold convulsion went through her. Suddenly she had no breath with which to make a reply.

"I'm sorry." He took off his spectacles and set to polishing them with a cloth from his pocket, probably that he might have somewhere other to look than at her. "I fear he's heard tales of . . . how a man in his situation might be cheated of his due. He speaks of protecting his interests." His brow creased. "I'll do my utmost, I promise, to convince him of what your character is, but without his having met you I fear he is prey to these wild sorts of speculation in forming his suppositions of what you might—"

"When?" That word, at least, she could manage.

"When did I hear from him?"

She swallowed. "When will he come?"

"Not immediately." He folded his polishing cloth, put it back in his pocket, replaced his spectacles. "His business concerns will keep him in Derbyshire through the month. I'll do my best to dissuade him altogether, as I said, and if he remains resolved, I shall know, and tell you, when he sets out for Sussex." His mouth twisted as though it were full of foul medicine. "He asks me to monitor your actions meanwhile, and report to him." He examined his own hands for a moment, and then looked up. "Your husband had some objections, I believe, to his brother. Were you aware?"

She shook her head. That the brothers had not been close was of course hinted at by Mr. James Russell's absence from both the wedding and the funeral, but never had Mr. Russell mentioned any reasons, and never had she asked.

He gave a quick nod, and appeared to confer with himself over whether to say more. "He had concerns, as I understand, in regard to Mr. James Russell's character, and great hopes of being able to leave Seton Park to a proper heir. I assure you he would never countenance such insult as his brother now makes to you."

"Did he ever tell you the nature of his concerns? What doubts he had of Mr. James Russell?" Barely breathing, she watched for his response.

Again he took an interest in his hands. "I only gather he thought him unfit to take charge of the estate." The tips of his ears went pink as he said it.

He knew. Just as Sheridan had known, and all the servants had known, and Mr. Russell had known. Everyone knew what infamy had been in this house—what infamy threatened to infest it again—and no one had troubled to tell her a thing.

The long-case clock chimed. Mr. Mirkwood would arrive in an hour. They must be more than ever careful, now Mr. Keene had been told to keep watch of her.

"I appreciate your telling me so much." He was a good man, the little solicitor. He deserved better than to be a sort of shuttlecock, batted back and forth between Mr. James Russell's villainy and her own scheming deception. "I know your professional bond is to the Russell family and not to me. I'm grateful for the personal kindness, and the respect for Mr. Russell's memory, that must have led you to grant me such consideration."

"It's no more than I would want someone to do for my own wife, if she were in your place," he said, his eyes averted and his voice uncharacteristically gruff. She'd embarrassed him, on top of everything else. So she only thanked him again, and said nothing more.

A WEEK AND a half have gone by since I addressed the women servants." She sat at her dressing table while Sheridan unpinned her hair. Mr. Mirkwood would arrive in minutes, and she would go down a back hallway from her own rooms to the east wing to meet him.

"A week and a half, to be sure." The maid's voice soothed as surely as her hands, letting down and loosening the plaits.

"Do you know that none of them has approached me for help in finding a new situation?"

"Indeed." She sounded thoroughly unsurprised.

"Nor does Mrs. Kearney report that anyone has notified her of an intent to leave."

"Everybody's waiting." Sheridan met her eyes in the mirror as she took up the hairbrush. "They all think it might be a fine thing to go on here under your charge."

"I'm . . . touched . . . to hear of their faith in me." Through a suddenly tightening throat she said the words. "But Mr. James Russell's visit puts a new complexion on things. To feign pregnancy—if that should prove necessary—and acquire a baby will be next to impossible under his watch. And his mere presence in the house might be a threat to the servants. I shall tell everyone to give strong consideration to leaving."

"I've considered already, and I don't mean to go." With skittish bravado the girl spoke, ducking her head and glancing up from under her lashes. "You've borne so much with Mr. Mirkwood. I can't think it was for nothing. I'll wait until the end of the month at least." She drew the brush to the very ends of Martha's hair. "Now you'd best be off to the blue rooms."

*S*OMETHING PREOCCUPIED her today. He could feel it in her skin, everywhere they touched. He could feel it in the weight of her hands on his back. He could see it in the lines of her face, even as she closed her eyes to give him privacy for that last, most undignified capitulation.

"Is something the matter?" he said afterward, lying on his side to face her. She lay on her back as usual, propped on the pillow, gaze somewhere distant.

Her eyes came to his and she gave a quick shake of her head. "Only I've had some estate business on my mind. Forgive me. I make you a poor hostess."

"Nothing to forgive." He touched his knuckles to her arm. "I could distract you from your cares."

"No, thank you." A smile flickered over her lips and was gone. Still, she'd smiled, and that was a start.

"In small ways, I mean." Yes. Why shouldn't he? "I can help you dress, and plait your hair while you read. I brought something by Humphry Davy today. You've heard of him? Everyone in London attends his lectures, even fashionable people. I have a book of his lecture notes. You might read from it, and try out your oratory style."

She eyed him with that half-disbelieving look that queens must have used on the court jester, once upon a time. But if she was finding him preposterous, well, that was so much attention drawn away from her heavier concerns. Court jesters served a purpose, after all.

"You'll dress yourself first, I hope." She glanced down his body. "I have no taste for anything exotic."

"Naturally I will." He pivoted away from her to go after his clothes, and also to hide the triumph that must be suffusing his every facial feature. He would make her forget her troubles, in the ways that suited her best.

And so he was attentive to her modesty, and her strict sensibilities, as he laced the corset and tied the petticoats and sat her in the low-backed chair at the dressing-table, book open before her, to fasten the hooks of her gown. But halfway through the fastening he stopped. He'd parted her hair and put it forward of her shoulders on either side to be clear of the hooks. The gown fell open to the left and right, baring a triangle of skin above the corset. Pale, smooth skin with an elegant ridge of back-bone down the middle. Perhaps there were more effective ways to distract her than merely dressing her hair.

He hesitated, fingers playing at the next open hook. She might be angry, and rebuke him. But she might not. He glanced in the mirror at her downcast eyes. Then, fluid as grain poured from a bushel, he sank to his knees and pressed his lips to her spine.

He might as well have prodded her with a hot iron. "What are you doing?" she said, her voice dashing to the upper end of its register. Distracted, beyond any doubt.

"I'm unhooking your gown. Don't panic." He eased the black bombazine down just past her shoulders. "And while you read, I intend to kiss along your backbone, from the top of your chemise to the nape of your neck. That is the whole of my plan." He touched his mouth to the place where the parting in her hair began, for illustration.

"It's a poor plan." Over her shoulder, he could see her face in the mirror, tight-lipped and severe. "You'd do better to plait my hair. You're liable to work yourself into a state."

Miracle of miracles, she hadn't actually said *no*. He gripped the chair-seat at either side of her, and drifted down some four inches to fix her with a second, softer kiss. "I've just been satisfied. Remember? A *state* is unlikely." A black, black lie. "Now tell me this: have you thought of your business concerns since I began?" Her face gave him the answer. "Very good, then. Relax. Take a few deep breaths. Read."

She sat perfectly still, deciding. He set his mouth at the top edge of her chemise and stayed there. He felt her rib cage expand and contract, and then, as she picked up the book, he could feel the words resonate in her body at the same time they came to his ears. "*To understand the mode of procuring from a given quantity of land, the greatest possible proportion of such vegetables as are necessary for human food, the food of animals, or for other purposes connected with human wants, is the great desideratum in agriculture.* I don't think you're paying attention."

"Of course I am. *Desideratum.* Can you please relax?" Her shoulders were rigid, and halfway up to her ears. She smelled of lilacs again.

"To obtain this desideratum, it is necessary to study with accuracy . . ." She put the book down. "Mr. Mirkwood, I think this may be the worst idea you've ever had."

But how could it be, when he'd coaxed her so quickly away from her preoccupations and back to her affronted self? "You haven't given it a fair trial." Still gripping the chair with one hand, he unpinned his gold watch from his waistcoat with the other, and flicked it open. "Allow me ten minutes." He reached past her to set the watch on the tabletop. "I'll stop the very second you tell me it's time."

"I cannot read while I'm watching the clock."

"Then you're not as accomplished a lady as I supposed. But perhaps you can forgo the reading for these ten minutes. I'm sure I'll pay better attention afterward anyway."

She closed her eyes. Through her vibrant muscles he could feel her warring with herself, casting about for some response that wouldn't be plain surrender. "Five minutes," she said.

Haggling. He could do that. "Seven." He flexed his fingers on the chair.

"Six." One small crease appeared in her forehead.

"Seven and a half." He breathed the words next to her ear.

Her eyes snapped open, all coffee-colored impatience. "You're supposed to go lower, to meet me. Six and a half, you should say."

"Eight," he murmured into her shoulder. "And I'll go

lower, to meet you, any time you like." He flicked his tongue across her spine and caught the little shock that went charging up from her tailbone to the base of her skull. When he lifted his head to look in the mirror, her cheeks were red and her chin was down, all fierce attention leveled on his watch.

Eight minutes it was, then. He kissed her, and kissed and kissed and kissed her until he knew that narrow path of skin, and the knobbly scaffolding underneath, the way he knew the lines on his own palm. He knew her scent, and he knew her taste, and he knew which vertebra put a catch in her breath when he brushed it with his lips. He could learn her whole body by mouth, if she would but let him, and distract her all out of her mind.

He tightened his grip on the chair-seat. Her skin had grown warm, and her muscles pliant, and his hands, his intractable hands, were every moment threatening to loose themselves and steal up to settle on her thighs. How well they would fit there, his thumb and middle finger arcing to compass her, his forefinger tracing elegant patterns, his palm discerning the knot of her garter through her layers of dress.

Someone was breathing harder. He was. He did that. And someone was breathing more softly, the slow, languid breaths of a person half-drugged. He glanced up at her reflection and a jagged bolt of desire shot through him. She'd closed her eyes—so much for the watch—and her face was unfurrowed, supple with pleasure, the face of a woman just waiting to be taken.

He could—No. He wouldn't. She didn't want that. But the longer he kept at this, the likelier he'd be to forget the fact. To forget himself. He unclenched his hands, one, then the other, from the sides of her chair, and began to fasten her gown.

Her eyes opened, hazy with confusion. She looked

down at the watch. She looked up at his reflection. "It hasn't been eight minutes." Possibly the sweetest words she'd ever said to him, and absolutely no help at this moment.

"No. But I've done as much as I think I ought." Planting his hands on her chair again, he levered himself up. "Excuse me." If this were any other woman, they'd be on their way back to bed. Instead he'd have to shift for himself, possibly the minute he got home—but was that allowed? Hell. Even when things went the way he meant them to, this bargain managed to make his life difficult. He went out to the sitting room and sank down on the sofa.

*T*HE WOMAN in the mirror was no woman she recognized. Cheeks flushed with pleasure. Hair tumbling in wanton waves down either shoulder. Eyes empty of all but mindless acquiescence.

Martha pivoted away from the image. She would not be that woman. Weak. Susceptible. Forgetting every vestige of principle the minute a man—a disrespectable man at that, and not even two weeks acquainted!—put his mouth to the back of her neck. A lady of purpose couldn't afford such frailty. Men ran roughshod over one's prospects as it was. They didn't need encouragement.

Over her shoulder she consulted the mirror again, this time with determination. Gradually her eyes came to look like her own eyes, brimming with unreadable thoughts. Her mouth let go its softness in favor of a firm line. She put her hair back behind her shoulders.

They'd established a way of managing, she and Mr. Mirkwood had, and she wouldn't muddy it with fleshly weaknesses that could benefit no one. She stood, caught up her book, and followed him out to the sitting room.

He slouched in a corner of the sofa, one arm flung across his face. His state was unmistakable, even from this distance. That distraction business had been a bad idea indeed.

She advanced to a spot near his knee and cleared her throat when he didn't uncover his face. "Are you ready to hear more of Humphry Davy?"

"Not so near, if you please." With his free hand he made a flicking motion, as if to rid himself of a housefly. "If you will go sit in your chair you may read whatever you like."

One was not without sympathy, everything considered. She sat and paged through the book. Perhaps Mr. Davy had outlined a lecture on uses of manure, or some other topic suitable for settling a gentleman's state.

"Before you begin, Mrs. Russell, may I clarify one point of our arrangement?"

She looked up. His elbow bent just over his brow, and beneath the shade of his arm, his eyes were on her. She nodded once.

"If I find myself with needs beyond what we've agreed to . . ." He touched his lips together and consulted the bend of his elbow as though to find the right words there. "Am I permitted to take relief elsewhere?" His eyes came to her again.

Every ounce of blood in her body rushed to her face, roaring past her ears on the way. "With other women, do you mean? Absolutely not. How can you even ask that, when you know the dangers of disease, and of—"

"No." He held up a hand, his gaze steady on her. "I'm not referring to other women." His fingers flexed.

"Oh." She couldn't blush any harder, but she could drop her attention to the carpet, and speak in the voice of some faint-hearted stranger. "Well, no. You can't do that either."

"Please tell me why I cannot."

"Because I've purchased the rights to your seed. All of it. What if you were to spill the bit that would have made my child?"

"Not likely." He shifted about on the sofa. "I think I need to do it."

"No. The discomfort is a trial you shall just have to bear."

"I think I need to do it this minute."

She looked up from the carpet. His free hand was fingering the first button of his trousers, and his eyes were still on her. Was he teasing her, or was he in earnest? No matter. She would tolerate neither. "I've said you cannot. Now put your hand somewhere respectable while I read."

"You make things worse, you know, when you speak to me that way." He sat up, finally dropping the arm from his face. "I'll just go into the bedroom for a few minutes. You can read through the door if you like."

"No!" She threw down the book and rose to block his path. "For Heaven's sake, get ahold of—" No. "For Heaven's sake, what is the matter with you?"

As quick as a striking cobra he caught her hands and pulled her down on the sofa beside him. "This." He pressed the back of her hand to where his condition announced itself through his trousers. "This is the matter with me. But it's easily remedied." His eyes glowed with unadulterated purpose. He'd be good for nothing until he'd had his relief.

"Oh, very well." His parents, or his governess, had fallen down badly when it came to acquainting him with self-denial. "We can go back to bed, and finish reading afterward."

"Too much delay. You take an age to undress."

That stung, surprisingly. She'd never supposed he might decline such an offer.

He turned her hand to cup her palm to his bothersome part. "You could help me."

Help him? What fresh indecency was this? "I haven't the first idea how."

"Fastidious Mrs. Russell." He spoke caressingly, and idly he was caressing her fingers, too, as though to seduce the hand away from her control. "I'll show you what to do."

What choice did she have? If she refused, he would almost certainly go home and disport himself regardless. "I'll do it if you will end by giving me the seed. I needn't undress for that." She rose. "And tomorrow you must take me to call on your laborer families."

"Laborer families." He was striving to contain his smile, like an unseasoned gambler who'd just turned up a royal flush. "By all means."

$\mathscr{I}$F SHE hadn't already consigned her soul to perdition, she was surely booking its passage there now. She lay flat on her back, overdressed for the occasion, and let him take possession of her right hand.

"We'll proceed gradually, shall we?" With his thumb and first two fingers he held her at the palm, and grazed her knuckles against his pertinent part. Thin, fragile-feeling skin slid about under her touch, but this was nothing new. In her marriage she'd learned more than she ever cared to know about the properties of the male organ.

"You implied there was some urgency to this. Am I to conclude you were deceiving me?"

"Do you know there are men who'd pay handsomely to be scolded so? You might consider that, if you ever find yourself in want of a profession." He wrapped her hand round the appendage and pressed it with his own.

"You didn't answer my question. And you need not introduce tasteless subjects."

"Pardon me. I'll converse with as much gentility as I can, while showing you how a man pleasures himself." He shifted her hand to a place higher up and gripped over it again. "And as to the question of urgency, perhaps you've felt enough now to judge for yourself."

There was nothing, really, one could say in reply to that. Urgency throbbed formidably in the palm of her hand.

He took her fingers to the end, where he'd begun to be damp, and drew them through the wetness, one by one. When he squeezed her hand over him again her fingers slid and he drew in a sharp breath. He guided their two hands up and back, slowly, and up and back again. "You see how it's done." He closed his eyes and spoke in a near whisper. "Not so hard, is it?"

"Not so difficult." Since these distinctions mattered.

"No. Not difficult at all." His hand tightened on hers and he made the movement faster.

She stared straight up at the canopy. This was four hundred kinds of wrong. He ought not to have involved her. She didn't want to hear his unchaste breaths, or to notice the way his hips moved. With brazen vigor they moved, as though he pushed into a greedy lover instead of one dumb hand clasped in another. She didn't want to notice that.

The crisis must come soon, surely. Already he sounded near to immolating himself in lust. And finally he did roll toward her, came up on one elbow, and let go her hand.

"Are you ready?" She drew up her skirts with the other hand, and put her knees apart.

"Soon. Don't stop." The look in his eyes could scorch a meadow to bare earth. His hand reached over and across her to the mattress there, and all her insides shrank and shriveled as he left her to make the motion on her own. His angle changed when he got above her. She had to turn her hand, then turn it back, groping for the least awkward way to hold him.

She might perish, literally, of mortification. Because she wasn't a mere passive hand anymore, prodded about by him as by some puppeteer. She was engaged in this, a participant, working to please the man who crouched over her so big and bestial.

He breathed in long, pleasure-drunk draughts, more unchaste than ever. Worse than this, he bent his head to watch her hand on him. And worse, worst of all, he said some words as he watched. She would not hear them. She would refuse to remember them. Soft words, they were, gentle words, all about how well she did the thing she was doing, and each one fell like a firebomb, leaving a swath of devastation that *cock* and *swive* and *corpse* could only dream of.

At last he leaned down and got his arm under her shoulders, to lift her partway from the pillow. "One thing more," he said, his voice tight and intent. He knelt, pushing his knees under her legs and bringing her hips up in a rustle of skirts. He took her hand off him, finally, only to bring it round, past her own leg and underneath him where it met with the soft weight of another alien part. Parts. "Here," he muttered against her ear. "Squeeze when I say so. Not too hard."

Was he serious? "Why on earth would you want me to—"

"Just . . . please . . . do it." With one last grim look he pushed in.

Once, he thrust. Twice. Three times. "*Now,*" he gasped, mouth at her ear.

Not too hard. Gingerly she compressed her fingers. "Like this?"

He swore, and brought his head down to her shoulder

and swore again, ferociously, an alarming string of every curse she'd ever heard uttered by man, and several she had not.

Oh, dear Lord. Too hard. She'd hurt him. His arms convulsed round her and his head fell back in some kind of agony as he pulled her nearly upright. But no, it was the right kind of agony. She could feel a quick rhythmic pulsing where he was inside her, the seed let loose.

He sank down with her to the mattress, and when the pulsing was done he rolled off and dropped to the place beside her, slack and spent, his eyes closed as though ever to open them again would simply be too great an effort.

"Yes," he said. "Exactly like that."

Chapter Eight

How EXTRAVAGANTLY he enjoyed his pleasure, Mr. Mirkwood. But then he was extravagant in everything. Undisciplined and unconstrained. Generous as well. He might turn that tendency to some more useful end. She might help him to do so.

Help him. Martha felt an inward flinch. She lay awake, some hour after midnight, staring into the darkness of her bedroom. For as mortifying as the memory of what she'd done this afternoon might be, she must admit he'd succeeded in taking her mind from her cares. The specter of Mr. James Russell's visit had wavered, like morning mist under a climbing sun, once he'd set himself to distract her. Distraction kept it at bay even now.

Her hands ached with restlessness. She lifted one, and stroked her fingertips across her belly. Certain acts ill became a widow in the first weeks of mourning. But mightn't those same acts serve to blunt a woman's appetites, and keep her from succumbing so readily to a man's touch and to his indecent suggestions? She hesitated, and sent her fingers lower.

There was a man she conjured for these occasions. He bore some resemblance, perhaps, to Mr. Atkins. His features weren't entirely distinct. But he was a man of principle, and conducted himself as a gentleman would who'd not been given to squandering his affections, but rather saved them up against the day he could join himself to a likewise principled woman, and spend all that treasure on her. He knew, without telling, every right place to touch. He gasped and shuddered, all wide-eyed wonder, as he found his bliss in her arms. And he evaporated, dependably, the instant his offices were no longer required.

But tonight her dependable man was possessed by some spirit of mutiny. He had things to say, things that would make any lady blush right down to her toenails. He made dark promises of what he would do with his mouth. He watched everything her hands did, and urged her to do more. And his eyes glinted blue in the moonlight, his hair pale like split wood, as he drove her to extravagant heights.

That was to be expected, maybe. So she told herself afterward. She'd got out of practice, not having done this for a month or more. Next time it would go nearer the usual plan, and in any case she could surely count on its inoculating effect.

She turned onto her side. Tomorrow promised more decorous distractions, with the visit to Mr. Mirkwood's laborers. She would watch for opportunities to work on his native kindness, and help him turn it into the foundation for responsibility. Her thoughts of him would be virtuous and improving, and she'd take her best satisfaction in thinking of how he'd go back to London a better man than when he'd come.

H<small>E WAITED</small> just inside the familiar copse of trees, eyes on the corner of the house round which she would appear, fingers fidgeting with the clasp of his watch.

Would she be distant today? Cold-mannered, or too

embarrassed to meet his eyes? Sorry for what he'd persuaded her to do? That would be cruel to bear, because for his part, he'd never been less sorry in his life. Indeed he could not see how he was to pleasure himself at all in future, his great paw a pallid substitute for the inordinate eroticism of her cool careful grip.

The brown-brick walls of Seton Park glowed warmly in the noonday sun. He flicked his watch open and glanced down at it. When he looked up again, she was there, a small black figure just come into view at the house's edge.

Why in blazes had he waited until six and twenty to dally with a widow? What a piquant, forbidden pleasure she looked, her black draperies marking her as another man's property even while they encouraged his eye to linger on her pale, sweet skin. Her skirts swayed in time with her sturdy gait, their fluid motion hinting at the shape of her legs.

He knew the shape of her legs. He knew how it felt to stroke a hand up her shin, with its small soft hairs, over the rounded knee and to her thigh, smooth and silken. He knew which muscles flexed when she drew her thighs apart, and which ones stretched and clenched when she crossed her legs behind him.

He gave himself a quick shake. No profit in this line of thought unless he was intending to back her up against one of these trees, and he was not quite low enough for that.

When she reached the edge of the woods she peered in, a quizzical cast to her eyes, before she discerned him and came on. "So," she said. She carried a basket, covered with a cloth, and now moved it from one arm to the other. "This is how you go, every day."

"Didn't I tell you it was convenient?" He took the basket from her. "Good God, woman. What are you bringing to these people? Bricks and rocks to make an insurrection with?"

"Only some bread and cakes and fruit from my orangery. Perhaps a few books as well, in case they have an interest."

"I see." Under his gaze she rather resembled a child caught with her hand in the jam pot, albeit a defiant one. "You aim for the slow and subtle style of insurrection."

"I do no such thing." She answered with an ease that seemed nothing short of miraculous. No fretfulness. No blush. No undercurrent of reproach. "I only picked out a few volumes such as I thought the women and children might enjoy. Not *Waverley,* because I've given it to Jenny Everett. Though I will gladly lend it to any of your people, once you've finished it yourself."

What very optimistic hopes she had of this visit, and of his cottagers. A pity Mr. Barrow would be away at work—she wasn't likely to find much conversation in any other house.

"You said you have families on the parish relief, didn't you?" Today's bonnet flared outward, to show more of her face, and as she turned partly toward him he could see her cheeks flushed with happy purpose. "I'd especially like to visit them, if we may. We ought to begin where we can do the most good."

He'd take her to the Weavers, then. Left to himself, he would have avoided that cottage for the rest of his term in Sussex—but she wished to do good, and residual tender gratitude would bend him to her will.

$\mathcal{T}$HE YARD was just as he remembered. Geese and more geese. "Watch your step," he said to Mrs. Russell, though that implied there was any clean place to set her foot. The pig came jogging from behind the house, clearly scenting opportunity. Through a window, he could hear the baby's squalls.

A glance at his companion found her to be preparing herself in little ways; ways a man less acquainted might not notice. Shoulders back. Head up. A deliberate deep breath.

"They'll be honored by your visit," he said quietly. Could she really be doubting? He touched her elbow once, in case she wanted courage, and came away with new courage himself. They went to the door.

There the farce of the pig repeated itself, to greater inconvenience this time as he was the one doing the introductions, but they got inside—Mrs. Weaver lapsing into this much civility, at least—and the door shut behind them.

"I'm sorry I've never called before now," said Mrs. Russell, all polite determination. "With nobody in residence at the house, one isn't quite sure what's proper. But I've been speaking with Mr. Mirkwood on some matters of land, and the opportunity finally arose."

He looked about him as she spoke. The same disposition of children, and—this gave a jolt to his stomach—in the corner, the eldest daughter, her face turned to the wall as though meaning to hide. She must have done that the instant he came in.

" . . . close to eleven months now, and I know so little of my neighbors. I shall be glad to know more." She allowed a little pause, which Mrs. Weaver made no move to fill. The baby replied in his usual style. Theo set the basket down on the kitchen table's one clear spot. Perhaps she'd like to get on with dispensing the gifts and bring this call to a merciful end.

But she had other ideas. "What a beautiful baby," she said. "May I hold him?"

He would bet money that no one had ever expressed that sentiment, nor made that request, before. Mrs.

Weaver looked as though she weren't quite sure of having heard it. Probably she must often be uncertain of what she had heard, with that constant squalling in such proximity to her ear.

"What is his name?" She did have an admirable focus once she'd made up her mind to want something. She went without hesitation to where Mrs. Weaver stood, and petted the baby's few wisps of hair.

"Job," said the woman. Yes, it would be. She let Mrs. Russell take the child from her arms. The widow arranged its head and limbs to suit her, and turned his way again.

Well. This was how she would look, holding a baby. Though of course her baby would be handsomer. It would have hair. It would have wide inquiring eyes, dark brown like her own. Or perhaps dark blue with flecks of gold. Odd to think of. One would be able to see the eyes, at all events, which was more than could be said for Master Job, who registered the change in arms as an outrage against which he must screw all his features into disorder and bring some cryptic modulation to his yells.

Undaunted, she smiled down at the baby and bounced it lightly in her arms. Give her a better infant model and she might sit for one of those Madonna-and-child paintings, all grave lovely radiance and almost painful to look at.

Why should she be painful to look at? What was the matter with him? But he did look away, when she raised her eyes from the baby to beam at him as though they shared some marvelous secret.

She had every right to beam. They did share a marvelous secret. He was the means by which she would get her heart's desire and secure her future. And perhaps in the years ahead he might come sometimes into Sussex, to manage something or other at Pencarragh, and then pay a visit to Seton Park to see how the child—Mr. Russell's heir—got on.

"It's a sign of health, isn't it, to have a good strong voice?" the widow was saying, raising her own voice to be heard above the baby. He returned his gaze to her, now she was looking elsewhere.

"Is it?" said Mrs. Weaver. Her now-empty hands made a half-hearted reach toward one of the table's dirty dishes, then fell slack.

"May I carry him outside for just a minute? It's such a fine day and I'm sure the fresh air would do him good."

"Take care not to let the pig in," was Mrs. Weaver's only response. Likely she wouldn't object if Mrs. Russell proposed to carry the child as far as Scotland.

"I'll come with you," he said, because even the ear-splitting society of young Job was preferable to the sullenness that polluted the air of this room. "I can open the door and keep the pig at bay while you walk out."

The pig waited just outside the door, poised against the moment. But he was ready. He flung the door open and advanced on the creature, managing by the element of surprise to drive it back long enough for Mrs. Russell to slip through.

He made a mental note. They'd have to pass once through the door to carry the child back inside, and once more to take their leave. He needed two more ways of outwitting the pig. To such things were gentlemen brought, when they came to the country.

I HOPE YOU'RE not planning to abduct that child." Mr. Mirkwood, having terrorized the pig to his satisfaction, caught up and fell into step at her side. The pig for some reason followed him.

"Of course not." *I should need a younger one than this.* She turned the baby so he was upright, head against her shoulder and bottom in the crook of her arm. "I thought to give Mrs. Weaver a moment of peace by taking him outside."

"Is something wrong with him? He's been like this every time I've seen him."

She shook her head. "One of my sister's babies was this way. Some babies just are. They grow out of it. It's difficult for the mother until they do, though. Enormously difficult, I should think, for a mother who hasn't the luxury of handing her baby over to a nurse." Poor Kitty could have done, but she was stubborn as a garden weed. That did run in the family.

He had hold of her arm suddenly and her heart leapt up her throat. She'd wadded up the memories of yesterday and last night, and stuffed them into a remote corner of her mind; now all at once they sprang out and billowed like the sails of a destroyer. For an irrational instant she was sure he knew all. He knew what she'd done last night and what part he had played and now meant to hold her to account—but no, he was only guiding her round a goose that had planted itself in her path. She swallowed, and wadded the unruly memories small again.

They gave the goose a suitable berth, she and baby Job and Mr. Mirkwood, with the pig shambling along on his other side. "You're an aunt, then," he said, dropping her arm. "For some reason it never occurred to me you might be."

"Several times over, I am." Her pulse had calmed. Her breathing was regular. She was speaking, companionably, with a man she hoped to improve. "My eldest brother has children as well."

"Is that the brother with whom you would live, if not blessed with a son of your own?"

"Andrew, yes." She dipped her head for a furtive whiff of Job's scalp. Baby scent, like no other scent in nature.

"Your eldest brother is Andrew. And your sister is . . . ?"

"Kitty. Katharine. She's next in age after Andrew." They'd reached the end of the small yard, and turned left to walk along the fence. The pig turned too, neat and nimble as a horse in dressage. The baby's howls were subsiding into hiccupping sobs of exhaustion.

"Andrew and Kitty. And you have two more brothers besides."

"How do you know that?" She looked up in surprise.

"You told me. I asked. Don't you remember?" The sun shone behind him, making it difficult to look into his face, and also casting a kind of halo about his pale hair, where it showed beneath his hat. "The second time I called on you, I asked after your brothers and sisters."

"Did you? How on earth do you remember?"

"I make space for it. Ask me what I recall of the Loudon we were reading three days since." He would be wearing his mischievous-choirboy smile now, if she should look that way. Not outright wicked, that smile, merely full of high spirits and the disinclination to take anything seriously.

"I'm persuaded that space in your mind would be better filled by Mr. Loudon's teaching than by the number and order of my siblings."

"Undoubtedly. Who are your remaining brothers?"

"Nicholas and William. A barrister and a soldier." Gently she moved the baby to her other shoulder, and patted his back. "Now what bit of knowledge did I just drive out from your head? Schemes for optimal crop rotation? That design for a greenhouse with an adjustable roof?"

"Both, I should think. One for each brother." A cloud softened the sun's vehemence and she could see his eyes, fixed on her with an almost hungry curiosity. "Does he enjoy that, the baby? To be tapped in that manner?"

"Most babies do seem to like such rhythmic actions.

You see he's growing calmer." Only the occasional ragged inhalation betrayed how he'd been sobbing, and his head lolled heavy on her shoulder. "Have you never carried little nieces or nephews about yourself?"

"Never any so small." Both their voices had dropped to a level that would promote Job's slumber. "They make better company when they're ambulatory. Better yet when they can speak in sentences."

"But you'll have children of your own one day. You'll be expected to produce an heir, at least." She stopped, and waited for him to stop as well. "You ought to practice." Indeed he must wish to hold the child, and felt awkward, as a gentleman, in asking. She would give him permission. "Put your arms the way I have mine and I'll settle him on your shoulder."

But he stepped back from her hastily, as though she were proposing to saddle him with a sack of moldy potatoes. "Thank you, I don't care to have him use my coat for a handkerchief. I'll wait to practice with a tidier infant." They walked on, and after a moment he added lightly, "Perhaps I'll practice with yours, when he comes."

"You'll be well back in London by that time, I should expect."

He shrugged. "I might come for a visit, though. I imagine I'll sometimes have business in Sussex."

A chill stole over her skin at the thought. He was a well-meaning man, but so careless: did it really not occur to him that someone might notice his taking an interest in a baby who like as not would bear some resemblance to him? "I cannot think that prudent." The chill had somehow stolen into her voice as well. "I shouldn't want anyone to connect you with my child in any way. If I'm so blessed."

Silence dropped between them, what sort of silence she couldn't say, as once again the sun's glare made his features unreadable. When he finally spoke, it was merely to recommend a change in course that would take them wide of the privy.

$\mathcal{D}$AMNABLE PIG. Fiendish, black-souled, fraudulent pig. It trotted beside him with a beatific look, quite as though it were a faithful companion, when surely its true purpose was to guard against his surreptitious reentry into the house through some window or back door. Or perhaps to spring at him, if he should happen to stumble. It took him for a fool, that pig, and in truth, in grim and mortifying truth, the pig was not far wrong.

He would have no claim whatsoever to the child his seed produced. He'd known that from the start. Now was no time to discover objections to the plan.

And yet he wasn't seeking to have any claim recognized, was he? He was only proposing to call, as any civil neighbor might, and admire the baby in the privacy of her parlor, out of view of those suspicious neighbors who concerned her so.

Children liked him. Confound it all, they did. Anne's children had thought him the most wonderful uncle in Creation, when he'd visited there last month. Robust young Harry, whom he'd taught to skip rocks; delicate Jane, who begged him to read stories in comical voices; the very small ones who climbed on him whenever he sat down—those children were pleased to know him, and wouldn't Mrs. Russell's child be too?

"Have you any plans to replace that roof?" She was eyeing the summit of the Weaver cottage, the previous subject folded up and put away. "I'm sure it must leak in places."

"I think so. I don't know. I think Granville wanted me to speak to you on the subject. You have new roofs on your property, isn't that right?"

"We replaced them all just this summer. You ought to meet with my steward, and he can tell you more of how it was arranged and carried out. Give you his thoughts on the workmen we used. I'll introduce you."

What could he say in response to so stultifying a prospect? He only nodded at the baby. "That child's gone to sleep. I shouldn't have thought it possible. Well done, Mrs. Russell."

She smiled at him over its straggle-haired pate, her eyes aglow with womanly pride. "Shall we chance putting him down in his cradle? I do hope the pig won't wake him with another commotion, trying to come in."

"You heard the lady, and don't pretend you didn't." He rounded on the animal, which raised its bristly chin, all attention. "We'll tolerate none of your nonsense. If you know your own interests, you'll reconcile yourself to staying outside."

The pig sank onto its haunches and never stirred as he caught Mrs. Russell by the elbow and whisked her back inside. Job shuddered with one agitated breath, but didn't wake.

The widow looked about the one front room. "Where is your mother?" she said to the children, and, indeed, Mrs. Weaver was nowhere in evidence.

"She went to lie down," said one of the older boys.

"Oh," she said. She glanced at Theo, then stepped nearer to the children. "Is there some cot or cradle where . . ." Her voice trailed off. She'd been approaching the eldest daughter, and her face betrayed confusion, then a quick shock of comprehension. Hurriedly she turned to the other children. ". . . where I may put him down to nap?"

The same boy pointed silently to one of the doors on the back wall. She went through it. Theo smiled vaguely at the children, none of whom smiled in answer, and after several eternities Mrs. Russell returned empty-armed.

"She's deep asleep." She stood near him, her voice low, her brow contracted with concern. "I don't think we ought to leave the children with their mother so deep asleep, do you?" Obviously she'd never encountered this predicament when calling on her tenants.

"I'd lay odds they're used to it," he answered at the same volume. "But if it will make you easier, we'll stay."

"I think we ought to. Perhaps we can call on the rest of the families some other day? I'm sure this family can use all I have in my basket, anyway." She didn't mention the books. Neither did he. "Well." She stepped away from him and addressed the children with bright resolve. "Who will help me clear these dishes from the table?"

One or two of the children looked up. None spoke.

Good God. He'd had enough of this whole clan. "You, there." He jerked his chin at a girl who looked to be ten or so. "Come and show Mrs. Russell where the dishes are to be scraped and so forth."

She responded well enough to a direct command. Just as the pig had done. Maybe that was the way to manage them all. He sat down at one end of the table when the widow waved away his help, to watch how she got on with the girl. Her name was ascertained, and her age, and favorite this and that, the child replying with gradually less hesitation. Not Mrs. Russell's favorite topics of conversation, clearly, which made her awkward effort rather endearing.

The plates taken away, he spied something on the table he hadn't before noticed: a scrap of paper folded partly into pleats. His stomach lurched at the sight. Cowardly stomach. He would teach it tenacity. He kept his eyes on the scrap.

The girl had gone wrong by folding two successive times in the same direction. She must have abandoned the paper after that, because no more folds followed. He sat perfectly still for a moment; then, careful not to look toward the corner where she sat, he leaned forward and possessed himself of the scrap.

To correct the wrong-way fold was the work of five seconds, and once he'd done that he finished the pleating. His hands did like occupation of the insignificant kind. He angled his chair a bit so she could see what he did, if she chanced to look this way—he would not look, himself—and ran his thumbnail along each pleat to sharpen the crease. He'd neglected to show her that, before. Of course it hadn't been practical when he had no table and must do the folding on his—well, he wouldn't think any more of that. His stomach was not so stalwart.

The paper all corrected and creased, he gave it a push back to where it had been. Then something caught his eye.

On the floor against the opposite wall was another paper, just like the first. So was there one on a windowsill. Under the stove. Poking out from behind the cushion of the frayed, sagging armchair. And in with the firewood, perhaps a dozen more.

Mrs. Russell and the little girl would be several minutes longer in tidying up. He must have something to do, or look indolent, and set a bad example for the children. He got up from his chair and gathered the papers, one by one. Old bills, the wrapping from tea, even a letter or two: the girl appeared to have been folding every bit of paper she could get in her hands. He took them all back to the table and set to repairing them.

When the dishes had been cleaned, and the dirty water thrown out the door (into the pig's astonished face, it was to be hoped), the widow and her young friend sat down at the table, deep in conversation on the subject of cats and kittens. Mrs. Russell watched him while she talked. Her eyes went from his face to his fingers and back to his face. Finally, without asking what he was doing or why, she took a paper from the pile and began fixing its folds.

He felt as though he were suspended in air, or floating on a strange warm sea. Time might stop all round them and here he would be, washed with the music of soft feminine modulations, working away in the pleasure of unspoken companionship. Why she should have such confidence that his project must be worthy of her own industry, he could not fathom. He would not try. He kept pleating and creasing, and so did she.

When the papers were all properly folded, and the cats of the world given their due, Mrs. Weaver at last emerged from her bedroom looking somewhat less drawn, perhaps, though not very much more civil.

Mrs. Russell got quickly to her feet. "I fear we've overstayed. I was so charmed by your Carrie here, I quite lost track of the time." She reached for the basket. "I brought a few things with me. I'd be honored if you'd take them. I hope your children like cake."

How kind of you. I can't thank you enough for getting the baby to be quiet. Please forgive me for falling asleep in the middle of your visit. Mrs. Weaver said none of these things. She eyed the pile of pleated paper and said, "Christine does that to all the paper in the house." Like everything else, the subject seemed to weary her.

"Well, I think I may have—here." She rummaged through her basket. "It's a book of fashion plates, altogether useless to a lady in mourning. You could take out the pages and give them to your girl. Then your bills and account-lists might be spared." She put the book down next to the cakes and other food she'd unloaded. "It was so nice to meet you all," she said, and little Carrie, at least, looked sorry to see her go.

"I'll deal with the pig, shall I?" Theo got up from the

table. He could find no words of civility for Mrs. Weaver or any of her brood.

On their exit they encountered no difficulty from the pig, who now seemed more than a little in awe of him and in fact walked at his side across the yard and to the gate. Very good. Three visits here and he'd succeeded in making one favorable impression, with a creature who sat on its young. He latched the gate behind them.

"I'm ignorant," said Mrs. Russell when he turned. "Disgracefully so."

This was an unpromising start to any conversation. He raised his eyebrows and made a noncommittal sound in his throat.

"How could I think to bring books and cake? I knew they were parish poor. I ought to have brought meat, and milk."

"They might welcome milk. They don't keep a cow." He wouldn't touch the subject of meat. Too clearly he remembered that last packet, heavy in his bag, as he'd made the long walk back to the house after his previous call on the Weavers. "And at least one of the books did come in useful. You'll have to work up to *Waverley*, that's all."

"Those people don't want *Waverley*." She strode with even more vigor than usual, swinging the heavy basket as though it were a kind of ballast. "I'd be surprised if the children can even read. I didn't see a book in that house. I ought to have anticipated as much."

He stopped her by catching hold of the basket as it swung by. "Don't berate yourself so. I don't want to hear it. You were mistaken in what you expected, and now you know better. We learn that way, don't we?" She'd said something to that effect, once.

"All I've learned is the extent of my naïveté." She hadn't let go of the basket, and they stood facing one another, each gripping on to the handle. "I've been that family's neighbor since I settled here. I ought to have known their circumstances before now. I ought to have interested myself in that oldest girl's welfare."

"Let me propose a bargain." He pulled gently at the basket until her hand released its grip. "If you cease blaming yourself aloud, I'll submit to whatever sermon you want to make on education. You may take up the whole of our walk to your house in telling me what ought to be done for the children on my land."

Her smile went through him like a fever-chill. What a strange, strange thing, to give a woman such pleasure without touching her. For the second time that afternoon he had to avert his eyes, and then he had to speak gruffly, as well. "But I advise you to put the best bits up front, because you'll only have as long as it takes us to finish this walk. When we reach your house we'll have other things to do." And he set off in full stride.

ᴬNDREW," said Mr. Mirkwood when the coupling was done and he lay stretched out beside her. He lifted one lazy hand and counted off on his fingers. "Andrew, Katharine, Nicholas, and William."

They'd got back to the familiar routine. He'd enjoyed himself without proposing anything untoward, and she'd enjoyed his enjoyment. That was what she'd wanted, of course. If some small part of her had hoped he might build upon the liberties of yesterday, well, that part must learn forbearance. "I'd be more impressed if you recalled what I told you of my curate's school," she said now.

"Shhhh." Without turning he touched a finger to her lips, finding his way by feel. "I'm missing one name."

"No, those are all my siblings." But her heartbeat skittered. She knew what he meant.

"My name is Theophilus." Now he did turn, addressing her as if he were a mannerly boy at a birthday party, albeit a naked one nearly six feet tall. "Though only my father calls me that. Brothers and sisters and intrepid ladies call me Theo."

"I know your name already. A servant told me."

"Then you have the advantage of me." He waited. He didn't tease or demand. He took a strand of her hair between thumb and forefinger and twisted it slowly round the finger, like a python's lapping coils, bringing his hand ever closer to her head. His eyes, patient and pacific, stayed trained on hers.

What would she give up, if she gave him her name? He might think himself her intimate, and he wasn't. For all the commerce of bodies, for all that he might intrude into some of her private thoughts, they were not intimates.

"Martha," she said nevertheless. "Andrew, Kitty, Nick, Will, and Martha. In that order. Our family name is Blackshear."

"Martha," he echoed on the softest breath. His lips wore the ghost of a smile and his eyes chased here and there as though attempting to see every part of her at once. "It suits you."

"I should say so. A plain, solid name."

"If you wish it to be. Or music, if you prefer. All composed of breath and murmur, and sounds that never stop until you want them to."

Was that true, about the sounds? Why, so it was. "Such things you notice! I've lived with the name for one and twenty years, and never noticed that."

In reply he only brought his smile to blossom, and settled his hand against her head as his wound-up finger made its final twist.

$\mathcal{M}$ᴀʏ I ask you something? I fear to offend you, but curiosity is getting the better of me." Three days later they were out of doors again, this time walking the long way, over the road, from her house to his. Mr. Mirkwood was to tramp about with Mr. Granville, reviewing all the land he might enclose, and he'd taken it upon himself to invite her along.

"I didn't realize you were capable of that particular fear. Your question must be grave indeed." She could speak so to Mr. Mirkwood. They'd attained an unexpected ease with one another, a black-humored camaraderie, perhaps, in the absurdity of their misalliance.

"Not grave, exactly." In the pause she could picture him rummaging for the proper words—her bonnet, constructed after the fashion of a horse's blinders, prevented her seeing the picture firsthand. "Blunt, though. Forgive the bluntness. Why don't you enjoy yourself with me? In bed, I mean." From the trajectory of his voice she knew he'd turned toward her in asking the question. "I put it down to dislike, at first, but I don't believe you truly dislike me anymore."

Discretion must have a different meaning among the

married ladies of London, if he'd made his reputation there. She swiveled to look about her.

"No one is near. I looked, already. And I'll keep watch as we walk. Of course whether to answer at all is your decision." His voice reassured in four or five different ways at once. He'd looked. No one was near. No topic was beyond discussion, if they wished to discuss it. And if she shrank from his question, he would let the matter drop.

She filled her lungs, settling her eyes on the far horizon where verdant green ended and blue sky began. She would start with the truth least slighting to him, awkward as it would be to say. She angled her bonnet a few degrees toward him and lowered her voice. "That particular act, I find, does not produce the proper sensations in me. Not as it does in you. Or in other men. Or in other women, I suppose," she added before he could supply this point out of his own experience.

"Improper sensations would be more to the point than proper ones, I should think." Yes, she'd known he wouldn't be able to resist that. "But you do have an idea, then, of how it ought to feel?"

"I do." Now he might guess at her private habits. Better that than to have him think her ignorant and pitiable. "I believe there may be something irregular in how I am made up."

Her half boots and his top boots had a dialogue of their own in the ensuing pause, creaking rhythmically as they struck the hard-packed earth. What a poor, old-fashioned road this was, pure mud when the rains came and impassable some days. Someone ought to see to putting down rocks, as was done on the larger roads. "Forgive me," he said. "I'm not quick. You're speaking of anatomy?"

"Anatomy. Yes." She would be blushing ferociously if she'd said this indoors. Out here, it had all the significance of a single leaf on a single tree in the distant great Weald.

"Forgive me again. You mean, because your chief pleasure-point isn't on the inside?"

He was quick enough on certain topics. "You've encountered this before?" Her bonnet canted several more degrees his way.

"It's common. Not at all irregular." He spoke with an authority that left no room for dissent. "Most ladies require a bit of attention there to reach a proper climax. Some require more than others."

Well, really. One couldn't think much of whatever planning process had resulted in human reproductive design. Men with their parts dangling like stockings on a washday line. Women with their pleasure put away from the main event. One might easily conclude people weren't really meant to—

"There are things I could do." His words came out low and intent, freighted with hope, but cautious, too, because he knew her well enough to guess at her probable response.

"I know." She'd dwelt altogether too much, recently, on the things he could do. "But my conscience would object."

A bird was calling somewhere nearby. Three high trills and a low one, counterpoint to the tireless rhythm of their boots. Mr. Mirkwood made a soft throat-clearing sound. "I don't mean to argue. But I don't understand. Surely you and your conscience must have come to terms before you engaged me."

Now he would think her foolish. So be it. "My conscience permits me to do what is necessary to get a son, because the good that will come of that outweighs the transgression. More people than myself will benefit, I mean. If I were to seek my own pleasure, this bargain would be something else. Something unworthy of the person I have tried to be." A quick glance round the brim of her bonnet caught his profile, scowling into the distance. "We're very unlike, you and I, and I don't expect you to understand entirely."

"And so I do not." His stride had lengthened, so that she must work harder to keep up. "To my way of thinking, if you must offend against your principles by lying with a man, you ought at least to have the pleasure that's meant to come along. There's meant to be pleasure, Martha." It was the first time he'd used her Christian name since gently prising it from her grasp.

"It's not so simple for me. First of all, I only laid eyes on you two weeks since."

"Two weeks and two days."

"Sixteen days, yes. We'd scarcely consider ourselves acquainted, in normal circumstances. And acquaintance may be sufficient for you—well, obviously it is—but for my part, I should have to know a man very well before making that surrender to him."

"Must it necessarily be a surrender?" He'd got a bit ahead of her and now turned to peer over his shoulder, plainly baffled by her notions.

How could he ask such a question? Men. So caught up in conquest, in the thrill of the hunt and the chase, they never paused to consider what might be the experience on the other side. "I think it always is, for a woman." She met his gaze steadily until he dropped back beside her, his gait more leisurely again.

"Well," he said. One gloved hand came out, palm up, fingers spread, while he counted off with the other. "I haven't been addressing the right part of you. We know that can be corrected. Your conscience interferes. And you haven't known me very long, but we've two weeks or so remaining to our bargain. Are those all my obstacles?"

For Heaven's sake, why couldn't he apply such energy

to something worthy and useful? She pointed her bonnet straight ahead, eyes on a distant bend in the road. "The greatest obstacle is the difference in our natures. You're correct in perceiving that I don't dislike you. In fact I like you better than I ever expected to do."

"But that isn't enough." His hand, with three fingers' worth of obstacles counted, still stuck out before him as if he'd forgot it there.

"For me it is not." How did one go about saying these things gently? "You're not a bad man, Mirkwood. I do think you have promise. But while I find I can be cordial with a man who lives for pleasure, and even come to feel a certain regard for him, I cannot, in the end, truly admire such a man. And I don't care to give myself up to a man I don't admire. Pardon my frankness."

"Not at all. I'm the one who opened the subject." His hand went slack, the three obstacles just three among five fingers again. He turned it, and turned it back the other way, and let it fall to his side.

A certain regard. What a paltry place for a man to hold in a woman's esteem. And yet some women could cultivate desire on such flimsy ground. Some women, for that matter, went about claiming just such a preference for upstanding men, and fell into the arms of the first willing scoundrel.

Though Lord knows, with a willing scoundrel hired to attend her, Mrs. Russell had had every opportunity to take that fall. She wasn't so susceptible.

"Did you admire your husband?" What the devil did he think he'd accomplish with that question? Did he mean to console himself with the disappointments of a dead man?—because he knew, even before asking, what the answer must be.

"No," she said without any particular emotion. "I did not."

He tipped his head back to watch the aimless clouds. Like those wisps of sheep fleece caught on shrubbery all over the widow's land. Sheep scratched themselves on bushes and left those slight markers behind. So she'd told him, walking one day.

Had Mr. Russell hoped to be desired by his young bride, and had he ratcheted steadily down into despair? He mightn't have cared. Some husbands didn't. Some availed themselves of their conjugal right and no more thought of the woman's feeling than one would wonder at a chamberpot's sentiments on being similarly used. Some thought passion in a wife unseemly, and saved up all their best attentions to spend on a mistress.

But many, many husbands must feel otherwise. Many a man must make a mistress of his wife, or at least wish to do so. That could be quite pleasant, a mistress in one's house day and night. Flirting with a man over the breakfast table. Sleeping but two or three doors away. Sleeping in his own bed some nights. Poor miserable Mr. Russell, if that had been his hope.

"We'll see my drive from this next rise." He gestured with one hand. "Granville will likely be outside already. I've called on you four times, remember, and always with land business to discuss."

*H*ere's our first bit of roadside waste," Granville said as they approached it. "In general this will be less useful land due to the location. Some of these pieces are thick with trees too." He was in exceptionally good spirits, the agent, with twice the expected number of young people to lecture, and one of them actually paying rapt attention.

"What are its boundaries? Besides the road, I mean."

Mrs. Russell, too, appeared to be having as delightful a time as could be allowed to a woman in mourning, as she unrolled her dashed map—his dashed map—to see how this spot was represented.

Theo walked a bit away from the others, bending shrubbery branches and letting them spring back as he went. Roadside waste. What man would want to add anything of that description to his holdings? Better to leave it for the turf-cutters' use. Indeed, here was a place where someone had been digging it out. He poked at the ragged edge with the toe of one boot.

"Why do you suppose the ground drops off there?" The widow had noticed his wandering attention, and swiveled to address him, rather loudly as she still stood beside Mr. Granville with the map. "It looks as though part of it were peeled away."

"Cut away, yes. Someone uses this turf." Someone else he could deprive by enclosing. He kicked idly at a loose bit of ground.

"Uses it?" She lowered the map and took a step toward him, her face written all over with astonishment and her voice almost indignant. "For what purpose?"

"To burn. This is the sort of turf people use for fuel." Didn't she remember? They'd spent too much of an afternoon reading some tract on the usage of common land, just last week.

"For fuel, really?" Her eyes narrowed at him and she marched over to inspect the ground's cut edge.

"Fuel, to be sure." Granville trailed her at a distance. "Among people too poor for firewood, it's quite common."

"Do your laborers burn this, Mr. Mirkwood?" She was bending over now, to pick up a crumb of dirt in her gloved fingers, and he looked quickly away from where her skirts gave a sudden elegant delineation to her form.

Fuel. Turf. No, a plain vision came to him of the Weavers's firewood box with all those folded papers scattered among the sticks. "I believe all our people burn wood." He glanced at Granville, who nodded. "I presume your tenants do as well, Mrs. Russell?" *Martha*. Her name, the name that said nothing of her husband, lingered unspoken on his tongue like an aftertaste.

"They do." She frowned at the clod held up between her thumb and first two fingers. "I wonder which of our neighbors does use this."

"Perhaps none of them. Gypsies come through a neighborhood sometimes, and take turf away in pieces to sell. Or so my reading tells me." The gentlest of jabs. She really ought to remember this detail. He recalled quite clearly that she'd been reading aloud when they came to that passage, and had stopped to poke him in the ribs on suspicion that he dozed.

"Gypsies. Indeed. I have seen them about on occasion." She dropped her bit of dirt and dusted her gloves together, tucking the map under one elbow. "Does your reading tell you anything of how such people would be affected by enclosure?" She angled her head to look at him, bright-eyed with interest.

Ah. Sudden daylight. There was nothing accidental about this question, or about anything she'd said. She remembered exactly what learning he'd acquired. "In fact that's one of the arguments put forth by the defenders of enclosure," he said, and only now did he notice the way Granville listened, nodding almost imperceptibly. "Enclosing reduces the presence of rootless people in a neighborhood, by eliminating the common land where they might camp."

"I collect the practice has its detractors as well, then." She glanced from one man to the other. "What are the arguments on their side?"

Theo hesitated, to give Granville a chance to answer,

but the agent dipped his head and held out a hand, palm up, to indicate he should proceed.

"Well, it tends to mean more cropland, to the loss of pastureland. More of the land held by the few wealthiest families in a region."

"Though that hasn't been an unmixedly bad state of affairs," Granville put in, directing his words to Mrs. Russell. "Many of the last century's advances, in knowledge of drainage and crop rotation for example, came about through the curiosity of gentleman farmers of ample means and acreage on which to try out their theories. A yeoman farmer hasn't the leisure to conduct such experiments."

"I see." Her brow furrowed. "I'm sorry, though, to think of anyone losing the independence of making his own living on the land. So many young people must go to the city now for work."

"Work that not so long ago was done in cottages." Here was something he could add. "Fifty years since, tenants on your own land all had spinning-wheels or looms, and Seton Park was known for its finished cloth as well as the raw wool you produce now."

"How do you know that?" Genuine surprise flickered in her eyes. "I'm sure it's not in any book."

"I should think he's been speaking to people who remember it so." The agent smiled with undisguised satisfaction. "Visited Mr. Barrow, have you?"

"He has a great many interesting stories to tell." He looked at the ground, to avoid the sensation that he was somehow preening under Granville's approbation. He'd visited the old man to be sociable, after all, not for any high-minded educational purpose.

"You do well to listen." The smile came to him, even with his eyes averted. "Books make an excellent foundation, but they haven't the immediacy of a man's own experience. To hear the stories of Mr. Barrow, and others both like and unlike him, will give a complexity to your understanding beyond what you could pick up from a book." The agent's address broadened to include Mrs. Russell. "Shall we go on to the next piece of land?"

Theo threw a look to the widow as the other man turned his back. Such a piquant stew of sentiments on her face. Pride at his showing and at her own part in it, surprise that he'd learned something worthy without her assistance, and poorly suppressed disapproval over the implied disparagement of book-learning.

"*Complexity,*" he mouthed with a tap at his temple, just to pique her further, and her features resolved themselves in favor of disapproval. His arm wanted very badly to sling itself about her waist, so he clasped both hands behind his back and they walked on.

Thus the morning went, from one patch of enclosable land to the next, Mrs. Russell framing questions and remarks that would show off the fruit of his study, Mr. Granville hearing it all, and dispensing supplementary wisdom, with a gratified good cheer, and one or another of Theo's limbs clamoring to touch his subtle mistress every minute.

A man might get used to landowning, after all. Not only to being outdoors on a morning like this, to see how the little wildflowers, curled indistinct and glistening with dew, gradually opened to reveal their shapes and colors as the sun climbed higher in the sky. A man might get used to discussing things with his agent, for example; to seeing his opinions received and considered as though they had actual weight. He might get used to the company of a neighbor who wished him well. He might even come to welcome the decisions and responsibilities themselves.

Nobody expected much of him, in London. Nobody ever had. He'd been spoiled from two different directions, really. All the privilege and consequence that went with being an eldest son, yet young enough to be doted on by fond older sisters. Such a boy must necessarily grow up believing himself to be wonderful just as he was, mustn't he? Then the mistresses and friends of one's young manhood only reinforced the view. Even his father's disapproval made but one more tributary to the same stream. Everyone expected him to be feckless and trivial, and all his life he'd gladly obliged.

At their final stop—another, even less promising piece of waste—he hung back, mulling over these novel conceptions while Granville showed Mrs. Russell how to measure a boundary, until his attention was caught by the unhurried beat of approaching hooves. He looked up the road to see a figure in a black coat on a frankly pitiable horse. "Is that your curate coming?" he said over his shoulder.

The widow left off her measuring, and came to step round him into the road. She shaded her eyes with one hand. "Indeed I think it is." She looked . . . God, but she looked pleased to see the fellow, shabby horse and all, despite the fact that she must see him often enough in the course of his regular business. She let her hand fall and stood where she was, fairly beaming. She must have felt his stare because she glanced his way and smiled, radiant and unself-conscious, as though certain that he, too, had wanted just this chance encounter to make his morning perfect. Then she turned back to the road.

Something unfurled in him, something base and bitter, as he watched her watch the curate. She'd never looked at him that way.

For God's sake, why should she? She's known that man longer, and she doubtless likes his preaching, and she's pleased about his school. That's all. Besides, plenty of women had looked at him, over the years, in plenty of exceedingly agreeable ways. He needn't command the admiration of every woman on the planet.

Admiration. Good Lord. Like a fist in the belly, that word. That name for what he saw before him. *Admiration* it was that put a light in her eyes, and touched her upright, expectant posture with simmering grace. His mouth went suddenly dry.

Stop it. He's not a rival, and she's not yours to guard. He bit down on the inside of his cheek, to will in some discipline and common sense, and only let up when the curate stopped—though really the man needn't have done any more than raise his hat and keep to his errand—and greeted each of them by name, requiring some sort of civil reply.

Their outdoor business was explained to him. He listened with interest, and commended the idea of neighbors consulting one another on such decisions, with the slightest bow—an extra measure of endorsement— toward Theo, which might have gratified him had it not so obviously gratified Mrs. Russell. The widow and the churchman, a pair of grave bookends in their black garments, fell into some discussion of the imminent school then, as he'd expected they must. He removed a bit, with Granville, to let them speak.

The high opinion went both ways. That was plain. But then how should it not? What clergyman wouldn't think highly of a virtuous, serious-minded young wife or widow, and where common interests and nearness in age promoted it, how should some little bit of friendship not develop? If only he weren't so damnably interesting-looking, all light and dark and clean-carved angles. Wasn't that always the way with these country curates? Not one in three of them had the good grace to be ugly, and promote sober-minded attention among the young ladies of a Sunday morning.

Enough. She had a right to be friendly with other men, handsome as well as plain. And he, not the curate, was the one who would take her to bed an hour or so hence. He needn't waste these last few minutes in which he might be solidifying Granville's improved opinion of him.

But when at last he was at Mrs. Russell's house, busy in the blue-draperied bed, he was conscious of some additional vehemence, some barbaric will to leave a mark. If he bit her . . . if he made her sore . . . if he held her down and put his tongue to her, conspiring with her body's most mechanical response to drag her unwilling into ecstasy, then she would have cause to think of him when he was out of her sight. The bruise, or the intermittent ache, or the scandalized aftershocks of what he had made her feel, would stay with her as she went about all the daily business in which he had no part.

But he was no barbarian, and besides, he could picture all too clearly the way she would look at him afterward if he did do any of those things. So he did none of them. He made his solitary journey to bliss, helped her dutifully onto the pillow, and put on his clothes and went home, an unappeased hunger rattling round some empty place inside of him.

Chapter Ten

$\mathcal{G}$OOD MORNING, Mrs. Russell. This letter was misdelivered to my house. I broke the seal before I realized it must be meant for you. Will you take a look, please, and confirm that it's yours, or tell me whether I must carry it about to some other neighbors?"

What in Heaven's name could he be meaning by this? The time couldn't be much past ten o'clock. What purpose would get him out of bed so early to stand before her in this show of respectability?

With a quick glance at the nearby footman, Martha took the letter and unfolded it. Stark across the paper, in the appalling hand of a highborn gentleman, she read, *It's got to be now. Can you contrive to meet me in the room in ten minutes?*

"Yes." She lifted her eyes back to him. "Yes, this certainly is my letter. Thank you for bringing it to me." She folded it closed, her worried fingers pressing each crease tight.

"Just as I thought." His attention lingered on the anxious industry of her hands, and when he spoke again, she knew he meant to reassure. "I'll wish you good day, then. I'm sure some duty demands your presence, as it does mine." With a bow, and an almost conspiratorial smile, he restored his hat and let the footman show him out.

𝒴ou did too good a job in showing me off to Granville yesterday." Already he was shrugging out of his coat. "He thinks I've got serious about management duties. I'm to attend the threshing with him today and tomorrow. Never mind that it's been going on well enough without me for days—I must be present, and then come along while he takes the grain somewhere to be milled, and Lord only knows what else. All manner of tedium, and all of it seeming to take whole afternoons. I couldn't see how to get out of it."

"Nor ought you." Martha stood still, and waited for his eyes to come to her. "Mr. Mirkwood, that's wonderful news. You've worked hard, studying things you don't like. You're to be commended. I could see Mr. Granville was impressed with you, and he has every reason to be. You should be proud."

"And *you,* darling, should be getting out of your clothes. Must I manage everything?" He'd ducked his head, to tend to his waistcoat buttons, but the glow of accomplishment suffused his whole frame. Oh, she had every hope of sending him back to London a better man.

𝒯hey sketched out the details while he dressed. "I can't depend on being at liberty this time every day," he said, pulling on his trousers. "Perhaps I could come at night—after the households have gone to bed—if you don't mind waiting up for me."

"Do you propose to walk all this way and back in the dead of night?" She lifted her head from the pillows to make the admonition more forceful.

"What would I have to fear?" An indulgent smile creased his face before he disappeared under his shirt. "Ghosts?" he said from within its billowy depths. "Gypsies? Man-eating tigers?" His head poked through and his hands emerged, one, then the other, from the cuffs.

"Don't laugh at me. Particularly not on a subject where my experience of living in the country makes me better informed than you." Her neck was beginning to ache, at this angle. "You'd be in danger from poachers, to take one example."

He shook his head dismissively, tucking in the shirt and fastening up his trouser buttons. "I haven't any game. Surely the poachers of this neighborhood know better than to waste their time on my property."

"I still don't like it." She let her head fall back. "I would worry."

"Save your worries for the child." The mattress dipped; he'd sat on one end of it to style his cravat. "I'm sure he'll give you cause enough, particularly if he takes after me." She could hear the cloth whisking over itself as he arranged it. Most impressive. He wasn't anywhere near a mirror.

When he'd risen from the bed to sit down in the chair by which he'd left his boots, she spoke again. "Why can't you take a horse, and come by way of the road, and stay until morning? You'd be less time abroad, and only one trip in the dark. I can speak to my maid about finding somewhere to put the horse where it won't be seen."

No answer came. She raised her head to find him studying one boot, lashes lowered, fingers evening up the folded-over top part. "Come to your own bed, you mean?" he said, as though it were unclear. "And sleep there with you?"

"I think it would be best. You can come in the same way you do now. I'll show you how to get to my rooms from here. I'll give you a key. Of course you'll have to be . . . quiet . . . in my rooms, closer to the servants as they are."

He didn't speak, or even bring his eyes to hers. He finished with the boot and slowly pulled it on. Then he pulled on the other. He took his time straightening the seams of his trousers at either side of each calf.

Was he . . . looking for the politest way to decline? Maybe she'd offended him with that admonition about quiet. Or maybe this proposal transgressed the boundaries of their arrangement altogether. Well, how was one to know what was and wasn't done? It wasn't as though she'd made a habit of this.

He finished with his boots and raised his head. "Yes," he said. "I can do that." With a swipe of one hand he gathered his gloves from the table where he'd left them, and rose. "Without the horse, though. Even if we could keep it from your own stablehands, there'd be no way of keeping it from mine. I'll take along a pistol to ward off the poachers if that will make you easier." He crossed to where he'd hung his waistcoat and when he turned to her he wore his familiar teasing smile. "I do fear your days will feel interminable without me. You'll listen to the chatter of your lady-callers and secretly count the hours until bedtime."

"I'll do no such thing." She propped herself up on her elbows. "Even if I did have callers, my mind would never wander so."

"No callers?" He stopped, one arm in the waistcoat and one arm out. "But you have friends in the neighborhood, surely?"

"I haven't really formed any such attachments. You've seen how it is, I think. People wish me well, but we keep a distance. I haven't a . . . confiding temperament, I suppose, or whatever those qualities are that promote affection and friendship." How the words stumbled about,

ungainly on her tongue. Foolish, this reaction. One val-
ued one's solitude. One asked for nothing from one's
neighbors but the best opinion one could earn.

"They still ought to call on you." He busied himself
with the second arm. "You're widowed. It's the proper
thing to do, whether they know you well or not."

Of all the men to concern himself with propriety!
What a ridiculous conversation this had become. She
swallowed her smile and made her voice level, to respect
his sentiments. "Don't fret on my behalf. I'll find occupation. I have visits to make to my tenants, and I can
help Mr. Atkins get his school ready."

He frowned at his gloves as he worked his fingers into
them. "You ought to have a wider acquaintance. More
people to visit than just the tenants and the curate."

"Perhaps, but that would have complicated my arrangement with you. We shouldn't have been able to
study so fruitfully in the afternoons. Now help me dress
and I'll show you the way to my rooms."

*H*ER BASKET wasn't so heavy, this time, but its contents
did require more frequent attention. Some box or basket
with a lid should have been more to the purpose than
the cloth she was constantly having to stop and rear-
range. So be it. She would know better the next time she
undertook this sort of errand.

On Monday Mr. Atkins's school would begin, and the
following Sunday would bring his first attempt at instruction for young ladies. She'd thought to work upon
Mr. Mirkwood in the matter of enrolling some of his
cottager children, and perhaps supplying a stipend, but
with his time taken up by duties, well, one must take
certain matters into one's own hands.

The trees whispered about her, stirred by some faint
breeze, as though conspiring with her purpose and

cheering her on. At a place where sun dropped through sparse boughs to light a clearing, she stopped, again, to extract a set of tiny claws from the basket's rim and push their owner back under the cloth. As pets went, a cat was a useful one. This individual should have earned its keep honorably in the Seton Park stable; now, if luck held, it would know not only the satisfaction of honest labor, but the tender affection of a young girl.

Some two dozen yards beyond where the woods trickled down to mere shrubbery and then to rolling pasture, the Weaver cottage came into view. Her breaths wanted to go shallow; she forced them deep and steady. How much less daunting this had been with Mr. Mirkwood, who made himself at home in any household, and made himself liked by even the pig. But mission could carry a person forward, even if she floundered a bit along the way. She set her shoulders and marched on.

Baby Job was outside today, somewhere back of the house, voicing his complaints to any who would listen. She let herself through the gate. The pig, busy at its trough, raised its head just long enough, one could easily believe, to ascertain that she was not Mr. Mirkwood before returning to its feed with a dismissive-sounding grunt. Three or four geese waddled toward her with a clear interest in the basket, and followed as she made her way to the backyard.

Several clotheslines crisscrossed the scene before her, half hung with fresh laundry. The eldest daughter stood over a copper tub, stirring its contents with a washing-stick, while four other children busied themselves in wringing the smaller garments taken from a second tub, presumably already gone through the rinse. Their mother was hanging an apron over one line, baby squalling in a basket at her feet. She turned, her attention no doubt caught by the increasingly vociferous presence of the geese, and, without a word, set both hands expectantly on her hips. Mrs. Russell had called; Mrs. Russell must be the one to speak.

Martha advanced. "Good afternoon. I'm so glad to see I've come at a time when I might be of use to you. I'd be happy to help wring the larger things. Or to hang them up, that you might rest and hold the baby."

The woman glanced down at her baby and frowned, as though she'd forgot he was there and didn't appreciate being reminded. She said nothing.

"Only I shall have to dispose of my basket first, or rather, what I have within it. I've brought a present for your daughter, and it's the sort of gift that must be put into safe hands. Do you see?" She lifted the cloth to display the kitten, its fur on end and its spine standing out in a ridge, probably as a response to the yard's general clamor. Quickly she covered it again. "He comes of good mousing stock. His aunts and uncles and cousins live in all my outbuildings and some of the tenant cottages. Your Carrie mentioned you didn't have a cat for the pantry, the last time I was here. When I called here before, with Mr. Mirkwood." Good Heavens, would the woman never speak? She herself could not seem to halt her tongue, if the alternative was this crushing silence. "I'm sorry Mr. Mirkwood wasn't able to accompany me today. But he has a great deal to learn of estate management. Indeed I don't believe he knew it was proper to call with gifts, before I told him so."

Finally the woman looked up, and rather sharply at that. "You told him to call with gifts?"

"Some while ago, yes. But if he hasn't found the opportunity to do so, I'm sure it's due to all the other demands on his time. Mr. Granville keeps him busy with a variety of lessons. He does mean well, Mr. Mirkwood."

Mrs. Weaver scratched the back of one hand. Both hands were rough and reddened. She would have been busy with laundry since yesterday, soaking and scrubbing and plunging her hands in hot water. Her brow contracted slightly. She reached into the basket and picked up a corner of the cloth, exposing the kitten again. "Carrie's inside watching the smaller children. I'll take this in to her. You can hold the baby if you like."

Martha let her take the basket, and picked up the howling infant. Well, that bit was done, though perhaps the gift had not softened Mrs. Weaver quite to the point where she would entertain a discussion of schooling. If she could get the baby to sleep again, that might put the woman in a pleasanter frame of mind. "Such lungs your little brother has!" she said to the other children as she walked a path along one clothesline, but the observation was apparently not novel enough to merit any reply.

Job was quieter, if not exactly quiet, by the time Mrs. Weaver emerged from the cottage's back door. With a single glance at Martha she set the now-empty basket on the ground—two geese rushed over and poked their heads in—and went to the tub, where she hauled out a sheet and set to twisting it.

This woman wouldn't smooth one inch of her way. Henceforward she simply wouldn't look for that. Doubtless this was how Mr. Mirkwood had felt, in his first few days with her, and doubtless he would laugh if he could see her now, grimly slugging down her own flavor of medicine.

"She talks of you sometimes." Mrs. Weaver turned her head halfway, not enough to face her. "Carrie does. Since you came to call."

"Does she?" Like an angel's breath sent down through parted clouds, these few civil words. Yes, Mr. Mirkwood must have felt this too. "I'm so pleased to hear it. She charmed me utterly on that visit. You may tell her I've thought of her as well."

No answer. But she wouldn't be stopped by that now. She hoisted Job higher on her shoulder and found a

place along the fence where Mrs. Weaver could see her
without turning. "I've thought of all your children, in
fact. I don't suppose you'll have had the chance to hear
this, but my curate is opening a school. Boys of all ages
and young girls will be educated during the week, and
Sundays after church he'll even provide some instruction for older girls. Religious instruction, of course, but
in addition to that—"

"We've no use for your church." Not even raising her
head to see how Mrs. Russell took this piece of effron-
tery, she began to untwist the sheet.

"Let me help." Martha hurried forward, baby on her
hip, to grasp one end. Gradually the sheet was un-
twisted, pulled out as flat as possible, and draped over
the line, the scent of lye wafting up to trouble her nose.
She cleared her throat. "You're . . . Methodists . . . I suppose?" Gingerly she pronounced the word. So many
poor families did seem to go that way. "But Mr. Atkins
believes in education for all, I'm sure. Why, he's studied
some of Mr. Wesley's sermons himself." Yes, studied
them in order to build arguments against them. But she
needn't say that.

Now Mrs. Weaver did face her. She put one hand to
the small of her back, and regarded her bluntly. "We've
no use for the Methodists, either."

"Oh. I see." She could feel her face coloring. Nobody
had ever said such a thing in her presence, and in front
of children at that.

And yet it was said, and would not be unsaid, and still
she stood here, and Mrs. Weaver stood there, and the
children continued untroubled in their work. She might
let it pass. She hadn't come here to examine the state of
the woman's soul, after all.

"Well, to be perfectly honest, the spiritual instruction
is secondary. Our hope is to enroll the older girls, eventually, alongside their brothers in the weekday school.

Only that's a new idea for many parents, to educate young ladies, and so we thought to bring it on gradually."

No telling whether Mrs. Weaver attended any of this. She'd hung something else—a child's dingy smock—and was picking at the neckline, where the drawstring went, to spread the cloth flat. Suddenly she drew a deep breath and closed her eyes. Her hand went to her belly and the color left her face.

"Mrs. Weaver. Are you quite all right?"

She gave one quick nod, and set the back of her other hand against her mouth.

"Forgive me, but you don't look at all well. Shouldn't you sit down? Can I fetch you something?" Martha looked to each child, but none sprang forward to help. None showed any sign of concern.

Behind her hand the woman was breathing deeply again. "It will pass in a moment. It's always like this, the first few months."

"The first few . . . Are you expecting another child? So soon?" Job, who'd gone nearly to sleep, emitted a fresh wail as though outraged by the prospect.

"Eight months, minus a week or two. Soon enough." She turned her hand and pressed her palm to her lips.

Eight months. For one shameful instant she was all taut, quivering attention, like a gun dog scenting grouse. A child. In eight months. Perhaps a boy. And this family had more than they could manage already.

How low she'd sunk! Mrs. Weaver's churchlessness, Mr. Mirkwood's decadence, were nothing to this vile, covetous design. She must force her attention elsewhere, decisively. "But your baby can't even be a year old yet." She lowered her voice, mindful of the children. "Shouldn't you have time to recover before you're brought into this condition again?"

Mrs. Weaver shook her head, finally opening her eyes.

Her color was returning, but she looked wearier than ever. "Ask your curate why God saw fit to make it so. Why children are visited upon women who never asked for them. If there's a divine purpose in it, that's more than I can tell." She let both hands fall, and took a wrung chemise from the little boy nearest her.

Martha bit her tongue. There was something that needed saying, though it was impertinent, and probably not in her interest: if she offended Mrs. Weaver, then she might have no hope, eight months hence, of—

No. She would not let *that* hope constrain her words. She would say what deserved to be said. "I should think your question had better be asked of a woman's husband than of a clergyman." A step nearer, to spare the children such scandalous talk. "If men could learn to value their wives' health and comfort above their own appetites, then we would see fewer deaths in childbed, fewer poor orphaned children, and fewer women with bodies worn out before their time. Is it so much to ask of a man that he show some restraint?" Men could fend for themselves, after all. She'd seen how it was done.

Mrs. Weaver picked and pulled at every gathered place on the garment with fierce concentration as she made her answer. "It's different for you, I'm sure. But some women are grateful to get a husband at all. Mr. Weaver was very good to marry me. He's borne a great deal. I've nothing to say to him of restraint." She wiped her hands on her apron and met Martha's eyes fully. "I thank you for your help with the baby. If you'd be so good as to take him to his cradle, you may give your greetings to Carrie. Mind the pig if you leave by the front door."

The woman had thanked her, at least, she reflected on the walk back to Seton Park. She must count that as progress. She might do more, at this cottage and others, now her days were wholly her own. If Mr. Mirkwood's presence in her bed tonight proved unsettling, she would think bracing thoughts of all she might accomplish tomorrow.

𝓗ᴇ ᴄᴀᴍᴇ in some time near midnight, on a wave of masculine vigor she could feel even from her place in the bed. She'd sat up reading; now she put her book aside and watched as he closed the door, locked it, and dropped the key into his pocket, one continuous move imbued with the satisfaction of a man who'd passed a day in upright pursuits and would now cap it in debauchery.

He took in her bare shoulders with one glance. "Naked already, are you? Very good."

She bent her knees and wound her arms about them, careful not to let the sheet fall from her upper body. "I expected you might be too tired to help me undress."

"Tired? Ha. Brace yourself." He dropped into the armchair and started wresting off his boots.

She hitched the sheet a bit higher. "What did you think of the threshing?"

"I think it ought to be taken out of human hands as soon as someone can invent a capable machine. Good God." He abandoned his boots and threw himself back in the chair. "Have you ever seen it done? Backbreaking work, bent over swinging that flail at the floor, and all that chaff flying about getting into everyone's eyes. Lungs, too, I don't doubt, despite the cloths they must tie about their noses and mouths. I'm surprised my laboring men aren't every one of them consumptive." He leaned forward again and resumed tugging at the first boot.

"I suppose there's a certain pride in the work of one's hands, though, that might be lost if it were given over to a machine."

"Bother pride. Bother the work of one's hands." The first boot came off. "One of those men is old enough to be my grandfather. I disapprove entirely." The second boot slipped off and he left it askew, just where it was. "Do you require more of this conversation, or conversation on some other topic? Or may we proceed?"

What fine funny spirits he was in. She allowed herself to smile. "I think that will do for tonight. Go on and undress."

Immediately he was up out of the chair and over by the candles. "You'll want the light doused, I presume? So you won't have to cast your eyes here and there to avoid the sight of me?" Candlelight danced in his pale hair like sunshine on the ripples of a lake. His skin looked lit from the inside out, and his eyes told her no more than if they'd been made of glass.

"Whatever you prefer. I think I'm growing used to the sight of you."

"Words to inflame any man." He licked his fingers and pinched out the candles one by one, leaving the extinguisher where it lay. "We'll try it in the dark. For the sake of novelty."

Another damp hiss and another, and the candles were all out. He was nothing but a shadow then, a shadow among shadows in that dark, dark room. Fabric whispered and rustled as he unclothed himself, and something metal clicked softly—a cuff link striking a button, perhaps. In the narrow space she'd left between the drapes, so they'd know when morning approached, only the faintest cloud-blotted moonlight seeped through. Enough, perhaps, to see his outline once her eyes had adjusted, but not enough to read mood and intention from his face.

Not that she needed that. She knew what were his mood and intention. She'd seen them often enough. She lay back, and waited.

* * *

*N*OVELTY. HA. With lights out and voices kept low, he might be any man. She could pretend he was another, if she had a taste for such imagining. Perhaps she'd imagine that curate, shy and eager on his wedding night.

She might respond, then.

Theo hesitated, wrapping his fingers round the bed-post. Her soft, patient breathing came to him through the dark. He tightened his grip, and relaxed it.

How would an innocent man approach her? A man who'd saved himself for his wedding night must be ravenous. He might go pell-mell, particularly if his bride was a widow who needed none of that gentle shepherding a bridegroom owed to a virgin on her first time. Rush through it, and save the niceties for a second round. Did she imagine it that way?

He set one knee on the mattress and gave it his weight, gradually. She'd know she wasn't alone in the bed now.

If a man had denied himself all the way to something-and-twenty, though, he would have some skill at self-mastery, and might put it to use tonight. He might like to go slowly, the better to savor each secret disclosed. His knuckles skated up the length of the sheet to the hemmed edge, and he took hold, and drew it slowly down to the foot of the bed. Nothing but air separated his skin from hers.

This would be his first experience of bare shoulders, the self-mastered man. He got his second knee on the bed and carefully set his palm to the mattress, just where her pillow ended. His free hand wandered—shyly, scarce believing it had the right—down from where it had hovered, and found the soft flesh of her upper arm. He fit his fingers round it. Slid them upward. His thumb felt its way to her collarbone and traced. The hollow above. The graceful ridge. Soon, when he'd plucked up the courage, his whole hand would steal lower. He bent, and pressed his lips to the curve of her shoulder.

She stopped breathing for several seconds, and started again. Confusion, maybe. Maybe something else. He lifted his knee and brought it gently down between her legs, the better to center himself above her.

She'd never liked him to kiss her, on the mouth or anywhere else. But the rules might be different tonight. The rules might be different for a man who had everything to learn from her. He brushed his mouth over one wing of her collarbone. Then the other.

Her breath hesitated again, for a shorter span this time. One hand came up and took a tentative grip on his arm.

Let her be tentative. So would he be. He ventured to set his lips on the column of her throat, lingering to feel her warm pulse. His hand went back to her arm and his fingers stroked reassuring paths from shoulder to elbow and back. *You are no more anxious than I,* said his touch, and the idea of it, of approaching a woman in trembling wonder, was beginning to be unbearably erotic.

He brought his other knee between hers and lowered his body carefully, not to overwhelm her, until they lay with skin touching, the shaft of his sex resting against her warm, tender flesh, because he was not so bold as to go straight in. Also because if he pressed against her just so, he might make her go molten at the core.

Her hand tightened, almost imperceptibly, on his arm. Her other hand settled, butterfly-light, at his shoulder. She made a tiny adjustment of her hips—her first small concession to desire—that brought him more firmly against the place where her pleasure lived. He shifted against her slightly, as though by accident, or as though he were a beginner just working out how to proceed. She flinched and went marvelously supple.

Good Lord. He'd finally found his way. All it wanted

was darkness and silence and infinite restraint. Nothing he couldn't do.

He kissed her jaw, dotting a line from under her ear to her chin. Her body rippled beneath him. His thumb marked the corner of her mouth and then his lips took the place of the thumb.

She didn't invite his tongue, and he didn't impose it. Time enough for that later. He went back to her jaw, the side he'd neglected on his first pass. Somewhere between the sounds of his breath and hers, he heard her lips part, and he might have heard her tongue flick out to sample where he'd been.

"You taste like liquor," she said. He could feel her muscles stiffen everywhere they touched.

"Brandy, yes." He whispered, to make his voice the voice of any man. "I needed it for courage tonight."

"Mirkwood." Her whisper sharpened. "Are you drunk?"

"Drunk on your scent, I am. Drunk on the feel of your skin." But even as he fought to keep the game going, he could feel how she was shrinking into her cool, brittle shell. The tilt of her hips changed and she sank into a mere passive posture, her responsiveness gone like an evanescent dream.

"You're perfectly acquainted with my scent and skin. I think the brandy has addled your brain." How badly must she have wanted an excuse to flee her own desire, that she would seize at one so flimsy as a mere drink of brandy?

He was acquainted with her indeed. He ought to have known better than to suppose he could lure her into pleasure through a pantomime of virtue. She wasn't the woman for that, and he wasn't the man. Small wonder she couldn't believe him in the role. What did he know of innocence? He'd flung his away at fifteen, the very day he'd finally grasped the import of those glances and stares cast his way by a neighbor's dissatisfied wife. It was long gone and irretrievable, and he'd never even thought to regret it.

Nor would he regret it now. "To business, then?" He didn't bother whispering anymore.

"As soon as you like."

And that was that. He raised up on straight arms and sought his own pleasure, like the careless wastrel he was. Devil take shyness. Devil take shy men, too. With one hand he clawed to the top of the headboard and gripped there to brace himself, panting or hissing between clenched teeth when he wanted to shout. Climax rushed up to meet him and he threw back his head and shook like a sapling in a gale, silently, because the servants mustn't be alerted, and he would show her even a brazen man could know something of self-mastery.

Fool, SHE reproved herself in time with his carnal rhythm. *Fool. Fool. Fool.* She'd known, not so long ago, all the reasons to resist a man. All the great and small ways a person could find herself betrayed. Appetite could cause a lady to give herself away until nothing remained but a shell of regret. Everything that had been hers would belong to the man on whom she'd bestowed it, and she would never have it back again. Nor would he prize it at all.

Trickery. Brandy-fueled trickery had come so close to undoing her tonight, with the crafty sweep of lips along her collarbones, the perfidious machinations of his hips. But she'd pulled up in time, and now she could remind herself of what she did and did not want.

He finished and lay panting beside her. She waited only until certain he would hear her over his own labored breaths. "I wish and hope you will not come to my bed drunk again." Her voice sounded stiff; brittle. Of course it did. "That habit offends me."

"I'm not drunk." He sucked in more air. "Just pleasantly fortified. And as to habit, one can enjoy a drink of brandy without making a regular practice of it."

Bitter laughter boiled up in her and she had to fight it down. "Men always think they control their habits, and never see that the reverse is true."

"I tell you it's not a habit." Now she heard some irritation. "I had Granville up to the house for a glass or two. I thought to be sociable. That's the first time I've indulged since the day I met you. And if you need further reassurance, I'll abstain before I come to you tomorrow. Now can you cease to address me as though I stood before you in the dock on charges of public dissipation?"

She turned his words over in the darkness. He might be telling the truth. Admittedly she lacked objectivity on this topic. And she'd never known him to be drunk before, though of course some men were skilled at hiding it. Maybe she should suspend judgment until tomorrow, when he would keep or break his word. She drew a clean breath. "I'm sorry. I have very little tolerance for any form of inebriation."

"So I apprehend." His voice went mild as he turned his body toward her. "Who had that intolerable habit? Your father? Your husband? The brother with whom you don't care to live?"

Her insides recoiled from the forward question, but her tongue had already got started. "Andrew?—that's absurd. He's so strict as to make me seem lenient."

"Then I hope I never meet him." He spoke in a calm, pleasant, conversational tone. "Is his nature, and yours, a reaction to growing up with an intemperate parent, perhaps?"

None of this was his concern. *None* of it. She sealed her lips into a tight line. But if she chose this juncture to keep quiet, she would encourage him to a conclusion that wronged her father. "How can you ask?" She couldn't bear that injustice. "John Blackshear was a serious, Bible-reading, abstemious man." She ought now to make a defense of Mr. Russell. That would logically follow. She stayed silent.

"Ah." The syllable was lush with comprehension. He thought he knew all, now. She could feel the way his mind worked in the silence. Reviewing every scene they'd played together, with this as the secret subtext. As though this one facet of her marriage could account for everything he'd previously found unaccountable in her. "Do you care to speak of it?" he said after a moment.

"No."

"Have you ever, to anyone?"

"No."

She heard his mouth doing something mobile, perhaps making a false start or two before he spoke again. "Did he beat you?"

"No." For Heaven's sake. "I told you I don't care to speak of it."

"Did he have an evil temper?"

"Nothing of the sort. Nothing like you'd read of in a novel." He would conjure a melodrama of Gothic proportions if she didn't give him some better idea of the truth. "It was a kind of absence, more than anything. And an impediment to my feeling that degree of respect that a wife would like to feel for her husband. Because I believe a man ought to be dependable, and have some command of himself."

"Not much chance of that, with a man in thrall to the bottle." His words drew a soft underscore to her own, encouraging her to go on.

"Precisely. The drink made him changeable. It put

great gaps in his memory. He would forget whole hours and everything that had passed in them."

"But he remembered the way to your bed."

Her breath caught. He'd gone right to the core of it, surely as though he'd sliced her open and laid a finger on her beating heart. For all that she framed Mr. Russell's habit as a bothersome inconvenience, something that could not truly touch her, the fact had remained: *he,* her husband, could touch her. Whenever he wished, he could. A man who made himself a stranger to his wife still had that right. A wife had no right to refuse.

It could have been worse. He didn't beat you. He wasn't cruel. That stern self-reproach never did have the bracing effect one would wish. Her eyes were blinking with loathsome rapidity, their will to expose her frailty luckily thwarted by the dark. She breathed in, sharply, and dug her nails into the meat of her palms.

"Martha." Across the distance of a pillow his attention flowed, a warm, buoyant bath inviting her to linger.

"Mr. Mirkwood." She made the words like a hand held upright, commanding him to halt. "Your kindness and concern do you credit, I'm sure. But I've said all I care to on this subject. I suggest we go to sleep now."

The air stirred with movement. Unerringly through the dark, his hand came and set itself against her head, palm at her ear, fingers spread and sunk into her hair. Just for a moment his hand remained there, just long enough to hold her steady as he brought his lips to her forehead. "Good night, then," he said, and she felt his warm breath at her hairline. He lay back, with nothing more to say, and she listened to his breaths as they lengthened and turned to light snores.

*S*OME TIME in the night, turning over, she collided with part of him. His arm snaked promptly across her and pulled her close, as though she had belonged on that part of the bed all along, and had somehow wandered. She held her breath, waiting for what would come next, but nothing did. His arm had acted of its own accord, perhaps as a reflex honed from countless nights spent with a woman in easy reach. Or perhaps her presence beside him coincided with a dream of some other lover.

That was not her business. He could dream whatever he liked. Only she'd prefer not to be drawn in as some kind of surrogate, her body ensnared in so many places by his. His legs tangled with her own. His arm across her, high on her chest. His chin and throat making a space just right to fit the top of her head. She could feel his pulse through her own scalp, and again through her shoulder where it rested against the middle of his chest. His breathing too: the soft rise and fall of his ribs; the slow, faint rush of air from somewhere over her head. Soon, surely, he would turn the other way and release her, but for the moment she lay there, trapped in bonds all made up of him, and there was nothing to do but consider the predicament.

If one loved a man, one must wish for this. Such a strange notion. One would wish for this clasp of the arm. This space his body made for hers. This little song, hushed and rhythmic, played by his pulse and his breath as though for the purpose of lulling her to sleep.

But what lady could ever sleep this way, surrounded by so much male? She could feel the appendage, slumbering against her hip. Her breathing, and his, might create movement enough to wake it. And from there, to wake him.

Slowly she drew her leg out from under his, and worked her way in a lateral slither toward her own edge of the bed. Scarcely had she gone six inches before his arm tightened and pulled her more firmly against him. He grumbled something incoherent; twined his leg again with hers. His lips pressed once to the top of her head. The appendage didn't stir.

"Mirkwood," she whispered. He couldn't possibly do all that while asleep, could he?

He made no answer, and in the quiet she shaped her mouth, her lips and tongue and teeth and palate, to something new. "Theophilus." The name floated out like milkweed fluff blown from her palm, wayward and ephemeral.

He grumbled again—she felt the thrumming of it in his chest—then fell silent save for the breaths, in and out.

She closed her eyes to wait for sleep or sunrise. Probably the latter. Her breathing arranged itself in soft accord with his own. Well, if she didn't sleep, they would at least be assured of catching that early-morning hour at which he must rise and make his quiet departure. She'd speak to him then about schooling his limbs in restraint.

WOMAN. SOME base animal part of his brain gave him the news. *Woman, not two feet distant.*

His nose confirmed the report. Sweet scent of naked woman, with an overlay of something floral. Lilac. A powder made to smell of lilacs. Ah, yes. *That* woman.

His eyes eased open. Faint gray, in the strip of window between the curtains. No sunrise colors yet, but they'd come. Then he must be off.

He had time. He needn't even wake her.

Her back was to him, her hair spilling all ways over the pillow and one shoulder exposed where the covers had slipped down. He tugged at the sheet and draped it over her shoulder, restoring her modesty. In trade, he took away every inch between them. His chest met her back—*gently*—and he draped an arm over her rib cage to keep her there. His knee pushed—*slowly*—between her knees. His hand grasped her thigh, lifting it up and back to rest atop his leg. His cock brushed against her, lingering on the threshold of where she opened to him, and—*quiet as snowfall*—slipped in.

"What are you doing?" Awake and alert in an instant. "You did this already, last night."

He cursed softly. "Can't you just sleep through it?"

"*Sleep* through it? Are you mad? You could wake a churchyard with that thing."

"Good Lord. If I'd known you awoke with a sense of humor, I should have been spending the night long before this." He thrust once and then twice. Christ, but he ought not to do this. The things she'd told him last night were coming back now, as was a vague, ardent resolve to respect her bodily reticence, and prove himself a better man than her husband.

And now here he was imposing himself on her—in her—and demanding she go back to sleep. Still, she hadn't stopped him. She would, wouldn't she, if she really objected?

He thrust once more and drew almost all the way out with a shuddering breath. "Truly, do you want me to stop?" He sounded like he'd just run from Vauxhall to St. James's.

Her ribs expanded into his chest, slowly, while she thought it over. "I don't suppose there's any harm. And this might be the right bit of seed."

"Good thinking. This might be the bit." *I'll do my best to make it the bit.* A place, after all, for worthy intentions. He paused to set his lips to her shoulder, careful to keep his rough cheek clear of her smooth one, before he resumed.

Chapter Eleven

$\mathcal{A}$ SECOND DAY of threshing only solidified his opinions. How was he to properly enjoy a slice of toast again, knowing the terrible drudgery that lay behind it? And what primordial coxcomb had first grown discontented with the earth's bounty of fruit and game, and cast a calculating eye on stalks of grain? He should like to meet that man, and fetch him a sound knock to his shaggy head. If he hadn't lost all his quickness, that was. Nearly four weeks without a bout at the parlor might have done irreparable harm. Each in turn he took his hands from the traces to flex out the fingers and clench them in fists.

"Should you like me to take the reins, sir?" Mr. Quigley, a slight whippet of a man, had clearly been non-plussed by the master's inclination to drive the wagon instead of riding alongside on a horse, as Granville had the decency to do, and was every minute watching for signs that he might be required to take over.

"Not at all. You did your part with the threshing this past week. You're to sit back now, and enjoy what scenery we encounter on the way to this mill."

Quigley set his wide-splayed fingertips on his knees,

and frowned at the road before him. Something in the attitude brought Mrs. Russell to mind. Not much for the incidental pleasures, these denizens of Sussex.

But the scenery rolled past, for those capable of enjoying it, until finally a town loomed into view, and at its near end, a smallish river with a gray-brick mill on its bank. A fall in the river sent water over the top of the wheel, driving it round and round with presumably enough energy to turn a grindstone. Gears came into it somehow, or so Granville had said. Large gears and small gears interacting in some mysterious way to make the stone turn faster than the wheel itself. Sideways as well. The waterwheel sat upright while the grindstones, both the fixed one and the one that moved, lay horizontal. Granville had sketched a diagram and Theo had nodded sagely at it while daydreaming of the widow's bed.

At the mill they unloaded their sacks of grain—let Quigley eye him as dubiously as he would; he could match muscles with any laborer—and watched a wheel-driven chain hoist them one by one to the sack floor, where some mill fellow stood ready to pour the grain down a chute to the grindstones. There would be nothing to do now but wait for the wheat to come back as sacks of flour.

He looked about him, reaching for the hat he'd put off while unloading the wagon. "I might go take a walk through that town, if you can spare me," he said to the agent. "I've been used to going for long rambles this time of day, but never yet to any of the neighboring towns." A superfluous lie, perhaps. For all he knew, Granville hadn't even noticed his pattern of absences in the afternoons. At all events, the agent could indeed spare him, and Quigley raised no objections to his going, and so he set off up the road to where the hamlet properly began.

The town was a pretty thing of its kind, a hodgepodge of brick, whitewashed, and half-timbered buildings all shouldered together in cheerful ignorance of the modern age. Carts cluttered the curving high street: he'd come on market day. A flaxen-haired child was leaning out an upstairs window, wide eyes taking in all the bustle below. Theo raised his hat when the child's gaze came to him, and was rewarded with as joyous a wave as if he'd been some beloved uncle just returned from a sea voyage with presents in his pockets.

Presents. He felt through the coins in his coat. He might buy a thing or two here. Decent cheese for Mr. Barrow, perhaps. Maybe something for Mrs. Russell. He started for the far end of the street, to make his way slowly back and see what was on offer.

More than one pretty girl glanced up at his passing. Speak of what was on offer. Even in the plainer clothes he'd put on for today's chores, he must cut a notable figure in this town. He gave a little straightening tug to his coat and smiled at the girl nearest him.

Things could begin this way. Things so often had. Glances exchanged, a gaze held half a second longer than was proper, a smile in which she could read everything, or nothing at all.

Confound his shallow soul. Was he no better than this? He'd thought he'd detected, of late . . . well, he rather thought he'd detected a certain tenderness in his thoughts of Mrs. Russell. A certain something that ought to preclude such speculative attention to other women. Such full-body notice of the russet curls escaping this one's bonnet. Of that one's lips, quirked up at the corners and lush in between.

Well, his body looked out for his welfare, didn't it? No profit in tender thoughts of Mrs. Russell. If he were foolish enough to fall in love—and Lord knows he was foolish enough for most uses—his would be a solitary plunge. He would blink up at her, as from the bottom of a well into which only he had been careless enough to tumble, while she peered down at him with a disapproving face, because she liked a man to be dependable and he could not be relied upon even to watch where he set his feet.

Regardless, he would be faithful. He'd pledged the widow a month of exclusive attentions, and a man's word must be worth something. He turned deliberately to a cart at which the only female present was an untempting sort, a solid-looking matron in the lavender of half-mourning. Another widow, like as not. So much the better. She was picking, with a stately aspect, through the cart's assortment of leafy things. Lettuces. Watercress. God only knew what. She threw one quick sharp look at him, and he bent his attention to the leafy things too.

"I beg your pardon." Why not make a friend of her, if only for the minute or two they must bear each other's company? He spoke softly, to omit the vegetable-seller from the discussion. "I'm not at all sure of how to choose a good lettuce. Are the darker leaves better?"

She looked at him again, assessing this time. Then she jabbed at a lettuce. "This is as good as you're likely to find," she muttered at the same confidential volume. "But don't pay more than tuppence for it, no matter what he asks."

Now what could he do but buy the lettuce? With one hand he hefted it; with the other he fished out a few coins.

"A lettuce for you there, sir?" said the vendor, all affability. "That's five pence."

Presumably he was to insult the vegetable, and its seller into the bargain, in hopes of threepence saved. He glanced at his neighbor, but she was picking with concentration through some parsley and didn't glance back. He paid the five pence.

"Badly done," she said through pursed lips as soon as the man had turned his attention elsewhere. "He saw your fine clothes and raised up the price. They'll always take such advantage, if you allow it."

"It's only threepence lost. I've thrown that much away just cleaning out my pockets."

"And didn't he know that, too, to look at you. You look like you don't know the cost of anything, pardon my saying so."

"That's only too true." To be lectured by a lady in mourning had almost a cozy familiarity to it, these days. "I thought to buy a bit of cheese, and I haven't the least idea what's reasonable to pay."

This subject drew her in further. "You'd do better to buy your own cow. There's only the one dairy in these parts, and their cheese is inferior. You'd be sure to overpay for it, too, just as you did for that lettuce."

"I can't regret the threepence. I can't begrudge the man a little profit. If he can get an extra few pennies here and there from those who won't miss it, won't that help to keep the price low for everybody else?" That was really a rather solid argument, all the way around.

Her eyes ran critically up and down his face. "I frankly fear for you at the dairy stall. They'll have your pockets inside out before you've half begun."

"Then might I prevail on you to go there with me and keep me out of danger? I'll give you this fine lettuce for your trouble." Notions were beginning to form; hazy notions of more than one good deed in which this woman might play some part.

"Keep your lettuce. I couldn't enjoy it at the price, even paid by someone else. I can spare you five minutes, I think."

They started up the high street. He introduced himself. The woman was a Mrs. Canning, a widow of some years who had apparently seen no reason to ever put off her half-mourning. "I'm neighbor to a widow myself," he said, "though a much more recent one. Are you acquainted with Mrs. Russell of Seton Park?"

He could see her revising her opinion of his intelligence another notch downward. Yes, he was used to *that* from a woman in mourning as well. "She's landed gentry," came the answer. "Our paths haven't crossed."

"Ah, of course. Only you strike me as so much alike in your manner, in your common sense and plain way of speaking, and then of course the gravity with which you each approach widowhood. I had supposed you might know one another." This gambit took him as far as the dairy stall, where he came to a stop, arms folded, and made a show of studying a wheel of cheese.

"I shouldn't eat that if it stood between me and starvation." Mrs. Canning dismissed the cheese with a single swift gesture. "Do you mean to say you've been calling on Mrs. Russell yourself?"

"A time or two, I have. How much will he ask for this inedible cheese?"

"Eight or ten pence a pound is what I hear. They've no shame. I'd lay my soul it's half sawdust." She frowned at the cheese with some ferocity. "It's not proper for an unrelated man to call on a widow."

"My point exactly. I wish I'd brought along a sister to keep house for me, so I could send her to call. A gentleman on his own isn't a very useful kind of neighbor in these cases. And then, I don't seem to make the right sort of conversation." He rubbed a rueful hand over his jaw.

"You ought not to be making conversation at all. Hasn't she any family come to stay with her?"

"None, I'm afraid. They're mostly occupied with professions." He moved along the stall. "Barrister and soldier and some such. And she was married too short a time, I gather, to acquire proper friends among the neighboring gentry. Ought the butter to be that color?"

"Don't start me on the butter." She shifted her glare to where it sat. "Do you know what they add to get that color? Copper."

"Copper, indeed? Singular. You know, Mrs. Russell takes an interest in just these things. The diet of those too poor to keep a cow, and so forth. I shall have to tell her—but no, it's better I don't call. You're quite right. Though she did serve me the most delectable cake. Now would you be so good as to ascertain the prices of some of these items for me?" He brought out a pencil and pocket-book. "I daren't ask myself, or I'll end by buying one of each."

Mrs. Canning obliged him in fearsome fashion, demanding to know the cost of everything and repeating each price in ringing tones of incredulity, that he might have time to hear and copy it down. Here was grist for an idea, indeed, if the grindstones of his brain were up to the task. He pocketed the book and pencil, thanked the woman for her time, and insisted she take the lettuce, if only to feed to her pig.

He'd meant to buy presents. Perhaps he'd done better than that. Still, because a gentleman ought to finish what he set out to do, he stopped at the bakery stall and picked out a currant bun. At the street's end he pitched the bun upstairs to the flaxen-haired child, who caught it, laughing, on the first try.

I HAVEN'T THE least idea of how to broach the subject." Martha stood in the bay-window alcove of her dressing room, watching Sheridan put away some underclothes just back from laundering. "Her manners aren't encouraging. And once she knows I'm seeking a child, she will surely deduce the reason, and then I'll be at the mercy of her discretion and her sympathy, the latter of which seems to be in decidedly short supply."

Sheridan brushed at the mourning gown hung over the wardrobe door. "I doubt she'd give it that much thought. I don't think farm people care a great deal about intrigues among the gentry. Probably it's all the same to her who owns Seton Park."

I doubt . . . I don't think . . . Probably . . . These were not the foundations upon which to go forward with such a risk. She set her hands on her hips and tilted her chin to study the ceiling. "I wish I knew how long Mr. James Russell meant to stay. If he means to be here at the time of confinement, then I don't see how to manage at all."

"If you give birth to a son, there'll be nothing to manage." The maid knelt to brush the ruffle at the gown's hem.

"Yes, but to count entirely on that outcome would be imprudent." Though really, the deeper she got into this undertaking, the more imprudent every bit of it seemed. Mrs. Weaver's child could very well turn out a girl. How was a desperate widow to proceed? Bargain with a dozen different women for the right to their unborn babies, to be certain of getting at least one boy?

And yet she wouldn't regret her course. Not when the alternative had been to sit idle and watch everything fall into Mr. James Russell's hands. "I shall have to cultivate that woman's goodwill first of all." She folded her arms and shifted her gaze to the view from the window. "*There* will be challenge enough to occupy all my resources, I don't doubt. I can worry about how to broach the pertinent subject after I've accomplished that."

"Indeed. Only save some resources for Mr. Mirkwood." Sheridan was sober-faced when Martha shot a glance her way, though the words did sound as if they'd been sieved through a smile.

"Mr. Mirkwood has grown quite reasonable." She looked out the window again, to the woods through which he would come late tonight. "And he has more sense than I first credited him with. Altogether he is among the least of my worries at present."

*T*ALK TO me the way you did that first morning." His face, above her, was half in shadow, half washed in shifting light. After two nights of darkness he'd chosen this evening to put out all the candles but one. Its illumination chased across his aristocratic cheekbones, warming his skin and kindling a diabolic glimmer in his eyes.

"I don't know what you mean." Opposition was a pleasure all its own, one she could allow herself and one that seemed to amuse him as well.

"Yes, you do. *You could wake a churchyard with that thing.*" He tilted back his head to look down at her from under half-lowered lids. "Only this time name it. Wake a churchyard with what?"

"With your male appendage. Obviously." For Heaven's sake.

"*Appendage.* Good God. Did your husband never teach you any proper words?"

"My husband was a respectable man. He knew the difference between a wife and a filthy-tongued harlot."

"No wonder you never enjoyed yourself with him." He eased in to the hilt, raising up on his arms and arching his back as he went. Candlelight danced over the squared muscles on his chest; the bands of sinew on his stomach. He might stay like this for a very long time and she would not grow tired of looking. Nor of the slight, sweet pressure where their bodies met. She knew what she would and would not do. But she could imagine how he might rock his hips against her, perhaps with a circular sort of motion, and she could imagine the motions with which she might answer.

He tipped his head forward and looked straight down into her eyes. "Tell me what you want me to do to you."

Hot panic flared under her breastbone. He knew. He knew what was in her thoughts. "I only want the seed. You know that. Have you been drinking again?" All one hasty stream the words poured out.

In answer he sank his mouth to hers. His tongue swept over the seam in her lips, from one corner all the way to the other. "Taste," he commanded, retreating an inch or two. "See for yourself."

"That wasn't necessary." She tasted while fumbling back to the firm ground of opposition.

"Ha. Not to you, perhaps." He oughtn't to take such liberties. Doubtless she'd encouraged him by allowing him to help himself to pleasure that first morning, and the second morning as well. But he didn't, admittedly, taste of liquor tonight. "I'm waiting." His voice was soft as a spring shower, coaxing her to leave shelter for the uncertain out-of-doors. "Say something wicked, Martha. Something you'd never say to your husband."

She twisted, though of course escape would be nothing to the purpose. "I have no idea what you're hoping to hear."

"Haven't you, really?" His gaze alone pinned her. The weight of his body was superfluous. "I'll give you a hint. It begins with *F*."

She could feel a blush creeping right up into her hairline. Confound the lit candle that would let him see it. "I cannot say that."

"No?" His smile creased deeper, iniquity incarnate. "Put your top teeth to your bottom lip and blow. That is how you begin."

"You know what I mean. I don't say vulgar things. Nor pointless things, for that matter."

"Pointless." His head tilted left and one eyebrow went up.

"Quite." Yes, here was a bit of self-assurance. "Why on earth would I bid you do something you're already doing?"

"Very well, then." He drew back his hips and the appendage left her to press importunately against her thigh. "Just as you like. Now you must bid me. Or beg me, if I should prove recalcitrant."

She would forget he'd said that. She would not allow her conjured man to say it later, for all that it sent a shameful tremor down her spine. She met Mr. Mirkwood's intractable gaze with her own for several seconds. Then she sent up her right hand and trailed a finger across his nipple.

He shivered. "What are you doing?" Instantly his voice was hoarse.

Foolish irreverent pleasure boiled up in her, and through his skin she could feel how he, too, took the joke. That *he* should be the one, this time, to say those words. That he should be the one off balance, wondering what she meant to do. "I'm touching you." She dragged her finger back the other way. "In this one spot."

"There are two." His lowered lashes cast shadows, exaggerated candle-flame shadows, on his cheekbones. "Two such spots. In case it's escaped your notice."

Like a cat demanding to be petted. Well, why not? She put her second set of fingers to work. He closed his eyes and leaned into her touch, yes, very like a cat. His breaths went slow and even, as though every last bit of energy in him must be diverted from its usual occupations, and applied to receiving the sensation. His head tipped right and then left. "I don't suppose . . ." His brow furrowed slightly, his eyes still closed. "Can you be persuaded to employ your mouth?"

Her mouth. Indeed. If she put her mouth here, he would soon want it elsewhere. Any woman who'd been a wife knew how that went.

So be it. If he made impertinent demands, she would simply say *no*. She slid her hands round to his ribs, found a grip, and brought him down to her. Her lips met his skin, the taut-drawn coin-sized circle, and he let out a ragged breath.

She would make him forget entirely that he'd wished her to say indecent things. She dragged her lips across that inch and heard a hitch in his inhalation. Men. Men and their weakness for women's mouths. Her tongue ventured out and found his taste not unpleasant. He growled low in his throat and squirmed, the hairs on his chest brushing ticklishly over her lips. "More," he whispered, so she let him feel the edges of her teeth.

A strangled sound came out of him. He pulled back, and fumbled to put himself inside her again. "Witch," he muttered, thrusting. "Sorceress. You won't rest until you've unmanned me utterly, will you?"

Sorceress. Witch. She was nothing of the kind. But she put her mouth back on him, that she couldn't be expected to use it for any bidding or begging, and through her lips and tongue and teeth she felt every tremor of his thorough, exultant, unbridled capitulation.

"Good Lord," he said when he'd caught his breath. "I was already prepared to call this my best day since I've come to Sussex. I haven't the words to do it justice now." He heaved himself off her and sank stonelike at her side.

"You enjoyed your trip to the mill? Will you tell me

about it?" That seemed the safer part of the day to discuss.

"In fact I hope to be shut of the mill altogether in time." He pulled the covers back over them both and rested an idle hand on her thigh. "I've had an idea." His eyes glittered hopeful and a bit apprehensive in the scant light, as though he cared very much for her opinion and feared it might not be a good one. "I think to give up the wheat field in favor of a small dairy. Not one of your large modern concerns with cowsheds and so forth. Just something modest, to supply the neighborhood with purer stuff than what's sold here now."

For a moment she couldn't speak. She had never, to her shame, supposed him capable of coming up with such an idea. "It's not good at all, what's sold at the market in town," she then said. "They water the milk, I'm told."

"Yes, I know." Good Heavens. He'd informed himself. "And if I had cows, instead of crops, I could graze them on the common land. No need to enclose. Only I've everything to learn about the enterprise." His hand flexed absently on her thigh. "I don't even know where to get milch cows, or how much they cost."

"I'll help you. We can ask my steward, to begin." So many poor people in the neighborhood could benefit from better milk.

"And I suppose I should have to persuade Granville of the scheme. And persuade my father to the expense." His hand twitched again, settling farther up.

"We'll study numbers. You'll show him how it can bring a better profit than wheat." Now he'd had the idea, she would not let him lapse in carrying it out.

"I expect we'd better ascertain that fact before building a case for it." He smiled, clearly enjoying her pleasure in his scheme. "I do know what they ask for everything in town. I copied down the prices. And at least one of my laborers has experience in a dairy of the old style."

"That's wonderful. That's an excellent beginning. What is your hand doing there?" She might have said nothing. She might have carried on with the conversation and never acknowledged the upward migration of his hand until suddenly she was gasping in the middle of some observation about butter. If she were frail and foolish, she might have done that.

"Martha." His voice sank, and his finger drew an exquisite small circle. "Give me eight minutes."

More trickery, this time cloaked in the kind of conversation he knew she liked best. She felt cold at her center, even as part of her wished he would trace that circle again. "We've discussed this." Her voice didn't sound cold. It sounded panicked and desperate. "I've told you I don't want it."

"I think perhaps you do." He spoke carefully. His fingers swept up the clefts at either side of her most sensitive flesh, navigating her with absolute ease. "You're wet, Martha. Can't you feel it?"

"You did that." He always spilled an overabundance of seed.

"Decidedly I did. But not the way you mean." One of his fingers went into her. Two of them did. That didn't matter. What mattered was his thumb, steadily circling, determined to leave her in pieces. "Can you not trust your body to know what it wants?"

"My mind rules my body. Not the other way round." That wasn't *no*. Why hadn't she said *no*? Her hips flinched as though to give the lie to her words.

"I'll pleasure your mind as well. I'll speak of land management the whole time."

"You're depraved beyond my worst conjectures." That wasn't *no* either. How had she lost the ability to form one short syllable?

"Tomorrow we'll visit your steward, that he may advise me on cows and cottage roofs. Perhaps I'll even speak to your curate about educating my laborer-children." Too much triumph in his voice. He'd glimpsed her frailty and now he was smug as a lion surveying a lame-footed deer. "Let me do this." His thumb was relentless. "Let me. Though it may sound like supplication, that's actually a command."

"You are not in any position to command me." The candle was beginning to gutter, throwing fantastical shadows all over the room. Something similar was going on inside her. She flinched again, harder.

"On the contrary, I would say I'm in exactly that position." He smiled, so sure of his victory, and finally she had the grounds for resistance she'd needed.

"No. Stop. I want you to stop."

His fingers stilled at once, though he kept them where they were. Foolish disappointment shot through her, there and gone like quicksilver. The candle flame perished and he spoke in the dark. "Martha." His voice was tender with pity, insupportable pity. "Why must you fight it so?"

She had answers. She'd learnt them by heart. "You're all but a stranger. My conscience objects. And you're not a man I can . . ."

"Admire." He supplied the word on which her own tongue had failed. "Do you really have to, though? Pretend the touch is your own." He pressed delicately with his thumb. "Follow your body's promptings for eight minutes. It needn't be any more complicated than that."

Now he was lying to them both. "It can't be anything but complicated. You want to command me." Why did she even try to explain? "You would have me give myself up to you."

"Only for a little while. And I'd give you back." But

he lifted his hand away and she heard him sink onto his pillow.

"I'm sorry," she said into the darkness. How could the loss of something she didn't even want leave her feeling so desolate?

"Never mind about it. Perhaps one day you'll have a change of heart." Such unfailing optimism. She must hope he continued so confident, that she might read it for arrogance and find the means to resist.

Chapter Twelve

$\mathscr{O}$NE DID not like to be illogical. One did not like to review one's words or actions, and see how any impartial observer must find them inconsistent.

Surrender. Command. So zealously she guarded against giving herself up to a man who gave himself up to her every day. Every night, now, and every morning as well. She hadn't told him to desist from that style of waking her. Nor had she said anything of how his limbs roamed while he slept, catching her body and reeling her in.

All the more reason. So Martha told herself, her mind newly disposed to wander, while Mr. Smith expounded on all he knew of dairy cows and the local thatching labor, and Mr. Mirkwood scribbled notes. *You've ceded so much ground already. Keep what you can.*

Ceded ground to whom, though? He wasn't her adversary. If he did want to command her—and only for a little while—was that any worse than what she herself had enjoyed with him?

She would not deceive herself on this point. She had enjoyed, to a certain degree, his loss of mastery. His helpless response to what she did with her mouth. His wholehearted renunciation of the quest to make her say vulgar words. She'd triumphed over him, absolutely, and how could she blame him for wanting a turn at that triumph himself?

Of course it was different for a man. A man could play at surrender, safe in the knowledge he still had more power than the woman with whom he played. He could overwhelm her physically. He tread a wider path in the world. For a man—particularly a man like Mr. Mirkwood—what happened in bed was all one great game.

He said something, scratching away with his pencil. Some question about cows. His head bent toward his paper, he looked up at Mr. Smith from under those six-pews-away lashes, studious attention limning his profile. Women in London no doubt thought him beautiful. Poor short-shrifted women of London, never to have seen him looking like this.

A GENTLEMAN KEPT his word. Even careless words scattered in a failed attempt at most deviant seduction. So Saturday he let her introduce him to her steward, and Sunday after church they sat down with the curate in his makeshift schoolroom.

"A boy who grows up on a farm today cannot count, as his father and grandfather did, on farming in his own turn." Mr. Atkins perched on the edge of the table where presumably he would hold court once the school began. He'd changed his cassock for a black coat. Probably he looked rather dashing to feminine eyes. "With the advances in machinery, and the gradual vanishing of the small farms, many such boys shall have to leave home and work for wages."

"Girls do too. The eldest of the Cheatham girls went away to Lancashire only this spring." Mrs. Russell sat in a straight-back chair a little to Theo's right, hands folded in her lap, feet flat on the floor.

"Indeed." The curate sent a bow in her direction. "Mrs. Russell has been a fierce champion for the young ladies. We'll come to her part presently." A smile, a wholly unnecessary smile, volleyed between the two of them before he went on. "Education is more than ever important in broadening opportunity for a rural boy. If the time comes when he must look for a situation, then instead of ending in a mill or a mine, he might find a place as a clerk in some establishment, and work his way up from there." Now the smile came his own way, with a rueful edge to it. "That's the kernel of the argument I made to the families here, and that I would make to your families if you desired it so. However I'm lacking in arguments framed to persuade you the venture would be worth your while. Mrs. Russell can tell you I made no headway with Mr. Russell until she came along and involved herself in the persuading."

"Mr. Russell had many demands on his attention." She said this with her eyelids lowered, as though addressing her still hands. "He saw the merit of the scheme from the beginning, I'm sure, and only wanted some near person to urge it above all the other schemes and pursuits in which a landowner might make some investment."

"I'm sure I'd like to hear from Mrs. Russell." *And she knows just what words I'd like to hear.* He covered that thought with a bland pensive look. "Will you tell me what hopes you have for the educated girls? I presume you don't foresee them as clerks."

"One day, perhaps. Now women go to work in mills, who can say what might come next?" She angled her body toward him, eyes lit with ardent determination. "But chiefly I hope to equip these girls for marriage to educated men. When such a man goes to choose a wife,

I'm sure he will prefer a woman with whom he can discuss all the matters on his mind, to one with whom he can discuss only the evening meal and the health of the baby."

"Mrs. Russell has a most noble vision of marriage." Mr. Atkins's mouth quirked up as he watched his own hand run along the edge of the table where he sat.

"On the contrary, I have a practical vision." She spoke to both men, though her body still faced his. "I'm thinking, too, of those cases in which a marriage should prove unequal to the hopes with which it began. A man in that marriage might still find a full life out in the world, perhaps in some occupation that allows him to do good. But what of his wife, who has no occupation but the marriage and the household? Even without she can have a profession, an education will teach her to take an interest in things beyond her own smaller sphere. And surely that could serve as consolation in her less hopeful hours."

She'd been lovely the first time he'd spied her, distant and disapproving in church. She was lovely each time he peeled away her clothing, and when she lay in his arms, and when her features went dim and unfocused as he lost himself. But she was never lovelier than when she spoke this way, all afire with the knowledge of wrongs to be righted and good to be done.

"You see, I think, how she convinced me." The curate was watching him, and probably seeing altogether too much himself.

"It wasn't so easy as that." She flashed a smile at both men. "I also had to argue for the utility of older girls in a classroom where their younger sisters will be taught."

"We plan to follow the Madras system somewhat, if you're familiar with the methods of Mr. Bell and Mr. Lancaster. A school in which the older pupils help to teach the younger."

"Only not their methods as to punishment."

"No, no black book filled with every least transgression. No miscreants hung from the ceiling in nets. I should lose my place in the lesson, if I had to look at that."

"And of course the older girls won't be present at first. We've had all we could do to convince a few parents to an hour of instruction on Sundays. We shall have to begin there, and work our way forward."

"Mrs. Russell has done wonders." The man bowed at her again. "I think we may almost count on seeing the Farris girls next week."

Didn't she glow at *that*. The easy rapport between the two of them; the way they all but finished one another's sentences; the evident fruit of hours engaged in intellectual discourse—and this at a time, surely, when her marriage offered no pleasures of companionship—could make a man cast up if he were subjected to very much more of it. Theo put a knuckle to his frown, massaging it into a merely thoughtful expression. "There's one child in particular for whom I'd like to be able to do something in order to broaden her narrow prospects as far as possible."

He could feel the widow's warm attention like a torch held in an outstretched arm. "That eldest girl in the Weaver family," she said.

He inclined his head to her. "One of my laborers has a simpleminded daughter. A young lady of fifteen or sixteen. I have no idea whether such a child is teachable, but perhaps that will have come up in your own research?"

Mrs. Russell's gaze lingered on him a second or two more before swinging, bright and hopeful, to the curate, who was raking a hand through his hair. "I don't know of any scholarship on what can be done for such children in the way of education." His attention had gone somewhere inward, reviewing everything he'd studied on the topic. "But why shouldn't we try? If she has the mind of a younger child, she might learn alongside the primary class. I should like to meet her parents, and hear what they think of her capabilities." He couldn't be happier, Mr. Atkins, now he faced a new challenge. Little wonder the widow liked him.

But Theo himself could not quite dislike him to the degree he'd intended. "You might come by my property two days hence," he said. "We'll be rethatching their roof and another, and as the families will be turned outside for the afternoon, I thought to throw a sort of picnic for them. It should be a festive occasion; good opportunity for you to make the families' acquaintance and begin to lay the groundwork for your schooling recruitment. I hope you'll come too, Mrs. Russell. You may see what you think of the young ladies."

She was staring at him now with force enough to singe his hair. Stunned, no doubt, that he'd arranged the thatching on his own, and planned the picnic too. Really, she must think very little of him, to suppose he had no capacity for responsibility but in her presence. He would show her he could do a few things by himself.

MR. MIRKWOOD," she said late that night, when he'd begun to think of sleep. "I want to tell you something. Will you listen?"

"Of course." He turned on his side, just making out her shape in what moonlight seeped between the curtains. She hadn't proposed moving their assignations back to daylight, and to the other set of rooms. They'd made their visits to Mr. Smith and Mr. Atkins in the afternoon, and she must surely have concluded he was free again by day. But she hadn't said anything, and neither had he.

"Mr. Russell never agreed to the school." He could hear that she was facing straight up, addressing the canopy. "Do you remember I told you he lost the memory of things?"

"I remember."

"I waited for a day when he was particularly not himself. And then the next day I told him how commendable was his decision to provide for the school."

"Neatly done." Something told him not to caress her, as his hand was demanding to do.

"I suppose I ought to be sorry, but I'm not. Someone needed to see that his resources were put to good use."

A thought occurred. "The cottage roofs as well?"

"Exactly so. I told him what a generous thing it was, replacing every last roof from the rafters up. And he couldn't remember enough to gainsay me."

"Generous indeed. We'll only be replacing a layer or so of the thatch." His fingers, restless for her, swirled about in small patterns on the sheet, filling the lapse in talk with a rhythmic soughing. "Does the curate know?"

"He hasn't the least idea." The sound of her voice told him she'd turned her head his way. "He wanted to halt the school when he learned how the will had come out, and that everything was likely to pass to Mr. Russell's brother. But I told him I would write to Mr. James Russell and secure his approval for the school."

"And did you?" One finger, just one, set itself in the crook of her near elbow.

"He thinks so, Mr. Atkins. But I never did." She faced the ceiling again. "He'll think very poorly of me if he finds out. When he finds out. It's almost a certain thing."

"That's a pity. I like you the better for it."

"You like bad behavior wherever you find it." Her words had the shape of a smile.

"Perhaps. But in your case it's something else." His finger stroked a line across her inner elbow. "You risk yourself for what matters to you. You risk the good opinion of people for whose good opinion you deeply care. That's to be admired."

She inhaled, and exhaled, probably turning over his words. "Mr. Mirkwood," she said, and hesitated. "Theo. I can't tell you what it means to me, your taking an interest in the school. My hope is that, if I should fail . . ." Her voice quavered suddenly, and he took hold of her elbow with all his fingers while she collected herself. "If the house does go to Mr. James Russell, or if Mr. Atkins, on discovering how he has been deceived, should decide . . ."

"You'd like me to take your place in supporting the school, you mean. If circumstances render you unable to continue in that role yourself."

"It's a great deal to ask, I know."

"Not really. Not between a man and his mistress." Finally he let himself reach for her. "And besides it won't be necessary. We're going to disappoint your Mr. James Russell. Don't forget that." His arms drew her against his chest, his leg tangled with hers, and his chin fitted itself to the top of her head. Her breaths stayed calm and her pulse untroubled; indeed one might think she had been only waiting for the moment when his limbs would gather her in just so.

MONDAY BROUGHT a surprise. The footman found her in the library, where she'd gone to gather any book that might have some reference to dairy farming, and he presented three cards announcing three women whose names she did not recognize.

Mrs. Canning. Mrs. Kendall. Miss Leigh. "Did they state their business?" She turned a book sideways to mark her place along the shelf for when she might resume this project.

"They're callers." The footman cleared his throat. "Social callers," he added, as though unsure of her familiarity with the concept.

And well might he be. Martha brushed her hands together to rid them of dust. "Is there cake?"

"Cake, madam?" A single faint line impressed itself in his otherwise impassive brow.

"Yes, cake. Mr. Mirkwood quite enjoyed that lemon cake, when he came to call. And I think you'd better send the tea things as well. I'll give them tea and cake." The more she could occupy them with this novelty, the less conversation she'd have to make. Heavens, but one wished for the aplomb of Mr. Mirkwood, who would view unknown callers as just the latest in a string of marvelous adventures. "I'll go to them, then. The peony parlor, or the larger one?"

Mrs. Canning, Mrs. Kendall, and Miss Leigh had been shown to Seton Park's large formal parlor where they sat in a row on a white velvet sofa with gilt arms and legs, craning about at the room's Moorfield carpet, heavy chandeliers, and gilded plasterwork. "What a charming room this is," said Mrs. Canning once the introductions were done and all four ladies seated. She made an impressive presence in it, solidly built as she was and equipped with a gimlet eye.

"Charming, to be sure." Mrs. Kendall was a little dormouse of a woman, bright-eyed and quick in her movements. "Just the word I was going to choose."

Miss Leigh, tall and thin as a sapling, made one more sweeping survey. "Did you manage the decorating?"

"Oh, no." Martha poured hot water to rinse the teapot. Really, *charming* was the last word she should choose for this ornate cavern. "Someone in my husband's family did that. It's after the style of Robert Adam, I'm told."

"Ah." Mrs. Canning inspected the ceiling afresh. "And what does that mean, exactly?"

"Well, the plasterwork, I suppose. The decorated walls. These arched tops to the doors and windows, perhaps, and . . ." Her words trailed off as she swirled water in the pot. She looked up. "To be honest, I haven't the faintest idea." She poured out the water. "I grew up in a plain country house, and should never have heard the name Robert Adam—or Capability Brown, for that matter—but that I married and came to live here."

This admission seemed to put the ladies at some ease, thank goodness. Condolences were exchanged for Mr. Russell and Mr. Canning, though the latter proved to have departed some great while ago, and recommendations were given on the best ways for a widow to pass the early part of mourning, while Martha measured tea from the caddy into the pot, filled it with boiling water, and put on the lid.

"You live in town, I collect?" Eight minutes for the tea to steep meant eight minutes in which she must find more right things to say. One wished again for Mr. Mirkwood's easy manners, for his quick light tongue. "I'm afraid I've spent little time there and of course I cannot now venture abroad. I'm sure there must be so many opportunities to do good in town too."

Indeed there were. The three ladies had strong opinions of what could be improved in town, from the vicar's overly expressive sermons to the landscaping on the green to a young man or two who'd been stringing a young lady along and ought to hurry up and come to the point.

"I cannot approve of that conduct." It wasn't her business, of course. But the other ladies had brought it up. "If a man doesn't mean to offer for a lady, he ought to withdraw his attentions and let her move on to other prospects. I'm sure I should say so to any young man who presumed to trifle with one of my tenant-daughters here."

"I'm all but resolved to say something myself, at our next assembly." Mrs. Canning lifted her chin and delivered this fact in a tone of royal decision. "If young Nelson and young Warrender haven't come up to scratch by then, they may count on hearing from me between dances."

"Very good." She picked up the strainer and teapot. "I doubt such careless young men even recognize the grief they may cause. To point it out to them must be a kindness." What sensible, sensible women. The young ladies in town were lucky to have their patronage.

"We should be glad to see you at an assembly one day." Mrs. Kendall spoke with sudden shyness as she accepted her tea and a plate of cake. "They're quite respectable. The gentry do come sometimes."

"Mrs. Rivers and Miss Atcheson have sat down to cards more than once." Miss Leigh, too, took tea and cake.

"Perhaps next year." Mrs. Canning eyed Martha as though fitting her for a new gown. "You'll be in lavender then, I expect, and looking both distinguished and presentable."

"I'm sure I should like that. Thank you." *Distinguished and presentable.* One would like to be thought of that way. One felt oddly touched by this kind invitation, and one felt an utterly unsuspected hunger, too, for the chance to take one's place among these matrons at a humble town assembly, conferring over which young man or lady must be pulled aside for a judicious word, and furthermore scheming ways to better the public landscaping, and inspire the vicar toward subtlety.

The conversation continued more sensible by the minute. What odd quirk of whimsy should have brought them to call on her, a perfect stranger with only her wid-

owhood to recommend her? But she would be grateful
for whatever quirk had done the deed.

"My son is in the infantry, you know, and we're daily
hoping to hear of his return home." Mrs. Kendall chased
the last crumb of cake about her plate. "Do you hear
anything of when to expect your brother?"

She paused, cup halfway to her lips, and felt color
coming to her face. Only one person in Sussex knew
that Will was a soldier. Only one person even knew of
that brother's existence. Her quirk of whimsy took a
shape, tall and fair-haired. She dropped her eyes to the
cup, and set the cup in its saucer. What question had the
woman asked, exactly?

"I'm so sorry." She could hear Mrs. Kendall leaning
forward. "He's not in any danger, is he? I shouldn't have
brought it up, if—"

"Oh, no. Not at all." She looked up and forced a smile
through her confusion. "Indeed with Napoleon imprisoned at Elba I expect we should see him before very
much longer. His regiment is at Antwerp, I believe, just
waiting for orders. And your son?"

Something was said of Mrs. Kendall's son. There followed a number of remarks, some of them even contrib-
uted by herself. Other things came under discussion.
The tea and cake, almost certainly. The weather, perhaps. But if someone had asked her, a minute or an hour
or six hours later, to tell what they'd spoken of, the last
ten minutes of that call, she could not have done so to
save her soul.

$\mathcal{S}$HE SAT on the foot of the bed when he came in that
night, cross-legged in her nightrail, with a plate of lemon
cake and a fork and an impossibly radiant smile.

If only she'd inoculated him with more frequent
smiles, he would not lose all his conversation. But she

was sparing with her smiles, so often holding them back or hiding them with an artfully placed hand, and the result was he had no more defense against one than he would against some fever from the wilds of farthest Feejee. He stood wordless, smiling back at her just as though he knew the cause of her pleasure. And then, all at once, he did know.

He took the cake from her upraised hands and stepped back away from her radiance. "Well," he said, forking up a bite. "And what worthy things did you accomplish today?"

"I didn't accomplish a thing." Her smile deepened, sweet and bracing as a bite of lemon cake. "I had callers."

𝒯HE CLASSROOM, clearly, was Mr. Atkins's element. Here he did not make speeches that went on a bit too long, but came every few sentences to a question, and delighted in coaxing or prodding an answer from his flock. He moved about, now at a map, now at a great sheet of copperplate lettering, and often down the aisle between the tables where the pupils sat. Martha sat in an empty place at the back where she'd been the last half hour, listening to the industrious squeak of slate-pencils on slate.

Everything was turning for the better. Everything. The passage of a few months might see the school's enrollment double, with the addition of children from Mr. Mirkwood's property and—one must be hopeful—the presence of older girls. She might, given time, shepherd a dairy into being on the very next property and then turn her attention to all the good she could do in town. If only things fell out so that she remained at Seton Park, the days and years ahead could be gratifying indeed.

Today, while Mr. Atkins made himself known to the first of the laborer families at Pencarragh, she would work at befriending Mrs. Weaver. Somehow or another, she must.

The curate's high spirits lingered even after he'd dismissed the pupils and taken the reins of the pony cart. For the entirety of their drive he spoke of this child or that, praising one's quick perception or furrowing his brow over another's disinclination to sit still. On the walk from their cart he turned his attention to laborer children, and what differences, if any, he might encounter in teaching them. One suspected he couldn't be more pleased if he were granted a living of a thousand pounds a year.

The Weaver cottage, as they approached, was all in disarray, with men on its roof, straw thatch thrown down in the yard, and seemingly half the furniture dragged out to the open meadow. Small Weavers raced back and forth with small children from another family. Larger children sat clutching plates, eating their fill of what appeared to be roast fowl and potatoes. Baby Job sobbed on the shoulder of a laborer wife she didn't know. From habit she looked for the pig and found it stationed at the foot of the ladder, its head canted up as though to keep careful surveillance of the interlopers above.

Mr. Granville, sitting among the other adults with a mug of ale, rose at the sight of them and waved them over for introductions. "Is Mr. Mirkwood not here?" she said, once she'd made the acquaintance of Mr. Weaver and Mr. and Mrs. Quigley. "When he invited us I assumed he would be present."

In answer the man flung an arm up and out, directing her gaze back to the half-undone roof.

He sat atop the very ridge, bareheaded, his hair brilliant as an unspent shilling in the sun. His back was against the chimneypiece and one knee bent up before him, foot planted on the ridge tree as though he were relaxing on a riverbank somewhere. In his coarse-gloved hands he held a bunch of split branches. While she watched he twisted one, bending the ends near together. Then he swung himself down the slope of the roof to hand the implement to one of the roofers, who used it to secure one bundle of straw to another. Surefooted as though he'd spent most of his life on rooftops, he scaled a rafter back to the ridge.

Three weeks and two days now since she'd first seen him. Not long enough for a lady to truly know a man. That obstacle still stood. The objections of her conscience, too, had not grown any less valid. And as to admiration—Her thoughts fled suddenly as he twisted and caught sight of her. Of her and Mr. Atkins. He grinned like a boy looking down from a treehouse, one hand making to lift his hat before he remembered he didn't wear one.

"I believe I've finally got his measure." The agent was at her elbow, looking up. "If you take the *duty* and *responsibility* out of a thing, and give him a way to get his own hands on it, he's entirely willing to learn. I confess I took him for an idler at first."

Mr. Granville wasn't the only one guilty of that. "Even the duty and responsibility may come in time, I think. He's young yet."

"To be sure. And then, he might choose a wife strong in those qualities, and she might shore him up. Altogether I have every hope of his turning out well."

Mr. Mirkwood was down the ladder by this time, his branches given over to one of the thatching-men. He stepped nimbly round the pig and climbed over the fence to greet them. "Sit down, won't you, and have something to eat." He waved to a table laden with dishes. "I put my cook to a great deal of trouble. And someone was asking after you," he said to her. "One of these girls." He looked about him. "Ah—there you are. No

more hiding behind your sister. Here is Mrs. Russell,
just as you demanded. Now come sit by her and tell her
all about your cat." With something very near a wink he
left her, vaulting over the fence to go back up on the
roof.

Little Carrie had much to say of the kitten, who was
apparently equipped with a full repertoire of such antics
as were common to kittens and delightful to those who
cared for that kind of thing. She was a charming child
indeed, and would surely benefit from the broadening
effects of education. Once or twice Martha felt Mrs.
Weaver's eye upon them, but when she turned to smile,
hopeful of inviting her into their conversation, the woman's glance had gone elsewhere.

Mr. Weaver, however, presently took his daughter's
seat, consigning her to a place on his knee. He was a
great boulder in human form, Mr. Weaver was, with formidable knuckly hands and a heavy, low brow. "It was
a handsome thing to do," he said of the cat. "He's killed
a mouse already and the child's taken him to heart."

"I'm so pleased to hear he's been of use. I wonder if
more families here might be in need of one. We have a
surfeit, altogether. I could probably supply as many as
were wanted."

"Mrs. Russell lives at Seton Park," the child put in.

"So I heard, Mischief." Affectionately he tugged one
of the girl's plaits. "My Livia worked there for a time.
Has she mentioned it?"

"Mrs. Weaver, do you mean?" She swung about to
look at the woman, who had turned her back. "Why,
no. I had no idea she was ever even in service." Could
that pinched, haggard figure really have once worn a
starched cap and apron, and bustled about managing
things?

"She was. Before she married me, of course." He was
watching his wife as he spoke, and suddenly she threw

him one sharp look over her shoulder. He sighed, and boosted the child from his lap. "Run along and play with the others now. I'll have to get back to work presently. Mrs. Russell," he said when Carrie had gone, "you'd do me a kindness if you didn't try to speak to Mrs. Weaver on that subject. I suppose I oughtn't to have brought it up."

"I'm sorry, I don't understand."

"Nor do I, entirely. Only we disagree over what should and shouldn't be told." He tipped his hat and stood, and shortly thereafter he and Mr. Quigley went back to whatever work they had in the field that day.

The sun crawled steadily westward while people had second helpings of fowl or moved on to cake and fruit. She sometimes spoke to the people near her, sometimes settled back to watch others speak. Mr. Mirkwood came down from the roof again and played at boxing with some of the boys. Mr. Atkins told a story, with goats and giants, to three small children and the eldest Weaver girl. A ball of sorts was brought out from somewhere and even Mr. Granville was dragged from his place to join the children and the younger men in kicking it about.

Martha patted baby Job, who'd finally found his way to her shoulder and into sleep. She and the other women sat in peaceful silence as the shouts and laughter of the ballplayers rang out over the field. Repeatedly, though, her sidelong glance went to Mrs. Weaver. For the husband's sake, she said nothing that even remotely referenced the forbidden topic. But it clung like a cobweb at the back of her brain.

*E*ARLY THAT evening she ventured to Mrs. Kearney's room. Irregular. One ought to summon a housekeeper to the drawing room, and leave her the sanctity of her own chamber. Nevertheless here she was.

The woman was busy with silk thread and a small hook, making lace, she said, for a family christening gown. Martha admired the intricate pattern of loops, and insisted she keep on with her work as they spoke.

Another chair sat opposite Mrs. Kearney's, so she sank into it. Light still shone through the window, burnishing metal surfaces—a mirror, the ring round a clock face on the mantel, a silver tray with tea things at the housekeeper's side—and warming the autumn-colored carpet beneath them. She took a breath. "I've met someone who once worked in this house, so I'm told." Her hands folded together in her lap. "I wonder if you will have any memory of her."

"There've been so many come and gone." Still plying her lace hook, the woman sent a quick glance to the row of ledgers on a shelf along the wall, testimony to all her time at Seton Park. "But perhaps. Did she say when she worked here?"

"I'm afraid I didn't speak to her at all on the subject. Her husband is the one who mentioned it. But they have a daughter of fifteen or sixteen, so it must be at least that long since."

She could see Mrs. Kearney striking a slew of names from her list of possible answers. The housekeeper pursed her mouth, and looked up. "Where did you meet her?"

"On the property just east. They're laborers there. I don't know what would have been her name, but she married a Mr. Weaver, and her Christian name is Livia, or perhaps Olivia."

Mrs. Kearney was nodding already. "That's one of the two." She hooked another tiny loop of thread. "One of the two as was ruined. The other went to London and never came back, but she stayed in the country where she'd grown up."

Yes. This was the suspicion that had chattered in some

dark corner of her thoughts. She hadn't yet allowed it into the light. Her fingers flexed, and tangled with one another. "Does her husband know?"

"That he does." Another nod, as her hands worked steadily on. "He'd known her from a girl, and loved her nearly that long, I suppose. But once she got a post here, it should have been a comedown for her to marry a farmer's son."

"I can't blame her for that." Odd, this compulsion to defend a woman who surely would not welcome any such charity from her. "We're not men, with so many ways to pull themselves up in the world. A woman has a duty to make the best marriage she can."

"She was lucky to make any marriage at all, after what befell her. No one expected Mr. Weaver to renew his proposals. No one would have blamed him if he turned his back on her. But he loved her just that much."

"That's . . . commendable of him." It was something more than commendable, but she couldn't quite find the right descriptor. "Do you ever speak to her?"

"Not once in sixteen years." Mrs. Kearney sighed, and let her hands go still. The lines about her eyes looked deeper. "I never faulted her for what happened. None among the staff here did. But if I pass her now on the road or in town, she fixes her eyes straight ahead and won't know me."

Chairs and tables and tea things went hazy as the world boiled itself down to two mere words. "Sixteen years." But of course. *Dismissed all the same, because of what condition they found themselves in.* So Sheridan had said.

"Twice cursed, she was." The lace hook started up again. "Any child should have been a painful reminder of the business, I expect. But an idiot child who'll need care all her life . . ." She shook her head on an angle, and twisted her mouth. "I don't know how she bears it. I never could."

But one bore what one had to bear. *Could* never entered into the bargain. Though sometimes . . . perhaps . . . one might share out one's burden among friends and well-wishers, and feel it lightened by the sharing. One did hear of that physic as efficacious. Even for a woman so chilly and inflexible as Mrs. Weaver, sympathy might do some good.

And why stop at sympathy? "Seton Park owes reparation to that woman. We owe something to that girl." Her imprudent tongue kept pace with her thoughts. "Where Providence has failed someone, it falls to the rest of us to step into the breach." Mopping up after the failings of Providence. Wouldn't Mr. Atkins grow pale with horror if he heard her now.

So be it. Justice had a claim on her. Mrs. Weaver and her daughter had a claim to justice, long in arrears. She thanked Mrs. Kearney for the information, and took her leave. More than ever, she must find a way to keep control of the estate.

Chapter Thirteen

*S*HE MIGHT have told Mr. Mirkwood. Taking an interest in the laborer families as he did, he would probably like to know of this sad history. But when he came in that night, so taken up with what he'd learned of roofing and with the pleasures of the picnic, to burden him with dark secrets seemed cruel. Then after he'd had his satisfaction, and she her seed, he wanted to speak of the dairy project.

"The central difficulty is that I've got to make a profit." He lay on his back, arms folded behind his head, a vague shape in the moonlight. "Granville and my father won't stand for turning Pencarragh into a charitable endeavor. Though Lord knows we get income enough from our other properties, not to mention the ancient family fortune. Forgive me." His face pointed itself toward her. "I really ought *not* to mention our worth."

"Given how our acquaintance began, I believe a reference to money can be forgiven."

His hand came across murky space to tweak her nose, then receded. "If I want any custom, I've got to set my prices low. But the larger producers can effect certain economies I cannot. Cows crammed together in sheds can be kept in greater numbers than cows that roam and need so much grazing land apiece."

"Thinning the milk with water must reduce their expenses as well." They stared into the same thoughtful distance. One had a not-unpleasant inkling of how an ox in yoked partnership must feel. Or a horse in harness, pulling alongside a fellow striver.

"If the market were different, I might hope people would be willing to pay more for superior quality. But families like the Weavers haven't that luxury."

"And any family who can afford that choice will almost certainly have their own cow." There was the core of the problem. He would have a worthy product, but in the wrong place. "What you need is a pack of wealthy people who don't keep cows."

"Londoners on holiday." She could hear his enjoyment in painting the fanciful picture with her. "Can we start a fashion for jaunts to the rural middle of Sussex?"

"We'll cry up some local pond for its healing properties, and establish a spa."

"Yes, and entice the Prince Regent into visiting. Then the rest of the *ton* will follow."

"Theo." She turned to him and came up on an elbow. "The Prince Regent already comes into Sussex. The *ton* does follow."

"To Brighton." He'd caught her caravan of thought and fallen right in line. "Brighton has as many wealthy people as any merchant could wish."

"And they don't travel with cows." Her pulse quickened. "What if you were to take your products to market there—perhaps once every month or two weeks—and sell at such prices as wealthy people are accustomed to pay?"

"Then I could keep my prices low in this neighborhood." His hand lifted from the pillow and wound itself in her hair, but without any solid purpose. His attention was elsewhere. "Only it might be too much to ask of my laborers, to make that journey. I think I must talk to them. After I've talked to Granville. Perhaps after I've approached my father in regard to the capital outlay. Or no, perhaps I'd better talk to the laborers first of all. I don't know. Where had a man best begin with this sort of thing?"

Serious, conscientious, and seeking her opinion: he could have had anything he wanted of her in that moment. She pressed her lips together. Generosity demanded generosity in return. "Think on it. Sleep on it. You'll make the right choice."

She felt his pleasure as surely as though his skin were shuddering against hers. He was all but a virgin in this, the experience of being taken seriously. Perhaps no woman—perhaps no one at all—had ever gazed at him with quiet faith, and encouraged him to believe in his own abilities.

She oughtn't to touch him. She ought to let him bask in this satisfaction, and not muddle it with anything else. Nevertheless her hand rose to clasp his wrist and carefully, very carefully, she leaned in and put her lips to the crest of his forehead. Nothing more than that. "Good night, Mr. Mirkwood," she said, and turned over to go to sleep.

*S*HE WOKE the next morning to a half-empty bed. He was up already, moving about in the sluggish gray predawn. "Did I wake you?" he said, coming in from her dressing room. He must have gone to splash his face. He certainly hadn't gone to dress: he wore not a stitch. In this light his body looked like something chiseled out of marble. Somebody's statue come to life and now reaching for clothes, weary of its naked state. So different from the candlelit nakedness to which she'd grown accustomed. By candlelight he was nothing like a statue, his skin warm and vivid under that lambent illumination, and all alive with appetite as well.

"You didn't wake me." She rubbed a fist over her eyes. Thoughts were not coming quite coherently. "You do, usually, though."

"Miss that, do you?" He tossed his shirt and trousers onto the armchair and stepped into his drawers. "Then I'll be sure to not omit it tomorrow."

Of course I don't miss *it*. She didn't have to say that. He knew, and was only teasing.

She watched him dress. Gradually he covered his chiseled self, sitting in the armchair at last to pull on his boots. When that was done he came to the bedside and sank all the way down on his knees. His arms folded atop the mattress. His chin sank onto his arms. He looked at her, wordlessly.

His eyes wore the raw marks of too little sleep. His hair bent in odd directions. He needed to shave. Her hand, without awaiting her permission, strayed from the mattress and settled against his cheek, to know what that texture was like.

He turned his head and pressed his lips into her palm. Soft, unutterably soft, his kiss, where her skin tingled from the coarse touch of his tiny beard-bristles. Eyes closed, he stayed just so for several seconds, as though breathing in her hand's particular scent. "Are you at liberty this afternoon?" he then said. He caught her hand in his and laid her palm once more against his cheek.

"I expect so. Unless you've recruited more callers."

"Not yet." His cheek rasped pleasantly over her hand as he angled his head to and fro. "And today I'd like you to come pay a call with me. I've wanted you to meet another of my laborers. An older man with some expertise in dairy farming."

"Mr. Barrow. You've mentioned him before."

"Indeed." His fingers laced with hers as though he meant to keep her hand against his face forever. "He ought to be at home during the dinner hour. We might make a short visit."

"I'd like that."

"Very good then. I'll call for you." He turned her hand over and kissed her knuckles one by one. And she found she was sorry when he came to the last.

$\mathcal{I}$F SOMEONE had told him, that first day in church, the course things would take between himself and the woman across the aisle, he should have roared with laughter until he slid right out of his pew and was ejected from the premises. If he'd been told to anticipate seduction, he should have imagined himself the seducer, gradually coaxing her to loosen her stays and let down her hair and learn to give over to pleasure.

"Is he a widower, Mr. Barrow?" She marched beside him, asking such questions, methodically preparing herself to make a good impression. He knew her habits by now.

"Never married and no family living nearby. All the more reason to call." With one finger he crushed the painstaking folds of his cravat to bare his neck to the breeze on that side. A month ago his cravat was sacrosanct.

August had finally drawn to a close, and the air brought promise of cooler fall weather. He might not see much of it. The more he undertook to better things at Pencarragh, the higher he would rise in Granville's estimation and the sooner he would be deemed worthy of a return to London. That had been his goal, not so very long since.

At Mr. Barrow's cottage the geese and pig had some

sort of commotion going, from their separate pens, and the volume increased as he and Mrs. Russell passed through the gate. Uneasiness glanced up his spine, like a skipping-stone over the surface of a lake. "Is something wrong with the animals?" the widow said. Another stone, skipping in the tracks of the first.

He knocked at the door, to no answer. "He may have brought dinner with him to the field," he said. "He can't come home and find it waiting, after all." This explanation had everything of reason to it. Nevertheless his hand closed round the knob and he gave it a turn.

The door opened onto a stench so overpowering that he had to step back and put a hand to his nose. Beside him the widow gasped aloud and his arm, independent of thought, swung out like an iron bar in front of her to prevent her going any farther. God. The animals. How long since they'd been fed? "Feed the stock," he said to her in a voice he didn't recognize.

"Later, for Heaven's sake. We have to go in and find out—"

"No." She shrank from his tone, and so would he most likely have done, had he been able to hear it through the blood now pounding in his ears. "I'll go. Wait here."

She nodded once, folding her arms across her chest. Pale and rigid, she stepped aside and left him to proceed.

He breathed with his mouth, through the six strides that took him across the kitchen to the bedroom doorway, sparing himself the smell but tasting rank air all the same. He'd never been in the presence of death. He'd never breathed its scent. And maybe . . . the thought stood firm through the haze of panic . . . maybe this was not that scent. Some lower part of his brain was beginning to unplait it into more than one strand. Several scents, fetid sickroom scents, mingled together.

He stepped into the bedroom. Mr. Barrow lay unmoving, a crumpled bit of refuse under a fouled sheet. Theo looked reflexively away—what man would want to be seen in this state?—before willing his eyes back with the reminder that the man might be beyond such cares, forever. He went to the bed.

He'd been ill, Mr. Barrow had, in every way possible for a man to be ill. Too weak, apparently, to reach the chamberpot. Mother of God, how long had he lain here, unmissed and unattended? Had no fieldworker noticed his absence and thought to look in on him?

One unsteady hand went to the frail throat, feeling through papery skin for a pulse, and . . . Yes. Undeniable. He lurched suddenly to the wall to lean there, and then bent forward, hands on knees. Relief had a weight all its own, staggering as worry but infinitely more welcome.

"Theo?" She didn't sound like herself either, now he thought of it. Fearful. Tentative. Faint. Everything the widow was not.

"Stay where you are," he called. "It's not the worst—not yet, at all events. But don't come in."

Mr. Barrow stirred at his voice. Theo dropped to his knees by the bedside. The old man's lips moved, and moved again, and on the third time he finally made out the word: *water*.

For God's sake, of course. The man needed something to drink. How could he be so stupid as to need telling at all, let alone three times? He shoved to his feet and made for the kitchen. Where would a cottager keep his ale? And would ale be safe, in his condition? Perhaps cider would be gentler on a weakened constitution. Devil if he knew.

But the question was moot. There was no bottle of anything in the larder, and in the kitchen he found only an empty jug. He'd fetch water from the stream, then, and . . . boil it, or something, to make it safe to drink. So people did with tea, didn't they? Yes. He must do that.

No fire in the stove. He'd have to make one. God. He must lay a fire, go to the stream, bring back water, find some vessel in which to boil it . . . and then how long would it take to boil, and how long after that to cool to a temperature fit to drink? He must probably strain it as well, and with what? Despair reared up like a tidal wave, and he set down the jug and put a hand to his forehead.

No. Forget about the water. He'd find a doctor. Devil take him, why had he wasted even three seconds trifling about water when he ought to have gone for a doctor at once? Curse his useless, impractical soul. He was unequal to this in every way.

*T*HEO." THE longer he stayed in there, the tighter panic gripped. "Please tell me what I can do to help."

And suddenly he was there at the door, pale but determined. "He needs a doctor. I don't know where to get one."

"I do." At last, a way to be useful! "I know where to get more than one."

"Good. Run and find a boy. Tell him to go to the stable and send someone on a horse to fetch a doctor as quick as can be." He paused for breath, and she could see the effort with which he kept calm. "If any of the cottagers have cider, or very mild ale, we need some. Tell the boy to have it sent."

"Shall I instruct them to tell the doctor you'll pay? Sometimes a doctor won't come to a poor man's house."

He swore, and put his fist to his forehead, half turning away. "Have the doctor sent to my house. There can be no doubt, then. I'll move Mr. Barrow there. He ought to be removed from that room anyway."

"I'll tell the boy to have the stable send a cart." She started off.

"No." His voice stopped her like a hard curb on a horse. "I don't want him jounced. I'll carry him. I'll clean him up as best I can, and carry him to the house."

Are you mad? That must be nearly a mile. Only to herself did she say these words, and she was already running as she said them. As she'd never run in all her years, she ran, skirts caught up in both fists and boots pounding over the uneven terrain. She found a boy, a lad of twelve or so, and gave him her commission, drink and doctor both. When he'd lit out with a boy's blessed fleetness, she hurried back to the Barrow cottage, the pain of exertion biting into her side.

Mr. Mirkwood was adamant in his refusal to let her in. "He wouldn't want a lady to see him this way," he said, and that was that. But she could tend to the animals, at least. Poor hungry clamorous things. She might pick a few vegetables from the garden, and perhaps there would be bread in the kitchen, suitable for throwing in crumbs to the geese. Water to begin, though. Round back was a pail, and Mr. Mirkwood was able to tell the way to the stream. Water, vegetables, bread: to shape a plan, even one so small, and put it into execution had its usual fortifying effect. She would conquer this crisis, a task at a time.

Mrs. Weaver, apparently, would conquer it with her, for here she was scattering bread to the geese when Martha came back lugging water. "I'd be of more use in the house," the woman said in lieu of a greeting. "I'm sure he doesn't know the first thing about a sickbed, but he came and took the cider from me and insisted I stay out."

Of all the moments to finally find a speck of kinship. "He said the same to me. As though modesty would matter at a time like this. Can you keep the geese away while I pour their water?"

They worked with a comforting efficiency, getting geese and pig watered, choosing the poorest stuff in the garden to toss into the trough, until Mr. Mirkwood appeared at the door. "I've got him in a clean nightshirt and I'll take him to the house." His hat was missing, his hair half on end as though he'd been running anxious fingers through it. "I think we must burn all the bedclothes and the mattress, and open any windows we can. Is there firewood enough?"

Mrs. Weaver shook her head. "Better to launder the things. I'll look them over and see what can be salvaged."

"No." His eyes were the eyes of a stranger, resolute and terrible. "Burn them. Burn them all."

"I doubt he's got more than the one set of sheets." Resolute and terrible didn't daunt Mrs. Weaver. "I know for certain he hasn't got another mattress. Where is he to sleep if we burn everything?"

His face contorted. "I'll bring him a blasted mattress from my own blasted house." He leaned a forearm into the door frame, and his brow against his forearm. She recognized the posture from that awful day on which he'd called her a corpse. "Please just burn everything. Or if you cannot, tell me, and I'll delegate the task elsewhere."

"We can do it. I can." What was she saying? She'd never built a bonfire in her life.

"Thank you, Mrs. Russell," he said, weary and grateful, and he vanished into the house.

Well, where to begin? Somewhere downwind, and far enough from the house that sparks couldn't jump to the thatch. She must get firewood, and some tinderbox or other fire-starting tool. If luck was with her, Mrs. Weaver would take pity and join in. If not, she would manage by herself, just the way she always—

Movement in the doorway interrupted her thoughts,

and then thought scattered altogether and she stood as though staked to the spot.

Mr. Mirkwood with a sick man in his arms. She had known to expect this sight. But to expect, and to see, proved two vastly different things. Expectation did not prepare one for the details. For the ashen color of the old man's face. For his arms, slack as a baby's, laid across his chest. For the sad fluttering hem of his nightshirt. For the dreadful ease with which the younger man carried him, as though he were nothing but bones in a bag.

So had Father looked in his last months. For all that he must have been twenty years younger, he'd had this same poor diminished weight. Diminished color. Perhaps Mr. Russell, too, had worn a similar aspect, his limbs hanging limp when a farmer found him and gathered up his broken body.

Something . . . shifted . . . in her. Something sheared away, thunderous as a shelf of ice in a spring thaw. She sucked in a tremulous lungful of air and felt tears coursing down her cheeks.

Mr. Mirkwood heaved a half-step forward. "Martha." Oh, he sounded as though someone had his entrails in a clenched fist! And he made an awful mistake, using her Christian name before an onlooker. She scrubbed at her cheeks with the back of one hand, turning her face from him.

"She'll be fine." An unexpected hand on her shoulder. "It's just the shock catching up, and alarm at the sight." An unexpectedly calming, strengthening voice. "Go on. I'll help her with the fire, and she'll be fine."

She stole a glance. He nodded at Mrs. Weaver, his face reddening—too late, he'd caught the mistake—and strode off with his burden.

Dear Lord. What to say now? "I'm sorry." She pressed fists against both her eyes. "It was alarm at the sight, just as you said, and then I was put in mind of my father before he died."

"It will pass." The hand fell from her shoulder. "I'll go see what firewood we have."

"Mrs. Weaver." What in Heaven's name was she doing? She saw the words she was going to say, like stones bouncing down a steep hill, farther and farther beyond her reach as she chased after them. "I know what happened to you at Seton Park. Or rather, what was done to you. What Mr. James Russell did." With titanic effort she forced her face to pivot ninety degrees, and let her fists drop.

Mrs. Weaver stood hard and expressionless. She didn't speak.

"I'm sorry, so sorry for it."

"It's nothing to do with you." Her eyes flickered away, to the pen where the pig had finished its meal and now scratched its back along the fence.

"I mean to make you amends one day. And to prevent Mr. James Russell from ever inheriting, and coming back into this neighborhood. I will do whatever I must to prevent that."

Mrs. Weaver glared through the pig now, her brow contracting and the corners of her mouth working as she cast and recast Martha's words. Or, perhaps, as she revisited scenes from sixteen years past. "It's none of my concern, what you do," she said finally. "And as to amends, I don't know what form they could take. We'd better start the fire."

They didn't speak again of that subject, but worked in brisk concert, building the fire and dragging every grim artifact of Mr. Barrow's illness out from the house. After an hour or six of this—could she recall ever being so tired?—Mr. Mirkwood returned, more rumpled than before, to say the doctor had been and gone, and pronounced Mr. Barrow out of danger. "I didn't know whether you'd still be here," he said, "but I saw the smoke. I wanted to tell you, and to thank you both for your help and forbearance." He held out a hand to Mrs. Weaver.

She took it, eyes averted, and let it go after one brief shake. "Next time he misses even a day of work I'll send one of my boys to look in on him."

"We'll get up a system. The burden won't be entirely on your family." He turned then, to face her, and his eyes brimmed with a hundred things he couldn't say in front of Mrs. Weaver. "You're feeling better, I hope, Mrs. Russell?"

As though Mrs. Weaver would forget how he'd addressed her before. Absurdity tugged at the corners of her mouth and she brought a hand up to mask it. "Much better, thank you, Mr. Mirkwood. I hope I shall be able to meet Mr. Barrow another day."

"By all means." His eyes went to the ground between them and he was briefly silent, like a young man who'd encountered a lady he fancied and was wracking his brains for conversation. "Shall I have someone drive you home? I'd offer my own services but I think I'd best go bathe before I'm in company with anyone."

"Of course. No, I'll walk, thank you." Now she looked at the ground as well.

Bathe. If she were his wife—Heaven above, where had that thought come from?—but if she were his wife, they would go to his house together and she would attend him in his bath. On the tile or marble floor she would kneel, taking the soap from his unresisting hand, and she would scrub him while he bent his head forward, all the burdens of the day floating off. With her thumbs she would knead away every knot that care had worked into the muscles of his back. His breaths would grow looser, telling her without words what comfort she brought. And her hands would tell him how proud she was, how very proud, of all he'd done and been today.

Nothing to the purpose. She would never be his wife. Even should she come to wish for that, and he to wish it too, it could not be. The safety of Seton Park depended on her child—however she procured one—being known as Mr. Russell's heir. Other men in their baths did not bear thinking of.

And yet one did think of it. On shaking his hand good-bye, on the long walk home, and for great swaths of the afternoon one imagined him sinking into warm water and turning lazily this way and that. His soap would be scented. Citrus, probably, or one of those musk-like smells men favored. His hair would curl more than usual in the steamy air. In water he would be naked yet a different way. Not like marble, nor warmed by flame, but subtle and obscured. Leaving parts to the imagination. One would admire the vague sum of him, and wait for the moment when he must rise into plain air.

He would grip the sides of the bath when that moment came, and unfold to his full height. Water would sluice off him. It would trickle from his hair, drops dancing in the sunlight that would just then happen to flood the room. And his eyes would come, unerringly, to the woman who watched.

In the library she pictured this, a forgotten book open on her lap. Over supper, as she speared peas on the tines of her fork. And in her bedroom, in broad brazen daylight, and again when she retired, she lingered over every lush detail of the scene to repeated and shattering satisfaction.

What had the Romans been thinking, with their Venus? Love ought to have been a man, tall and broad and glistening as he broke the surface, not to drift about on an insipid clamshell as the painters had it, but to stride under his own power out of the waves up onto land, the ocean's bounty made manifest for every woman in a fifty-mile radius.

One had things to do. One had a hundred and five more productive ways to spend time than in sinful reverie. But it wasn't altogether sinful. Images of a love-god rising from the sea gave way, and then somehow conflated themselves with the memory of Mr. Mirkwood as he stood on that cottage threshold, muscled arms tenderly cradling a fragile old man. He'd never looked so powerful. So capable. So suffused with grace and might.

He would offer to touch her tonight. She would send signals that would prompt him to it, and when he offered, she would permit him, just for a while. He knew the right place. He knew what to do. "Don't let me lose myself," she could say, and he would know when to stop. She could trust him with that.

Then why not with the rest? The query popped unbidden from some impertinent place in her mind. Even her own brain conspired against her now. She let the question hang unanswered, and drifted back to thoughts of long limbs in water.

How was your bath?" Mrs. Russell wanted to know the moment he came in. She sat up in bed, sheet clutched carefully at her shoulders.

But he was beyond polite remarks about the petty details of his day. He strode to her, set his hands at either side of her jaw, and bent to kiss her, full on the mouth.

She was startled, clearly. She didn't shrink away, though, or even stiffen. Her mouth accommodated his, soft and steady, until he drew back for breath.

"I'm sorry to have put you through all that today." He half-knelt on the bed, one foot on the floor, hands still cupping her face. "But I'm glad you were there. You braced me up beyond telling."

"I'm glad too. You were so brave." Her hands came up to find a grip on his wrists. The sheet fell away to expose her and she didn't even notice.

"Brave? You must be joking." He tilted her face up and kissed her chin. "I was frightened nearly out of my wits."

"Yes." Her grave dark eyes watched him on a downslant. "Frightened, and so brave. I was proud of you."

"Enough of this." He pulled away and started on his buttons. "Let's see to your seed, and then I'd like to hear your opinion of a new idea I've had."

The seed changed hands with more dispatch even than usual. She helped, sweet generous woman, arching against him and tangling her fingers in his hair. But then she always had liked it to go quickly. Willingly he obliged her, charging to his crisis with a haste of which he would surely be embarrassed, had his partner been anyone but Mrs. Russell.

"Now it's your turn to be pleased," he said afterward, stretching out beside her. "I've had a thought as to the financing of this dairy scheme."

"Dairy scheme." He hadn't stopped to put out the candles, and he could see by her expression he'd taken her aback.

"I told you I wanted your opinion of an idea, recall? But perhaps you're worn out from your exertions of the day. I can wait until morning if you like."

"No . . ." Her lips compressed for a moment. Her whole face went fierce with concentration, like a drover trying to get a hundred head of oxen to change direction. "No, I would like very much to hear your idea. Is it a new argument by which to persuade your father?"

"In part, yes, because it will reduce his share of the expense. I think of seeking investors."

"Investors." She slipped her hand beneath her cheek,

propping her head partway up. Here came the eager curiosity a man could learn to crave. "As people invest in a merchant vessel, do you mean, and take a share of the profits?"

"Precisely. It's long since time I called on some of the neighborhood's better families anyway. If I could fix them with a stake in the venture's success, then I expect they'd be inclined to direct any cowless tenants to buy from us. Perhaps to buy from us themselves, if we were to produce some special variety of cheese, or any other thing not readily available."

"Emphasize the aspect of benefiting our poorer neighbors. Particularly if you're speaking to ladies." She'd got all her oxen turned the right way now, and all the force of her attention was on him. "That will be more palatable than if you were to frame it only in terms of commerce. Speak of the hard work involved, and how that will promote virtue among the laborers."

"Virtue. By all means."

"And have you thought of making your shares small? That way your wealthy investors could buy a dozen or more, while even a person of modest means might buy one, and feel that same sense of stake in your success. Your dairy could have champions in every house in the neighborhood." But no better champion, ever, than the one who lay facing him, her eyes warm with the satisfaction of wrestling a cloud-castle down onto solid ground.

Lucky the man who persuaded her to remarry. He could go through life forging one nebulous idea after the next, and know that she would hammer each one into practical shape.

His hand reached across the pillow, and two fingertips brushed over her smooth cheek. "I'll miss this, you know. When I've gone back to London." To say these words aloud periodically—to remind himself he must go back—made a worthy exercise in discipline. "This business of planning and talking. It's not a way I ever thought to spend my time in bed. But I'll miss it all the same."

He made her glow. Were he just meeting her, he would mistake her flush of incandescence for carnal invitation. And he would proceed, and be hauled up short for his mistake.

Instead he brought his fingertips back to touch his own lips, then hers. A chaste goodnight, absurd between a man and his mistress, preposterous between a woman and her hired stud, but suitable, perhaps, for two ill-matched strangers who'd improbably found their way to friendship.

Chapter Fourteen

*Y*OU'RE SURE she knew what it meant, him calling you by that name?" Sheridan sat at the dressing-table, paging through a book of plates that showed mourning attire for fall and winter weather.

"She certainly knew it meant something improper, and I as good as told her the rest. I said I meant to keep Mr. James Russell from inheriting." Martha paced to the bay window and set her palm against a warm pane of glass. Not so warm as it had been one month since. "We must hope she desires that outcome as well."

"Living on the next property, all this time!" One could picture the maid shaking her head. "Mrs. Kearney never said a thing."

"I commend her discretion." She turned, letting her hand fall from the window. "Do you know, Sheridan, for as unsavory as the last few weeks may have been, I've seen so much of noble nature in all the people about me. Mr. Keene, for example. I had a most gracious letter from him only this morning, assuring me he's working to dissuade Mr. James Russell's visit. Why should he go to the trouble? He scarcely knows me. It's a kindness beyond anything I could expect."

"Do you think he may succeed in preventing the visit?" Sheridan used a narrow slip of paper to mark one page as she flipped to the next.

"I begin to hope he may." She paced again to the room's other end, her restless hand trailing over the wallpaper. "If an heir presumptive were truly concerned with the prospect of a widow's defrauding him, he would come in the first month, wouldn't he, to hinder her effecting the sort of scheme I've been about."

"Or he might come at confinement, as you said before, to hinder you in other schemes."

"True. But that gives Mr. Keene more months to work upon him." With one finger she stirred a tray of little-worn jewels that sat on the table. "I can't help but be hopeful. So many things have been aligning themselves with my wishes of late."

The girl's eyes rose briefly to hers, and fell again to the book. "You're keeping watch of the calendar, I suppose?" She spoke in low, tentative tones, as though unsure of whether she ought to broach the subject.

"I'm trying to think of anything else." Martha speared an agate ring and turned it round twice on her finger. "Today makes four weeks since the start of my last courses." She needn't say so aloud. An abigail knew the mistress's private business as well as she knew her own.

"Does Mr. Mirkwood know?" Sheridan turned a page without marking it.

"Not the exact date. But it's been three weeks and a half now since he began calling. He must have some idea."

"Will he say anything, do you suppose? Or will he wait for you to tell him he needn't call anymore?"

Here was something else from which her imagination shrank. The way their bargain would end. She tapped a fingernail against the agate and finally shook her head. "I'm long past attempting to predict what Mr. Mirkwood will do." In one motion she stripped off the ring and cast it back on the tray, where it pirouetted on end for several seconds before clattering down flat. "Now, must you mark so many plates? You know I only want two gowns and a spencer, the plainest possible."

MR. Barrow owes his life to you, I don't doubt." Granville sat with his hands folded on the table before him, his tea and toast sadly neglected. "I shall see that Sir Frederick hears of it."

Theo spooned raspberry jam from the pot to his own toast. "He owes his life to sheer luck. I cannot now look back on that picnic with anything but shame, knowing he lay so unwell not a half-mile off while we enjoyed ourselves in light pursuits."

"I bear that shame as well." Sun slanted into the breakfast parlor, bathing the agent in mellow light. "Management is a new undertaking to you, but it's my profession. I ought to have known what was his condition."

"In future you shall." With a butterknife he spread the jam to all corners of his toast. "I mean to work up some scheme by which the other laborer families will look in on him, if he ever falls ill again, and keep you apprised. Certainly I cannot afford to lose him just now." His blood hummed and tingled as though tiny benevolent hornets were racing through his body. The moment had come. "I've had an idea for a new use to make of this land, and I shall be wanting his expertise nearly as much as I'll be wanting yours."

Granville was all attention. He sat forward in his chair and listened, plucking out his ever-present pencil to take down a note or two. He agreed as to the pitiable condition of milk and butter available for local purchase. He opined that all but the wealthiest wheat-farmers would always be at a disadvantage, not having the option to hold back their grain and wait for prices to rise. He nodded thoughtfully over the idea of selling in Brighton, though he cautioned they must ascertain what sort of products were already brought to market there. And at the bit about investors, he immediately wanted to make columns of numbers, working out what would be the cost of a share and how soon a shareholder might expect to see some income.

"I think of five and twenty cattle to start, and two bulls, and I'd hope to pay no more than eight pounds a head." His spoon tapped deftly round the shell of his egg, a pleasing industrious sound to go with the agent's scratching pencil and murmured calculations. "We might purchase at the fair in East Grinstead come December, though I understand most of the cattle there are brought from Wales. I rather like the sound of these cows from Jersey: good milk-producers, and small, so they won't need as much fodder as your larger breeds."

Granville put down his pencil and sat back. "Well." Finally he picked up his tea. "You *have* been studying on the subject, haven't you?"

Theo took off the top of his egg and spooned out a bite. "Mrs. Russell's steward—the fellow who got me started with the thatching—has been helpful. And I've acquired a few documents. I don't doubt my father will have a hundred questions, when I ask him to advance this money, and I'd like to be prepared with as many answers as I can."

"I won't discourage you from educating yourself." The agent sipped more tea and set down his cup. "However you won't need to persuade Sir Frederick of anything. When he arranged your stay here, he authorized releasing a certain amount of money in support of any such schemes you might conceive."

"He did?" His spoon stopped, suspended halfway between his mouth and the plate. "He never said anything to me."

"No, and he asked me not to broach it either. He didn't want you looking for a way to spend the money. He preferred that the idea come first, the financing after."

"Good Lord." Silver clinked on china as he set the spoon down. "What on earth gave him the notion I would ever come up with any scheme?"

Granville lifted one shoulder, the suggestion of a smile just visible on his lips. "He's had six and twenty years to observe you. He must have formed some idea of your capabilities."

"Good Lord," he said again. Beyond the agent, dust motes swirled idly in a sunbeam, inviting a man to drift away in thought. He would have laid money he knew exactly what Sir Frederick thought of his capabilities. Indeed he would have concurred with the assessment. Even now his father's good opinion—if such it was—felt odd and ill-fitted, like a borrowed coat.

A coat borrowed from a woman, at that. None of this would have happened without the influence of Mrs. Russell. Would it? He might have wished, vaguely, for people to live a more comfortable life on his land, but he would never have applied himself to bettering their state. Would he?

"In fact you have funds enough at your disposal to forgo the investors altogether." Granville sawed his toast into strips, his appetite at last making an appearance now Theo's had been forgot. "But I confess I like the idea too much to recommend your dropping it. It strikes me as characteristic of the kind of landowner you will be."

For an instant he wanted to laugh. Then the instant passed. There was nothing ludicrous, after all, in his being thought a certain kind of landowner. The kind who knew how to weave disparate interests together to make something for the benefit of all. He did, perhaps, have that talent.

"Then let me try your opinion on another possible use for Sir Frederick's funds." He reached for his tea. "The Reverend Mr. Atkins of Seton Park has spoken to me of the school he's starting. What do you think of encouraging our laborers to send their children to him?"

*M*ORE CALLERS came. The magistrate Mr. Rivers and his wife that afternoon; a Miss and Mrs. Landers the next. The calls were of a proper duration, and the conversation just what it ought to be. Everyone approved Mr. Mirkwood's benevolent aims. Everyone was pleased to know her. They insisted—such unsuspected kindness— that she must send to them for help with tenants, or servants, or any other matters difficult for a young lady to manage on her own. All but strangers until Mr. Mirkwood had rousted them out, they were true neighbors of a sudden, ready to look out for her interest in the name of duty and, perhaps, something more.

"I've never known a man to promote affection the way you do," she said to him the night after the Landers ladies had called. "Not only toward yourself, I mean, but among people generally. I think this will be a better community for your having come." Again she hadn't sent the right signals, and he'd gone to his satisfaction alone. Likely he'd long since given up hope of bringing her with him.

"Go back to the bit about my promoting affection toward myself." He lay beside her, sated, his hands absently plaiting a lock of her hair. "Do I do that, indeed?"

"Of course you do. Everyone who's called has spoken of you so graciously. They're fond of you already." Coward. That was neither what he wanted to hear, nor what she truly wanted to say.

You have not known him four weeks. Any feelings a lady might develop for a gentleman in that span can only be illusory. The admonition had truth behind it, and still, what but affection could make her wish she might say words more gratifying to them both?

Touch me, she might say. *Promote what feelings you will.* The signals weren't working, and she wouldn't have many more opportunities. Thirty days now since the start of her last courses. Not unprecedented. Failure could announce itself at any time. Enough days without failure, too, would signal the end of their relation.

She closed her eyes, bringing on a citrus-scented darkness with starlike pinpoints of pleasure: the thousand tiny tugs to her scalp as he laid her strands of hair over and over each other. Occasionally his fingertips came in accidental, exquisite contact with her skin.

Touch me. Tongue to the back of her top teeth would be the beginning. She could even say it with her eyes closed if she wished.

"You'll come tomorrow, won't you?" Of a sudden his hands left her hair. "When I meet with the laborers? I've asked Granville to be there and I'd like your presence as well, since you've been in on the thing from the start." When she opened her eyes she saw him up on his elbows, regarding her as though he meant to will her into attendance.

Such absurd torment: never did he tempt her so strongly as when he forgot to be libidinous, and turned all his earnest attention on some responsibility or another. But she must follow his worthy lead, and let other thoughts go. "Of course I'll come," she said. "I wouldn't dream of missing it."

*T*HE FACT is, I know nothing of dairies but what I've read, or heard from others." Theo sat at the head of his immense dining-room table, elbows on the tabletop and hands shaping the air as seemed appropriate to accompany his words. To stand would probably have lent him a more suitable air of command, but to sit this way encouraged his listeners to be at ease. "Also we must bear in mind that I shan't be here to oversee things. I hope, at some point, to make my home in London again." He gave a quick smile to Granville, at the table's foot. Exile did take on a different cast, now he knew his father had put money aside in expectation of his turning out well. "Therefore the success of this venture will not be in my hands, but in all of yours. That being the case, I should like to hear what you all think of it. No deference, please. If you find it a harebrained scheme you must say so. Mr. Barrow to begin."

He picked up his tea and sat back. At his right hand Mr. Barrow sat in an armchair brought from the drawing room, a counterpane over his shoulders. Not entirely recovered yet, but nearer every day.

Beyond the old man, who began to speak now of various dairy methods, he had a clear view of the far corner where Mrs. Russell perched in a second conscripted armchair. She'd declined a place at the table, preferring to observe from the periphery. She watched with keen attention, hands folded in her lap, back straight as a fireplace poker. Not really an armchair sort of woman, the widow.

Three weeks ago—hell, even two—he would not have recognized how she was enjoying herself. Her pleasure didn't look like the pleasure of any other woman he knew. Well, sometimes it did. She'd taken unreserved delight in her callers, if one could judge by her manner on later recounting the visits to him.

"Have you thought of keeping a she-ass or two, in addition to the cows?" Mrs. Rowlandson said, drawing his attention back to the table. "Their milk is the best thing for sickly children, or motherless children, and I don't believe we have any at all kept in the neighborhood."

"There, now; I knew I had something to gain by including the ladies." He set his elbows on the table and leaned forward again. "I've never heard of this. Will you tell me more?" From the corner of his eye he could see Mrs. Russell following the exchange. Had he harbored thoughts of her likely approval, in deciding to invite the laborers' wives? Perhaps. And he wouldn't be sorry for that. How could he be sorry for anything, watching a roomful of humble people gradually claim their own consequence?

$\mathcal{M}$ARTHA SAT all the straighter, her posture sufficing for her and Mr. Mirkwood both. If he had asked, she would have told him not to sit so. Elbows on the table. Back and then forward in his chair, hands flourishing about as though he sat at a club among his fellows, debating the best way to style a cravat. She would have told him authority wore a cloak of cool decorum.

And she would have been wrong.

When had he become this man, as easy about command as though he were born to it? He gave respect in extravagant handfuls, never fearing he might diminish his own store—and indeed he did not. The more he deferred to the expertise of others, the farther they would follow him down any path. One could see that in the way people stepped up to undertake this or that part of his plan. Mr. Quigley and Mr. Weaver would drive to Brighton to survey the market there. Mr. Tinker would write to a drover cousin, investigating where to acquire the Jersey cows. And several of the wives already had ideas as to the best cheese varieties to produce.

He was in prodigious good spirits as the meeting

ended, and would undoubtedly have come to speak to her but that he was waylaid by Mrs. Weaver, of all people. The woman put out her hand to him and said something to which he listened, grave-faced, before delivering his answer with a smile and a shake of his head.

"What did Mrs. Weaver have to say?" she must ask when he finally cleared a gauntlet of handshakes and well-wishes to arrive at her side. One couldn't help remembering the woman's all-but-certain knowledge of how things stood between them.

"Oh, nothing very much." His happiness had a charge she could feel, as though he were a tree where lightning had struck and stayed to race through the branches. "We had a misunderstanding, early in my stay here, but we've put it to rights. Some other time I'll give you the details. Just now I'll see you home if you like, and you can tell me on the way what you thought of everything."

And yes. That was exactly what she would like.

*O*H, BUT the meeting had gone well. No one had thought his plan ridiculous, and what was more, he'd known they wouldn't. This management business was not beyond him, after all. Nothing, perhaps, was beyond him today.

With a stride that could cross subcontinents, he left the house behind. Mrs. Russell kept pace at his side, stealing looks at him in what she must suppose was a surreptitious way. "What is it?" he finally had to ask, turning to face her square. "Why do you look at me as though I've suddenly grown a second head?"

For all her attempts to be furtive, she did not look away now. "You're a leader of men, Mirkwood. I should never have guessed it."

They were the most thrilling words a woman had ever said to him. What suitable answer could he possibly give? He laughed and shook his head, lengthening his stride to pull a bit in front. "If so, I've only just become one. So there wouldn't have been any way for you to guess."

"No, I think you always have been." Her own step quickened. She wouldn't be left behind. "You only wanted the proper field on which to show it."

Now *that* was the most thrilling thing he'd ever heard from a woman. His head felt light and his legs unsteady: who'd have known a man could get drunk on a lady's good opinion?

The wooded path loomed up before them and as soon as they were under cover he reached for her. He would tell her, without flimsy words, how very much he—

"Please don't." She twisted and slipped from his grasp. "Not where we might be seen."

"Where we won't, then." *For the love of reason, don't make me wait until tonight.* "Is the bed still made up in that blue room, do you suppose?"

She glanced down his body as though to gauge the urgency of the question. Her glance skittered away. Urgency in spades.

Miraculously, then, she nodded. "I've nothing else planned today. Would you like to come for a visit?"

"You've had a look. What do you think I'd like?"

More miraculously yet, she smiled, a delicious, secret-keeping smile, and walked on without a word, leaving him to follow.

*W*ITH DISPATCH that would put a lady's maid to shame he got her down to her stockings and chemise, but he lingered in undressing her hair. She enjoyed that—any man could see—so he gave her a good long while of it, unwinding every plait and combing through the tresses with his fingers. He'd sat her in the middle of the bedroom, on the stool he'd brought in from her dressing room, and he could see her serene, shut-eyed reflection in two different mirrors. His reflection as well. A nearly unclothed woman and a man with intentions for her, the tableau warmed and gilded by a handsbreadth of afternoon light.

He flicked his wrist, and a hairpin skipped and settled on a distant tabletop, its delicate percussion a garnish to the moment's languorous mood. "I'd like to see you with your cap off under full sun," he murmured, soft enough that she could take the words for indistinct music if she preferred. "All those plaits bound up, glowing in facets like honey in a cut-glass jar. And then, let down, like honey poured out."

"You needn't seduce me with compliments, you know." She was smiling, eyes still closed. "I've already given my consent."

"Consent doesn't preclude seduction. What a lot you have to learn." He worked his fingers in at her hair's roots, massaging her scalp. "Shall I teach you something new today?"

"Yes." Susceptible girl. What wouldn't she agree to, with his hands in her hair?

"I advise you to ask what I intend before agreeing to it. Or at least to stipulate a few things you will not do."

"I don't have to." Her eyes opened, their irises like fresh-turned earth, and found his in the mirror. "I trust you, Mirkwood." And no woman, ever, would say any words more thrilling to him than those.

As though he had all the time in the world—perhaps he did—Mr. Mirkwood drew his hands from the roots of her hair to its ends, letting the locks fall in shiver-inducing caresses against her neck. Then he walked deliberately away from her and sat down in the arm-chair.

He would ask her to do something. She would say *yes*. He might like to command her, and she might say yes to that too.

His head slanted a bit to one side, considering her as he would a courtesan hired for his entertainment. He sank back in the chair, his hands light on its armrests. One finger drummed speculatively. "Take off your stockings," he said.

Yes. She bent forward and felt for the first garter.

"Not like that." His voice floated, soft and dusky, across the room to where she sat. "Turn profile to me. Lift your foot up before you. Ease the stocking down slowly, and look at me while you do it."

Like a courtesan, indeed. She turned profile. "Your wife will never be bored."

"Don't mention my wife. You'll make me feel unfaith-ful."

"Unfaithful to a wife with whom you're not yet ac-quainted?" The garter, untied, fell loose about her thigh and she pushed her stocking down.

"Unfaithful to you both. A little slower, if you please."

She crept the stocking down her calf while he watched, a lascivious smile playing on his lips. Doubtless he'd en-acted this same scene with more women than he could count—but she wouldn't think of that. The stocking slithered over her toes and off. She folded it loosely and tossed it to him.

His grin spread into something wolfish. "I knew you'd be good at this. Now the second one, please."

He confounded her from the inside out, directing her in lewdness and peppering the commands with *please*. One couldn't be sure, moment to moment, of who ex-actly was in charge.

"Throw me that one too." He snatched the second stocking out of the air one-handed. Then he got up and went to the bed, where he laid both stockings across a pillow.

For the first time her pulse quickened. He might have things in mind to which she would not be equal. "What do you intend to do with those?" She folded her arms across her chest.

"I? Nothing." He turned and faced her, already busy with his cravat. His eyes shone dark and shameless. "You, however, will use them to tie my wrists to the headboard before having your way with me."

For an instant she felt as though someone had flipped her skin raw side out: she was one furious blush head to toe. Did men really . . . And how was she to . . . No. No. This was not a thing she cared to do. She rose to her feet, arms clamped about her ribs in the posture of intransigence. "You must have me confused with some more adventurous lady."

"I don't think so." The cravat fell unheeded to the floor. "Consider a moment, darling." He tugged his shirt free of his trousers. "I won't be able to do anything you don't approve, will I?" The shirt went over his head. "I'll be entirely in your power."

Curse his handsome shirtless self. He didn't doubt for an instant she would comply. And curse her for having agreed to something new.

Refuse him. Tell him to suggest something else. He'll understand. But stubbornness rose up in strange moments these days, and now it had hold of her tongue. "That doesn't sound very . . . diverting for you," was all the demurral she could make.

"Oh, Mrs. Russell, you'd be surprised at what diverts me." He'd sat down on the bed to pull off his boots. "Come here and let me show you how to make the knots."

He showed her—one didn't like to ask where he'd acquired the knowledge—the sequence of loops and twists
round one carved mahogany spindle, and left her to tie
the second while he shed his trousers. "Now," he said,
and she felt the mattress dip as he climbed onto the bed
behind her, "you'll do those same knots at my wrists.
Not too tight. Not too loose." With the grace of a
prowling animal he crawled to the bed's middle. He
lowered his body to the sheets and turned over, arms
snaking up above his head.

She looped the stockings one at a time round his wrists
and knotted them. This was madness. For all that he
was naked and bound, he didn't look compliant in the
least. His arm-muscles alone were a taunt to her puny
soft hands. He lay before her like some creature of cata-
strophic power, something she ought to have thought
twice about capturing. "Take off your chemise," he said
as soon as she'd secured him, and there was nothing of
entreaty in his voice.

But her stockings held him fast. She need only obey if
she wished to. Did she wish to? Yes. She stripped off the
garment and dropped it to the floor.

"Good." He drank in her nakedness, fervent as a man
downing ale after three days in the desert. His eyes,
gleaming with unholy intention, came to rest on hers.
"Now fuck me."

The command knocked her back like a handful of
dust in the face. But only for a moment. He was the one
tied up. She folded her arms again. "If you want my
cooperation you had better address me more politely
than that."

"Fuck me." Like the world's wickedest elocution pupil he articulated the words, lips and tongue and teeth
put to such nefarious use. "Fuck me until I thrash and
shout beneath you."

"It was shocking the first time. It's not shocking now."

"Fuck me like the whore I am."

"That's not shocking either." Heaven help her, there was some pleasure in this. In resisting him so. "And I told you your role is closer to that of a stud animal."

"Indulge me this once." His whole body twisted and roiled, serpent-like. "Let me be your whore if I want to be."

Let me. "You mean that as a command, I suppose." She loosened her arms and touched one finger to his near hip bone.

"Always. Use me, Martha." His voice invited her into unspeakable things. "Ride me until you've got your seed, and then take your pleasure from my mouth."

Well. Apparently not unspeakable, to him. And not, after all, too terribly distressing. The deeper he went into iniquity, the greater one's reserves of mulish aplomb.

"You're considering, aren't you?" Hopeful to the last, Mr. Mirkwood. "You're imagining how it would be. You've got me captive." He flexed his hands to remind her. "You could keep me at it all afternoon if you liked. And grip onto the headboard for balance when the sensations grew too strong."

"I'm *reconsidering,* in fact." Without haste she trailed her finger over the hip bone, into the adjacent hollow and among his coarse curling hairs. "I don't believe I would have agreed to restrain you, if I'd known you would take it as license to be so wicked."

"Wicked, to be sure." He repeated the word as though tasting it, his gaze now following her finger's progress. "Perhaps you'd better punish me."

Good Lord, what next? "Punish you, indeed." She advanced her finger just to the base of his erection and stopped. "Suppose I were to walk out of this room and leave you here alone until you remembered your decency. Would that be punishment enough?"

He smiled as though he were teaching her chess and

she'd just made a clever move. "Maybe." His eyes came to her face, and wandered in leisurely, thorough fashion down her body and back to her still finger. "Or maybe you ought to touch yourself. Pleasure yourself, and force me to watch."

"Now I know beyond question that you've confused me with someone else." Aplomb had company: his every shameless utterance was waking strange—or not so strange—sensations that spiraled from her core on out. "And I doubt you'd take it as punishment, quite."

"Darling, I would take it as *torture*." Again he twisted against his bonds, so much power at her mercy. "Because you'd taunt me with it, wouldn't you? You'd place yourself where I could nearly reach you. And you'd say things to inflame me, but never touch me at all. I'd have to lie here helpless, watching you give yourself what you won't take from me." He sucked in a breath. "Start now, if you would."

What a dreadful man he was, all intemperate appetites and no decorum to speak of. And what foolish affection she felt for his libidinous excess. She skimmed her finger, and a second and a third, up the length of his appendage while he watched, eyes narrowing at the sensation. "No," she said. Her hands went to the pillow at either side of his tied-back arms. She let him see her poised above him for a second or two. Then she bent her elbows and brought her mouth to his.

HELL AND damnation. She'd never kissed him before. On the forehead, once. But never for pleasure—and whose pleasure was she about? No matter. No matter. Her lips brushed over his and he lay back to take it. Even without the use of his hands, he might have gained control of this kiss; might have led her through it as through a dance. Not today, though. Today he'd see where they went if she had the lead.

Her mouth was small on his. Her lips were careful and her breath was warm. His pleasure. Almost certainly. She went meticulously along his lower lip, giving attention to every fraction of an inch in light touches and delicate strokes. His mouth softened for her. *Invite. Don't demand.* He let his lips part, just the width of a suggestion, and—like a sunbeam through London fog—felt the sweet trespass of her tongue.

A shiver surged through him. Her lips pulled taut as their corners ticked up. Her right hand left the pillow to feel its way to his nipple and torment him there.

Too much. He had to have his hands on her. "I've changed my mind," he said against her mouth. "Untie me."

She lifted her head enough to look into his eyes. Every inch the terrible uncloaked fairy, at last. "No," she said, and bent to kiss him again.

Devil take her. She enjoyed this. She relished the spectacle of his thwarted desire. With one hand he scrabbled at the knots on the spindle. He'd free himself without her help, and then she'd see—

"No." Her fingers closed about his wrist. "This was your idea. You've no one to blame but yourself." She gazed down at him like a governess out of someone's perverse boyhood fantasies, not to say his. "Perhaps next time you'll think twice before proposing such sport."

Good God. She was enjoying this indeed. She'd had to shift up to grasp his wrist and he could see now, not twelve inches from his mouth, where her nipples swayed, ripe and heavy as fruit ready for tasting. He could—no. Not yet. "Go on, then." He let the words drift lazily through the air between them. "Do what you will to me."

She let go his wrist. Her fingertips skated down the length of his arm to his shoulder, then slipped off to find purchase in the pillow. She knelt at his left side; now her left knee went up and over to straddle him. His breaths were shallow. His heart pummeled his chest like a sparring partner with a twenty-pound advantage. What was the matter with him? Breathless as a virgin bridegroom when he'd possessed this woman how many times?

Well, zero, to be exact. For all the times he'd spilled seed in her, he'd never yet possessed her. That was the matter.

Her eyes fixed to his, she felt down his belly with one hand and closed her fingers round the base of his cock. She held it steady and—thanks be to whatever divinity had put her in this mood today—eased herself down onto him, her soft parts yielding magnificently, embracing him with a warmth and wetness he'd once expected from a woman and would never, never take for granted again.

He breathed in. Breathed out. Held her steady gaze.

"You want me," he whispered.

"Yes," she said.

𝒮HE COULD still say *no*. One could go partway down the path and pull up. Almost certainly she *would* do that, in fact, because without help from his fingers, no other outcome was likely. She took her hand from his appendage—his manhood—and put both palms to the mattress, feeling for the proper balance. This wasn't . . . was it like this for him? Surely the fit didn't feel so precarious when he was on top.

"Is something the matter?" Her eyes had left his, to watch her hands place themselves, but he apparently had nowhere else to look.

"It's only . . . I don't see how . . ." Assurance leaked away like air out of a balloon. A crude ungainly vision was coming clear, her naked body bouncing away atop his and losing the appendage more times than not. "The angles are all wrong."

"Not wrong. Just different." His voice was impossibly gentle, as though to stand in for the reassuring caress he could not deliver. His face, if one could bear to look at it, would probably radiate kind understanding. "Would you like me to close my eyes?"

Yes. "No." One did not give in to craven cowardice. And half his enjoyment was in seeing things; she would not take that away.

"I'd like to, just for a minute or so. For novelty." Piece by piece, he burned through what was left of her resistance. He closed his eyes indeed, and the strong, patient lines of his face touched her resolve like a candle flame held to so much cheap paper.

She moved. She would show her gratitude by making a mission of his pleasure. The angle wasn't so difficult, once one got accustomed. She might not look altogether ungainly. And he helped, thrusting up to meet her, showing her the pace and depth he liked best.

Use me, he'd said. Her body took what it could from the long strokes of his manhood, and clamored for more. His mouth. His hands. His scalding gaze, at the very least. She took a breath. "Mirkwood. Open your eyes."

His eyes opened. He knew just what she wanted, and he gave it. If eyes could devour a person there'd be nothing left of her but a cracked bone or two. She sat up straighter, that he might see right down to the scattering of curls, feral and primitive and private, where her body joined his. She would hide nothing from him.

"Martha." Her name *was* music—dark, voluptuous music—the way he said it. His arms strained, every minute forgetting their bonds. "Martha, put your hands on yourself. Touch your nipples."

She set a hand on her shoulder and trailed her fingers down . . . and no. She wasn't his puppet. What was the good of a man in one's bed if one had to see to oneself? "No," she said aloud. In one surge of motion she leaned down to him, palming up her breast. "Take it in your mouth."

A groan tore out of him as his head whipped up from the pillow to obey. Good. She'd pleased him. Now he could please her.

Oh, and he did. He roughed her nipple with the flat of his tongue, and teased her with the tip, and nothing in the world mattered but that he keep on. Chains of fire ran from where his mouth worked her to where his manhood—his cock—filled her up. She drove down onto him, her hands leaving the mattress to grip the spindles where he was tied, her fingers willfully entangling with his own.

"Martha," he gasped. The nipple slipped from his mouth and his head fell back. "Untie me now."

Now? She panted, stupidly, struggling to bring him into focus.

"The seed." His face contorted. "You need to be on your back."

Yes. Yes. She did. With a great effort she wrenched herself off of him—he sucked in a tortured breath through his teeth—and pulled at the first knot.

"Quickly," he said. The first wrist came free. Before she could reach the second he was on it himself, fingers laboring with fiery intent. Then that stocking too fell loose, and he used both arms to roll her beneath him, and pushed into her again.

He kept his strokes shallow, as though holding himself back. His hand, no longer captive, found its way down to where their bodies joined and his fingers made splendid mischief there. His face was all watchful, ravenous, half-unbelieving hope.

"Yes," she said, that he might have no more doubt. She tipped back her head, pressed her arms and shoulders into the mattress, and arched her hips, twisting, to chase the touch of his fingers, to urge on his cock. His rhythm was going ragged, his breaths were all gasp and pant; dimly they came to her through the heedless sounds her own mouth made—and she saw him naked above her, and she saw him dressed at his dining table, graceful leader of men. She turned her head then, and bit into a corner of her pillow as the whole world went up in white flames.

Chapter Fifteen

$\mathcal{H}$ E FELL hard to the mattress beside her, eyes closed against the still-spinning room. He'd emptied himself in her. He had nothing, absolutely nothing left. He was a gimcrack shell of a man, dumb elation rattling about where his lungs and liver ought to be.

Damnation. *Orgasm.* What a painfully inadequate word. Like some dull scientific process involving plants, some abstruse topic for a Humphry Davy lecture. Nowhere near to capturing that bone-jangling glory. The way his very soul left his body and went into hers. The savage, transcendent triumph in her pillow-stifled cries.

Pillow. He opened his eyes. He ought to help her onto the pillow. Though really, what need? She was with child by now, or she wasn't. She would know soon enough, and then so would he. Then everything would be at an end. But he needn't spend this moment thinking of that.

"Mrs. Russell." Between labored breaths he sent the words up toward the bed's canopy. "Please don't tell me it's been that easy all along. Bind my hands. Put you on top."

She rolled to her side, her whole body facing him. Her

hand found his and laced their fingers together. "That may have helped. But chiefly I needed to know you, I suppose. To learn what you really were."

"Ah. Well." God help him, he would never get used to her saying things like that. His throat felt as though he'd swallowed a plum-sized rock. "Indeed, if you said I'd always had the means at my disposal, I believe I should have to hurl myself out your window in shame."

She laughed, the lovely knowing laugh of a satisfied woman. Her eyes, now he let himself look, were dark and delicious as Turkish coffee. "Only don't hurl yourself today." Her thumb stroked over his palm. "Neither from my window nor any of yours. I want you to come again tonight."

"I can come again in fifteen minutes if you like." With his free hand he took hold of her waist, pivoting her closer. "So can you."

"Irredeemable man." Her voice simmered with indulgent affection. "I knew you'd make that joke."

*T*HIRTY-ONE DAYS. Too soon to declare victory. Too soon to give in to hopes that could be crushed with proportionally greater devastation, the more time went by. Though she did imagine, or perceive, a faint nausea midmorning of late.

Martha sat in the back of the schoolroom, one absent hand at her belly, watching yet another scheme come to fruition. Seven young ladies. The two Farris girls, Jenny Everett and her sister, two girls from two other tenant families, and—what a wonderful surprise this had been—Carrie Weaver, her plaits put up and her eyes bright with eagerness.

She could barely read. "Do you think we ought to tell her parents she must go to the weekday class with the younger children?" Mr. Atkins came to the back of the room to ask. His brow knit with kindly concern. He'd kept up a pleasing habit of consulting with her on questions regarding the girls' school.

Opinions presented themselves with their usual dispatch, but she silenced them. "What do you think?" She sat forward, elbows resting ungracefully on the tabletop. "It will be you, after all, who must contend with her in class."

"I hate to move her." He glanced back at the seven heads bent over slates, each girl inscribing her name. "I can only think she'd be shamed by it, and then too her mother may not be willing to spare her more than one day a week."

"Then we must find a way to keep her in this class. She must learn to read at the same time she learns English history."

"Perhaps if one of the Seton Park girls were willing to tutor her . . ."

"Try Jenny. She's an excellent reader and she might make time while she's out with her flock."

"Very good." With a quick nod he moved back up the aisle to the schoolroom's front. "We'll begin with kings and queens today." He stood beside his desk, one hand resting on its top. "Working backward from our present King George. Can anyone tell me in what year he came to the throne?"

The voices, earnest teacher and fledgling pupils, wove themselves into a sort of soothing counterpane that settled over her as she drifted away on her own thoughts.

She wasn't a bit sorry for what she'd done yesterday. And again last night. And once more this morning, hurried and direct, that Mr. Mirkwood might go home and have a few hours of sleep before church.

He'd acknowledged her with a single nod before slipping into his pew. His countenance had betrayed no sign of improper recollections or imaginings; still she'd dropped

her eyes immediately and felt her face grow warm. His
every shift and fidget distracted her throughout the service, pressing on her attention like a hot hand laid to her
cheek. Inconvenient in so many ways, this business. And
still she was not sorry.

*N*OT SORRY, to be sure. Perhaps a bit melancholy,
though, after another night spent in similar fashion, and
another day notched on the calendar. One heard of that
as a symptom. Tender inexplicable moods. One noted
the possibility, and did not dwell.

The mood persisted, however, and took her that afternoon on a long walk to all corners of the property. Up
hills and down, along the farthest hedge, past tenant
cottages, and finally to the bank of a stream where she
sat, picking up twigs from the ground and dropping
them into the current. Some sailed out of sight, allowing
her to imagine them borne along to where the stream
joined a river, and from there, journeying all the way to
the sea. Many caught on rocks, though, or ran aground
in the shallows, their voyage brought to an ignominious
early close.

Things ended. Sometimes sooner than one would like.
Mr. Russell must have walked about this land countless
times in his life, envisioning its transfer down his direct
line. Never dreaming of this intrigue in which he must
exit the stage too soon, letting his prized estate fall into
the hands of a reprehensible brother or a faithless
widow.

*I've given myself up to a man as I never gave myself
up to you, who were my husband.* The words shaped
themselves and demanded to be spoken aloud, though
for whose benefit, one could scarcely say. She was not
penitent. If enjoying herself with Mr. Mirkwood was a
betrayal of the dead, then she would knowingly make

that same betrayal again, as many times as remained to her.

Still, she threw a last twig into the water and then stood, brushing off her skirts, to wend her way to where the churchyard sat, with its generations of Russells all resting in rows. Mr. Russell lay beside his first wife, a little distance from the iron fence. Short green shoots stubbled the ground above him, like the cheek of a man overdue for a shave. By the time her child was born—if she was so blessed—his grave would look like all the others.

He'd wanted a son. He'd objected to his brother's villainy, when so many men only shrugged at such behavior, and he'd hoped to prevent Mr. James Russell's inheriting Seton Park.

She knelt before the headstone, tracing the dates that bracketed his life. *The child won't have your blood.* Soundlessly she formed the words. *Maybe not even mine. But he'll be raised as a Russell and he'll honor your line.* Singular, when one considered. Even a loveless, forgettable marriage could result in something worthy. Mr. Russell had wed her in pursuit of an heir, and she would see to it he got one.

"I wondered when I might see you here." There was Mr. Atkins, just come through the gate with a set of shears in his hand. The afternoon sun fell sharply on him, lighting his frame and features with peculiar radiance. As though he were some earthbound angel consigned to work among the dead.

Martha sat back on her heels. "I've been remiss." She brushed her gloved hands together.

"I didn't mean to imply that. Forgive my choice of words." His footfall advanced to within a row of where she squatted. She heard him hesitate before he veered off to the grave of a Rodney Russell, where he knelt to snip some weeds.

Partly obscuring her view of him was the nearest headstone, engraved—as hers one day would be—with the name of Mrs. Richard Russell. *Beloved wife,* it also said. Those words might be omitted from her own. "Was his first marriage happy?" The question spoke itself, with no regard for circumspection.

Mr. Atkins twisted to glance at her before returning to his work. "I believe it was. Certainly her death came as a terrible blow to him." His shears sang on in the ensuing pause. "That juncture marked . . . a distinct worsening in his habits." He too spoke almost unwillingly, the thought stealing out, pirating his tongue, and stirring what had been the placid churchyard air.

"I wasn't aware you knew." She knelt again, her legs suddenly craving as much steady ground as she could get beneath her.

"I learned, quite young, to recognize those symptoms." He stilled the shears and just sat, looking down at them, for a second or five. "If I may ask something very intrusive . . ." His eyes lifted and came round to hers, his brows like those accents with which the French marked their letter *E.* "I never supposed him violent. I was not mistaken, I hope?"

"He wasn't violent." Her body felt frozen, immobile as the gravestones and those who lay beneath them.

"Good." He dropped his eyes again to the tool in his hand, and moved it idly to his other hand. "No woman should be made to bear that." She could all but see the memories back of those words, hovering like a malevolent cloud round his shoulders. So busily had she kept secrets from him, over the months, and never once had she paused to wonder what secrets he might keep in his turn. "I ought to have been a better friend to you, understanding your circumstances as I did."

"You were an excellent friend."

He twisted his mouth and shook his head once. "I

shrank from broaching the subject on which you could surely have used some sympathy."

"We both did. We both chose propriety over an unseemly intimacy. You've nothing to regret." And propriety had gentler claims now. They could converse with more openness hereafter. "I'm sorry for what you must have suffered. Have you ever spoken of it to anyone?" So had Mr. Mirkwood asked her, to little avail.

"My brother and I speak of it when we see one another." He brought up a hand and pushed back the hair that always would fall forward. He'd left off his hat. "From the distance of years we can even laugh at some things, truth be told." With his other hand he wielded the shears again, bending to trim the grass at the gravestone's edges. "Our mother had ways of managing. My brother wished for an Oxford education, though every Atkins man had been to Cambridge. On his own he should never have brought Father round. In fact he didn't." He told the story with the same meticulous care he employed to clip the grass. "One day Mother simply told Father he'd agreed to Oxford. And his memory was such that he never knew he hadn't."

Her gloves might split along the seams, she was clenching her fists so hard. Her heart might crack her ribs. She would be candid now. They would build a better friendship, a real one, with truth and forthrightness where deceit and evasion had been. "Mr. Atkins." Her voice vibrated with hope.

"Mrs. Russell." His hand came up, palm toward her. His face didn't turn her way. "I cannot know. You understand, do you not? I cannot know." Gradually, in response to her silence, his hand slid back down to the grass as the shears snipped on.

But he did know, obviously. Perhaps she'd never deceived him at all. And the message was plain: openness between them could go only this far.

Disappointment swirled round her insides like the muddy bed of a stream stirred up. For no good reason. Reticence was proper. One couldn't go about like Mr. Mirkwood, saying every forward thing that came into one's head.

Her fists uncurled and she laced her fingers, letting the shears and the distant converse of sheep fill the pause until he spoke again.

"You ought to know I think of leaving the Church. As a profession, I mean," he added hastily in response to what must have been her astonished look. "I find I want to give more time to the school."

"Teaching suits you." Yes. They could speak freely of this.

"I've been lucky enough to find the work for which God created me." A mischievous smile blossomed on his countenance. "There is my answer to anyone who disapproves of this step. Rather difficult to dispute, isn't it?"

"I wouldn't dare try. But will you manage?" She inched to the left, to see him better round Mrs. Richard Russell's marker. "I shall certainly increase your stipend if I can, but until the succession of Seton Park is settled, I haven't that power."

"It won't be necessary. Mr. Mirkwood has been most generous. If you'll let me a cottage at the rate the other tenants enjoy, then between the stipends from Seton Park and Pencarragh, and a bit of farming, I shall make do." With the satisfaction of a man who knew his future, he went on trimming the grass.

When had Mr. Mirkwood offered a stipend? He must have called without her, or had private correspondence. At all events it was handsome of him. She would tell him so. He was coming to visit this afternoon, on some pretext of dairy business, and she would see to it he knew how he'd pleased her.

* * *

*N*o lust, it developed, was so gratifying to a man as the lust that blossomed only after esteem had taken root. He might have gone his whole life without finding this out, if he'd never been exiled to Sussex. Now, in stray moments, he allowed himself to imagine enjoying this delicacy for the rest of his days.

She'd like Lincolnshire. There she would find all the amenities of Seton Park—crops, stock, tenants, a living to bestow—and if she ever felt nostalgic for the Sussex landscape, they need only come for a stay at Pencarragh. She might even like London, with its lectures and libraries and great pockets of poverty just waiting for industrious, noble-minded women to push up their sleeves and set things right.

Over the top of his pamphlet describing symptoms of cowpox in unfortunately vivid detail, he eyed her. Round the corner of her *Communications to the Board of Agriculture,* she was just as often eyeing this or that part of him. His call had taken a most agreeable turn, and now he sprawled naked atop the covers of the blue-room bed, his pillow propped against one of the bottom bedposts. She sat up against the headboard, counterpane tucked high under her arms. A smile hovered perpetually at her lips these days, as certainly it ought.

She hadn't cared for the sight of him, in the beginning. There was another triumph. She might forgive a bit of gentle gloating. "Do you see something that catches your fancy?" he said, turning a page in an offhanded manner.

She colored. "Your body is so unlike mine." Her eyes came to his face. "I thought you strange at first. But now I discern a certain logic to your form."

"Glad to hear it." He lowered the cowpox pamphlet

an inch or two. "Did your marriage not acquaint you with the masculine physique?"

"Indeed it did." He could see by the pursing of her mouth how she felt about that. "But I find one man might differ in significant ways from another."

"One might have a larger appendage, you mean."

"That's not at all what I meant." The corners of her lips twitched nonetheless. "Though I'm sure you'll be gratified to know you do best my late husband in that arena."

"Darling, I best most men there."

"My felicitations." She put her reading down altogether. "What I mean is more to do with a woman's response. How a set of limbs may be plain or handsome depending largely on who inhabits them." Her eyes strayed briefly to the counterpane. "How certain . . . acts . . . might seem distasteful with one man, but not wholly unreasonable with another."

"Acts." He cleared his suddenly dry throat. "What acts would those be, exactly?"

"Ask your appendage." Impishness sharpened her face. "It seems to have a few ideas."

Indeed his blood was racing now, on a mission to converge where it could be of most use. "My appendage always has ideas, and has never met an act it didn't like." Carefully he set the cowpox pamphlet aside. "I remain in suspense."

Her gaze held every womanly secret the world had ever known. Her lips played at smiling but didn't quite give in. Without hurry she pushed her shoulders off the headboard and sat up straight. The covers swished beguilingly as her legs swept round to one side and bent under her. She was kneeling. Providence be praised.

She glanced down and up. "You bathe it sometimes, I hope." Mrs. Russell to the core.

"Daily. With precisely this purpose in mind."

"Because at any time you might meet a lady who wants to put it in her mouth?"

"I'm of a hopeful disposition." He put out a hand to touch her arm. "Have you done it before?"

She nodded.

"But not with any relish, I expect?" When she shook her head he flexed his fingers to grasp her arm. "Martha, don't do this if you think it disagreeable. I don't need it."

Her brows edged together. She stared at him for a moment, the familiar severity in an unaccustomed context. Then she leaned low, the counterpane still pinned under her arms, and pressed her lips to his most susceptible skin.

Hell. "Martha." She turned her head, still bent low, looking up at him like some supplicant conjured out of his untidiest dreams. "I won't want you to stop, if you begin this."

"I imagine not."

"But you must. If you find it unpleasant you must stop, even if I'm begging you to keep on. Promise you will."

"I promise." All soft-eyed, naked obeisance, his supplicant. Counterpane clutched to her front but the splendid curve of her back laid bare to his view.

"Well, then." He sank a little farther into his pillow and closed his eyes, listening with his whole body for the exact instant when she—*there*. Her lips, halfway along his length, brushing over him and leaving a trail of sparks under the skin. Then a narrower touch that could only be the tip of her tongue. Then nothing at all. Her breath. He could feel her breath, quiet and warm, where her tongue had dampened his skin.

He waited. "Is it—?" The words came out of him jagged and untidy. "Have you decided you don't want to?"

She answered with her tongue. He jerked, under her.

Then he slid down the bedpost until he lay flat. Again she stopped, and breathed.

Good Lord. She'd kill him with this. "Please," he whispered. Ha. He hadn't expected to be begging quite so soon.

Her breath fell on him unevenly. Laughter. "Is that a command?"

"Woman, it's whatever will get your mouth back on me the soonest. I had entreaty in mind. But if you prefer command, then yes. Please me without further delay. I command it."

He didn't need to say more. Still as still water he lay and felt the touch of her mouth, here and there, like sparse raindrops on a pond's smooth surface, the gentle beginning of what would end as a deluge. "It's best on the end," he muttered. "Where it's rounded, there. Especially on the underside. That's where it feels the best."

"Patience." She spoke against his skin, so he felt the syllables. Idle and unhurried, she worked her way from the base of his cock to the head, exploring him with her lips and her tongue. Patience, indeed. Already his body was beginning to seethe in the middle, arching that scant inch or so to find her mouth again every time she was so cruel as to take it away.

He wouldn't last. He'd be undone the second she took him inside her mouth—or—ahh—maybe not. He might stand it a few seconds longer. Bloody hell. Had Mr. Russell taught her this? These quick, wicked patterns her tongue inscribed? The way her lips closed over him and welcomed him in? He'd have to thank that man in the afterlife. Of all things.

He lifted his hands and wove his fingers into her loose hair, his fingertips playing over her scalp in the way she liked. She'd have more pleasure than this, a few minutes hence. He'd see to that. She couldn't refuse him now.

One more second, he could hold out. No, two. And

three. And—No. Here was his limit. His hands slipped down to cup her jaw and push her face away, then settled on her shoulders. She blinked at him, all confusion, as he scrambled to get her on her back; to yank off the counterpane; to fumble his way to the right place. "Seed," he explained hoarsely, and gave it to her, half a second before he must have given it to the sheets.

Strange images came and went on the long slide back to consciousness. A child. More than one. Taking after him and her in every possible combination. A boy, tall and fair-haired, but with coffee-colored eyes. A girl of impeccable posture, her stern countenance marred by a mouth shaped for laughter. Child after child, each one more beautiful than the last.

He pushed off her and sank to the mattress at her side. One hand lifted to stroke her cheek and put a loose lock of hair behind her ear. He had something to say to her. But first, he had something to do.

Her brow quirked when he sat up and sent his arms to gather her, one behind her shoulders and the other under her knees. Her forehead furrowed in earnest when he stood and lifted her, but she made no sound. Only when he set her in the armchair, and dragged it up before the room's largest mirror, did she speak. "What are you doing?" Yes, that, for the rest of his days, would be the only reasonable response from a woman surprised.

"Watch and discover. Hook your leg over the chair's arm. Either leg."

A tremor went through her. "I don't want to. I don't care to look."

Less command. More coaxing. He modulated his voice. "I'll give you something worth looking at. I promise. But meanwhile let me look at you." He stood behind the armchair, one arm resting atop its back, and leaned down to speak close to her ear. "How imperious you look, sitting there. Keep your eyes on your face. Or mine." In the mirror he loomed over her, one hand snaking down the back of the chair, along its arm. He leaned round to the left, reached farther, got hold of her knee. Her mouth tightened. "I wish I had a crown to put on your head. I think you must imagine yourself a queen now."

"And are you my king?" Her eyes, in the mirror, stayed trained to his.

He shook his head. "Stablehand." She didn't resist as he brought her knee up; draped her leg over the chair's arm. "Great strapping stablehand who's caught the queen's eye and been summoned to service her in her chambers."

"That's very shocking of me." Another tremor went through her; a better one this time.

"You're a shocking, shocking queen." He let her see his eyes travel down her reflection, down her naked body to where she was most naked of all. "Every man in the palace, from the prime minister to the rat-catcher, knows your habits and lives in hope of being chosen one day."

"I'm not sure I approve. Am I married?"

Too much thinking. As always. "Nominally." He pressed his mouth to her shoulder, to the sensitive skin of her neck. "The king minds his own business, as long as you don't give him any bastards. And we won't." Out again to her shoulder, and down her arm he set kisses as his body twisted from behind the chair, advancing with devilish grace toward its purpose.

"Here comes the bit you'll want to watch," he said, and sank to his knees before her. Back and forth her eyes went, from his face to the mirror. She'd gone pale with some emotion only she could name. Paler still were the inner sides of her thighs, where he set his splayed fingers. And between them, of course, the flushed pink of her sweetest flesh.

He bent his head, and put his mouth on her. She sucked in a startled breath. Good. Then he was the first. "Shame on your negligent husband," he drew back just far enough to say, and after that there was nothing to do but drive her mad while losing himself in her, in these soft parts, so secret, so exquisite, so clearly made to be a match for his tongue.

Her body opened to him like a hothouse flower. She set one hand at the back of his head, and eased herself to the edge of the chair to get more of him, to get all he had to give.

And he had plenty. He pushed her second leg over the chair's other arm to spread her wide—she was beyond offering even a token resistance—and clamped his hands over her hips to still her when she wanted to move. Likely she'd be outraged at this, but the more he controlled the pace and pressure, the longer he could keep her going.

She fought his grip, voicing her frustration in guttural animal tones. He drove her harder, and higher, his merciless tongue in three places at once, his merciless hands holding her fast. Every move he thwarted—every twist, every thrust—rippled out to the rest of her body. She kicked and flailed, no longer human or even animal but elemental, pure and raging under his touch. Air, fire, earth, water: his whirlwind, inferno, his avalanche, his own private tropical storm.

Oh, but he was a selfish man. Selfish to keep her imprisoned in her pleasure, and selfish because it was his own burgeoning need that finally made him loosen his hold, and let her go from that peak where he'd kept her over the edge and on down.

She fought for breath. She looked, wild-eyed, into the mirror and then down to where he still knelt between her legs. "That was . . ." Again to the mirror. "That was . . ." Again to his face. "What was that?"

"A woman's greatest trick. I wish to God you could teach me how." He came to his feet, scooping her up on the way, and made for the bed. "And now, milady, I'm your king. With royal seed to plant and a royal lust that will not be denied."

She wasn't the woman to deny a man anything, now. She laid herself out on the bed and took him, all of him, for the third time that afternoon. Damnation, but she did make him feel like a king. She made him feel as though he'd always been one, muddling along just waiting for her to kiss him out of some enchantment into his birthright. He spilled into her, breath arrested in his throat, time suspended all round them, and slid off, pulling her to his chest, settling his chin on the top of her head.

"Martha," he said on his first steady breath, "I love you."

𝒫ULSE TICKED in his throat, not an inch away from her eyes. Carotid artery, was that? Or jugular vein? A girl's education didn't include internal anatomy. But she might look it up in a book. At all events the pulse looked hurried.

She shut her eyes.

One had known this might come. One had seen certain signs. And he was a naturally affectionate man. A month spent in the exclusive company of any woman should perhaps have produced the same effect. It would pass, undoubtedly, when he was back among the fair distractions of London.

Her heart, as warm toward him as any sensible heart could be toward a man of only a month's acquaintance, demanded she speak. She had a delicate confidence of her own to impart.

Gently she edged away to a distance from which she could properly address him. "I have something to tell you," she said.

*W*HAT WERE the chances she would choose those words to preface *I love you too*? Not great. He nodded, and waited.

"I expected my courses some five days since. I begin to believe I've conceived." Her face glowed, as it had been wont to do lately. This had been the reason all along.

"Martha, I love you." He'd said that already. "I want to marry you."

She put a hand, tender and sympathetic, to his cheek. He felt a fearsome urge to knock it away. "You're fond of me." As though she were a wise adult correcting an errant boy. "As I am of you. But we've both known the limits of this bargain from the beginning. It cannot end in anything like marriage."

"I do not refer to anything *like* marriage." With effort he kept his voice calm. "There is nothing *like* marriage. There is only marriage, and I know of nothing in our bargain that rules it out. Only your own heart can do that."

"My heart has nothing to say in the matter." Those words could raise gooseflesh in a feverish man, even as her tone grew warm and earnest. "I've pledged to keep Seton Park out of Mr. James Russell's hands. I cannot marry, and give it up."

"Why, for God's sake? Will he raze it to the ground? What do you fear from him?"

She hesitated, her lips pressing together. Would she not even tell him this? "I have nothing to fear," she said abruptly. "But I believe the housemaids do. I know he has been guilty of villainy in the past."

Ah. Here was what had driven her to undertake something so disagreeable to her sensibilities in the first place. He might have known it would be some such crusade. "You cannot be certain, though, of what he'll do in the future. And must the burden of the servants' safety fall entirely on you?"

"Who will bear that burden, if I don't?" Every word took her deeper into righteous conviction. "Nobody takes an interest in the welfare of such women. Your own Mrs. Weaver can tell you that. And I will not gamble on the threat's uncertainty. The stakes are too high." Every word pushed him farther away. She'd kept from him this central mission. She'd apparently had confidences from Mrs. Weaver to which he was not privy.

"Martha." He would not ask after the confidences, and be distracted from his purpose. "I believe I could make my happiness with you." Best to put it plainly. "I hope I could make yours, too. And you and I and this child are a family. Will you really throw all that away?"

She swallowed. He could see—he could feel in the pit of his stomach—her slow descent into despair of his ever understanding. "There are more important things than happiness," she said. Of family she said nothing.

He rolled onto his back. The canopy filled his vision, blue brocade only slightly less impressible than the woman at his side. He'd foreseen this, hadn't he? This preposterous outcome. Only he hadn't known the bottom of the well would be chest-deep in frigid water that made every breath a chore. "Will you not even say you might accept me if you bear a daughter?" The image came back with painful clarity, a girl with her posture and his smile.

"I cannot." Something new colored her words. Shame. "If I don't have a boy baby, I shall procure one by other means."

"Good God." She flinched at the utterance but he could not help himself. "Are you really capable of that?"

"I am capable of doing whatever I must to uphold the trust these women have placed in me." An edge crept into her voice, angry and desperate. "I should think you of all men would know that to be true."

Of course. Now she would recast their entire relationship, including these splendid past few days, as something she'd borne, teeth gritted in her noble countenance, for someone else's sake.

Weariness dropped over him like a sodden wool blanket. He had no more questions to ask. How exactly she would procure a boy baby—not his concern. What she knew of Mrs. Weaver—that was Mrs. Weaver's business. He'd cared to the point of fatigue and now he would not care anymore.

"Then I have only to wish you happy." One more ignoble sentiment came, settling like a sharp missile in his throwing hand. "And wish the curate happy too, I suppose."

"I beg your pardon?" God in Heaven, that engaged her like no other bit of this conversation yet had. She turned to him, eyes narrowed and brow creased.

"I see what will be the outcome." He shrugged and sat up. "Several more years of chaste conversation and yearning glances; then after a decorous mourning has passed, the fulfillment of romantic dreams that have probably been in place since—what would you say?—a month after your arrival here as Mr. Russell's bride?"

With whipcrack speed she sat up, but he was on his feet just as quickly, reaching for his shirt and not looking her way. "You do Mr. Atkins and me a terrible injustice." He'd never heard her voice like that. Interesting. "I suppose pure friendship between a lady and a gentleman may be a foreign concept to you, but I—"

"Friendship." He pulled the shirt roughly over his head. "If you will call it that."

"You have no idea of what you speak." From the corner of his eye he could see her, pale and still and cold as alabaster. "Mr. Atkins is a worthy, honorable man. I consider myself privileged to provide him with employment."

Employment. Devil take it. "You provide abundant employment for his right hand of an evening; I'll grant you that." He snatched at his trousers.

Her silence had weight and texture; it stretched out for seconds. Doubtless she was willing herself into composure. "Do not suppose I will respond to such a mean, scurrilous remark," she said at last. "When you've finished making yourself decent—or rather, when you've put on all your clothes—you may leave. I will not be at home to you tomorrow, nor on any other day I can imagine." She didn't even spare him a glance.

Anger and—damnation, but he ought to have more sense—asinine grief clawed at his insides. In the space of five minutes he'd wrecked what little they had. They might have gone on a few days more, and parted on friendly terms, at least.

No. Not one more speck of sorrow, not one more scrap of sentiment wasted on a woman who would never be able to repay in kind. Damn it all, a man owed something to his pride. Unhurriedly he buttoned his trousers, shutting away the body whose indecency offended her so. Cravat. Waistcoat. Hose. Boots. Piece by piece he covered himself, as calm and methodical as though he were alone in the room.

When he paused before the mirror, a last cruel impulse gripped him. With a sweeping gesture she could not miss, he drew out his handkerchief and scrubbed the taste of her from his lips. Then he tossed away the crumpled linen and—so this was how it ended—strode from the room without once looking back.

Chapter Sixteen

$\mathcal{D}$AYS PASSED. Two days, or maybe three. One did one's best to think as little as possible of Mr. Mirkwood, even when one's callers mentioned him by name. He was keeping busy, clearly. He was pursuing his dairy project without her involvement, and, for all the cruelty of those last few minutes with her, he was still sending callers her way.

Not that this could excuse the vicious things he'd said of Mr. Atkins. Vicious, and with no shred of truth behind them. Indeed if there was a guilty right hand to be spoken of, it most certainly was not the curate's. Perhaps she ought to have said so, answering pettiness with pettiness.

Perhaps not. Mechanically she nodded and smiled at Mr. Tavistock and his wife, who sat side by side on the best parlor sofa. They were well-meaning people, but they did weary one with comic anecdotes in which the amusing points were not immediately evident. One had constantly to watch the wife, when the husband was speaking, and follow her lead as to laughter. Mr. Mirkwood should have laughed at all the right places, and wrong ones too, and never have felt burdened in the least. But she must give up thinking of him.

And indeed, when the Tavistocks had gone, something occurred to absorb her thoughts altogether and drive out such small cares as had troubled her. The footman brought a letter in Mr. Keene's careful hand. He'd not dissuaded Mr. James Russell after all. She must expect him in a week's time.

*F*IRST, WE will see that every lady's door can be bolted from the inside." Martha paced back and forth at the head of the dining-room table, the women servants assembled to hear her as they'd been one month before. "A keyhole lock alone isn't enough. Please hold up your hand if your door doesn't have a bolt, and Mrs. Kearney will write your name." Her pulse jogged erratically, as it seemed to have done almost from the moment of reading Mr. Keene's letter. So be it. If she could not command her body into calm, she would ride its unruliness the way one posted a trotting horse.

What a wonderfully clarifying thing a crisis was. One knew what had to be done—keep the servants safe from Mr. James Russell—and every small action and decision fell efficiently in line. "For as long as he should remain here, be assured you owe him no deference." She wheeled to a stop, facing down the table. "If he addresses you in a familiar manner, you may answer him as strongly as you like. And then tell me at once."

Sheridan sat forward in her chair, bright-eyed at the prospect. "May we strike him as well?"

Certainly someone ought to. She took up pacing again. "I shall leave that decision to you. Just be mindful of your own safety."

"Men like that don't give you a chance to strike them," said a grave-faced lower housemaid. "They pin your arms first thing."

"Then you must shout for a footman." She set her

palms flat on the linen-covered tabletop and nodded to Mrs. Kearney, sitting at its far end. "Will you apprise Mr. Lawrence of this matter, that he may put the footmen on notice?" Now the men-servants would know too. The whole house would be united against this menace.

"Only I wish I knew how to escape being pinned in the first place." Sheridan set her troubled gaze on the strip of tablecloth between Martha's two hands. "If we could learn the best places to strike or poke a man so as to disable him . . . if we had someone with some knowledge of boxing, for instance, to instruct us . . ."

"We don't, however, so we shall rely on what resources we have." Crisply she spoke over whatever nonsense Sheridan had meant to hint, and the girl sat back, her slightly protruding lower lip the only sign of argument.

She'd known somehow, Sheridan had, that things had ended badly. For all that Martha claimed the bargain had served its purpose and been finished, she frequently caught a pitying look in her maid's eyes as she dressed her or did up her hair, and occasionally these unsubtle allusions came; these poorly veiled suggestions that she might take some step to bridge their rift. As though that were what either she or Mr. Mirkwood wanted, now.

She'd hurt him. Obviously. He'd offered her his heart and she'd declined it the way she might decline a second helping of turnips. What man would bear that with equanimity?

But he wasn't the only person disappointed. She'd shown him her best self—the one capable of prodigious sacrifice for a worthy cause—and seen how he did not prize it. Chagrin knifed through her every time she allowed herself to remember. How could he claim to love her, when he did not love what was essential in her?

Not that it mattered. With marriage out of the question, love must be beside the point. "We'll begin on the locks tomorrow." She straightened again, and clasped her hands behind her back. "If you have other ideas for how we may brace this household, I shall be glad to hear them."

I'M TOLD we may lose Mrs. Russell. Had you heard?" Granville dropped this remark while sorting through the various dairy implements stored in one of Pencarragh's outbuildings.

A week now since he'd spoken to her, and as though she didn't trouble his dreams enough, she must intrude here too. "Was there some complication with the will?" Theo poked at a cheese-press. Cheese-making had lost a deal of its luster. He hadn't known the bit about the calf-stomach until some recent reading. Poor blameless doomed calves.

"It develops the estate may go to Mr. Russell's brother. She's not provided even a dower-house in that case, according to the family solicitor." The agent paused to make a note. "That's four good oaken pails. Have you come across a syle dish?"

"That milk-straining thing? I think this may be one. Have a look." He held up the odd contraption, like a bowl with its bottom cut out, for Granville's inspection. "How does this fellow come to be discussing Mrs. Russell's private affairs? I should certainly hope for better discretion from my own solicitor."

"To be sure. The topic only came up because this brother—the present Mr. Russell—will be at Seton Park within the week. Mr. Keene wanted me to know, particularly as his residency there may eventually be permanent."

"He's coming now?" Not his concern. Not his concern. Mrs. Russell could look to her dashed curate if she wanted masculine aid.

"Not the most gracious thing to do, is it? He looks as

though he were anticipating his inheritance, and thus anticipating Mrs. Russell's disappointment. I could see Mr. Keene disapproved. Ah—good. These setting-bowls have a tin coating. I've heard the bare iron sort can rust."

He didn't owe her anything. She, in fact, owed him five hundred pounds. Four times that sum, if things worked out the way she hoped.

But he'd acquired inconvenient proclivities over the past month, and now his thoughts went to the Seton Park housemaids. He couldn't stand by and pretend no knowledge of the threat they might face. He must call, at least, and hear what, if anything, Mrs. Russell planned to do.

Bother responsibility. He sighed, and felt for his pocket watch. If he could hurry Granville along with this inventory, then he could perhaps make the visit this afternoon.

*M*ARTHA SAT at the library table, tapping a dry quill on a sheet of paper. She'd addressed the servant-women four days since, and every one of those four days Sheridan had seen fit to make some mention of Mr. Mirkwood. How he must be struggling in his dairy plans without Martha's sensible advice. How he'd done a respectable job, for a gentleman, of arranging her hair, on those days he'd chosen to undertake that task. All manner of foolishness, transparent in its motive and fit to be ignored.

Still, she sat at the table with paper and pen. She might just send a note. He would perhaps wish to know of Mr. James Russell's imminent arrival.

Yet why would he? He'd cleaved his cares from hers. Or maybe it was she who'd done that. At all events, she could not expect him to trouble himself over this development that did not affect him. She tossed the pen down and was just rising from her chair when a footman appeared in the doorway.

"Mr. Mirkwood asks to see you, madam. I've put him in the smaller parlor."

She stopped where she was, half risen. Her heart dashed and halted like an indecisive squirrel.

I shall not be at home to you on any day I can imagine. What errand could bring him here in defiance of those words? Perhaps he'd come for his five hundred pounds. "Very good. Thank you. I'll go to him." Mechanically she lurched to her feet, and let them carry her, one step after another, from the library down the long hall and to the peony parlor at the front of the house.

He stood at a window, one hand pushing back a curtain to gain the broadest possible view. He would always be that man, wouldn't he?—drawn to vistas and pleasures and all things light, in absurd contravention of his name. At the sound of her slippers on the oak floor he let the curtain fall and pivoted to face her.

Those eyes had seen all that her gown now concealed. That mouth had done things past description. That chin had sheltered the top of her head, night after night, his pulse and his breath murmuring in soft concerto with her own.

She blushed, even as she went to him, one hand held out. He took the hand and bowed, and let it go as he put both his own hands behind his back. "I've heard you're expecting Mr. Russell's brother." His head tilted down, his solemn blue gaze taking the shortest path to her eyes.

"Indeed. By the end of this week. Will you have a seat?" She'd told him not to call. He'd called anyway. Now she was inviting him to stay.

He shook his head. "I've only come to ask what you plan to do, and what help you may need." With a conscious formality he addressed her. "I don't mean to intrude."

Stupid squirrel of a heart. He spoke of love, and she answered with stoicism. He dragged himself over here in deference to duty, and her knees went weak. "You're kind to inquire." She sidled a step or two to where she could steady herself by gripping the back of a chair. "We'll manage. We've put bolts on all the maids' bedroom doors, and I've instructed them to shout for help if he attempts anything by daylight."

"Very good, then." He nodded. Now he would go.

No. He couldn't. He'd offered help despite their angry words. He'd set aside whatever he felt for her in pursuit of a greater good, and he'd probably had to swallow a deal of pride along the way. Abruptly she let go the chair and took one long step to block his path. "We do need help. The women want to know how to strike a man most effectively. I need someone to teach them."

A smile of pure boyish pleasure started across his face. He checked it, and bowed again. "Of course, Mrs. Russell. I'm at your service."

W HAT IS a woman's greatest weakness, as compared to a man?" Like a corporal reviewing troops, Mrs. Russell strode back and forth before the women assembled to hear her. They sat, half eagerness and half apprehension, on straight chairs in Seton Park's ballroom. Theo stood along one wall, with a handful of footmen and grooms who'd been conscripted to the cause.

"Frailness of body." That was Mrs. Russell's maid, the girl who managed all her dressing and undressing now. "Speed as well. Men are stronger and quicker than we are."

"Indeed they are and yet, for our purposes, that can be overcome." Crisis only seemed to increase her self-assurance, odd woman that she was. "The weakness we must conquer, ladies, is our propensity for mercy." She threw him a quick look. They'd spent a good hour just strategizing, and agreed this should be the cornerstone of their approach.

"Has any among you ever struck a man?" She stood still, her index finger sweeping across their ranks as though to count the response. But no woman said she had.

"Has anyone ever borne insult from a man, and later wished you could have struck him?" Now five or six servants nodded, putting up a hand to be counted. Mrs. Russell laced her fingers behind her back and stood taller. "Would anyone want her daughter—if we should all be so blessed—to bear such insult without defending herself?" Triumphant in the force of her argument, she let her eyes roam emphatically over her audience before she spoke again.

"We must protect ourselves with the same ferocity we would wish for our daughters. Our neighbor Mr. Mirkwood has graciously offered to show us how we may best hurt a man. We shall repay his kindness by promising not to shrink from using what he teaches us." She took a step backward and held out a hand, palm up, ceding the floor to him.

He pushed off the wall and came forward. "Even the smallest lady may disable a man, at least for an interval that allows her to escape, by striking him in one of several vulnerable places. I'll show you these places, and how to deliver an effective blow." The widow's maid, and a few other women, were clearly keen to see that. "But first I'll show you, with Mrs. Russell's help, a number of ways to get free of a man who has seized hold of you. If you please, Mrs. Russell."

They'd rehearsed all yesterday afternoon. In careful civility they'd worked together, the widow insisting she must set the example for ladies who would be wary of practicing such maneuvers with a man. Again and again he'd grasped her wrist or elbow, again and again wrapped his arms about her, first mindful of their perished intimacy, then of the child, tiny and unformed, somewhere in the depths of his embrace.

She'd slipped away from him every time, child and all, by his own tutelage. And so she did now, dropping like a plumb bob and breaking his encircling hold, much to the servants' delight. Her cheeks flushed with industry and excitement above her somber weeds. Her eyes shone like oiled mahogany. "Now if we may have everyone on their feet, and if the gentlemen will join us, you'll see how quickly you can master this." She nodded once to him—her partner in this mission—and they threaded their separate ways into the company.

If he'd ever spent a more useful hour in his life, he could not now bring it to mind. Oh, he'd accomplished a few things with the dairy venture, to be sure, and perhaps he'd made some difference to Mr. Barrow, but only through much grappling and toil. To be of service to these women by doing what came so easily to him was a pleasure beyond reckoning.

Round the room he went, instructing this kitchen maid as to the placement of her feet; that laundress as to the fatality of hesitation. He could see Mrs. Russell, meanwhile, circulating, encouraging, coaxing the more reluctant ladies to take a turn. She stepped in and demonstrated, with a footman, how to wheel one's arm about and break a grip at the wrist. What a formidable creature she looked, straight and strict as ever even while she allowed manservants to put their hands on her, and urged other women to do the same. A fierce, black-clad warrior for her sex, her un-tender nature finally finding its proper sphere.

At a certain juncture their paths crossed. A bit outside the fray they both stood, catching their breath and considering where they were needed next. "I think it's gone well so far," she said in an undertone. Her cap-strings had loosened, and the roots of her hair, uncharacteristically, framed her face. "What do you think?"

That was new. The earnest appeal to his opinion. He nodded, arms folded, eyes on the maid and groom nearest them. "They're quick learners, the women of Seton Park."

"And game, for the most part. I count only three maids I cannot persuade to try."

"You'll have them by the afternoon's end."

"Do you think so?" He could hear how she'd like to believe it herself.

"I haven't a doubt." He angled his face a few degrees toward her. "You're a leader of women, Mrs. Russell. I've known that for some time." With a brief bow he moved off to make himself useful again.

*T*HREE DAYS later he stood in the window of one of Seton Park's closed-up sitting rooms, watching a coach-and-four pull up the drive. "Didn't spare any expense on those horses, did he?" he muttered. At his right shoulder Mr. Perry, one of the stablemen, craned for a better look. "Has he got a fortune of his own?"

"I've heard he married into money." That was one of the more senior housemaids, a Miss Morehouse, standing at the next window.

"Married, is he? Contemptible dog. I wonder if his wife knows."

"Look at Mrs. Russell." Miss Sheridan, just to his left, went up on her toes. "Don't she look just like a queen getting set to play host to an enemy."

"And have him beheaded in his sleep, one hopes." He felt the familiar small wrench—really, not so bad as it had been—as he watched her slight black figure, erect and resolute on the walkway from doors to drive. The day had dawned cool and she wore a shawl over her shoulders, her hands drawing it round her like a royal mantle.

"There come the steps," said Perry, and they all put noses to the glass, keen for a first look at Mr. James Russell.

From this height he appeared a nondescript sort of man, middling in size and with no notable style to his dress. "Is that all he is?" Miss Sheridan's voice sprang up an octave from where it had been. "I'd expected some hulking monster."

"You'll thrash him, if he gets hold of you." A pity he couldn't do it himself.

"That I will." She tapped her fist to a diamond-shaped pane. "Provided Mrs. Russell don't do it first."

She looked capable, the widow did. She didn't advance to meet the man but stood, regal and forbidding, just where she was on the walkway. *I know what you are,* said everything in her aspect, even from this distance.

"Here's the wife," Miss Morehouse spoke up. A stout, richly dressed woman stepped out of the coach. Then a plain thin one. A governess, this second woman must be, because two boys followed, perhaps ten and eight years old.

He saw Mrs. Russell give a tiny start. Apprehension slithered up his spine. "She didn't know he had children." He swiveled to face Miss Sheridan.

She spoke simultaneous with him. "She didn't know he had sons."

HE HAD sons. How had it never occurred to her that he might? She dropped her eyes to her own hands, on pretext of making some adjustment to her shawl, and then forced herself to look again.

They were bright-eyed boys, both of them, the younger with his mother's fair coloring and the elder—the one she would rob of his rightful expectations—dark-haired and ruddy-cheeked like his father. They stood straight as little soldiers beside their governess, who had no doubt spent a deal of time training them in posture. Perhaps she favored the use of a board, as Miss York had done.

No. Any such sympathetic reflections would be detrimental to her resolve. That she must disinherit these children was unfortunate, but could not be helped. The sins of the fathers, and so forth.

The father himself was a surprisingly unimpressive figure. Shorter in stature than his brother had been, with a smirking sort of countenance and an insinuating posture. He would not have loomed terribly, the way she'd pictured, in a poor housemaid's bedroom doorway, his malign silhouette dimming the hallway's light. At most he might have come in weasel-like, shutting the door softly behind him, the click of its latch conveying all the menace his person did not.

Would that be worse? Violation at the hands of so insignificant a man? Her stomach performed some slight undulations as he approached. The business had been bad enough on a wedding night to which she'd consented. To compound that pain, that astonishment, that awful sense of exposure with such powerless terror as Mrs. Weaver and the other maid must have felt, was an outrage almost past imagining.

"Mrs. Russell." Neither did his voice bear any stamp of villainy. One might easily ignore it, in fact, and rest all one's attention on his wife while he droned on with his transparent false pleasantries.

Mrs. James Russell was plump and might once have been pretty. She wore a blue woolen gown abundantly trimmed with ribbon, and stood halfway between the carriage and her husband, hands folded before her and eyes lifted to consider the house. As though she'd felt Martha's gaze, she suddenly dropped her chin and appeared to consider the walkway's paving-stones.

Something in the action prodded at her heart, as did the way the woman stood, apart from both her husband, who had not brought her forward for an introduction, and from the children, who lingered by their governess, apparently waiting for her next instruction. What a dreadful thing, to know such isolation in the midst of one's own family.

For Heaven's sake no more sympathy! "I shall be glad to see what Richard managed in the way of improvements," Mr. James Russell was saying. He was, it developed, one of those men who directed half his remarks to her bosom instead of her face. She must make an effort to converse often with him during his stay, that this vulgarity could remind her of her purpose and shore up her resolve.

"Most recently he devoted his attention to the tenant cottages, rather than the house and grounds. I'm sure you'll be as gratified as I was by the results. But you must all be weary from your journey." She pushed past him, contemptible bosom-addresser that he was, and spoke to his wife. "Do come in and have some tea while I see to readying a few more rooms. To have you all with me is such a delightful surprise."

$\mathcal{B}$ Y THE time she retired for bed that night she was exhausted. To entertain even benign company for half a day—one must not succumb to gloomy speculation over how many such days stretched out ahead—should have taxed her resources considerably. But to be always watchful of Mr. James Russell, exchanging glances with any maid who happened to be in the room; striving to read him for signs of perfidious thought or intention, depleted her beyond anything she could have imagined.

If he'd reformed at all in the past sixteen years, he had not come so far as to be a good man. He paid little notice to his wife, and indeed had spent the whole of an awkward supper swilling Mr. Russell's best claret and regaling Martha with increasingly voluble tales of his Sussex boyhood, while Mrs. James Russell consumed her jugged hare with such steadiness as did not permit for conversation. He walked about the rooms, too, with a presumptuous step that suggested he already counted them as his. Though of course that was not beyond understanding. He'd grown up here, and inhabited the rooms much longer than she had. An objective observer, knowing nothing of his crimes, might even say he had the greater claim to Seton Park.

And an observer, indeed, would know nothing of the crimes. If only men wore the marks of such deeds in their faces, or gave off some appropriate stench! If only they did not have wives and children to share in the punishment for their wrongs. How much simpler this had all been when he remained at a distance, the unambiguous monster of her imagination rather than this perfectly ordinary-looking husband and father. Nothing in his appearance suggested him capable of the threat against which the whole household had mobilized.

Yet when she was awakened, hours later, by a hand over her mouth, her whole body convulsed in panic. "Don't be afraid," said a voice at her ear. "It's Mr. Mirkwood. It's Theo. There's no danger."

"What is it? What's happened?" she said as soon as he lifted away his palm. Her heart thundered like a runaway horse. She couldn't see a thing.

"Nothing. Shhh." His fingers pushed a lock of hair behind her ear, something he'd often done when he shared her bed, and she fought an impulse to grab his wrist and hold on. "I'm sorry to wake you like that, but I didn't want you to wake on your own, later, and be alarmed by my presence here."

"I don't understand." Panic was subsiding, but confusion whirled all the harder. She sat up, away from his hand. "How did you get in?"

"You gave me a key, remember?" The source of his voice moved; he must be getting to his feet. "And just as I suspected, you've put bolts on everyone's door but yours." Now she could hear him lifting something. "I'm going to sit in this armchair, just inside your door, until morning. Tonight, and every night until your husband's brother has gone away."

She rubbed at her face with the heel of one hand. Gradually his words were coming clear. "You don't owe me that service."

"No. Probably not." He sounded so very far away, though no more than a dozen feet divided them.

"I wonder if you oughtn't to be guarding the stairway to the maids' rooms instead, that we might catch him if he even attempts anything."

"Hawkins and Perry have that in hand." She could hear him stretching, making himself comfortable in the chair.

"Who?"

"Henry Hawkins. Second footman. Jack Perry. Groom." At some point he'd apparently made bosom friends of men who were mere nameless servants to her. "If Mr. Russell goes anywhere near that stairway, he'll be caught and brought to justice. If he attempts to enter here, worse than that will befall him."

"I really can't imagine I'm in any danger." Yes, she was thinking clearly again. "He hasn't a history of—"

"Martha." He could be addressing her from the moon, his tone was so distant. "I've no interest in arguing this, and you waste your time by doing so. You will not dislodge me from this chair without you raise an alarm and bring the whole household to your bedroom. Everything considered, I doubt you want that."

She lay back down. If she held her own breath, she could hear his. He didn't make any other sound.

"I'm sorry," he said after a minute or two.

"You needn't be. You're trying to do me a favor and I've been ungracious." For the sixty-eighth time.

"Not for that." His voice was almost too low to hear. "There are things I wish I hadn't said."

An odd thought struck: maybe *I love you* was one of those things. "Never mind about it. You've done me so much more kindness than unkindness. And it had to end one way or another, didn't it? Just as well in anger as any other way, I suppose."

"Mrs. Russell." His soft laughter carried across the room. "Are you drunk?"

"What?" She came up on one elbow. "Hasn't anyone ever forgiven you before?"

"Countless times." She could hear his face was turned toward her. "Only I never expected it from you."

Without question she deserved that. She lay flat again. "You're an excellent man, on balance." A yawn mounted up and she stifled it. "You were very good to think of putting those men on the maids' staircase."

"I didn't, though." He'd faced away and sounded as though he were pushing back a yawn himself. "It was their own idea." Some creaking came as he settled deeper into the chair. "You have more allies than you know, if you would only learn to trust them. Now go back to sleep. I'll wake you if there's any need."

H E LEFT a bit after daybreak. He slept four or five hours before rising to work with Granville. And when night enfolded all of Sussex in its dark embrace, he was back in the armchair by her bedroom door.

"He has sons." Without sight of her, he couldn't be sure whether she was talking to him or to herself. He'd arrived, this second night of his vigil, to find she'd left a single candle burning, but he'd long since put it out. Its smoke still faintly flavored the air.

"I saw them. I was in the house yesterday, watching out a window with some servants when he arrived." He felt absently for his watch, though of course he wouldn't be able to read it. The time must be somewhere near one.

"I didn't know there were sons." Her words drifted out into the room, subdued as the lingering scent of that candle she'd left to light his way.

"Would you have done anything differently, if you'd known?"

"I don't see how I could."

"You're sorry, though." In the pauses, he could hear the soft whistle of wind drawn into the chimney.

"I can't change my plans now. Everyone is depending on me." Her voice had a desperate undertone, as though she'd been arguing this with herself for some time.

"To be sure. But you can be resolute and remorseful both. You can hold fast to your mission, and still grieve what it will cost those boys."

"I do." Her hand did something to the sheet, linen whispering over linen. "Thank you."

"For what?" Even though he couldn't see her, he turned that way.

"You know how to say things I don't know how to say."

Undeniably. *I love you,* for instance.

He struck that unworthy thought. "What of the wife? Have you been able to form any impression?"

"Scarcely. I'm sure she's not happy. She talks very little, and eats a great deal."

"Yes, she looks as if she did."

"That's impolite." The terrible judge recumbent.

"I don't mean it to be." He stretched his legs, crossing one booted ankle over the other. "I've enjoyed ladies of similar proportion more than once. Enjoyed them thoroughly." In time he might do so again.

He'd go back to London. He'd find his next lover. And the widow would be, whether he wished it or not, just one more woman in his past. The first woman he'd ever loved, eventually, instead of the only one. That truth rolled round the room like a marble on a ramshackle floor.

The sheet whispered again. She was clutching it, perhaps, in her fist. "I won't forget you," she said.

"Of course not. You'll have a little reminder, won't you?" At least one of them would.

"Little, and then not so little. If we're blessed with good health." Her hair rustled on the pillow as she turned over. "But I shouldn't have forgot you anyway."

Four strides would take him from this chair to the bed. He could lie beside her one last time, breathing in her lilac perfume for remembrance.

He sank deeper into the chair. "How is your health of late? Do you suffer any indisposition?" If he made her blush, he wouldn't know.

"A bit, midmorning. It's not too bad."

"Ah. Good." Even a husband and wife might be shy and halting in speaking of these matters. He'd marry one day, and when his wife was with child, he'd find that out. He'd have that child to think of, then. To take his thoughts away from the other child, the little being manufactured out of love and determination, who would never know him.

Christ. He tipped his head back, blinking against the

dark. "You'll love him, won't you? Or her?" He sounded like he was speaking from the bottom of a well. And of course he was.

A pause, as she absorbed his question. "I know why you ask. I'm not affectionate by nature, and I conceived the child in service to a scheme, rather than for his own sake. Or hers." She took in a breath. "But I've always liked babies, and this one . . ." Another pause. Another breath. "He's mine. Or she is. I'll love this child as I've never loved anyone in my life."

"Well, then." His throat worked mutely for a second or two. "Very good." There was nothing else, really, to say.

$\mathcal{M}$R. JAMES Russell did not rise in time for church, which fact might be taken as a sign of Providential approval. The longer she could keep him from meeting Mr. Atkins, the longer she would postpone her final plummet from the curate's favor. In the front pew, beside Mrs. James Russell, the governess, and the two boys, she sat through a lengthy but rather heartening sermon on that adulteress against whom no one dared to cast the first stone. From time to time she closed her eyes and took deep breaths to propitiate her stomach.

From time to time also, she battled the urge to turn for a glimpse of Mr. Mirkwood, who sat in his usual place three rows back. She'd half-expected him to miss the service as well, after two sleepless nights. But there he'd been, looking a bit bedraggled even in fresh clothes as she passed him on her way up the aisle. And there was his voice—a fine, true one, she must allow—interlacing with the others on every hymn, proof he hadn't dozed off in his pew.

He'd sleep after church, perhaps. Collapse on his bed fully clothed. Or he might change into a nightshirt. Or he might wear nothing at all. To shuck his clothes would be all he could manage before he crawled under the covers, cool sheets caressing every turn of his rough-hewn frame.

She missed the sight of his body. Nothing could be done about that. Circumstances estranged them more decisively than any quarrel could do.

"That was a thoughtful sermon," said Mrs. James Russell on the walk home. "A bit long, perhaps, for the children, but well considered." It was the first opinion the woman had ventured in her presence.

"Not too long for your sons, to judge by their conduct." The boys trailed their governess in single file, a little way ahead. "They attended like perfect gentlemen."

"Thank you." The words came softly, as though she were unused to compliments of any kind. "Miss Grey does very well with them." She lowered her gaze to the ground. "You feel better, I hope, now you're walking and in fresh air?"

"Indeed. Forgive me if I distracted you in church. I fear I may have to give up going, sooner than I expected."

"So I did with my first child." Her eyes, as she glanced at Martha, were pale blue and framed with thick lashes. She would be pretty indeed if her face were not so care-worn. "I was sorry for it. Church is a great comfort." She blushed as if confiding something, and angled her glance away.

Her soft plump hand might as well have reached into one's chest and wrung one's guilty heart. She was worse than unhappy, Mrs. James Russell was. Disconsolate, forsaken, and entrusting her slight confidence to someone who would cheat her sons of their birthright. "You must miss your church in Derbyshire, then. I'm sure you'll be glad to go back."

Ruthlessness muscled those words out—ruthlessness might be all that remained of her, one day—and the other Mrs. Russell did not again attempt fellowship for the rest of their walk.

*H*E HOPES to set up here with a mistress, and leave her behind in Derbyshire." Miss Sheridan sat forward in the blue-and-silver striped armchair, hands clasped before her. "Her maid says he's even brought a mistress into their house sometimes."

"But a wife can divorce for that, can't she?" Mrs. Russell, on the sofa beside him, gripped its far arm with pale knuckles. Any observer would think she was the one who'd gone two nights without sleep, so drawn was her countenance. "For a mistress under her own roof?"

"She's got nowhere to go." Such an impressive compendium of knowledge, a lady's maid. "Her father won't have her back again and she hasn't any brothers to take her in."

Theo leaned back into the sofa's corner. He missed this sitting room, site of so much profitable study and of a few other things as well. From this very sofa she'd risen in that pink dressing gown, on the day he'd most needed such a gesture.

"I knew she was unhappy." Poor Mrs. Russell. Discovering she wasn't so heartless as she'd counted on being. "But I didn't know how dreadful were her circumstances."

Without thought he lifted a hand and settled it on her back, where it made slight comforting circles. Miss Sheridan averted her eyes as though by reflex. She knew what had been between them. A companionable touch could hardly shock her in the face of that.

"Miss Gilliam says he's always had one mistress or another." The maid brought her eyes back to Mrs. Russell. "She says he's never touched his wife since the second son was born."

He could feel the widow's spine sag farther. He sat straighter himself. "That's her good fortune, I should think. Does the maid say whether he's given any trouble to the servants?"

"Nobody likes the way he looks at them. But she doesn't know of his taking any liberties."

Mrs. Russell dropped her face into her hands. "I'd almost rather he had," she said through her fingers. "If he poses no threat to the servants, then I cheat those children without good cause. And if he were to inherit, and move here with his mistress, who is to say his wife and sons wouldn't be better off for his absence?"

"Martha." What had become of his iron-willed mistress? "You cannot be sure he poses no threat, and you cannot gamble on that uncertainty. So you told me yourself, I remember. You've pledged your allegiance to the women of Seton Park. You must do what you think best serves them, regardless the effect on anyone else."

"I know. Only I expected to feel grand and righteous, doing so. I had no thought of its all feeling so mixed-up and awful."

Miss Sheridan gave a small cough, as though to remind them of her presence in the room. He nodded to her. "Did you learn anything else?"

"Only that he suspected Mrs. Russell was counterfeiting her condition. But his wife is convinced she's not."

The widow's backbone came away from his hand as she brushed off her skirts and stood. "Thank you, Sheridan. Very well done. I hope you'll summon us both again if you have further intelligence to report." She paused, and half-turned to him. "You'll be back later tonight, I expect?"

"Indeed I don't plan to leave." He leaned over and grasped his right boot. "I remember this sofa as a fine spot for napping. Miss Sheridan, you'll send someone to roust me if I sleep past Mrs. Russell's bedtime?"

The maid rose and bobbed a curtsey. "Mrs. Ware says you may come to the kitchen if you're here through supper. She'll put something aside for you."

"Mrs. Ware. Splendid." He shed the second boot and brought both feet onto the sofa. The widow was staring at him, no doubt astonished he should know her cook by name. "Will you leave a candle for me again? That was quite helpful last night." She nodded, and both ladies left.

$\mathcal{M}$R. MIRKWOOD must have come during the night—the candle was put out—but he was gone, as he'd been the first two mornings, by the time she woke.

A pity, because she woke with an idea, and he was the one who'd planted it. *You have more allies than you know,* he'd said. What if she called on their aid? Other people, if given a chance, might take an interest in the fate of Seton Park. Or the safety of honest women. Other people might have a care for justice. They might step in, when her purpose wavered, and take up the cause on her behalf. An alliance of such people, with herself among their number, might after all accomplish more than she could manage alone.

She would finish, by whatever means necessary, what she'd set out to do. And if she wronged the sons, well . . . Well, there was no *if* in the matter. She would wrong the sons. Time enough for self-recrimination when Seton Park was secure.

She sat down at the library desk that morning, and she wrote. To stately Mr. Rivers and his wife she wrote, and convivial Mr. and Mrs. Tavistock. To conscientious Mr. Keene, and generous Mr. Granville, and to the three sensible ladies in town. The words, so very awkward at first—*I need your help* and *Forgive my opening such a subject as this*—came more easily with practice, one found.

And when the letters were all sent, she made some visits.

"I had no idea of this." Mr. Atkins had just dismissed his school, and sat on the edge of his desk, half-crumpling a paper he'd had in hand when she'd begun to speak. "No idea in the world. Had you?"

"Only recently. We were both left ignorant." She faced him from a desk in the front row. They'd been equal in ignorance. Natural allies. Why hadn't she called on his help long ago? "I believe such secrecy only abets that kind of man in his crimes, and shields him from the censure he deserves. I mean to end it."

"To be sure. You may depend on my assistance." His brows canted. "But Mrs. Weaver won't be named, I hope. For the sake of her children, particularly Christine, I think ignorance may be the kinder path." How quickly he'd taken on this protective concern for his pupils, even those who never came to his church.

"My instinct is the same as yours." She folded her hands before her. "But I shall leave that decision to Mrs. Weaver herself."

WELL, THIS sitting-up-all-night business would get him back in practice for London hours, at least. Though if Mr. James Russell stayed much longer, he'd have to make some account to Granville of why he slept so late in the mornings, or was nowhere to be found of an evening.

Theo glanced at his dressing-room clock. Half past two. A respectable hour for most pursuits. He'd just finished arranging his cravat and was entertaining thoughts of breakfast when a footman appeared with a card he'd first seen six weeks ago to the day. Plain black lettering on white; no border. No hint of the owner beyond her name.

He found her in his parlor, seated on the least comfortable chair, her gloved hands folded one over the other in her lap. Her gaze, staunch and decided, swung to him as soon as he crossed the threshold. "I have a plan," she said, "and I need your help."

"Of course. Tell me what I may do." Somehow, clearly, she'd found her resolve again, and he would help her hold tight to it.

A quick, grateful smile lit her face before she restored the air of purpose he knew so well. "First, I'd like your company for a visit to the Weavers."

Chapter Seventeen

Tell me what I may do, Mr. Mirkwood had said. *You may depend on my assistance* had been Mr. Atkins's words. These were friends, and perhaps bound to answer her summons.

What, though, could account for the beneficence of the other fifteen people ranged down the length of her dining-room table?

Not one person had refused her entreaty. There sat Mrs. Canning, Mrs. Kendall, and Miss Leigh, glancing about at the imposing portraits of Russells gone by. There were Mr. Rivers and his wife, respectable bulwarks against delinquency of any kind. There were Mr. Lawrence and Mrs. Kearney, longest-tenured of the household servants, looking quite the equal of the gentry among whom they sat. Everyone had risen to the occasion, almost as though they'd only been waiting for an occasion to which they might rise.

Mr. Mirkwood, halfway down the table on her left, caught her eye and vouchsafed her a private slight nod. He was responsible for making her known to all these neighbors, and he might have sat beside any of them. But he'd chosen a chair by Mr. Atkins, and now the two of them conversed in low tones, probably about the school. The sight put a bothersome prickling at the back of her eyes.

She needn't be overset now. She must make an example of steadiness for others. She turned to the place at her right. "Are you ready?" she said, and Mrs. Weaver nodded once as her husband, beside her, put a coarse knuckly hand over hers. "Mr. Lawrence." Martha pitched her voice to reach the rest of the table as well as the butler. "Will you have a footman fetch Mr. James Russell to us, please?"

𝒯HEO'S SEAT faced away from the door, but even had he been deaf, he could not have mistaken the moment of Mr. James Russell's entrance. Mrs. Canning's eyes and those of her two friends all narrowed in unison, as though it were some maneuver the three ladies had practiced. Attention sharpened all up and down that side of the table. He saw a rolling flex in Mr. Weaver's prodigious shoulder. Mrs. Russell's right arm went under the table at an odd angle, and he realized she was grasping Mrs. Weaver's unseen hand. Mrs. Weaver herself was red in the face.

"Have a seat, please, Mr. Russell." The widow had never sounded more regal. Doubtless she could dispense justice singlehandedly, if she had to. But she didn't have to. Seventeen comrades stood ready to do their share. No, eighteen. The footman Pinnock took up a position behind the end of the table, where Mr. James Russell was sinking into a seat.

Astonishing how a man could be guilty of such monstrosity and still go about looking like any other man. A bit weak in the chin, with a florid complexion and deepset eyes, and teeth just begging to be knocked out by a good punch or two.

"These are your neighbors." Mrs. Russell let go Mrs. Weaver's hand and wove her fingers before her on the table. "You may or may not know them, but make no mistake, they are thoroughly acquainted with you."

"What the deuce is this about?" The man's eyes shifted left and right, taking in the grim stares that surrounded him on either side.

The magistrate Mr. Rivers, with the air of one long accustomed to authority, inclined slightly forward. "Do you deny you committed vile indecencies against women who had no power of redress, when you used to live in this house?"

For a full second Mr. Russell looked startled. Then his face settled into a cloaked expression. "I won't sit and be subjected to this," he said, beginning to rise from his chair.

Theo was on his feet in an instant and Pinnock, too, closed in on the man. "I suggest you sit down." Was that his voice? Good Lord. He almost frightened himself. "These people have been at great inconvenience to come here, and you shall hear what they have to say." One day he must learn Rivers's brand of understated power. Today, this tone of barely reined-in violence would have to do. He waited for Russell to take his seat before returning to his own.

"There are things we will not tolerate." Rivers resumed almost as though there'd been no interruption. "This is a decent neighborhood. Those of us who have servants take an interest in their well-being. To let such abomination as that with which you are charged pass unremarked, is a stain on all our good names."

"I don't see that what happened in this house so many years ago, if it did happen at all, is any of your concern." Russell's truculent gaze swept round the table.

"It concerns me, to begin with." That was a balding, bespectacled man Theo had not met before, sitting at

Mrs. Russell's left hand. "You've disgraced a house with which I'd had a long and proud association. And your presence now, when you did not trouble to attend Mr. Russell's wedding or funeral, suggests exactly the sort of grasping suspicions you have already made plain to me. I fear I will be unable to continue as Seton Park's solicitor, if you become resident here."

"I'm afraid you'll have to find someone else to make the Sunday sermons as well." Sly devil, that Atkins. As though he weren't already planning to give up the curacy. So he'd said not fifteen minutes prior.

"I'm troubled by this talk of *suspicions*." Mrs. Landers, at his left, had a magnificent fastidious way of speaking, handling each word like a jeweler hefting uncut stones. "Does he dare to imply an aspersion on the character of the late Mr. Russell's widow?"

"No one can deny a gentleman's right to safeguard his interests." The man's gall was astounding. He was pushed back in his chair, arms folded across his chest, his posture a blunt defiance to the judgment of everyone in the room. "Widows will defraud a rightful heir sometimes. We've all heard of it."

"The time to think of a gentleman's rights was surely sixteen years since." Again the solicitor spoke, his spectacles glinting as he leaned into sunlight. "Before you chose to commit such grievous wrongs as have rendered you unfit to ever be called *gentleman* again. As to your insinuations regarding Mrs. Russell, I shall not dignify those with any response."

One must glance, naturally, at the widow to see in what spirit she took this defense. She rather resembled one of those martyr pictures that turned up in illustrated prayer books. Her arms made a graceful circle, fingers laced in the middle, and her downcast eyes evoked divine patience even while her uplifted chin suggested righteous pride. If he should announce, to the table at large, that he'd been to bed with that woman, not one person was likely to believe him.

He cleared his throat and grasped for as much innocence as he could contrive in his turn. "Am I to understand you mean to impose yourself here, hovering about and making an honest woman uneasy, until the event that will determine the property's succession?"

"It's my right." He'd gone a bit back on his heels, Russell had, like an overmatched pugilist. His fingers were twitching where they gripped the opposite elbows. "This isn't her house. She can't bar me from it."

"None of us can." Theo sent a glance to Rivers, to Mrs. Rivers, to Granville, to Mrs. Canning and her friends. "But we can make things uncomfortable for you here as long as you choose to remain. Regardless what your conduct is now, this neighborhood will regard you, and treat you, like a man who violated innocent young women and escaped justice. You cannot expect ever to be a gentleman of standing here."

"Nor in town." Mrs. Canning angled her baleful attention to the foot of the table. "You may depend on us to make everyone within ten miles aware of what you are."

"And if that were all you had to fear, you might say devil take it and stay on here all the same." Mr. Weaver's soft voice broke in. He'd kept his eyes to the tablecloth most of the meeting, and so he did now, even while speaking. "So let me put it plain: you've more than that to fear from me." He might not have been here, Mr. Weaver. Yesterday he'd said he would not come if Mrs. Weaver didn't wish it. But obviously she'd decided she did. "You brought shame on my wife that she'll never be free of. It was none of her own making, but she's borne it ever since, while you went about living a gentleman's life with never a look back. Don't expect me to let that stand."

"I'll put it plainer still." Mrs. Weaver lifted a gaze that could give a man nightmares. Her voice shook with sentiments too dark to have names. "If you stay in this country I'll stick a knife in your foul throat. Though I go to the gallows for it and leave my children orphans, I promise you I will."

Mr. Russell shifted, ducking from her basilisk stare. If he recognized her, he gave no sign. "They threaten me. You've all witnessed it." He sought for sympathy from one face after another. "Does nobody mean to do anything?"

It certainly sounds as though Mrs. Weaver means to do something. He bit his tongue, though the temptation was strong.

The solicitor bowed. "If you should after all inherit and decide, everything considered, that you'd rather not take up residence, I shall be glad to draw up a lease and help you find a suitable tenant."

No one else had anything to say. The widow gave a quick nod. "Very good, then. Mr. Russell, I thank you for your time and attention. We won't detain you further."

Without meeting anyone's eyes the man pushed up from his chair and went out of the room. Atkins exchanged a look with Mrs. Russell and got up as well.

"Are you going after him?" *Good Lord. To what purpose?*

"I'm a clergyman. I must believe no one is beyond redemption." He flashed a smile. "And if I can make him believe it too, I may serve Mrs. Russell's cause." With a bow to the company he left.

Other people got up as well. The solicitor fell into conversation with the three ladies from town. The Seton Park housekeeper approached Mrs. Weaver, one tentative hand held out, and said a few words. Mr. Weaver nodded, looking embarrassed, as Mr. Rivers spoke to him. He stayed at Mrs. Weaver's side.

Such tricky business, being a husband. Knowing when to be your wife's champion, and when to stand back that she might be her own. So many large and small skills to master beyond simply pleasing a woman in bed. Yet one more unexpected lesson from his time in Sussex.

Over Mrs. Tavistock's shoulder he caught the widow's eye and she smiled a thin smile. She looked exhausted. Likely her composure had tried her beyond her expectations, and likely she'd be asleep by the time he came tonight. Well enough. Not so very many things remained for them to say.

$\mathscr{S}$HE'D DONE it. No, they had. Allies beyond her imagining had rallied round her and now, with any luck, Mr. James Russell would go away. Corrupt he might be, but he was surely not so bold—not so stupid—as to stay in the face of Mrs. Weaver's threat.

Martha caught the loose end of her shawl to stop it flapping in the breeze, and wound it more tightly about her. All the kind callers had gone on their way except for Mr. Atkins who was, presumably, somewhere in the house attempting to set Mr. James Russell on the path to rehabilitation. One wished him luck, and left it at that.

Laughter came to her from somewhere in the garden ahead. She rounded the corner of a hedge to find the two young Russell boys throwing sticks for the same sheepdog she'd watched Mr. Farris training, the day the will was read. Their mother and the governess sat on a bench to one side.

She paused for a fortifying breath. Nothing could be done. She should not have disinherited them if she could possibly have avoided it, but there had simply been no other way.

Mrs. James Russell saw her and came to her feet. "I hope you don't mind the boys playing here. We've been careful to keep them away from any of the planted beds."

"Not at all. Most of those beds are done for the season, anyway." An awkward silence came. What on earth was she to say to this woman? "Do your boys have a dog at home?"

Mrs. Russell shook her head. "Mr. Russell has gun dogs, but he prefers they not be played with, or treated as pets. He finds it spoils their temperament."

"Ah. This one is a worker as well, though he seems to forget the fact easily enough." The smile with which she punctuated this remark felt taut as an ill-fitted glove. "Please do sit down. You may stay here as long as you like." *Here,* of course, meaning this garden, on this day, even while with all her might she schemed to make the woman's husband bundle up his whole family and be gone.

"Will you sit, too? I hope you've been warned against overexertion." Her cheeks colored prettily as she made the shy admonition. The governess removed herself to be nearer the boys, and Martha must sit beside Mrs. Russell's fruitless generosity.

They sat in silence, watching the Russell sons. A minute or so of observation and she should not have had to ask whether they owned a dog. They chased it, and ran from it, and scratched behind its ears with the tirelessness that could only belong to someone for whom a dog was novelty itself. Such unbounded, artless enjoyment, their every merry shout causing her to feel more like some ogress in a fairy-story. Plotting to make a meal of innocent children who came to the wrong house.

"May I ask you something, Mrs. Russell?" And then there was their mother, a timid shadow of a woman half-apologizing for everything she dared to say. Her pale blue eyes didn't meet Martha's but stayed steady on the boys. "You spoke to my husband this morning, I think. Was anything the matter?"

Gravity gathered in the pit of her stomach, tugging mercilessly at her heart. She pressed her lips together. "Nothing of consequence. Only I wished to make him known to some neighbors."

"I see. Thank you." Mrs. James Russell asked no further questions.

The woman would be no better off for knowing the truth. One must push pity aside, and forge ahead. Perhaps Mr. Atkins was even now convincing Mr. James Russell to reform. She would think of that, and surely it would ease the sense of poison creeping through her veins and corrupting her flesh.

$\mathcal{T}$HE CURATE met her on her return to the house, with such a look of priestly satisfaction that she could guess at his news. "You've talked him into leaving."

"It was Mrs. Weaver did that." He smiled, all generous modesty, as he pulled on his coat. "But I helped him, I hope, to conceive of the move as a principled withdrawal rather than a cowardly retreat."

"He listened to you, then?"

"I flatter myself he may have done. I don't expect him to take orders any time soon. But a sympathetic ear can work wonders for a man in such a state." He started down the hall and she walked with him. She still had her shawl; she could accompany him a bit of the way outside. "We've all done our wrongs, on whatever scale, and to be faced with them, when you may think you've left them behind, is a severe trial for any man."

"You'll pardon me if I save my sympathy for the women against whom the wrongs were done."

"No one can fault you for that." He inclined his head as they passed through the front door.

A thought came uninvited: what if she faced a tribunal, some sixteen years hence, like that Mr. James Russell had undergone today? Not with neighbors round the table but with the two Russell sons calling her out for fraud, lying, and adultery? *I had good reasons,* she would say. *It was all for the benefit of someone else.* But her reasons might be nothing to the wronged parties.

And would she convince anyone with the bit about someone else's benefit? Heaven help her if they chose to cross-examine. If they brought in Mr. Mirkwood to testify to the truth.

"At all events he says he'll leave tomorrow. Send for me if you suspect he's going back on his word." He put his hands in his coat pockets as a breeze swept in. "Truly, though, I don't expect you'll need to. I do believe you've come to the end of this business."

"Yes." She wrapped her fingers in the folds of her shawl. "I suppose I've finally reached the end indeed."

*T*HEO CAME in that night to find five candles burning, and Mrs. Russell sitting up. She'd waited for him.

"I'd say that meeting was a resounding success, wouldn't you?" He shrugged out of his coat and tossed it on the armchair before going to sit at the foot of her bed. Likely she'd want to relive this morning in all its glory.

She nodded, her hair gleaming in the soft light and shifting about her muslin-clothed shoulders. "The Russells are leaving tomorrow." She didn't smile.

No mystery in this subdued manner. She never had entirely reconciled herself to cheating those boys, and her heart still grieved for their mother.

He shifted higher up the bed and picked up her hands

to clasp in his own. "Don't doubt yourself. Think of the servants you've kept safe. The ones you've avenged. Think of the neighborhood's general good."

Again she nodded. But she'd have to work this out largely for herself, and he would give her room to do so. He loosed his grip on her hands and made to rise.

Her fingers clutched at his, arresting him. "Theo, stay. Please."

"You've nothing to fear. If he means to leave tomorrow, then I'll sit by your door tonight."

"I don't mean that." Her mouth compressed miserably. Her eyes glimmered with desperate intent. And just as he was piecing together the meaning of that look, of her disquiet, of the fact she'd waited up for him, she leaned across twelve inches of air and brought her mouth to his.

Oh, God. Didn't she know how hard he'd worked to not want this? He let her finish the kiss before he took her face in his hands and gently put it away from his. Then his hands sank, bereft, and he sat, suspended between one desolation and another.

*O*H, GOD. He didn't want to. She'd taken his ready desire for granted and now it was gone.

Mortified heat washed through her. His eyes flickered to her cheeks, witnessing her blush and causing it to deepen. So be it. Pride would get her nowhere now. "Please," she said again, craven and past caring.

He glanced away from her, to the candles. Glanced back. Infinite weariness sat on his brow; sorrow and resignation darkened his eyes. His hands half rose, hesitated, and came to his cravat. His gaze sad and steady on her, he started in on the knots.

I love you would be cruel in this circumstance. *I love you yet I will not marry you.* Cruel to them both. Perhaps she could make him feel the better part of it, though. Her hands came up and laid themselves on his, then trailed down to his waistcoat buttons. With a wife's tender care she helped him undress. As though he'd spent a taxing day in duty and now looked to her for respite. She might have given him that, if some very many things had been different.

His shirt came over his head. The hairs on his chest showed gold in the candlelight. His upper-arm muscles flexed as he reached for the ribbon at the neck of her nightrail.

They didn't speak. Their careful breaths, and the rustle of fabric against fabric, fabric against skin, were the only sounds in the room. "Should I put out the candles?" he finally said, barely loud enough to hear, when he'd stripped off the last of his clothes and stood ready to crawl in with her. She only shook her head.

He did not propose to be her stablehand this time, or demand any exotic attentions, or attempt to shock her with coarse words. He set his hands under her, her shoulder blades fitting into his palms, and he looked in her eyes. Probably—these thoughts would come stabbing through her consciousness—probably relations were like this more often than not between a loving husband and wife. Not the leaping blaze of a new-laid fire but the steady warm glow of embers that abided even when that blaze sank low. Probably. She would never know.

"Don't cry," he said. "Please don't cry." More than once he said so, kissing where her tears ran down, and each time she'd only know she'd begun again when she heard those words. He never asked what was the matter. He must be able to guess.

Pleasure came in sweet and bitter waves, too soon and for the last time. She clung to him through the crest of it, arms round his back, legs round his hips, as much of her

body as possible in contact with his. He shook with his
own release, stifling all sounds but his breath, in and out
through clenched teeth. And it was done. They'd come
to the end of the end.

Afterward he lay against her, chest to her back, spread
hand settling and resettling on her lower belly. "There's
nothing to feel yet," she said. He would break her heart.

"You're wrong." His fingertips swept an arc from hip
bone to hip bone. "You curve here a bit more than you
used to do."

He was imagining. Her body wouldn't have changed
so soon. And somehow this broke her heart even more.
"I'm sorry," she said through a throat thick with tears.

"I know." He sighed, and bent his knees in behind
hers. "But regardless what course you chose, you should
have had regrets. And you've done just what you set out
to do. Surely there must be consolation in that."

She would have thought so, once. But now, wrapped
in his embrace and looking to a future devoid of him,
she could not perceive where consolation was to be
found.

$\mathcal{T}$HE NEXT morning she woke with one last idea. One
brilliant hopeful idea that could only have come through
the machinations of love, the indefatigable industry of
her own heart while she'd slept in Mr. Mirkwood's
arms.

He'd gone without waking her. He wouldn't come tonight, so she must call at Pencarragh and tell him if her
idea bore fruit. Then, too, she'd be able to tell him everything circumspection had kept her from telling last
night.

She found Mrs. James Russell in the breakfast parlor,
a forlorn figure facing a plate of herring, alone but for

the footman. Without taking even toast from the sideboard Martha sat opposite her. The woman greeted her with understandable wariness, and she drew a deep breath. "I hope to do you a service, Mrs. Russell. I have a plan that I believe will benefit you. Of course you know best what you do and don't wish for." Under the table her hands were kneading anxiously together. That could be permitted, as long as the visible parts of her remained calm. "I've given you little reason to trust me heretofore, I know. Nevertheless I ask for your candor. I hope you will address me as Martha. And I'll begin by telling you I know what it is to be unhappy in marriage, with no prospect of escape."

$\mathcal{A}$N HOUR later Mr. James Russell sat across from her at that same table, scowling into his coffee. The footman, bless his heart, had drifted over to stand directly behind the man. "Proposal." He swilled some coffee. "Why would you bring me any proposal? You've already arranged it so I can't set foot in this neighborhood whether or not you produce an heir."

At some inmost layer of his being he was ashamed, Mr. Atkins had assured her, and he'd wrapped that shame in anger to blunt its irritation, the way an oyster fashioned a pearl. She'd never yet heard of anyone unpeeling a pearl to reach that central irritant, but surely Mr. Atkins knew best.

"I thought it right to apprise you of what your reception would be, if you came to settle here." Her folded hands lay calmly on the tabletop now. Odd how much more unsettling the wife had been, compared to the husband. "But I recognize that your interest in Seton Park has never been so much for your own sake as for the sake of your eldest son." She recognized no such thing.

Flattery, though, could sometimes prevail where plain honesty could not.

"It's natural for a man to protect his sons' interests."

"Natural and honorable. We have no quarrel there. In fact, I'm prepared to stand aside and let the estate pass to you, for your sons' benefit, regardless the issue eight months hence."

He choked on a swallow of coffee and put down his cup. "That's not in your power, to undo the terms of the will."

"Not strictly. However I could tell Mr. Keene and others that I'd lost the baby, and if I then removed to some distant place, no one would ever know otherwise."

His eyes narrowed with calculation. "You want something in return."

"No more than you yourself wanted." She unclasped her fingers, flexed them, and clasped them again. "You were planning, I know, to set up a separate household from your wife."

Whatever surprise he felt at her knowing this, whatever offense he took at the subject being broached, he managed to stifle for the sake of gaining the estate. "Perhaps." He lifted and dropped a shoulder. Then understanding broke across his face. "Ah. You think she, too, needs rescuing from me."

"I'm only proposing a variation of the arrangement you already had in mind." She leaned a degree or two toward him. Her barrister brother must feel like this, making arguments in court. "Install her here with your sons. You can continue to live on her fortune and what income you have in Derbyshire. You'll have control of the Russell fortune as well."

"And what of the income from this property?" Greedy, contemptible man.

"A share of it makes up my dower. I've no way to undo that. The rest can go to Mrs. Russell's support, with any surplus put aside for your boys. I'm sure Mr. Keene would be delighted to act as your proxy in drawing up a plan."

His gaze danced about the tabletop as though he thought to find some better option there. "If you don't have a son it shall all be mine anyway."

"Indeed. But if I do, you'll have nothing. And you'll know, every time you look at your heir, that you had a chance to guarantee him the estate and you let it fall through your fingers." She turned over her teacup and reached for the pot. "I know what I would do in your place. But the decision is yours."

*T*HE KNIFE-SHARP pleasure of sacrifice pierced her as she struck out across the lawn. This land she loved, these hills and house for which she'd so long schemed, would not be hers. She'd given them up to someone with a better claim, and preserved the servants' safety into the bargain.

She would come here sometimes. They would. Even if they settled primarily in Lincolnshire, they'd want to revisit this country where they'd found one another. They'd show their children, too, certain paths they'd walked or the church they'd both attended, though of course they would have to concoct some more seemly story to tell of how they came together. Well, they'd have time for that.

On the steps at Pencarragh she got out her card and had it ready, held between finger and thumb, when the footman came to answer the bell.

He bowed without taking the card. "I'm afraid Mr. Mirkwood isn't here anymore, ma'am. He left for London just this morning."

"London?" She put a hand to her chest, where a panicked hummingbird had suddenly taken the place of her heart. The other hand still offered her card. "I had no idea he meant to go."

"No, he's always meant to go back. His stay here was only temporary."

"Of course. Only I didn't realize—" She stopped her tongue. Nothing would be gained by letting this servant guess just how close was her acquaintance with Mr. Mirkwood. "He and a number of other neighbors met with me yesterday. I should have wished him a good journey, if I'd known. I don't suppose he gave any indication of when he might return to this neighborhood?"

"Didn't say a thing. Just packed up and left early this morning."

"I see. Thank you. You'll give him my regards, I hope, if he should come into Sussex again." Finally the footman took her card and she retreated down the stairs. On the last step she set a foot wrong and went sprawling onto the drive, all the breath knocked out of her lungs.

For a moment she just lay still. The frantic hummingbird grew to something like a barn owl, its wings beating mercilessly against her ribs. No one came—the footman had already closed the door—and no one would. Mr. Mirkwood should have come running to help her up, if he were here. But he'd gone away without even saying good-bye. She shut her eyes. She'd made a plan that depended on a husband, and she'd neglected to secure the husband first.

Bit by bit her breath came back, and her heart subsided to hummingbird size. She opened her eyes to the vast Sussex sky. Then she got to her feet and began the long walk back to Seton Park.

Chapter Eighteen

𝓘T wasn't that he'd lost his enjoyment of London. The Bond Street shops, the billiards and card games at White's, the seedy bustle of Covent Garden after dark, all delighted him as much as they ever had. His lodgings welcomed him home with elegiac autumn sunlight, just fashioned to coax a man gently and gradually out of bed in the morning. And the opera transported him, mysteriously as it ever had, raising gooseflesh and making him blink even as he scanned the audience below to see what notable characters were in attendance tonight.

No, the trouble was the wistful edge that came with his enjoyment, now, as he wondered how she would receive each novelty. He should have liked to come home to her, and tell her something droll that had happened at his club. He should have liked a reason to linger in bed of a morning. He should have brought her to the opera, his arm about her to keep her safe through the Covent Garden crowds, and she should have sat in a chair beside him, rapping his knee with her closed-up fan when she saw his attention wander.

Well, no, she shouldn't have. Her condition would keep her from going out in society for some time.

Theo stretched restlessly in his chair as the fool of a soprano launched into an aria grieving the loss of her faithless husband's love. Five days he'd been in town, and at odd moments the knowledge would come in like a swift uppercut: he'd abandoned a woman pregnant with his child.

By her choice, of course. By the original agreement. Indeed *abandon* was hardly the right word, when a gentleman asked for a lady's hand and was refused.

Still. Here he was in London, and if a time ever came when his child, or child's mother, was in danger or dire need, he would have no way of knowing. No way, ever, to be of service to the two. Love and family aside, there remained the question of duty, didn't there? Singular notion to have brought back from Sussex, but brought it he had.

Other duties pricked at his conscience as well. Other people. Granville, who'd been so encouraging in regard to the dairy operation and now was left to manage all the details of someone else's scheme. The laborers. Oh, he'd told them he would eventually go back to London, but they must have expected he would at least stay long enough to see the cows purchased.

And in truth he'd looked forward to that. To going along and paying Mr. Barrow or some other worthy man the tribute of his absorbed attention, and to learning just how to tell a good cow from a lackluster specimen. Really, why shouldn't that be every bit as interesting as judging horseflesh at Tattersall's?

"Mirkwood." The voice had an impatient edge, as though its owner had been trying to get his attention for some time. "Where the deuce are you tonight? I thought you'd liven up our box, but I'd have done better to invite my own grandmother." His friend regarded him through dark eyes, his brow lowered in an attempt at severity.

Ha. *I've seen dark-eyed severity practiced by a master. You, sir, don't come close.*

"I mean you might as well have stayed in Sussex for all the good you've been. What topic so engrosses your thoughts?"

And there it was in plain words. What the devil was he doing here? He ought to have stayed. He'd thought his attachment to Sussex had only to do with his attachment to Mrs. Russell, and he'd left when that tale had come to its end. But was he no more than the sum of his sentiments? Damn it all, he had things to learn and projects to carry out. He wasn't the sort of man to walk away from the dairy thing when it was only half begun.

"Cows," he said, while the orchestra threw up a swelling chord as if to underscore his coalescing resolve. "Cows engross me." Yes. He knew what he must do. "Or kine, I think, may be the proper term when one refers to a lot of them."

"Oh, I say." The brows bounced skyward; the eyes went wide with distaste.

"Summerson." He stood, unthinking, as though the music itself had heaved him to his feet. "Do you know any prayers?"

"Prayers?" Summerson gaped up at him. "Well, I did win a prize in grammar school for learning Bible verses, but—"

"Splendid." His pulse was pounding. He straightened his coat and made for the back of the box. "Pick out a few good ones and say them for me."

"What do you mean? Good God. Mirkwood, where are you going?"

One hand on the doorknob, he turned to look back. "Tonight, home, to get what sleep I can. Tomorrow—" The briefest pause as the aria reached its apex and swirled all round him like wild ocean waves—"Tomorrow, I go to beard the lion in his den."

* * *

Martha shifted from foot to foot, arms wrapped tight about her middle, as the closed carriage came swaying up her drive. Four horses, and these the last of several changes, no doubt. Northumberland was a long way off.

With the toes of her right foot she felt for the edge of the step. Three steps. She would descend them briskly, face bright with a sisterly smile. She would be the first to put out her hand. "How was your trip?" she would say, and from there proceed to all the pleasantries that were expected in such a meeting. What didn't come naturally could be mastered with practice, and she might as well begin practicing now.

The carriage halted and a footman jumped down to open the door. *Now.* He set the steps. *Go now. Smile.*

She forced herself forward, down the first step, as a poised, dark-haired figure emerged from the carriage. And all at once the actions came as naturally as could be. She pelted down the remaining steps and across the drive, into a pair of ready warm arms. Kitty, as always, smelled like jasmine.

"Goodness, Martha." Such an elegant voice, and so sweetly familiar. "Are you feeling quite yourself?"

"Oh, yes. I'm just so happy to see you." It was true.

"I set out the day I got your letter." She turned her head to nod back at the carriage. "Came by way of London, and see what I brought you."

"Nick!" Martha slipped out of one embrace to run into another as her brother sprang down from the steps. "I had no idea of your coming along."

"Good Lord." This voice, too, so richly redolent of childhood and home, as he spoke over her head to Kitty. "Who is this creature, and where do you suppose she's hidden our sister?"

Almost certainly she looked a fool, adopting girlish habits of affection at such a late age. So be it. Her heart had had its fill of moderation, and nothing—almost nothing—could please her more than the gentle teasing rapport of these people to whom she belonged.

"Truthfully, I'm relieved to see you so. I confess I worried for you after the funeral." Nick let her go and turned once more to her sister. "You ought to have seen her. So pale and drawn and hardly speaking at all."

"I'm sorry I couldn't come. Poor Martha, no one to comfort her but a pair of clumsy brothers."

"Never mind about it." The few servants had climbed down from the carriage, and Martha stepped away to relieve a nursemaid of her tiny bundle. "You had the best excuse in the world."

"Sweetheart, I didn't even have the best excuse in the family. Does either of you hear anything from Will?"

Nick had the most recent letter among them, and reported that the Thirtieth Regiment of Foot was still stationed at Antwerp.

"What can they be thinking?" was Kitty's reply to this intelligence. "I could understand if they'd posted him on Elba, to personally keep watch of Napoleon, but surely the war is over now, and English soldiers belong at home."

Nick had some dissent to make, and the two of them wrangled over the issue all the way into the house while Martha followed, head bent low to breathe in the scent of her newest nephew. Little Charles would have a littler cousin within the year, Heaven and her own constitution willing. In the far reaches of north England, from where no reports of the child were likely to reach Sussex and overturn her bargain with Mr. James Russell.

And some time between now and then—some time between now and when her condition became unmistakable—she would work out what exactly to tell Kitty and her husband. For the moment, she hadn't the least idea what that could be.

THIS WON'T be the first time you've disappointed him. Likely it won't even be the last. Theo set his shoulders and mounted the stairs of the family's London home. He'd sent a card, of course, upon his arrival in town, but not until now had he got round to presenting himself. And with such tidings.

Ahead of him a silent footman led the way, as if he needed to be shown. Left at the second floor landing, and right toward the back of the house. Sir Frederick would be in the drawing room, with assorted family members no doubt present to compound the degree of his disgrace.

So be it. His father's good opinion would be worth little, after all, if it were based on falsehoods or even strategic omissions. And if he lost Sir Frederick's regard, well, he'd got by well enough without it for most of his life.

At the sitting-room door the footman thankfully stopped short of announcing him, and took himself off with a bow. Theo went in.

In spite of his errand a sense of well-being washed over him as he crossed the threshold. So many pleasant hours he'd spent in this room, losing pocket-money to whatever sibling cared to play him at draughts, or simply idling while his sisters worked at their embroidery frames and one of his bookish younger brothers read aloud.

No brother was present this afternoon, but Sophia, his eldest sister, set aside her needlework and rose from the sofa to express her delight that they should both happen to be in town. Mother was likewise present, and likewise delighted. Father gave a possibly cordial nod

from the desk in the corner where he must always situ-
ate himself, surrounded by important-looking papers
and other tokens of consequence.

Now for it. He excused himself from the feminine
pleasantries, and crossed the room to take a seat before
the baronet's desk, hat in his lap.

What a fine brooding specimen Father was, even in
riper years. The same grim profile and hooded eyes that
marked all the portraits hanging in the gallery at Broughton Hall. Pity he'd fallen for a Nordic princess of a
woman and seen the Mirkwood features shouldered out
by blond brawn in most of his issue.

"Yes?" Sir Frederick angled his head to indicate half-
grudging attention, his pen still poised above a paper.
*I've made up my mind to be fond of him and he hasn't
succeeded in dissuading me yet.* Fondness was in his nature. It couldn't be helped.

"I've come to tell you I'm going to settle at Pencarragh. I've given up my lodgings in town and I plan to
stay in Sussex through next summer, at least. I thought
you should know."

Father took up the pen-wiper and cleaned his quill
with meticulous attention, but his mouth was threatening every second to draw into a genuine smile. "It gets
into your blood, doesn't it?" he said finally, arranging
the pen in a channel the desk provided for that purpose.
"Working with land. I had a suspicion things might turn
out so."

Such ill-contained pride and pleasure were like a rack
on which to stretch a guilty man's conscience. He cleared
his throat. "Granville wrote to you, I think, of our dairy
undertaking. There's a deal of work to be accomplished
in order to get the thing going, and I find I should like to
see it through."

He could stop there. These weren't falsified reasons
for his return, but sincere ones. Yet he was weary, after

six and twenty years, of always avoiding unpleasant-
ness. He wanted, lately, to be a man who shrank from
nothing. The sort of man a child's father ought to be.

"But there's another reason as well. Another obligation." He turned his hat round, one full revolution, and
tightened his fingers on the brim. "The fact is I've gotten
a lady into difficulty." A clatter reached him from the far
side of the room; Sophia had dropped her scissors. They
were listening, then. Splendid.

The pride and pleasure drained right out of Sir Frederick's face. He stared down at the desktop, as though he
could not bring himself to lay eyes on his son. His mouth
tightened. He rolled the pen a quarter-turn in its channel.
Abruptly he looked up. "Not the widowed neighbor."

Theo felt his own face fall. "How do you know?"

"I asked Granville to keep an eye out for such entan-
glements. He assured me he hadn't seen you to spend
time with any lady excepting the widow on the next estate. But he was certain of her virtue."

"He was right to be." He watched his hands rotating
the hat again. "I've never had such trouble seducing
anyone in my life."

"Regardless your private habits, you will at least feign
some decorum in your mother's presence." Like a thunderous pronouncement from on high, the reprimand.
The baronet was in his element now. "What does she
demand? Money? Marriage?"

"Nothing of the kind. Nothing at all, in fact." Here
came the worst bit. "Her widowhood is recent enough
that the child could be accepted as her late husband's,
and the resulting inheritance will provide quite well for
her."

"Good Lord. What kind of woman is this?" Father's
voice suggested he already had that worked out.

"An honest, upstanding one who was overset by her
loss and susceptible to the wiles of a practiced adven-

turer." Practiced, indeed. He'd practiced before his mirror these lines that would put all blame on his shoulders. He bowed his head in an attitude of contrition, studiously avoiding his mother's and sister's eyes.

"Where is the obligation, then?" Sir Frederick sat back in his chair, palms flat on the desktop. "Certainly there's shame enough in the business, but if she can call the child her husband's, where is the difficulty to which you referred?"

He'd practiced this, too. *Duty demands I find a way to be of service to that child. Whether you recognize it or no—whether she recognizes it or no—I have a responsibility in this case, and I will not run from it.*

He flipped his hat upside down, and right side up, and raised his eyes to his father's. "The difficulty is I'm in love with her. I don't want to be away from her." Oh, Lord, what was he about now? Across the room he heard a sharp intake of breath. Sophia. Maybe even Mother.

"The devil you are." A muscle jumped in Father's cheek. "If you think for a moment I'll countenance your maintaining any sort of relation with a woman whose want of moral character apparently exceeds even your own—"

"I'm not seeking your permission, sir." He spoke softly, and folded his hands atop his hat. "And I urge you, for your own sake, not to make any further remarks upon her character."

"Do you threaten me?" He looked capable, even at his age, of leaping over the desk and thrashing any man who did.

"Not at all. But when you've come to know her as a daughter, and love her accordingly, you won't want your affection tainted by the memory of such unbecoming sentiments as you might express today." From where did these words originate? He'd walked into this room

sure of what to say: *duty compels me back to Sussex.*
How had it turned into declarations and skyscraping
ambitions?

"Theo." Finally Mother must speak. "How can you
have any hope of marrying her if she means to claim the
child is her husband's?"

"And even without a child in the case, she couldn't
think of remarrying so soon." Sir Frederick adopted a
milder tone, as though to work in tandem with his wife's
gentle concern. "The pair of you would be received nowhere in polite society."

"Linfield and I would receive you." Sophia threw one
bold glance to his side of the room, needle working
smoothly away. "I'm sure all your married sisters
would."

His heart pooled with warm gratitude and for a moment he couldn't speak. "I hope to require your hospi-
tality eventually." He bowed to his sister. "But I expect
she won't entertain any talk of marriage for at least a
year." One more look at his father. "Perhaps that will
give you time to reconcile yourself to the idea, sir."

"Reconcile myself?" Again the baronet addressed his
desktop. "To a grandchild begot in iniquity and then
credited to another man? To a marriage brewed in six
kinds of scandal?" He shook his head. "For all your
years of folly, I never supposed you capable of bringing
such profound disgrace upon this family. I can only say
I'm sorry Edwin was not the elder, and you the younger."

As though *that* hadn't been plain since about the age
of twelve. Theo took up his hat, and settled it on his
head. "I regret that my actions have caused you distress.
And I know I haven't, in my life thus far, given you much
to be proud of."

"Of which to be proud."

"Yes. Quite." He got to his feet. "But I'm afraid my
mind is made up. I'm a better man for having known

Mrs. Russell. That you cannot perceive this doesn't make it any less true. I shall welcome your good opinion on the day you decide to bestow it, but I shall not lose any sleep in waiting for that day. With respect." He bowed.

Mother's face and Sophia's both shone with mute sympathy as he made his good-byes. He would have people in his corner. Devil take it. Sir Frederick himself would be won over once he met her. There was the silliest bit of the whole business: if he'd gone looking for a bride with the express intention of finding a temperament and sensibility agreeable to his father, he could not have done better than stern, single-minded Martha Russell.

Now all that remained was to persuade her as well. And if it took him a year—if it took him ten years, or twenty, or every year remaining in his natural life—he would find a way to do just that.

𝒫ENCARRAGH, CONFOUND its paltry acreage, looked like home when he pulled into the drive. He jumped down from his carriage without even waiting for the steps, and started through the house to see what might have changed in the week of his absence. Not much, and yet he saw the walls and windows and parquet floors through different eyes. Here was the place from which he would launch his campaign of unrelenting persuasion, and here he would celebrate when she finally agreed to join her life, and the child's life, to his.

In the library Granville was working at his desk. Theo picked up a few cards and letters that had been left for him, and sorted through them as he gave the agent a vague account of his time in London.

"We've had some sad news while you were gone," Granville said by the by. "Mrs. Russell was disappointed of her expectations and must leave Seton Park. I believe she goes to stay with a brother or sister."

His correspondence fell forgotten to the floor. He blinked, but saw only shifting colors where the agent ought to be. "She lost her baby?"

"I only heard of it yesterday, from Keene. The estate goes to the present Russell after all. I don't mind saying I'll be damned sorry to lose her. But I suppose everyone will."

He stood, unmoving and bereft of words. He'd thought he knew what the bottom of a well felt like. He hadn't known a thing. "Have you seen her?" Yes. These were the words he needed. "Is she recovered enough for callers?" Granville made some reply, but it may as well have been birdsong. If she were laid up in a sickbed he would force his way in to see her. He bent to pick up his dropped letters and then left them after all. No time for trifles.

He said something to Granville—God only knew what, let the agent make what he would of his haste—and was gone from the room. Stable. Horse. Down the drive and onto the road where they'd walked, the day she'd enumerated the reasons she could not enjoy him in bed. A fact presented itself, through his haze of grief, like a distant shore sighted through fog: *Her reason for refusing marriage is gone*. But his only response to the prospect was a stab of shame that his thoughts should turn there at all, in such a time.

Someone must have taken his horse, at Seton Park's front door, and someone must have shown him inside. But all was blur and desperation, and he only knew he was pushing past some servant into a drawing room even as he was announced. And there was Mrs. Russell.

She sat on the sofa, face turned toward him in astonishment. Other people were in the room with her. They didn't matter. Four strides took him to the sofa, where he hauled her to her feet and into his arms. "I heard of what happened," he said for her ears alone. "I'm so sorry I wasn't here. So sorry you had to bear it alone."

"Who in blazes is this?" said someone behind him, but at the same moment Mrs. Russell was speaking, and so he did not turn.

"I don't know what you mean." She twisted in a half-hearted attempt to get free of his arms. No chance, no chance in Hell or Heaven, of that. "What did you hear, and from whom?"

How could she not know immediately to what he referred? He found a grip on her upper arms and drew back to meet her eyes. "Granville told me you lost the child." He sank his voice as low as he could.

"Damn your impudent eyes, unhand her at once!" Vaguely he saw someone get to his feet.

"A moment, please." He held up a palm in that direction. "Martha?" Hope was suddenly pounding, uninvited, at his consciousness like an importunate caller on the front step. She hadn't known what he meant. And she didn't look, sound, or feel devastated as she ought.

With a quick sidelong glance at the room's other occupants, she shook her head. "It's not true." She took the same nearly unintelligible tone. "The child is with me, still."

Sheer relief bore him down and he sagged to a seat on the sofa, then dropped his face into his hands. He felt a slight weight depress the sofa beside him as she sat too.

"Martha, what's the meaning of this?" Through his fingers he spied the owner of that voice: a gentleman of about his own age, with honey-colored hair and coffee-colored eyes, half risen from his armchair. A lady with darker hair but identical eyes sat in the next armchair, holding a cup of tea.

Yes, that was what he'd like to know, too. "Why the

devil did Granville tell me otherwise?" He lifted his face from his hands. "He said you were leaving Sussex." Suspicion knifed through him. "What are these people doing here?"

"How do you dare to ask?" The young man was clearly spoiling for a fight. "Blood gives us a claim on her welfare. Damn you if you will assert any such claim."

"Please." He held up a weary hand. "Let me stay for just five minutes to speak to her. Then you may take me outside and thrash me for my damned impudence if you like."

"Nick." The lady spoke over her tea, her eyes bright with interest. "Let's give him the five minutes. I suspect they will be most illuminating."

"You're going away to live with one of them, aren't you?" He bent near her for privacy. "But why, if you haven't . . ."

"I've given up the estate to Mrs. James Russell and her sons." Her words reached him as barely more than a whisper. "I could only manage that if I told everyone . . ." She pursed her lips and waited for him to comprehend.

And comprehend he did. He sat bolt upright. "I agreed to this with the understanding that a son would inherit the estate, and a daughter would have a portion." A confidential tone was beyond his power now. "To say nothing of an acknowledged father. Don't dare tell me you mean to make an impoverished bastard of a baronet's grandchild."

"Oh, Martha." The woman looked from Mrs. Russell, to him, to Mrs. Russell's belly. "What have you done?"

"I had good reasons." Unrepentance stiffened her spine. "It was a sound plan. Only circumstances changed in ways I did not anticipate."

"Hang your five minutes. Hang your thrashing." The young man was up out of his chair again. "Find me a pair of pistols and we'll settle this now."

"Nicholas, sit down." In an instant he glimpsed the way she must have ruled her elders even from a young age, her cool aplomb unwavering in the face of temper or other outsized, combustible emotions. "Or if you insist on dueling someone, you shall have to duel me. Mr. Mirkwood is guilty of nothing more than agreeing to the business proposition I put forward. And your hotheaded, uncivil behavior must make this family appear to him a most unpromising prospect, just at the time when I was hoping he would entertain thoughts of joining it."

"Good Lord." Theo threw himself back, into the sofa's corner, to study her. "Was that a proposal?"

"It was the poorest one I've ever heard." The sister made this pronouncement, putting down her tea as the brother sank into his chair.

"I should say. I'll make you a better one if your siblings will grant us a minute of privacy. Eight minutes, rather." His heart was bounding all about his chest like a rabbit freed from a snare. She wanted to marry him. His child was well, and would be known to the world as his.

"You'll do no such thing, sir." She had a redoubtable streak of her own, this sister. Katharine. They might call each other by given name, in time. "She's barely been widowed two months. No clergyman who values his post would consent to marry you."

"I know a clergyman who will." She leveled all her resolute attention on brother and sister, but when he lifted a hand hers came immediately to grasp it. "Only we must do it by license, as soon as possible for the sake of the child."

"Think of the scandal. You could not expect any respectable person to know you."

Ah, but he'd been through this before. "My family comprises several more-than-respectable houses, and they will all be glad to admit us. I've just been in London preparing them." Her hand tightened deliciously on his at these words. "That will be enough to begin on, and I shall make it my mission to win your approval as well."

"Everyone in this neighborhood will accept us too." She edged forward, earnestly, still clutching his hand. "I've thought it all through." Of course she had. "Everybody has heard of my disappointment, and the change in my circumstances. Everybody thinks well of Mr. Mirkwood. They'll all believe he married me to save me from a pitiable dependent existence. They'll think better than ever of him." He could hear her tenacity grow with each syllable. "And even if they didn't, I would marry him."

"Duty demands it now." He flexed his fingers over hers. Together they could face down all the skeptical brothers and sisters in the world.

"Yes. Duty." Her whole body tensed with sweet, self-conscious effort, as though she must find the way to deliver her next words through a mouthful of rocks. "My heart as well. I love him." Her cheeks went scarlet. Any observer might conclude she'd just confessed to some mortifying mishap.

He wouldn't laugh, for all that he was grinning like a fool with a bucket of treacle. He pressed her hand once more. The sentiment was of consequence. That she voiced it gracefully, or voiced it at all, was not. All he could do was give her reason to tell him often, in the years to come, and discover whether her delivery improved with practice.

And late that night, when he crept up the servants' staircase and through three corridors into the room where she'd left a candle burning because she'd known, without telling, that he would come—then, she practiced and practiced some more. *I love you,* she said, in words and in ways that satisfied a man to his soul. And from his soul he answered, thoroughly and tirelessly. Because duty demanded nothing less.

March, 1816

THREE OF the courtesans were beautiful. His eye lingered, naturally, on the fourth. Old habit would persist in spite of anything life could devise.

Will leaned on one elbow and rested his cheek on his palm, a careless posture that suggested supreme confidence in his play while also allowing him to peer round the fellow opposite and get a better view of the ladies. Not to any purpose, of course. He'd come into this establishment on a solemn errand, and courtesans had no part in his plan.

Still, a man could look. A bit of craning here, a timely turn by one of the ladies there, and he could assemble a fair piecemeal picture of the four. So he'd been doing all evening as they'd sat down in different combinations at their card table, some fifteen feet removed from the great tables where the gentlemen played. And while every one of them—the sleek mahogany-haired temptress, the crystalline-delicate blonde—gratified his eye, only one thus far had managed to trifle with his concentration.

He watched her now, her eyelids lowered and her fingers precise as she fanned out her freshly dealt hand. Not beautiful, no. Pretty, perhaps. Or rather handsome: a young man could have worn that aquiline nose to advantage, and that fiercely etched brow.

She studied her cards without moving any of them—though the game was whist and all three of her companions were rearranging their cards by suit—and glanced across at her partner. Gray-blue eyes, expressive of nothing. She could hold all trumps and you'd never know.

"No sport to be had there, Blackshear." The words rode in on a wash of tobacco smoke from his right, barely audible under the clamor of a dozen surrounding conversations. "Those ones are all spoken for." Lord Cathcart switched his pipe from one side of his mouth to the other while inspecting his hand. A queen and a ten winked into view and out. Luck did like to throw itself away on the wealthy.

"There'd be no sport even if they were at liberty. A youngest son with no fortune doesn't get far with their kind." Will replied at the same low pitch and lifted a corner of his own card, a seven of clubs to go with his seven of spades.

"Oh, I don't know." The viscount's fine-boned profile angled itself two or three degrees his way. "A youngest son who's just sold his commission might set his sights beyond the occasional adventurous widow."

"Widows suit me. No taint of commerce; no worries over whether you've seduced a lady into something she'll regret." The words felt flabby and false on his tongue, a stale utterance left over from the life that used to be his. He nodded toward the courtesans' table. "In any case, your birds of paradise are a bit too rich for my blood."

"Ha. I'll wager your blood has its own ideas. Particularly concerning the sharp-faced wench with the Gre-

cian knot. Stick," he added to the table at large as his
turn came.

"Split," said Will, and turned up his sevens. His pulse
leapt into a hasty rhythm that had nothing to do with
any sharp-faced wench. He pushed a second bid forward, and gave all his attention to the two new cards.

An eight brought one hand to fifteen. Good chance of
going bust on a third card and not much chance of best-
ing the banker if he stuck. The second hand was better:
an ace gave him the option to stick at eighteen, and also
tempted him with the possibility of a five-card trick, if
he counted the card for one instead of eleven and if the
next three cards fell out in his favor.

Were the odds decent? Twenty-one less eight left thirteen. How many combinations of three cards came to
thirteen or less? With one hundred and four cards in
play . . . eight aces, eight twos, et cetera, and eleven
other men at the table who must already have some of
those cards in their possession . . . hang it, he ought to
have paid better attention in mathematics classes. Fine
return he'd brought his father on a Cambridge education, God rest the man's soul.

"I'll buy another on both hands." Twenty more
pounds in. Best to cultivate the appearance of recklessness early in the evening, when wagers were small. Pru-
dence could wait until several hours hence, when most
of these men would be drunk—make that drunker—and
inclined to put up sums they'd regret the next morning.

The new cards dropped in and he lifted their corners.
Five and three. Twenty and twenty-one. Or twenty and
eleven, with two cards and ten pips between him and the
double payoff of the five-card trick.

He flicked idly with a gloved fingertip at the corner of
one card. Was he really considering it? Buying another
card when he might stick on a total of twenty-one? His

first night in the place, not two hours yet at the table, and already he was goading Fortune to do its worst.

Well, there'd be no novelty in that, would there? He had a fair acquaintance with the things Fortune could do. A loss of thirty pounds would barely merit mention.

"One more here." He pushed another note out in front of his second hand.

A knave of hearts grinned up at him when he lifted the new card, and quiet relief poured through him, loosening places that had wound themselves tight. No five-card trick, but neither would he be dunned for his recklessness. Unless the banker beat him with a twenty-one of his own, he'd have at least one winning hand. Maybe two.

"Stick," he said, and leaned his cheek on his palm again as the play passed to his left. The ladies played two straight tricks of clubs while he watched, the sharp-faced one producing her cards with smooth efficiency from their disparate places in her hand.

Cathcart could needle him all he liked. She gave a man's mind places to go, did such a girl. Let beautiful women air their attractions like laundry on a line, flapping for all the world to see. The woman who kept something back—who wore her graces like silk underthings against the skin, and dared a man to find them out—would always be the one to set his imagination racing.

Even if he couldn't afford to let any other part of him race along. He heaved a quick sigh. "What's a Grecian knot?" he said, sinking his voice again. "Do you mean the way she's got her hair?"

"Hopeless," the viscount hissed round the stem of his pipe. "Must not be a particular lot, those widows you favor. Mind you, I don't suppose your hawkish Aphrodite is any too discriminating herself, judging by the company she keeps." With a jerk of his chin he indicated a fellow down the table, a square-jawed, blandly hand-some type who'd assured himself the next deal by reaching twenty-one on his first two cards.

Curiosity buzzed wasplike about Will's temples. He brushed it away. He hadn't come here to gossip. The lady's choice of protector was her own concern. "Hawk-ish, truly?" He leaned back and stretched his arms out before him. "Try to be civil."

Though admittedly this wasn't much of a place for that. Bottles at the table. More men than Cathcart smoking, despite the presence of ladies, or at least women, in the room. Granted, a true gaming hell was probably worse. Gillray, the artilleryman, had claimed you could actually smell the desperation by four or five o'clock of the morning. Rolling off the pigeons in waves, he'd said, a stinking sweat more acrid than the sweat of healthy exertion. And why not? Fear had a scent, reportedly—you'd think battle would be the place to find that out, but amid the perpetual cacophony of scents, no one had ever risen up and proclaimed itself as fear—so why not desperation as well?

Enough pondering in that direction. He rotated his wrists, flexing the tendons, as a corpulent fellow went bust and the next began his turn. At the ladies' table, the strong-featured girl took her third straight trick and calmly marked the point on a paper at her right hand.

Hawkish. Really. He folded his arms behind his head. And yet there was something undeniably birdlike about her nose, her blank eyes, her wren-colored hair. Cold little creatures, birds, for all their soft feathers and pretty songs. Eat your brains for breakfast as soon as look at you. The odd bits of knowledge one picked up in war.

The banker stuck on a total of nineteen, and Will was fifty pounds richer. One more small step up the mountain. He raked in his winnings and pushed his cards toward the hawkish girl's square-jawed protector.

Near his own age, the man looked. Five and twenty or thereabout, and bearing himself with fresh consequence now he had the deal. Making some minor adjustment to his cravat before tending to the cards. Tilting his head with an air of practiced condescension to grant an audience to his right-hand neighbor, who was, it happened, speaking on the subject of the girl herself. "I declare, Roanoke," the neighbor said in an audible undertone, "I should never have bet on you keeping her this long. Not half so comely as the one you were squiring about last summer. Pretty winsome thing, she was."

A small compression of Square-jaw's mouth was the only sign he took offense at the questioning of his choice. "That one gifted me with a bastard child." Green-jeweled cuff links glinted in the candlelight as he reached out to gather in the cards. "This one can't."

"Or so she tells you, I'm sure," was the first gentleman's rejoinder, his undertone abandoned to more generally air his wit.

"She can't." With the patience of a crown prince accustomed to dull-witted minions he made this correction. "Something's gone wrong with her insides. No monthly courses."

Charming. And quite a bit more information than any man at the table could desire to know, surely. Will threw a look to the viscount, who only lifted a shoulder in reply. Evidently this sort of discussion was usual.

And it quickly got worse. "I shouldn't mind one like that myself." A coarse-featured bounder in a bottle-green coat offered this opinion. "Available all days of the month, isn't she? Can't ever claim indisposition and turn you away. Where did you come by her?"

"Plucked her out of Mrs. Parrish's establishment." Roanoke took his time squaring the edges of all the used cards before putting the stack faceup at the bottom of the deck. "And you may believe they trained her up proper. If there's a thing she won't do in bed, I have yet to discover it."

Mrs. Parrish's. Even a man who'd never set foot in such a place knew a thing or two of its character. One heard certain reports. Accounts, for example, of a contraption that positioned a man to be serviced by one woman while another administered a holly-branch whipping. Rumors of women who'd submit to a whipping themselves, or to any foul debauchery a man could conceive. Through what perverse acts had Square-jaw made his mistress's acquaintance?

Devil take it. This was none of his concern, and to speculate so on a lady's private business ill became him. Indeed it ill became the men at the table who were now pelting Roanoke with crude questions—Would she do this? Did she allow him that?—while the lout deigned to answer only in monosyllables, vague in proportion to the heightened interest, as he dealt out the cards.

Temper sent its warning prickle down Will's spine. She must be hearing this. She must see first one head and then another swiveling to reappraise her. He could mark no change in her countenance, her posture, or the speed at which she played her cards, but with what effort did she keep that composure while hearing herself reduced to an object for the common gratification of a lot of jackals?

"Has she got a name?" That was his own voice, rising above the others. What the devil was he doing? Did he want to invite the suspicion of the entire company? A slight straightening in Cathcart's posture spoke of sharpened interest, though the viscount didn't turn.

Roanoke did. His patrician brows crept a fraction of an inch closer together, then relaxed. "Lydia is her name," he said, and spun out the next card.

Leave it alone, Blackshear. But temper asserted itself again, the cautionary prickle swelling to a ham-fisted *glissando* played on his vertebrae. "I mean a name by which it would be proper to address her." Damnation. He would never learn, would he, what was and wasn't his responsibility?

"Have you something particular to say to her?" The man looked at him with full attention, as did most of the men at the table now. A charge like incipient lightning thickened the room's air. Choose the right words, and he'd be addressing Prince Square-jaw at twenty paces.

Wouldn't *that* be a suitably ridiculous end. Called out over excessive propriety. Killed on account of a woman he hadn't even got to enjoy.

Ongoing chatter from the room's other tables shrank to something distant and obscure as the prospect took shape before him. A few insults, none too subtle, were all that was wanted. Easily enough he could probably provoke the fellow into aiming for his head while he sent his own shot ten feet wide.

How badly would such a caper besmirch the family name? Andrew wouldn't like it, of course. But Andrew's respectability could surely transcend any number of family scandals. Kitty and Martha were both already married, quite well. He couldn't blight their futures in that regard.

Nick, though. His second-eldest brother harbored political ambitions and depended on a good name even now to keep up his practice. He'd do Nick no favors with reckless nonsense.

Besides, he had a deal of money yet to win. "I've nothing whatsoever to say." He made his consonants crisp, and held Roanoke's eyes. No need to back down altogether. "I'm only unused to hearing a lady spoken of in this way, and called openly by her Christian name. But I've been out of society for some time. Perhaps the mores have changed."

"Were you in the Peninsula, do you mean?" A bright-eyed fellow who barely looked old enough to be out past bedtime piped up with this. "Or perhaps in the final battle at Waterloo?"

One encountered this sort with disconcerting frequency. Men who'd swallowed the bitter pill of staying home—heirs who couldn't be risked, unfortunates who couldn't scrape together the blunt to buy a commission—and now wanted to hear every detail of what they'd missed.

"Lieutenant with the Thirtieth Foot." Will nodded once. "In the actions at Quatre Bras and Waterloo." If the nickninny wanted to know more than that he'd have to drag it out of him with a grappling hook.

Fortunately a gentleman three seats down had some opinion to air about Wellington, which someone else countered with an insight into Blucher's actions, and from there the usual derision was heaped upon the Prince of Orange and the usual agreement ensued as to what a bright day in England's history had been June eighteenth of the previous year. The table's mood shifted; the tension between himself and Roanoke guttered like a spent candle and was gone.

Will sat back, drawing in quiet, even breaths. He could listen to such discussions, at least. Some soldiers couldn't. One heard of men who grew light-headed and must leave a room when the subject was broached. Or who flew into a rage at hearing the perdition of battle recast as some grand glorious sport, like a thousand simultaneous boxing matches improved with the addition of strategy, and flashy uniforms, and weapons that made a good loud noise.

"Slaughter," Cathcart murmured under a mouthful of smoke as he took out his pipe.

And there was that. Those men who didn't care to romanticize the event must remark upon how "near run" the whole business had been, with the best soldiers in far-off Spain or Portugal and only hapless youngsters and second-rate officers to fumble their way across the Hougoumont fields.

He'd heard it before. From a friend, it still stung. "A tremendous loss of life indeed." He steadied his voice, made it low and careless. "Slaughter on both sides, I can assure you."

The viscount shook his head. "Her name. Your barren nymph is Miss Slaughter." A card dropped before him and he lifted a corner to look. "Not the most original gambit, defending a Cyprian's honor, but usually effective for all of that."

Ah. The mistress. Yes, that made more sense. Seven years he'd known Cathcart and the man had always taken life as a string of great larks; why would he begin pronouncing opinions on military strategy now? "I tell you there's no gambit." The words tumbled out with a vehemence born of relief: he felt enough of a stranger already to old friends without introducing such rifts, and he would a hundred times rather argue over a lady than a battle. "Truly, am I the only man in this room with sisters? With any grasp of simple decency? No woman deserves to hear those things said of her." He couldn't help stealing another glance, but if Miss Slaughter had heard any part of his ill-advised gallantry, she showed no sign. Deftly she marked another point on her paper and sat back, her shoulders square, her head erect, her gaze, stark and pitiless as a falcon's, never once turning his way.

Neither did Fortune find him worthy of notice, this time. He enriched Mr. Roanoke by twenty pounds in one hand and thirty in the next, erasing over a third of the evening's gain. Let that teach him to get caught up in petty intrigues. He pushed away from the table in disgust.

* * *

*T*HIS HAD been someone's house, before it became a club of most lax membership. Walls had been knocked out here and there to create the necessary large salons and supper room, but some traces of the residential scale remained. A drawing room at the back of the second story, for example, currently occupied by ladies who did not care for cards. Will turned away from the brightness and chatter and, on the street side of the same floor, found a modest library, intact even to books. No candles lit, or fire in the grate, but that only increased the likelihood he'd have the room to himself.

A bookshelf jutted out at right angles to the single bay window, and on the shadow side loomed a shape that proved, on approach, to be an armchair. Perfect. He sank into it and closed his eyes. Through the open door he could hear the house's sounds, all remote and indistinct. Conversation. Laughter. A faint strain of music— violin?—from the ballroom one story below. No doubt there would be dancing later. Just one of those artful amenities that proclaimed this house to be no seedy Smith and Pope's, but a place of gentlemanly sport. Where a gentleman could waltz with courtesans, and drink himself into a stupor, and ruin himself to the benefit of his fellows instead of some impersonal proprietor.

And who are you to condemn them for it? He slouched deeper into the chair, folding his arms. It seemed sometimes he'd lost all ability to . . . enjoy himself, carelessly. As a man ought to do, indeed as he had used to do. Nearly eight months he'd been back in England, turning aside invitations and ducking from acquaintances, schoolfellows, with whom he couldn't seem to remember how to converse. Only thick-skinned, cheerful Cathcart had persisted, and the viscount had finally prevailed not through the power of friendship but because he'd dangled the lure of a gaming club just when Will discovered a need for several thousand pounds.

Some hard edge was imposing itself against his fore-arm. Some square shape in his breast pocket that he hadn't any recollection of—

Oh, Christ. The snuffbox. This was the coat he'd worn when he'd first called on Mrs. Talbot.

He felt inside his pocket and drew out the box, then stood and reached round the bookshelf until moonlight through the window bathed his open palm.

Such a pretty thing for a man of modest means to have owned. Gold clasp, gold hinges, the lid all enameled with a scene of horse and hounds. Probably it was worth a bit of money. That was why it had stayed in his pocket, once he'd seen the Talbot relations pawing over the other small items he'd returned. When Mrs. Talbot was able to be independent of those people he would put it into her hands that she might keep it for the child. She wouldn't want for money, so there'd be no temptation to sell it.

His fist closed over the box, and opened again. He tilted his hand and the enamel gleamed as the moonlight caught it just so.

Altogether too much thinking he'd done tonight. He'd be useless at cards if he couldn't quiet the rest of his brain. He closed his hand on the box again, and brought it back.

He was just stowing it in a pocket when footsteps sounded in the corridor. For no good reason he with-drew to the armchair with its shadows, whisking his legs back to keep his Hessians away from the spill of moon-light. Unaccountable reflexes a man brought back from war. It wasn't as though the French had made a practice of sneaking up on one soldier at a time. Nor, of course, was it likely that the footsteps, if indeed they were bound for this room, could represent any threat.

Two sets of footsteps there were, one lighter than the other, and unmistakably bound his way. A man and woman. Yes, he ought to have anticipated this. Often enough he'd made like use of a darkened room at some gathering in his carefree days.

Something stopped him immediately rising. The awkwardness, perhaps, of having to explain just why he'd been in here, alone, in the dark. The stubborn assertion that he'd been here first, and why should he have to give way to their sordid purpose? At all events he was still seated, all the way in shadow, when two shapes filled the doorway and came in. The taller shape swung the door gently to behind them, and as the swath of illumination from the hall grew narrower, a green-jeweled cuff link glinted faintly.

Roanoke and his mistress. Or perhaps Roanoke and some other woman—indeed that was the likelier case, given Prince Square-jaw could entertain his mistress at home, at his leisure, without need for skulking about. The door clicked shut and Will abandoned the idea of a prompt exit. They could get on with their business and he'd slip out while their attention was engaged. Perhaps he'd make some attempt to ascertain the lady's identity— for what purpose, though? If the man betrayed Miss Slaughter, that was nothing to do with him. Did he propose to finagle a seat next to her at supper, and drop vague dire hints of what he'd seen?

The question was moot. The pair made straight for the bay window and he knew her by her posture alone. Erect and somehow remote, as though holding herself apart from the very air through which she moved. They passed into the bay—he could almost have put out a hand and touched her skirts as she went by; thank goodness their eyes were not so well adjusted to the dark as his—and the draperies creaked along their rod; the thin gruel of moonlight grew thinner. Then, silence, save for a few vague rustles. Whatever their next order of business, it apparently required no preamble of conversation.

Doubtless there were men who would enjoy sitting here, clandestine witness to such goings-on. A pity one of them couldn't take his place. All he'd wanted was a quarter-hour of darkness and silence; now he must tax his weary brain by calculating how best to retreat undetected from this room which he, by any measure, had the better right to occupy.

He'd make his try in thirty seconds. Any sooner, and they might not be sufficiently oblivious. Much later, and he'd be more visible to their dark-acclimated eyes.

An indistinct utterance added itself to the rustles. His hands settled carefully on the chair's arms and gripped there. Twenty seconds. No more.

Confound these rutting fools, both of them. Confound her especially, for letting Prince Square-jaw make this use of her not forty minutes after he'd bandied her name about so despicably. Did she have no care at all for her dignity? Then henceforth neither would he. No more misguided gallantry for Cathcart to twit him with.

Nineteen, twenty. They sounded absorbed enough. Slowly he eased up from the chair, angling round the bookshelf for a furtive glance to assure himself they wouldn't notice him.

He stopped, half-risen.

He'd been prepared for something sordid, a brute coupling between an importunate boor and a harlot who'd learned her trade at Mrs. Parrish's. And of course it *was* sordid by its very nature, this retreat to the library, and Square-jaw himself was everything sordid, with his mouth at the juncture of her neck and shoulder and his hands groping here and there.

She, though. She was . . . Confound him if he could even begin to find the right word. He only knew *sordid* wasn't anywhere close.

She stood with her back to the drapery, eyes closed, chin lifted, whole person swaying with pleasure. While he watched she sent her arms—ungloved, he could now see—up the wall behind her where they twisted overhead, wrists crossing with serpentine grace. Like one of those dancers in a story who bewitched men into cutting off other men's heads. Her naked fingers closed over a fold of the velvet drapery and he knew how that velvet would feel to her, thick and lush-grained, a cat's purr made tactile. Knew, too, how it would feel to be the velvet, trapped unprotesting in her hand. He found a grip on the bookshelf and held on tight.

Down her arm he dragged his attention, down the sinuous curve until his eyes rested again on her uptilted face. Had he thought her less than beautiful? In moonlight, even in such scant moonlight, he could see the truth. Her bold features carved up the shadows and threw them helter-skelter, light and darkness dancing giddily over her nose and cheeks and chin. Her skin was pale as the moon itself, pale and tantalizing as an opal at the bottom of a clear still lake. Pale throat. Pale shoulder. Pale bosom, magnificently formed and half spilling out from the disarranged bodice. But he would not let his gaze linger there. Indeed he ought to be removing himself altogether, as he'd meant to do.

One last look at her face. Her head tipped a few degrees left and then a few degrees right as though to stretch the muscles of her neck. Her chin came down, rearranging the composition of shadows and light. And her eyes opened and looked directly into his.

She said nothing. She didn't jump away from her lover, or yank up the bodice he'd tugged down, or cross her arms modestly before her. Only her eyes, widened and showing an excess of white, betrayed her consciousness of exposure. And that, for only a second or two, though the interval was sufficient to make him feel like a thoroughgoing cad.

The bookshelf's edge bit hard into his hand. He couldn't seem to look away, let alone make an apologetic bow and hasten from the room. He stood, frozen, as she regained her composure and her face hardened into the unmistakable lines of defiance: *Judge me if you dare*. Then that expression too subsided and only her falcon-like blankness remained. She looked through him, and past him, and altogether away.

He'd ceased to merit her notice. Whether he watched, or not, was a matter of supremest indifference to her. Her hands came down from their place on the curtain—even now, with a dancer's lissome grace—and settled on the oblivious biceps of Mr. Roanoke, who had continued at her shoulder and neck through the brief drama but was now commencing to haul up her skirts.

And finally Will let go his grip on the bookshelf. He didn't want to see what followed. He'd probably see it in his dreams, and that would be torment enough.

Some impulse of obstinacy made him bow. She didn't look his way, and neither did she or Prince Square-jaw glance up as he stole light-footed to the door, opened it just enough to accommodate his long-overdue exit, and soundlessly closed it behind him.